God's Window

By

Tammy Watson and Melissa Phillips

God's Window
Copyright © 2012 by Tammy Watson
Cover Design by Jeremy Helm

Published by:
Helm Production
6411 St Leonard Dr
Arlington, TX 76001
USA

Library of Congress Control Number:
2012937960

ISBN-13: 978-0-9842287-7-5
ISBN-10: 0-9842287-7-2

www.TammyWatson.com

Dedication:

This book is dedicated to all my precious children who believed in it more than I did. Thank you for hounding me unmercifully until I gave in and finished it. You all dedicated not only encouragement, but work as well. You are my "Window".

– Tammy Watson

I want to thank my family for believing in me, especially my sister Tammy, without whom none of this would have been possible.

"Let's just write the first chapters and see how it goes..."

Love you Sis

– Melissa Phillips

Index:

God's Window

Prologue

Elizabeth had contemplated murder several times over the last few weeks. Going over every small detail of his demise, she knew there would be little room for error. She would simply tie him up and then stash his worthless body away in the hold of a ship, much like this one. It would probably be days, if not weeks before anyone found him, and by then it would be too late. Yes, what better way to punish him for all the wrongs inflicted upon her?

Slim, creamy fingers tapped thoughtfully against the railing as she looked down at the crowded dock. She could envision the headlines now, "Mr. Rawlings, prominent lawyer, dies mysteriously after forcing his client to travel long, grueling hours in a floating oven." She swiped at the bead of perspiration gathering on her brow. The unbearable heat from the September sun seemed to bare down on her, zapping her even further. She supposed there would be an inquiry, but felt certain they would let her off. Once, that is, they knew her motives; wilted hair and temporary insanity due to heat stroke.

"All ashore!" yelled a familiar voice in her ear.

Spinning around, she glared at the voice's owner. It was just as she thought... him again. The filthy sailor's toothless grin widened, as his bucket, full of smelly fish parts, tilted towards her.

Elizabeth backed up a step, in horror. "You wouldn't dare."

Her words ended in a sputter. Water oozed down her dark peach traveling dress and began to form a puddle at her feet.

She clenched and unclenched her fists. "You..." she stared unbelieving at her ruined skirt and snatched the bucket, intending to swing it at him. "You ingrate! You did that on purpose!"

The middle aged man's grin faded when he spied his captain coming up from the hold of the ship. He quickly doffed his worn cap, then with down cast eyes muttered contritely, "Sorry miss, I didn't see ya standing there."

His failed attempt at innocence only infuriated her further. Was this how he rewarded someone for a good deed?

She then saw the reason for his sudden repentance. The captain's familiar form walked past her. She closed her eyes and tried not to hit the insincere man with the bucket still clutched in her fingers. "Are you quite through, sir?" She spat. Angrily swiping at her wet skirt hoping to wipe away some of the awful stench coming from it.

Just do a simple act of charity, and this is your reward, she thought. Who would think one small suggestion could provoke this much antagonism. And to think she had sacrificed one of her best bars of lilac soap, discreetly slipping it into the sailor's blackened hand with an encouraging smile.

It appeared, however, the ungrateful man didn't appreciate her gesture. From that moment on, he had glared and grunted at her like a mule. Since his awful odor did not improve, she could only suppose there was a fish out there somewhere smelling of lilac soap.

Realizing the man fully expected her to retaliate by informing his Captain, she took a deep cleansing breath, before doing what Sister Agnes would expect of her.

"I forgive your ignorance sir," she ground out. Then after putting on her clean white gloves, she brushed past him toward the ramp with only one thing on her mind. The sooner she met with Mr. Rawlings, the sooner she could leave this awful place and go back home to Pennsylvania.

After an hour passed and still no Rawlings, Elizabeth came to the conclusion this was going to be a very long day. Feeling something drop into her lap, she looked down and groaned. This day was just getting better and better. Prying a gooey peppermint stick from her dress, she gingerly held it out between two fingers toward the small boy ogling her.

3

He stared seriously up at her, before snatching the peppermint from her and plopping it back into his mouth. She shifted slightly away from him, hoping he would go away. He didn't.

"Do you mind finding someone else to bother? I mean, don't you have a mother or something?"

"Yep," he responded solemnly.

"Wonderful," she muttered to herself. He must be one of those strong silent types.

Elizabeth searched the crowd milling around for a frantic mother. Seeing none, she tried again. "If you insist on staring at me in that rude manner, would you please move over you are blocking what little breeze there is."

He moved over a step and wrinkled his snub nose. "Why do you smell like fish?" he asked.

Horrified, Elizabeth turned beet red, "I most certainly do not smell like," she leaned in towards him to prevent being overheard, "Dead fish."

The little boy pondered that denial a moment before asking, "Well, then is it rotten fruit on the top of your hat making you smell funny?"

No wonder she disliked children, they had no manners whatsoever. Rising quickly from the trunk before he repeated it loud enough for the whole town to hear, she pointed with her parasol, "Do you see that ugly, rather large man loading those crates over there?"

The boy's eyes cut across to the sailor in question, before giving her a serious nod.

"There are at least two, rude little boys in those crates. If you don't want to join them, I suggest you disappear, and fast!" she emphasized.

Wide eyed, the little boy spun around and ran crying into the crowd. "Mama, Mama!"

Feeling a little guilty, she tugged at her gloves, and sat back down to wait. Where was that lawyer anyway?

Her light green eyes scanned the busy dock once again. Nothing. She huffed and sat back down on her trunk, watching the ship's crew unloading a massive cargo of food staples, as bales of cotton waited to be loaded in their stead. Blowing a wisp of wavy mahogany hair out of her eyes, and pushing her heavy purple hat back in place, she frowned. Galveston, she thought with disgust, even her hat appeared to be melting in this wretched heat.

How Rawlings had ever talked her into coming here she couldn't imagine. Looking back on it now, traveling hundreds of miles to settle her Uncle's estate was just short of idiotic. However, after trying for weeks to explain what she wanted done through letters, she was forced to come in person. Apparently something as simple as liquidating all her Uncle's assets, seemed a major feat for Rawlings.

Laying aside her parasol, she heaved a loud sigh, crossed her legs and propped her chin up on her hands. Her crossed leg began kicking the air in front of her in agitation. The first thing she intended to do, if that man ever arrived, was to have a nice soothing bath with lots of scented oils and soaps. Maybe then she wouldn't feel so out of sorts. It had been one awful day, and Sister Agnes always said that a bath was the nearest thing to heaven on Earth.

Wrinkling up her nose, Elizabeth paused in her kicking. No, that wasn't it. Now what was it she said…a frown marred her lovely face. It had something to do with cleanliness. Oh well, at any rate, a bath sounded lovely.

Thoughts of Sister Agnes made Elizabeth homesick for the Catholic boarding school where she had been raised. What she wouldn't give right now for one of Sister Agnes' lectures. Guiltily remembering the little boy she had terrified, Elizabeth cringed. Well, maybe not right at this moment.

She unconsciously smoothed out one of the hundreds of wrinkles in her skirt, remembering Sister Agnes' words concerning her temper, "Nuns do not rant, nor do they rave, Elizabeth."

However, even Sister Agnes would have to admit Elizabeth had held her temper better than a saint today. Besides, she did not precisely rant or rave anyway. It was more like…she raised her eyes heavenward and thought better of her denial, well, maybe she did rant. Just a little.

Recalling what else Sister Agnes told her, she was amazed at how the words still stung. "I just don't think you are nun material dear."

Hurt and shaken, Elizabeth remembered trembling to the point her fringe of black beads hanging off her hat shook. "Did God Himself tell you He did not want me?"

Sister Agnes had been at a loss for words, "Well, no, He didn't. However…"

"Then, I believe you should leave it up to Him. I am sure if He is against the idea, He will think of something to detour me." interrupted Elizabeth, more confidently than she felt.

And He had.

She reached into her tapestry travel bag and pulled out the familiar black book given to her that day. She stroked the Bible's worn cover before opening it and absentmindedly turning the pages. Now, because of her Uncle's fortune, her "calling" must wait another long month.

Maxwell Rawlings threw the reins of his carriage at the paid man beside him and reluctantly went in search of Miss Elizabeth Brown. Through their short correspondence there were only two undeniable facts he had gathered about her; she was impossibly stubborn, and entirely too hard to get along with. He yanked his pocket watch out of his tailored suit, checking the time, an hour late. If that judge hadn't insisted on being paid up front he would have made it in plenty of time. Crooks were such unpleasant people to work with.

A smug smile stole over his usually restrained demeanor. At first, he imagined marrying the girl would be easiest, but it took only a few letters to realize that marrying her was out of the question. After all, he didn't want to end up murdering her, just her fortune.

He stopped to catch his breath, and searched the crowd until his eyes rested on a petite young woman with mahogany hair and the most ridiculous hat he had seen in a while. She sat impatiently taping her foot and thumbing through a small book much too fast to actually be reading it. Elizabeth Brown. Thank goodness she was still here.

The young woman in question noticed his approach and rewarded him with a deep scowl. The insincere smile on Rawlings face faded.

Motioning for the two men behind him to catch up he smoothed his thick mustache into place. He always liked to look his best for a performance.

Hurrying over and taking her hand into his, Rawlings gushed, "Miss Brown, I must say it is a pleasure to finally meet you."

Elizabeth coldly ignored his charming smile and firmly pulled her hand away. "Well, I can truthfully say with certainty it is a pleasure to *finally* meet you as well. I do not think you realize how comforting it is for me to know my fortune lies in such competent hands."

Rawlings' eyes narrowed at her sarcasm. "Miss Brown, I assure you. I had no idea…" he began, raising his black eyes to hers. Uncontrollably they flew to the large fruity hat on her head. The thing was massive. He would wager a month's salary a man could park a carriage in its shade.

"Mr. Rawlings, I'm much too tired and hot for your chit chat. If you would be gentleman enough to fetch my trunk and take me to the hotel, perhaps then we can talk."

Mr. Rawlings' eyes were instantly drawn back to the woman speaking to him, or at least what little of her he could see. "Of course Miss Brown, how thoughtless of me, you must be exhausted."

Moving aside, Elizabeth received a certain amount of satisfaction when she saw it took all three men to lift her trunk off the ground. Good. She refused to feel guilty about Rawlings, but she did feel a twinge of guilt towards the two men in his hire. By the looks of them, they were in sore need of a job, no matter the source.

She followed sedately behind Rawlings and his men as they weaved their way to a waiting carriage. Elizabeth could not help noticing that even under the strain of the trunk, sweat popping off his forehead, Rawlings was a handsome man. Yet, there was something about him that caused uneasiness in her. It was an uneasiness that the two rough-looking men with him did nothing to dispel.

Nervously shifting her parasol from one hand to the other, Elizabeth's eyes never left the two seedy men loading the carriage beside her. No doubt she was being unduly suspicious. It was her imagination again. Inventing danger where none existed. Many a time her friend

Susan had scolded her about that very thing. She gripped the smooth parasol stem in her hands, trying to ward off the feeling of approaching danger.

Finished at last with the loading of her trunk, Maxwell Rawlings climbed into the open carriage and collapsed into the seat opposite of Elizabeth and tried to look pleasant. "Martin, hurry up will you!" he shouted, "Let's get away from this foul smelling port. It reeks of dead fish over here."

Elizabeth stiffened self-consciously and tried to move further away, as the two burly men finished strapping on the heavy luggage and climbed in the front of the carriage. Pulling out a handkerchief to cover his nose, Rawlings waved them forward. As they moved the smell blew straight at him and he began to study her suspiciously. Elizabeth blushed. Oh! If that awful sailor were here right now she'd love nothing better than to drown him in a tub of lilac water!

Hoping to take his mind off the smell wafting around him, she changed the subject.

"Mr. Rawlings, I feel we need to talk. About my Uncle's estate…I have repeatedly tried…" Elizabeth's hat slid down her face muffling the rest of her words. This stupid hat, Elizabeth groaned, pushing it up out of the way. Rawlings appeared to look concerned, although she did notice a twitch at the corner of his mouth. Surely she imagined it.

She tried snapping her umbrella shut, but it hung like a limp dishcloth somewhere in between. She struggled with it for a few more moments, and then gave up. She rested it across her lap, the prongs catching on her gloves as she spoke again, "As I was about to say…"

Hearing a snicker, she narrowed her eyes. Was that dreadful man laughing at her? With a wary look, she flung her parasol half out of the carriage and began again, "As I was saying, this is a wasted trip. It doesn't matter what my uncle left me, I do not wish to have any of it."

Rawlings eyes shone, as he leaned comfortably back in his seat. He studied her and was obviously pretending to be interested in what she was saying.

"You see," she adjusted herself in the soft seat, "I plan to give all of the money to charity."

She attempted to smooth the loose hair flying about her face, and then giving up, continued, "I, of course, will need no worldly possessions when I re-join the order."

A glint of interest flickered in his eyes. He studied her serene features, and then shook his head in disbelief. "I beg your pardon?" He asked the shock on his face apparent.

Did people have to look at her as if she just announced blowing up a building, every time she brought up becoming a nun? Still fidgeting with her umbrella, she tried to reopen it. Seeing it was a waste of time, she gave up. The thing was making her look ridiculous.

"I said I am going to become a nun; therefore, I do not need, nor do I want my uncle's money."

Feeling put out by the look of total disbelief on Rawlings face. Elizabeth failed to notice the passing carriage until it was too late. She barely caught a glimpse of it as her umbrella was ripped from her hands. She looked down in stunned surprise at her now empty hands. "Stop!" she yelled to the unkempt pair driving the carriage.

There was no mistaking Mr. Rawlings' laughter now. Why, the hysterical man could barely catch his breath. Her hopes that only Rawlings witnessed her humiliation were dashed as a young man; top hat in hand rushed over and retrieved her bent parasol.

Barely managing a nod of thanks before they were off again, she let out an audible groan. What next. Then, halfhearted she again fought with her broken parasol until it opened; upside down, and tried to maintain some sort of dignity, while Rawlings wiped at his tears.

Unwilling to summit herself to more of Mr. Rawlings' detestable manners, Elizabeth chose to ignore him. She sat a little straighter and blinked back the tears threatening to fall. Why did everything she tried to do turn out so wrong?

Traveling the rest of the way in silence, she watched the busy wharf fade behind her as they headed out along a coastal road. The houses soon became more and sparser as the sun began sinking in the ocean.

Elizabeth looked around at the darkening sky and the empty beach. Her eyes cut across Rawlings' shadowy form opposite her and she became even more uneasy with every step the horses took.

She cleared her throat. "Mr. Rawlings, how far is this inn? Perhaps, you took a wrong turn somewhere?"

Rawlings looked up at her, and Elizabeth let out a small gasp. His eyes were cold and dark, completely void of any pretense to warmth. At that moment she knew – there was no inn. Her hands shook slightly and she gripped them together, willing herself to think.

By the time they slowly turned onto the crushed shell driveway of a deserted mansion, her heart was hammering wildly in her chest.

Crumpling the velvet purse in her lap, she whispered, "There must be some mistake."

Rawlings drew out a slim cigar from his jacket and lit it, while turning a chilling smile her direction. "Now you and I both know, Miss Brown, the only mistake made was by you."

His words slammed into her with deafening clarity.

Then, acting as if this was a pleasant outing and they were the best of friends, he jumped down from the carriage offering her his assistance.

Elizabeth simply stared down at him, her body frozen with fear.

Rawlings cruelly grasped her wrist and pulled her from the carriage. "Come, come Miss Brown. I haven't got all day."

Falling against him, she struggled from his embrace, real panic flooding her senses. He only laughed mockingly and leered at her. "What is the matter Miss Brown? Are you afraid of me?"

Frantically searching for some form of help, but finding none in the darkening world around her, she backed further from him. In an effort to muster up some small bit of courage, she answered untruthfully, "You're not significant enough to be afraid of."

Rawlings' eyes flickered with merriment. He actually enjoyed her fear. "Am I not, and I thought I was doing so well too. Now get moving." He ground out, shoving her towards the rotting porch.

Elizabeth's breath caught in her throat. Her mind refusing to accept what he was implying. The two ruffians from the carriage followed behind, not bothering with the pretense of unloading the trunk.

Rawlings walked around and held the unlocked door open for her, "After you, my dear."

Feeling outnumbered and uncertain what she could do about it, she bravely brushed his hand out of the way and walked through the door. One thing school had taught her was that a bully thrived on your fear. If she had to die, she would at least die with dignity.

Reaching the deserted hallway, she hesitated a moment before entering the musty interior. Her lungs closed in rebellion to the dirt-infested air. Removing a handkerchief from her purse, she quickly covered her mouth and nose. Her only consolation being that Rawlings suffered, too. She could hear him fall into a fit of coughing behind her.

"You idiots, couldn't you at least have picked a spot we could breathe in!" He shouted, ending in a round of sneezes.

Hurriedly the men set out a few fledgling candles, but they did little to dispel the gloom in the room or her heart. It was apparent this house hadn't seen life in years and she greatly suspected her own life might end here, without friends or even the comfort of knowing true fulfillment.

She forced such thoughts from her head. She needed to have all her wits about her if she intended to get out of this alive. Her muscles tensed, ready for flight. However, the front door slammed shut behind her, closing out any hope of escape with it. She physically flinched when the bolt slid into place.

Swallowing the lump in her throat, she faced the man responsible for her imprisonment. "This will never work. Everyone knows I have come to see you. Why, you'll be hanged. I know Sister Agnes will be impatiently waiting to receive a telegram of my arrival."

She stood waiting for the man to come to his senses. Even he must realize he couldn't get away with this.

Mr. Rawlings waved a hand in front of his face to see her clearly. Unperturbed by her outbursts, he walked right past her to a small pile of rags lying in the corner.

"Have you ever played poker, my dear?" he asked almost conversing, as he picked up the wrinkled mass.

Elizabeth shook her head slowly, watching his every move.

"Take my word for it dear, you would be a very poor player."

Elizabeth shook her head in weariness, "I am afraid I don't understand what a card game has to do with any of this."

Amused Rawlings toyed with the rags in his hands, "Well, you see Elizabeth, what you just tried to do is called a bluff, but any good poker player knows that I hold the winning hand. Therefore," he shrugged, "you, Miss Brown, lose. Now get dressed!"

Unbelievably, he flung the filthy garments her direction, where they landed in a heap at her feet.

"There, Miss Brown, is the change of clothes you requested, but I fear the bath will have to wait until another time," his voice held a note of humor in it. As you can see, we are rather short of tubs right now."

He smiled, but it lacked enough sincerity to actually reach his cold dark eyes. The setting sun's light sent an eerie glow through the dirt encrusted windows, bathing everything in a dull yellow hue. For the first time in her young life, Elizabeth was uncertain what to do next. Bowing her head in defeat, with heart felt words, she did the only thing she could think of, she prayed.

When several seconds passed and God didn't see fit to strike Rawlings dead, she had no other choice but to pick up the clothing lying at her feet and let one of the ruffians lead her into what once must have been the drawing room.

She looked around at the vast room. Nothing seemed real to her, her body obeyed her commands, but her detached mind hovered overhead watching. She noted how her vibrant gown contrasted with the faded red carpet. How the cobwebs clinging from the corners, and peeling wall cloth, made a fitting backdrop or Rawlings' plans. Almost certain she could force herself awake and this whole room would fade away, she looked to her captor for advice on how to proceed.

Rawlings strode into the room, forcing her to face this new reality. "I've had enough of your games, Miss Brown," he warned, "You have caused me to be quite late for a dinner appointment as it is."

No, this was not a dream. No dream she could conjure up could be this unfeeling.

She stared straight at him, "Sorry to have inconvenienced you."

His dark eyes bore into hers, the silent battle of wills clashing between them. His face showed a slight appreciation for her futile display of spirit. Yes, even in the dim light of the few candles placed about the room, she looked lovely and frightened.

He wanted her that way, he looked like a cat stalking his prey, cornering it, and then allowing it again and again to hope for escape, only to end the game by devouring the poor defenseless creature.

"I am still waiting Miss Brown."

Although she knew Rawlings meant every word, her body seemed perfectly content where it was. He gripped her arm, pushing her towards the back of the room.

"I have been extremely patient with you, far more than most kidnapers, I assure you."

His handsome face was cold and angry, "I will put it simply. You have a choice Elizabeth. Either you change clothes now by yourself, or my men will –shall we say – help you."

Elizabeth gasped. Her eyes flew to the two sleazy men blocking the doorway. A shiver of fear went down her spine at the mere thought of them placing one of their grimy hands on her. She swallowed heavily. She really had no choice.

"Would it be too much to ask, that you and your men turn your backs so I am afforded a moment of privacy?"

She didn't know what she would do if he refused. Surprisingly he did not, only shrugged his well-tailored shoulders, "Certainly Miss Brown, we are all civilized people here."

Elizabeth somehow failed to see how kidnapping fell into the realm of civilized.

"Besides," he smirked, "I doubt it would have been very interesting anyway."

Then, true to his dishonest word, he turned his back and motioned his men to do the same.

Elizabeth dressed hurriedly, but there were so many tiny buttons and her trembling fingers were barely able to grasp their slippery surface. She kept glancing over at the men surrounding her, wondering just how far one could trust a kidnapper.

Freed from the dress, she picked up the dirty clothing at her feet. She wrinkled her nose in distaste. Clothing was much too flattering a word for the cold dirty garment she forced over her head. She shivered. Whether from fear or the thin coarse material she could not tell.

She looked over at her captors, their backs still facing her. Okay, Elizabeth, think. Quickly she checked over her options, one rather bent umbrella and a velvet purse. She sighed. Not exactly weapons by any stretch of the imagination.

However, hearing the soft clank of money inside her purse, she had an idea. If she could hide the small bag in her blouse, maybe an opportunity would arise in which she could use it to buy her freedom.

Trying to hurry she fumbled with the drawstring of her purse costing her valuable time and drawing Rawlings attention.

"How naughty of you Miss Brown," he said turning around and clicking his tongue in disapproval, "I can't even turn my back for an instant, can I?" Sometimes I find it extremely disappointing how untrustworthy we human creatures all are. Now hand it over."

She faced him bravely, unwilling to plead for mercy and placed her purse in his hand. Though tears glistened in her eyes, she refused to let them fall. Tears were useless and impractical. The only thing they accomplished was making your eyes all puffy and red. Worse than that though, they caused people to pity you.

Rawlings returned to the business at hand, and began issuing orders to his henchman. He was becoming more impatient and Elizabeth gathered things were not running as smooth as he hoped. Apparently he did not intend on killing her here, for they began tying her hands and feet together.

Dreading the answer, but unable to remain silent any longer, she asked, "What do you plan to do with me?"

Rawlings looked pleased by her question. He came over and ran a finger down the length of her cheek.

"Why, my dear, I'm disappointed in you. I took you for a woman who enjoyed surprises."

Squaring her small shoulders, she gave him a cool look and jerked away from his searing touch, "I suppose you're right. It doesn't matter in the least. I am sure your plan is as horrible as you are. But, just for the sake of curiosity, what do you hope to gain by all this? I am the only heir to my uncle's estate and I very much doubt even you could touch that money. My uncle was extremely careful with his finances."

Rawlings raised an eyebrow at her. She cleared her throat. "Well, even if he did misplace his trust somewhat. I don't understand how you hope to get your hands on my money."

He roughly wrapped a gag around her mouth. "That no longer concerns you, now does it, Bootsie?"

"Bootsie?" she thought, was that some kind of criminal endearment?

Checking to make sure she was secure, he leaned in closer, his evil eyes chilling her to the bone. "You just make certain you're a good little piece of baggage and don't cause me any trouble. After all, you wouldn't want me to come finish what I've started, now would you?"

Elizabeth felt a chill run down her spine. This man was terrifying. Confused by his odd warning, she vaguely heard his last remarks as a blanket covered her head. "Bon Voyage, I hope you enjoy your trip. I know I will enjoy spending your money."

That was the last awful thing she heard before blessedly giving into her fear and passing out.

Awakened by a blinding light, as the blanket's heavy weight lifted off her, Elizabeth blinked in confusion. Taking in her surroundings, she noted the cluttered desk, the furniture bolted to the floor, and the portholes for windows. She was onboard a ship, and from the looks of it, a rather shabby one at that.

She turned questioning eyes toward he man looking down on her. He was small and wiry with a head full of snow white hair. He clutched a pipe between his bearded lips and pushed his captain's hat back on his head to get a better look at her.

His eyes were kind and his smile reassuring. Elizabeth felt herself relax. This man couldn't possibly be a criminal. Finally she was safe, and here at last was a man she could reason with.

However after several minutes passed and she still remained bound and gagged, She became worried. Then, when the man unbelievably began lecturing her, her worry turned into frustration. Her hands and feet had no feeling left in them, and he stood there conversing.

"Like I was saying, little Missy, I'm right sorry for you and all, having that terrible fever of the brain, but, well…crazy or not I won't allow no trouble aboard this vessel, understand?"

Elizabeth understood alright. This man was worse than a criminal, he was an idiot. Here she was all trussed up like a turkey for Thanksgiving dinner, and he was worried she would cause trouble.

He bent over and seemed to debate whether it was wise or not to unbind her. Finally, to Elizabeth's relief he began untying her. The whole time continuing to reprimand her and only pausing to gripe about the landlubber's ineptitude at tying a good knot.

"So, little lady, we will get along just fine as long as you cooperate and help us make this a pleasant voyage for us all." He patted her kindly, "Why, once you get to Oregon and meet your future husband, I'm positive you'll get your senses back."

Elizabeth started shaking her head wildly. "Now, the gentleman that brought you here explained everything, so don't go worrying that pretty little head of yours none." He chuckled. "Imagine believing yourself to be a fancy lady. I guess we all wish we were rich, no harm in that. But, the other thing, believing someone's after you… I won't put up with any of that foolishness, understand Bootsie?" There was that ridiculous name again.

Then, with that unbelievable statement ringing in her ears, he slipped the gag off her mouth.

Elizabeth just stared at him, totally at a loss for words. She finally managed to croak out. "Did you say Oregon?"

Smiling down at her obvious agreement to cooperate, he nodded, "yep, you're in for an adventure Bootsie."

"Captain, I assure you I have had quite enough 'adventure' to last a lifetime. My name is not 'Bootsie' and I, sir, am not going to Oregon to marry some stranger. So you can just take me off this floating woodpile and onto solid ground, immediately."

Feeling the ship lurch beneath her, she panicked. The captain pulled the pipe out of his mouth, studying it.

"Now Missy, I thought we had an understanding, me and you."

He placed the pipe back in his mouth, sadly retrieving the rope behind him. Elizabeth's eyes widened.

"But you don't understand," she tried again.

"I understand plenty. Now are you going to cooperate, or do I tie you up till we are out to sea?"

Well, maybe she was going to Oregon after all.

She sighed heavily, "I suppose I don't have a choice, do I?"

The captain grinned around his pipe at her. "Nope, can't say as you do, at that."

Reluctantly, she let him help her up before going over to the porthole and looking out over the dark churning water. Oregon.

"Captain?"

"Yes, Missy."

"I won't marry a complete stranger. You can't force me."

The Captain puffed on his pipe, contemplating her statement. "Don't reckon I could at that."

Elizabeth faced him, determined to show she had some control over what was happening to her.

"And Captain?"

"Yes, Missy?"

"My name is Elizabeth, not Bootsie."

Chapter 1

"As I was saying, Bootsie," she cringed at his insistence on using that hideous name, "I explained to your shipmates about your fever of the brain and they seem real understanding. Why, with their help and a couple of months breathing this brisk salt air, you will be fit as a fiddle. Before you know it, you'll be planting your foot in beautiful Oregon, with you memory intact."

"Speaking of memory, Captain, how many times must I remind you? My name is Elizabeth, not Bootsie."

"Why of course it is Missy," he said consolingly, "Now watch your step there Bootsie, it's a might steep."

Elizabeth gave up. It was no use trying to convince him she was anything other than Bootsie, mail-order bride. Rawlings had seen to that. No, she would just have to wait until she arrived in Oregon. Once there, she would head straight for the nearest telegraph office and wire Sister Agnes. Surely, the law would believe a nun. Elizabeth frowned. Did that obnoxious man say something about months?

Abruptly, the Captain came to a stop, and Elizabeth so intent on keeping up, ran smack dab into the middle of him. He laughed heartily, and gave her a sound whack on the back.

"Here's your quarters, Missy," he informed her indicating the heavy door before them.

Elizabeth took a cautious step forward. She was not eager to find out what lay next on her agenda of horrible experiences.

The Captain grinned at her wary face and swung the door wide. The color drained from Elizabeth's face. She stood in the doorway, trying to take it all in.

Gaping before her was nothing more than a dingy hole filled with poorly dressed women, a few scattered children, and half empty trunks littering the little floor space available.

He couldn't be serious. She looked back over her shoulder at the Captain. He answered her with a confident nod. Apparently he was.

The six women looked up from their unpacking in curiosity. Elizabeth immediately started backing out of the doorway. There were no way six women and three children could fit in that room.

"You can't possibly be serious?"

The good natured man wrinkled his brow in confusion. "Can't see as I know what you mean Bootsie."

"I mean," she yelled, then catching herself, lowered her voice back to normal. "I mean, don't you think that there are too many of us for this one small room?"

The Captain took in the ten bunks bolted to the walls, the scattered trunks, the five other females turning in unison their direction, and cleared his throat, "Well now, I…"

Recognizing the Captain's distress, a young blonde about Elizabeth's age came forward, stopping just inside the doorway, "I am afraid you have our Captain somewhat flustered."

With a welcoming smile, she stuck out her hand, "Hello, my name is Christina. I know how overwhelming this must be for you. I admit to being a little skeptical at first too, but when we get these trunks organized I am sure we will have plenty of room."

"For what, sneezing?" asked Elizabeth, ignoring the hand extended toward her. She was much too upset with how things were progressing to notice Christina withdrawing her hand of friendship.

The Captain frowned, "You're being mighty unfriendly Missy."

"Unfriendly?" Elizabeth slung her long tangled hair back over her shoulder, blinking back angry tears, "I think I am being extremely friendly after being kidnapped, tied up like a…"

"Now, now Miss Bottoms," the Captain interrupted, "We both know you were not kidnapped, let's not start that up again, hey?"

Elizabeth shook her head in hopes she was going deaf. "What did you call me?"

The Captain impatiently knocked his pipe clean against his leg, "I called you your name, what else, now I don't suppose you remember that either."

This was getting way out of hand. "Bottoms? Bootsie Bottoms?" She flung out, not bothering to answer his question. "What kind of simple-minded dolt would actually answer to an absurd name like that?"

There was a snicker from somewhere in the cabin. The Captain opened his mouth to speak, but Elizabeth raised a hand to cut him off, "Don't even answer that question."

"Now see here, Missy," the Captain was getting a little tired of her accusations.

"And stop calling me Missy!"

The Captain shoved his empty pipe into his mouth and clamped down in anger.

The other women waited in breathless silence for the Captain's temper to blow. At last, his temper barely in check, he leaned forward, pointing a calloused finger at the stubborn female.

"I am Captain around here, MISSY," he stressed the word, "and I say the only one wronged around here will be that husband of yours when he gets wind of what a hard-headed woman he paid good money for."

Elizabeth could not believe he acted as if she were being unreasonable. Why, she could have been killed tonight. "Captain," she spoke so softly, he wondered if he had heard her, "I am tired, dirty and discouraged beyond belief. I don't care anymore if you tie me to the mast, or cast me out to sea. I only ask one thing for my own sanity. My name is Elizabeth."

The Captain's face was growing redder by the minute. He waved his pipe at her, as if to make a point, and then abruptly changed his mind. "Women," he muttered, "and people wonder why I never got married." With that he glared at her one more time before spinning around and leaving her standing in stubborn silence at the doorway.

A small head peeked around the doorway, and asked curiously, "Ma is that the crazy lady everyone's been talking about?"

A dark-haired woman, rushed over, gave Elizabeth an apologetic smile, and then snatched up her wayward son. "Edward how could you...I didn't say crazy, I said she was a little confused."

21

"No, you didn't. You said…" a hand clamped down over his mouth.

Elizabeth brushed back a tangled auburn lock, and dared the uncomfortable woman to admit the truth. She may not be crazy, but they were making her seem that way, "Haven't you been listening to a word I have said?"

All six women gaped at her from the open doorway. They were uncertain exactly how to respond to a crazy woman.

"I am not touched, delirious, or confused," she felt awfully close to tears again. She bit her bottom lip harder in an effort to still them. She wished at least one person would believe her, but seeing the women's alarmed expressions, she knew it was hopeless. It was obvious they thought her totally insane.

A thin, older woman of about fifty cautiously approached her.

"Certainly not, dear, but I think you really should calm down. We wouldn't want you to have a seizure or something."

"Abigail," cautioned Christina.

Abigail was much too interested in what she was saying to heed Christina's warning. "Goodness knows what horrible things await us on this trip, without you adding to our worries."

Elizabeth noticed how her small beady eyes lit up through her think glasses at the mention of danger. "Why, I hear the storms are so fierce they literally rip through small boats like this one. For all we know, we could be tossed unmercifully into the churning sea to our deaths!"

Cornelia, a thin tall woman in the corner, gasped.

Abigail warmed by the subject, crouched down, a make-believe knife clutched in her bony hands, "And then there are the pirates. I hear they are so woman starved that…"

"Abigail!" A large breasted woman shouted, as she nodded toward the children, whose eyes were almost popping out of their heads.

Her story interrupted, Abigail transformed back into the older sedate woman Elizabeth first believed her to be. Innocently smoothing out her skirt, she elaborated, "Why Hannah, I was just trying to tell this young woman here, why she must cooperate. I certainly didn't invent pirates."

22

"I didn't say you did, Abigail," admitted Hannah, dragging her back into the room, "But, I hardly think scaring the living daylights out of a person is consoling, and there are children to consider."

"Are we really going to be attacked by pirates?" a nervous Cornelia squeaked, clutching her bed clothes against her.

"Of course not," Christina soothed

"Don't worry, ladies. I'll protect you from those nasty pirates!" said a small red-headed boy about seven, as he started wielding an imaginary sword around the room.

Cornelia burst into tears, "You're just saying that to spare my feelings. We are all going to die. Then be eaten alive by sharks."

"You can't be eaten alive, Cornelia if you are already dead!" piped Edward knowingly.

"For pity's sake." muttered Elizabeth, her own troubles forgotten for the moment.

"Oh Edward, how can you joke at a time like this?" Cornelia wailed accusingly. "Can't you see we are all about to die?"

"Lass, get a hold of yourself," ordered a freckle-faced Irish woman of about thirty. "Daniel, stop that swordplay this instant. Can't you see you are scaring your sister?" The red-headed boy who was the spitting image of his mother, plopped dejectedly on one of the trunks and replied, "Aw…Mom."

Elizabeth sighed wearily. It was obvious they had long since forgotten she even existed. What she needed was a moment to herself, time to gather her wits and form a plan.

Slipping off while they were still debating which would do them in first, the sharks or the pirates, she headed for the solitude of the deck. She needed a breath of fresh air.

Up on the deck, the crisp evening seemed to refresh Elizabeth's spirits. She leaned over the railing, watching the dark waves beat on the hull of the ship. Yesterday if someone had said she would have been kidnapped, crazy, and headed for Oregon as a mail order bride, she would never have believed them. This was the most absurd two days of her entire life.

She leaned her head against the cool railing. She had to think of some way out of this mess and back to Pennsylvania.

She looked up at the disappearing coastline. Surely there were lawmen in Oregon. Someone to help her, someone to care that her whole life was being taken away from her.

A salty tear dropped to the ocean mingling with its murky depths. The stars were bright and reassuring through her tear blurred eyes. How her heart ached, for she knew beyond a doubt that except for Sister Agnes, she had no one. Except God of course. She gave Him a trembling smile. Surely He did not mean for her to be a mail order bride in some untamed place like Oregon. She belonged in Pennsylvania with the only family she had ever known.

Just thinking about the good sisters and her school friends made her feel a little better. She pushed away from the railing, a new found courage straightening her spine. Two months... after that, she could go back home. Besides, she would be safe from Rawlings this way. He could hardly silence her once she reached Oregon. Yes, two months were not that long.

This ship was going to be the death of her.

"Well if you're rich and all that, where's all of your money and servants?"

Elizabeth sighed deeply. Maggie's son Daniel had decided to make her already long, miserable voyage even more unbearable.

"I told you, someone has taken all of my things, and I never had any actual servants."

"Rich people got servants," Daniel interrupted arrogantly.

"Rich people *have* servants," Elizabeth corrected.

"That's what I just said, boy lady, you really are crazy," bored, Daniel skipped over to little Edward to play jacks.

"I think you are a pretty princess," said Molly, peering up at her with trusting deep brown eyes.

"Don't go filling her crazed head with a bunch of muck, lass. She doesn't need your encouraging her stories," Maggie scolded her youngest child.

It amazed Elizabeth that a woman could have two such different children. She gritted her teeth. Of all the women on board, Maggie was the hardest to get along with.

"I'm going up for some air," Elizabeth announced.

"Why don't you stay and help clean up a bit for a change?" Maggie snapped.

Elizabeth stuck her nose in the air before heading out the door. "I didn't make this mess." She quickly slammed the door before Maggie could lunge at her, and sighed. Sharing a cabin with three kids and six unrefined females was not her idea of an 'adventure', as the Captain had put it.

Maggie was going to kill her.

"Let me at her!" Maggie roared trying to struggle free of the firm hold Christina and Alice had on her pudgy form. Cornelia quickly dropped the calico dress she had been washing back into the wooden barrel, before helping the two women tackle Maggie to the ground.

Hannah stood by watching the whole episode, agreeing whole heartedly with the struggling woman's sentiments. After two months on the ship, the girl was getting to all of them.

"That lass is driving me crazy! I came all the way from Ireland to escape servitude, and I certainly don't intend on becoming her very own personal maid!"

Hannah's clear brown eyes shot over to the girl in question calmly looking out to sea just a dangerous ten feet away.

"Just let me throw her over the side. No one will be the wiser." Maggie pleaded, pulling one arm free.

Abigail, standing clear of the tussle, sniffed with superiority.

Maggie struggled free of the two woman holding her, taking two steps before being blocked by Hannah. "Abigail's right, Maggie."

Abigail pushed her spectacles back on her nose with the back of one wet hand, "As I said before, Maggie, just ignore her."

"Ignore her?! How can you be ignoring someone who is constantly expecting you to wait on her like she's the Queen of England, that's what I'd like to know?"

Abigail flung her wrung out garment over the makeshift clothesline, saying with superiority, "You, Maggie O'Brian, have too hot a temper."

Maggie shoved past Hannah, her dark green eyes flashing fire, "And be telling me Abigail dear, is it easier to ignore her when you're chasing after the poor Captain?"

Abigail flung her garment back into the water barrel, "How dare you. I most certainly do not chase the Captain."

Hannah, trying not to smile, stepped up between the two feuding women. "Maggie I hardly see how Abigail's feelings for the Captain enter into committing murder."

"I do not have feelings for the Captain."

Cornelia snickered and Christina coughed to hide her laughter. Abigail glared at the two of them. "I tell you, I hardly notice the man."

The girl responsible for all the upheaval in the first place traced a delicate finger along the rough mast in the middle of a ship, looking up at the billowing sails. It was much too windy to wash. Goodness knows she tried telling the other women that not five minutes ago. Since they seemed so insistent, Elizabeth suggested they divide up the chore evenly. For once they actually smiled at her and listened to reason.

That is, until they found out she had no intention of helping them. This made no sense. After all, it was not her idea to do the wash in the first place. The sound of women's voices arguing brought a puzzled frown to her lightly tanned face. What in the world were they fighting about now? She shrugged. She would never understand them. In some more obvious ways she differed from the hardworking women she shared a future with.

For one thing, she was the only one among them who could read. This was why she offered to entertain them by reading poems by Emily

26

Dickenson while they washed. The Captain in an unusual bout of generosity had loaned her several books from his personal library. She greatly suspected that he had hoped it would keep her below deck and out of sight.

Regardless, the women were not in the least interested. In fact, Maggie's fair skin changed a bright red when she had made the suggestion. You would have thought she had suggested they commit mutiny from their stony responses. Maggie afterwards had lunged at her. Realizing it was no use explaining, she simply walked off to wait until they were finished with their things.

The noise behind her grew to such proportions, that she turned around to see what the commotion was all about. To her astonishment all five women were nothing more than a tangled heap of legs, arms and petticoats. Dirty water sloshed out over the barrel as they wrestled one another to the deck, one rising, only to be pulled back down by the others.

"Of all things," grumbled Elizabeth, "they can't be left alone for a minute."

By the time she reached them, clothes were everywhere. A corset hung off Cornelia's head as she grabbed blindly for Maggie's ankle.

Shaking her head at their lack of manners, Elizabeth tried to recover some of her muddy garments. Really, these women were impossible. They seemed to have no inkling of what the word lady meant.

Maggie was rolling around on her only petticoat. After several unsuccessful tugs, she burst out. "Whatever in the world are you doing? Have you completely lost your senses?"

The surprised women ceased their struggles, looking up at the scolding young woman, fire shooting from their eyes, "I can't for the life of me imagine why grown women would be rolling around the deck in that uncivilized manner. Why, just look what you have done to my things," she accusingly held up a crumpled, muddy camisole. "Honestly, it is no wonder you look forward to marrying illiterate backwoodsmen, you are no better than they are."

Saying her piece, Elizabeth tossed her long thick braid back over her shoulder waiting for an apology.

"Fish bait," was the only answer she received.

Christina threw up her hands in defeat. There would be no stopping Maggie now.

Maggie regained her footing and attacked about the time the good Captain rounded a corner. The sight that met his eyes stopped him dead in his tracks. Those brides were at it again. The two seamen with him took one look, and then tried to make a hasty retreat by disappearing behind some rigging.

"Oh, no you don't, mates." His loyal crew was fast becoming a bunch of cowards when it came to his ship load of brides.

Not that he could blame them. He studied the brides; all sprawled out like so many wet dish rags, and debated whether he should just walk away. Right before his eyes they were once more enthralled in a wrestling match. He silently cursed every woman the Good Lord created. No wonder men had banned them from ships citing 'bad luck'. Why, if left up to the troublesome bunch, they would spend all their time fighting over the wheel, while the ship traveled in endless circles.

He grudgingly moved forward and bellowed, "Lasses!" Then, the Captain laced his large rough hands on his hips and gave an intimidating glare to the hopeless lot of females. "I have had just about enough of all of you!"

All six women jumped guiltily. Cornelia found her feet first, rising as regally as possible, considering she has just a moment ago been sprawled face first on the deck.

"Captain, I am sure this must all look rather odd to you, but I can explain," she nervously looked around for a backup.

Abigail came gliding up, but not to help her faltering friend. She stared at the Captain in adoration and began batting her sparse eyelashes at him.

He cleared his throat and ignored her attempts at flirting. He focused instead on the irritated young woman off to the side, holding an armful of dirty clothes.

"Bootsie, do you have anything to say for yourself?"

Her eyes widened in disbelief, as she pointed a questioning finger at herself, "Me?"

"Yes, you. I don't know how, but you must be at the bottom of this."

He motioned to the mess around him, "Speak up, Missy."

Indignant, Elizabeth straightened to her full five feet, "For your information, Captain, I am completely innocent of any wrong doing here. If you would have taken notice, you would have found that my clothing is completely dry."

Puzzled the Captain studied her closely. She was dry. He looked confused, but every other time there was a commotion could be traced to the small, innocent looking female. He looked to his first mate, as if somehow he may hold the answer. The young man shook his head in disbelief, indicating that he hadn't put much faith in Bootsie's declared innocence. The Captain clamped down on his pipe for a long puff before turning to his first mate. "It reminds me of an old Irish saying, lad. 'Is minic a bhionn ci'uin ciontach!"

The young man rubbed at his rough beard thoughtfully, "What's that mean Capt.?"

The older man sighed as he looked straight at the dry innocent girl he said, "The quiet one is often guilty."

Abigail tugged on his sleeve, "Captain?" He groaned. To top everything off, this infatuated spinster had been forcing him to remain a prisoner in his own cabin to avoid her advances. Almost flinchingly, he asked cautiously, "Yes, lass?"

She smiled up at him, attempting to straighten the bun sliding sideways on her head, "Isn't it a lovely day for a stroll?" she hinted.

The Captain pried her fingers from his arm. "No, it isn't Miss Brewster, and I would appreciate it if you fluttered somewhere else as I have work to do and you will be married when we arrive."

Abigail burst into tears. Christina ran over, pulling her protectively away from the unfeeling Captain.

"Well, I for one don't know why you're so heart-broken, Abigail, you were practically drooling over the man," Maggie commented.

Abigail gasped in mortification, before wailing like a banshee.

Christina glared at Maggie.

"The poor woman was just trying to be pleasant Maggie, a trait you wouldn't know anything about."

Maggie bowed up, "Is that so?"

Hannah's large frame quickly stepped up between the two, "Now ladies, no reason to get yourselves all worked up in a lather."

Maggie shoved past Hannah. Christina stood her ground refusing to budge.

Elizabeth leaned forward tapping Maggie on the shoulder. "You have a real problem with your temper don't you? Sister Agnes suggests counting to ten. Believe it or not, it actually helps."

"I'll count to ten. Just before I toss you over the railing that is!"

"Of all the nerve, I was only trying to help," sputtered Elizabeth.

The Captain began rubbing his throbbing head. "Ladies, please."

Cornelia began wringing her hands in indecision, as Maggie pulled Elizabeth down on the dirty deck and into a headlock.

"Oh dear! Oh my!" Cornelia started waving her arms around looking for someone to intervene.

Christina, meanwhile, continued to sooth a wailing Abigail, as the other women tried unsuccessfully to explain things to the Captain. But, the confused Captain didn't have a clue as to how the new fight had begun, and he had been standing right there. If only they would decide to speak one at a time.

"Land ho!" shouted a relieved sailor from his perch above the commotion.

The bickering continued, unaffected by the good news.

"Land ho ladies," roared the Captain, trying to shout above their arguing voices.

Still receiving no response, the Captain stepped up behind the wheel, letting out a shrill whistle. "I said, land ho ladies! Oregon is..." but before he could finish Elizabeth picked up a sodden dress, dripping with soap and grime, slinging it towards Maggie, who had the good sense to duck.

30

Unfortunately, the Captain didn't. Elizabeth clobbered him in the back of his head with the heavy garment, sending him face first into the wheel.

In horror the women watched his eyes roll back into his head as he slowly slid to his knees, before blacking out completely onto the hard deck.

"Oh my, now you've done it," wailed Cornelia, "You've gone and killed the Captain!"

In response to Cornelia's announcement, Abigail flung herself prostrate over his unconscious form, weeping inconsolably.

Horrified, Elizabeth dropped the weapon in her hands.

Only Christina seemed to realize what the Captain had tried to tell them, just before his demise. She whispered almost reverently, "Did you hear what he said, girls?" All six women turned her direction, as if waiting for some great revelation. "He said 'Oregon.' Girls we are home!"

Chapter 2

Elizabeth clutched the sides of the white dingy with only one thought prevalent in her young mind. This was definitely worse than she imagined. Barely taking enough time to clean up and gather their things, the brides were quickly shoved into a life boat and headed for shore. Elizabeth had never seen sailors move so quickly. It was as if they couldn't get rid of the women fast enough. Elizabeth scanned the cleared section of trees for some sign of civilization with dismay. Unfortunately there wasn't any. That is, unless you counted the fifty whistling giants waiting to snatch them off the boats. She couldn't even see a town, she squinted harder, surely those two buildings separated by a muddy trail wasn't the town. She sincerely hoped not at least, because neither one of those poorly erected buildings even remotely resembled a law office.

Abigail leaned in to Alice and whispered, "I hear the men here are so strong they can snap a tree off at the roots with their bare hands, drag it to the mill and throw it on the ship, all before lunch."

Cornelia gasped, tittering worriedly, "Did you say the men are so strong they might accidentally snap you in two, as they drag you off into the woods? Oh dear, I don't believe I care for Oregon the least little bit."

Elizabeth placed a nervous hand over her fluttering stomach and took a deep breath to calm herself.

"A little nervous Bootsie?" asked Hannah beside her.

Elizabeth gave her a wry grin before her eyes strayed back to the ruckus the men were making.

"Did I fail to mention, I hate burly men," Elizabeth replied solemnly.

Hannah chuckled out loud, understanding the girl's fear. "Well, honey, I suggest you get used to them, because it looks like that's the only kind they grow out here."

Elizabeth looked uncertainly before her, searching diligently for a shiny star pinned on any of the rough looking men below.

Hannah reached over and squeezed her reassuringly. She was finding it a lot easier to get along with the girl knowing she wouldn't be living in her pocket anymore. Hannah raised her own trembling hand up to wipe the perspiration from her forehead.

"Don't let them frighten you honey, all men are basically the same. Why I even hear that the bigger they are, the bigger the heart." Elizabeth looked at her like she had taken leave of her senses. Trying to express herself better, Hannah added encouragingly, "You know, like horses."

Elizabeth was not encouraged. From her limited experiences with horses, she found them generally uncooperative with a tendency to run her straight through the briars.

Much more quickly than Elizabeth would have liked, she found herself on the splintered dock bunched up with the other women on one side. The men on the other hand were being unnaturally silent across from them. Desperate now, she scanned the sea of faces for a lawman. Who was she kidding? Right now she would take anyone with a uniform on.

Maggie caught her eye and looked pointedly down at her foot. Elizabeth looked down to find that she was nervously tapping away and forced herself still. If the Captain weren't glaring her in place she would have pleaded with the largest burly man across from her to believe she was not this Bootsie person.

She became even more edgy when the Captain, sporting a bandage around his head, stepped up in the midst of them. When he did, a heavy set bearded man hooked a thumb in his suspenders and let out a stream of spittle that landed in a puddle right at his feet. Elizabeth watched it land, turning a sickly green. Maybe she should have killed the Captain, and then she would be in a nice safe jail somewhere instead of the main course for one of these huge mountain men.

Clearing his voice, the Captain pulled a wrinkled piece of paper from his pocket. "Well, gents, I suppose you're all pretty anxious about now, wondering which one of these here ladies belongs to you."

Elizabeth wasn't paying any attention to the Captain's words as she rose on her tip toes trying to get a better look at the tree covered town. Even Oregon had to have a jail, didn't they?

The proud Captain called out a name, as if he alone were responsible for their union, "Maggie O'Brian."

33

Elizabeth grabbed hold of Maggie's shoulders, her small head popping up over the crowd to get a better look.

A tall, dark haired man opposite her frowned in puzzlement at the flash of auburn colored hair bobbing up and down.

"Bootsie, let go of my shoulder," hissed Maggie.

Bootsie gave her an exasperated look. Honestly, the woman was more volatile than a keg of dynamite. Now she supposed Maggie would start threatening her again.

However, Maggie ignored her completely. In fact, she even moved politely out of the way and joined the Captain in the midst of their group with her two young ones in tow. Bootsie was pleasantly surprised at her reaction, and that she now had a clear view of the proceedings.

"Mr. Patrick Sullivan," the Captain's voice rang out with authority. A large freckled man nervously stepped forward to join Maggie, wringing his large banned hat in his hands.

Elizabeth wiggled through an opening in the close knit group until she found herself in front of the cheering crowd. She looked back over her shoulder in confusion at the teary eyed faces of bliss. What was going on now?

A warning bell went off in her head, as she whipped back around. She took in Maggie, her arm looped through some strange man's, heading straight for the smiling preacher at the other end of the dock and her mouth went dry. Preacher?!

"But, Christina, I can't possibly marry one of these overgrown tree trunks. I told you, I am going to be a nun!"

Exasperated, Christina lowered her voice in warning, "Bootsie, not now. Can't you decide to be a nun some other time, you're ruining everyone's wedding day."

The Captain caught the slowly building tension out of the corner of his eye. Recognizing Elizabeth arguing with several of the women, he groaned as if in pain. That confounded woman was at it again. He had to do something and quick. His worried eyes scanned the list in his hand for her name.

Finding it at last, he shouted, "Bootsie Bottoms." Then sent a quick prayer heavenward that the man marrying her would fail to notice she was as loony as the day was long.

"What?!" shrieked a shocked Elizabeth.

The Captain instinctively ducked, clutching his head.

Alice and Cornelia pushed a protesting Elizabeth forward.

"Now wait a minute. I am not, I repeat not, this Bootsie person," all the women moaned in agony, well aware of where this was leading.

Elizabeth stamped her foot in frustration. "No, I mean it." Receiving only mutinous glares from the women she turned to the only one who could stop this madness, the preacher. "Please you have to help me," she pleaded, "I can't marry anyone. I am supposed to be a..."

"And Adam Reed," the Captain quickly injected. He was trying to get her quiet before she scared everyone off with her crazy talk.

The Captain looked as though he didn't know which of the two young people were more upset. The beautiful woman stunned speechless, or the embarrassed and obviously angry man, who seemed resigned to his fate as he stepped forward.

Elizabeth took one look at the man chosen for her and nearly passed out. The man was huge and...so masculine. His thick dark hair was long and wavy. In an attempt to tame it he had tied a thin leather band around the heavy mass. The effect made him seem more dangerous. Rather like a panther in a cage. Had the Captain actually meant to put her in a cage with him?

The Captain grabbed her arm and pulled her over to the large giant's side. She barely reached the shoulder of his tailored jacket. She was shaking uncontrollably now, whether from fright or anger she could not tell which. She felt his warm hand engulf hers in what could only be described as a death grip. She looked down. Why, even his hands were sprinkled with wiry dark hair.

When she looked up all she saw was...man. Total and massive man. His tan jacket, dark blue flannel shirt and tight fitting pants barely contained the muscles bulging to be free. His skin was a golden bronze from hours of felling trees, and his eyes, why they were so blue, they nearly took her breath away.

Dumbfounded, she met his steel blue gaze. To do so, she had to tilt her head back. He towered over her from a six foot plus frame. All she could think to say was, "Oh heavens."

The man didn't wait for her to say more as he propelled her forward toward the preacher and her doom. She could hear him cursing under his breath the whole way, while she tried frantically not to panic. Who was she kidding? She was panicking. If she didn't do something fast, she would find herself married to what must be the largest man in Oregon.

Think, Elizabeth, she encouraged herself. She dared a quick glance his direction, saying breathlessly, for the man was practically dragging her now, "Sir, unhand me this minute. If you would just stop and listen, I could explain about this terrible mix up."

His mouth formed a grim line and his eyes held a dangerous light in them. "I have heard enough from you already. I would suggest madam that you do us both a favor and learn when to keep your mouth shut."

Well, reasoning was definitely out.

Adam looked furious and embarrassed. Then, with a look of unadulterated challenge Elizabeth faced him raising her small chin in stubborn pride. She had no way of knowing, but that small show of courage cost both their freedoms.

She tugged on her arm, and he jerked her up against him never even breaking stride. Horrified, she watched the preacher come into clear focus. It was then she knew she had only one chance at freedom, so she forced herself to relax in the man's firm grip.

They stood before the preacher. Solemnly, he opened his big black Bible. Elizabeth could barely breathe she was so scared. Still, she forced a trembling smile to her lips and gently tapped the strong square hand still crushing her arm.

He scowled down at her.

"Excuse me," she looked through thick, sable eyelashes, her green eyes bright with suppressed anger   , "but you're breaking my arm."

36

"Sorry," he answered gruffly, loosening his hold on her.

"I'm not," she replied sweetly, before kicking him hard in the shin.

Elizabeth groaned out in pain when her small foot collided with the steel appendage he a called a leg. Bending over, she clutched at her sore foot and glared accusingly at Adam. Adam, on the other hand, looked a little stunned by her actions, but remained relatively unhurt.

"I think you broke my foot, you overbearing nincompoop."

"It seems to me you broke your own foot," he calmly pointed out.

She started to tell him just what she thought about that, when she noticed that he no longer held her in his steel clasp. Unable to believe her good fortune, she picked up her skirts and bolted for the nearest heavily wooded area.

The hoots and loud laughter of his men woke Adam from his stupor. His eyes narrowed on the small spitfire gathering speed as she neared the thick pines.

Isaac Moon, wiped tears from his eyes, "What cha do, scare her off Adam?"

Patrick Sullivan slapped his thigh in enjoyment at his friend's discomfort. "She seemed a little worried about bedding down with you Adam, or maybe it was being dragged to the wedding she didn't take kindly to."

Adam sighed at her retreating form, clenched his teeth, and turned to the stunned preacher. "I'll be right back," he said.

Elizabeth held only one thought in her mind. Reaching those clump of pine trees just five yards away. Of course, she had no earthly idea what to do after that. Right now all she needed was a place to hide.

Her breath was coming in short gasps, and the stitch in her side was beginning to hurt. It still only ran a close second to the pain in her throbbing foot. She quickly glanced over her shoulder to see if her beau was in pursuit. This is precisely why she didn't notice the huge log stretched out peacefully across her path.

"Uh-oh," she managed, just before flying through the air, doing a somersault, and landing face first in a disgusting, brown mud puddle.

"Honestly," she muttered, between spitting out clumps of mud, "what next?"

Shaking the dripping mud from her arms, she debated whether to attempt hiding in that monstrous log she had just tripped over, or take a chance on climbing that overgrown Fir tree. She certainly wouldn't make it very far running. She grimaced. Of course she could simply lie down; she should blend in quite nicely with her surroundings.

"Would you like a hand sweetheart?" Adam offered from his comfortable position leaning against the tree in front of her.

Elizabeth stared in surprise. Her hand covering her racing heart, "How dare you speak to me like that? You scared the living daylights out of me."

"Tell me, do you plan on keeping this odd habit of yours after we are married?"

When she looked perplexed he added, "Rolling around in the mud." A grin was tugging at the corner of his mouth.

Her body responded to the deep timbre of his voice, her stomach getting all fluttery. Confused, she pushed back a few muddy strands of hair, "You know it is not very gentlemanly of you to keep bringing up marriage, when I have made it perfectly clear that I am opposed to the idea."

He winked at her, crossing his massive arms in front of his broad chest. "Well in case you hadn't noticed, I am not a gentleman."

She glared at him, "Oh, I noticed all right. Are you going to help me up or just stand there grinning at me?"

When she received no response except his continued grin, she tugged on her heavy skirt, attempted to stand, only to fall right back down into the cool mud. She hit the mud beside her in frustration, "I really hate you. Do you know that?"

Adam bent down on one knee, his arm resting casually across his other leg. "Now sweetheart, how can you hate me? You don't even know me."

Elizabeth looked up at him, intending to give him specific reasons why she did too hate him, when their eyes met. Both of them froze in

38

wonder, neither one able to draw a breath as electricity filled the air between them. Adam was so close, Elizabeth could feel the very heat from his body, even smell the clean scent of him; she closed her eyes in an effort to concentrate. What was happening to her? She reopened her frightened green eyes, looking straight into his questioning blue ones.

Adam regained his composure first, shaking his head as if to clear it. He rose to his feet, putting some distance between them.

Elizabeth ducked her head in confusion. For some unknown reason her stomach was still doing cartwheels. She tried desperately to focus on what he was saying to her, but all she found herself doing was watching the way he moved.

He stopped his restless pacing to stand before her, legs spread apart, hands clasped behind him. His voice came out short and gruff, and he looked as flustered as she felt. "I didn't come out here to argue with you."

"Good because I have no intention of marrying anyone, you included."

Realizing she meant to be difficult, his voice became low and threatening, "You made a bargain with me, and I intend to see that you live up to your end of our arrangement. I spent all of our extra money on this crazy idea, and can't afford to wait another six months for a bride, so you Darlin' are marching right back there and marrying me, whether you like it or not."

Bristling at his insinuation that she was not one to keep her word, she struggled to her feet, prying her skirt from between her legs, "I haven't broken my word. I have been trying to tell you, I am not Bootsie Bottoms. And you're right; I don't like the idea of marrying you. But I assure you it isn't personal. I feel the same about all overbearing, stubborn men who chase me down in order to get their way."

Adam shoved his hands deep into his pockets, "Now, let's try this again, Sweetheart. Will you be walking, or do I carry you back?"

It wasn't a question. Perhaps she had pushed him a little too far. He was awfully big, and was staring at her impatiently.

39

Still, she refused to let this overgrown bully push her around. She attempted to stomp her foot, quite forgetting she stood in a good three inches of mud. The mud refused to release her wayward foot. In an effort to catch herself, she threw her arms out for leverage, but this only succeeded in splashing up an extra coating of slimy mud all over her. Her eyes shot to a face filled with hidden laughter.

"Don't even think about laughing," she threatened.

He raised his hands up in mock innocence, "I wouldn't dream of it."

She lifted one glop covered a hand, and admitted defeat. This was going to be another horrible day, she could tell right now. She pulled her knees in to her chest and gave him a resigned smile. "I suppose I must look quite a sight, huh?" she asked as mud oozed down her skirt.

He lost it then, his laughter rich and full, "Sweetheart, right now you could scare a bear back into hibernation."

Her sense of humor caused her to join with a giggle. It felt good to finally laugh at this whole ridiculous situation. Goodness knows getting mad wasn't helping.

Adam carefully reached out, making sure to avoid getting mud on his best shirt and jacket and hoisted her effortlessly up onto more solid ground.

Elizabeth blushed at the familiarity of his hands around her waist. He leaned back studying her for a moment. "Come here," he commanded, taking off his jacket and hanging it on a tree limb.

Elizabeth backed up a step. "I most certainly will not."

He frowned in the midst of un-tucking his shirt. She frowned back.

"I just want to wipe some off that mud on your face."

"Oh," she responded meekly, letting him wipe away some of the grime.

He was grinning at her again, when he finally unearthed her cheek, "What did you think I wanted to do?"

Elizabeth pushed his hand away, turning a guilty pink, "You sir, are incorrigible. I don't need your help, thank you very much."

"I'll remind you of that fact after you meet Nicholas and Chelsea."

"Let me guess, you have children."

This was getting worse by the minute.

Adam tucked his shirt back in, "Yep. Two of them."

Terrific, she thought, children. The only way this could be any worse is if he lived in a tent. She opened her mouth to ask, and then changed her mind. She didn't want to know.

Instead, she would beg for mercy. She had no pride left and they were talking about children, little creatures who loved to torture her, "I can't possibly take care of children."

Adam finished stuffing in his shirt, before grounding out, "Why not? Any normal female should be able to look after two harmless kids."

She chose to ignore that remark, "I can't. Even if they did like me, which they won't, I am going to be a nun. How many nuns do you know running around with children clinging to their skirts?"

"About as many as have husbands, I imagine. Look, Bootsie, it seems we already had this discussion. You are marrying me, and that's final."

Elizabeth huffed rather dramatically, "Would you stop bossing me around and just listen to reason?"

Frustrated, Adam ran a hand through his black wavy hair and leaned forward, "I would listen to reason, but I have yet to hear any coming from your mouth."

Elizabeth began roughly pulling twigs from her tangled hair, "Insulting me won't change the facts."

"What facts?" Usually even tempered, Adam was fast losing patience.

Elizabeth frowned at his tone of voice, "I don't like children, and I most certainly don't like you either."

She waved him off when he started to bellow at her again, "You will just have to get yourself another one."

"Another what?" She was irritating the fire out of him and it showed.

41

Elizabeth rolled her eyes. No wonder he still insisted on marrying her, the man was as dense as a doornail, "Another wife, of course."

Adam took her surprised face in his hands, to make his point clearer. "Listen sweetheart, and listen carefully, because I am only going to tell you this one more time," she hated ultimatums, "I don't care if you like children, me, or Oregon for that matter. You made a bargain and you are going to stick to it, regardless. Is that understood?"

She pulled away from him, crossing her arms determinedly in front of her, "Oh, I understand all right. I understand that you are extremely annoying and unpleasant."

"And you," he leaned forward, his nose touching hers, "are the most hard-headed woman I have ever met. But, I am going to marry you in spite of it."

"Please, don't do me any favors," she spat out.

Adam's mouth turned up at the corners. "You are marrying me."

She smirked back at him, "Oh no, I am not."

His voice was low and threatening, "Yes, you are."

Elizabeth refused to look away, "No, I'm not."

Adam leaned in closer, saying firmly, "Yes, you are."

Elizabeth was probably going to die right there on the spot, and it would serve the man right if she did.

She struggled up once more from her position, and then was suddenly slung across his shoulder! He slapped her backside and kept walking. Elizabeth closed her eyes in humiliation. Imagine being toted around like a sack of potatoes. The gall of this man was incredible.

Coming up on the cheering crowd, Adam started looking worried, but was apparently not dissuaded enough to put her down. He must have meant what he had said. As Adam reached the preacher and dropped Elizabeth to her feet, he stated firmly, "We are ready now, Reverend."

Elizabeth stood in open mouth shock as the ignorant man actually opened his Bible and began reading. Elizabeth looked around for someone to do something, but everyone was acting as if it were perfectly normal for a bride to be dripping with mud, standing beside a stranger who had chased her down and carried her back slung over his shoulder. Was she the only one who saw a problem with this picture?

She struggled against the firm hold Adam had around her waist. Well, he might force her here, but he couldn't make her marry him, that was for certain. Even she knew how marriage vows went. If he wanted to play this little game, they would just see who was the most obstinate and stubborn.

The other men were laughing so hard tears rolled down their cheeks, while the women looked on in shocked silence at Elizabeth's appearance.

"Hey, Reed, what ya have to do; mud wrestle her to the ground?"

Elizabeth felt Adam stiffen beside her. Apparently he was having a hard time keeping his temper in check. The men's reminding him of how foolish he looked was not helping the situation.

The preacher looked at Adam questionably. Adam gave a curt nod. Opening back up his book the preacher continued, "Will you take this woman…"

A fresh wave of panic hit when she heard Adam grinding out, "I do," like he was taking a dose of castor oil. Her eyes snapped back to the preacher, as he earnestly began reading her vows.

She waited patiently for the question to come. When it did, she took a very deep breath before answering in a loud and clear voice so there could be no misunderstanding, "I most certainly will n…"

To her horror, she realized Adam's huge hand was preventing her from finishing her sentence. He then snatched her up against him so hard she could barely breath, much less scream. Her eyes widened, and she began struggling in earnest when she realized the preacher had come to the end of the absurd ceremony.

He closed the big black book, with a resounding thwack. Then beaming down at her outraged face, he announced, "I now pronounce you man and wife. What God has joined together let no man put asunder." Then he added encouragingly, "You may kiss your bride, Adam."

Adam bent over to comply, but Elizabeth's furious face conveyed the fact that if he dared, he literally took his life in his hands.

Chuckling, he stepped back, "If you don't mind, John, I believe I'll take a rain check on that one. At least until my little bride here has cleaned up a bit."

His words brought forth a fresh bout of laughter. All at her expense, she noticed.

Adam didn't wait around to see her reaction at the turn of events. Bending down, he picked up her small bag containing one other dress, and grabbed her resisting hand. He then dragged her up the dirt road towards town. Elizabeth gave one last wistful look at the remaining brides. She hoped they would find it in their hearts to rescue her. They all responded with sympathetic nods. She felt a little better. That is, until she realized the nods were directed towards Adam, not her.

Adam waited until they were well out of sight, before jerking her between the only two buildings within walking distance and released her.

She responded by whirling around and slapping him as hard as she could.

Wincing in pain she instantly regretted her action. Why was it every time she hit him, she ended up the one hurt?

He cocked an eyebrow, not betraying the anger she saw in his cold, hard features, "I would have preferred a kiss."

Oh, the man was insufferable. Outraged she jammed her fists on her slim hips, "This marriage can't possibly be legal. I demand to speak to the sheriff immediately."

Grinning attractively, he replied, "All right. Talk away."

It took her a second to comprehend just what he meant, and even then, she couldn't believe it. "Do you mean to tell me, you are the sheriff?"

Her only answer was a satisfied smirk.

Horrified, she scanned the town around her for proof he was lying. Taking in the hastily erected buildings on each side of her, the muddy street with boards lying across it, and the endless expanse of trees, her shoulders sank in defeat. She asked reluctantly, "The Mayor?"

Adam's cocky grin only widened.

Biting her lower lip, Elizabeth couldn't bare for him to see the tears gathering in her eyes. How would she ever get back home? She picked up her worn bag, asking sarcastically, "Do you own this entire town, Mr. Reed, or just most of it?"

He looked into her bright eyes and then to her trembling hands as she stood facing him, and then for some unexplained reason, he gentled his response as if he could see into her very soul. "Pretty much all of it actually, I guess you could say you married a rich man."

She fell back against the crude building in defeat, "Then, I would hate to see a poor one."

He didn't seem too insulted by her honest observation.

Resigning herself to the inevitable, she unconsciously clutched her bag against her chest, "What do you call this place?"

"Reedsport."

She rolled her eyes, "Of course, what else."

Adam smiled at her again, then reached out and caught a stiff strand of dull hair between his fingers, "No offense, sweetheart, but you need a bath."

She jerked her long hair out of his hands. She didn't like him touching her; it caused a funny feeling inside. Rather like when you slide down a steep hill too fast.

"Well, at least we agree on something."

"I still have some work to do at the mill," he tried to pry the bag loose from her strong grip, "I'll let you freshen up at Sullivan's Saloon while I'm gone…will you give me that?"

She held on tighter, "A saloon?! Are you completely insane! I can't possibly go into a saloon, my reputation will be ruined."

"What reputation? I am your husband now, remember?" He reminded in exasperation, snatching the bag from her hands.

She snatched it back, "Will you leave my bag alone. And I am not going to set foot in such a vile place and that is final."

"You are my wife, Mrs. Reed," he pried her hands loose from the bag, "and that means that I carry your infernal bag." She glared obstinately at him. "And it also means you will take a bath anywhere I tell you to, even in the middle of the street if I so desire, is that clear?"

"Perfectly," she ground out. It was about as clear as mud.

"Good. Now come on, I have already lost most of a day's work as it is," he ordered, "I'll be back at dark to pick you up."

"Fine. Come whenever you want because I don't intend on being there."

"And what do you mean by that remark?"

She clamped her mouth shut and glared at him, "Nothing what so ever, sweetheart," she added mimicking his use of the endearment.

He sighed at the look of rebellion on her face. By the look of things, she meant to cause him as much trouble as possible until he could get her home.

"Look, Bootsie, I think we got off to a bad start here."

"Oh really, and what gave you that impression? Was it that you had to chase me down and force me into marriage, or was it the dress covered in hardening mud, that gave it away?"

"Never mind, I can tell there is no talking to you right now. Maybe later on the way home, we can work this whole thing out."

She turned away from him, too angry to speak.

With a shrug, he gave up. "Women," he muttered.

When he turned his back and headed toward the saloon, she stuck out her tongue at him. He whipped around so fast; she swore he must have had eyes in the back of his head. She in turn only gave him a wide eyed innocent look.

As they headed to the saloon she rebelled even further by taking her sweet time about following him. He finally became so aggravated; he reached a muscular arm back and pulled her along beside him. She in turn refused to even acknowledge his existence, sticking her nose in the air.

At last reaching the saloon, he pushed open the door and shoved her inside. "Sullivan!" His deep voice filled the musty room.

Soon, Maggie's new husband hurried in from the back. Elizabeth pursed her lips together in disapproval. Adam ignored her, focusing on his longtime friend, "My wife here needs a bath. I'll be back to pick her up around dark. And Sullivan? I want her to still be here when I get back."

Sullivan got his meaning and looked the little lass up and down, before giving his friend a curt nod, "Done, Adam."

Relieved, Adam faced her and pointed a warning finger at her nose. She was sorely tempted to bite it.

"And you stay put, do you hear me?"

Elizabeth refused to answer. She of course had no intention of obeying that order or any other for that matter. She was leaving.

Chapter 3

Well, maybe she wasn't leaving. Her green eyes, dancing fire, bore a hole through the large, freckled Irishman baring her path. Since he refused to move, she focused her frustration on the poor excuse for a washtub. From the looks of it, the man responsible for her imprisonment, probably picked the thing out, and then beat it with a rusty sledge hammer for effect.

He nudged her forward, and she dug in her heels. For some reason she felt if she gave in to this one thing, her past way of life would be gone forever.

Well, she would put a stop to this nonsense here and now. She wanted a real bath with sweet smelling soaps and oils. Not some fast dunk in a rusty tin cup. Angry tears sprang to her eyes, but she wiped them away with the back of her hand. Then, with shoulders squared she turned to face the man watching her.

"You can't possibly expect me to bathe in that. Why, I couldn't even fit my big toe in, much less my entire body."

Even though she tried to sound more haughty and indignant, her confidence was badly shaken. She was more out of control since her arrival then she had thought possible. All she had to do was look at her simple surroundings, the old metal tub, a worn small bed in the corner and one dresser that had seen better days. She unconsciously twisted the ring on her left hand.

"Mrs. Reed, I know how you must…" Sullivan pacified.

Her throat constricted with unleashed tears. He didn't know how she felt. She just wanted to go home. If not that, than at least to have one real bath.

As she looked at the chunk of lye soap lying on the floor beside the tub, a shiver went through her body.

"I know you can't help being an ignorant Lumberjohn," she began.

"Jack." He stated back.

Elizabeth stared at him, "Jack?"

The big Irishman, Pat, scratched his head, and explained, "It's not Lumberjohn, it's Lumberjack."

Elizabeth scowled at him. "Fine, Mister...Lumberjack. However, from now on I would appreciate it if you called me by my real name. Elizabeth Brown, not Reed. I am not married. Why is it no one around here grasps that simple concept?"

Pat shrugged his shoulders, and rolled his eyes. "Adam might have something different to say on the subject." He mumbled.

"If you say so, Lassie. Now about your bath... Being as this is the only tub about, I be wondering what ya be wanting me to do about the problem?"

Elizabeth looked at the exasperated giant, wiping sweat from his forehead. Even she couldn't argue with common sense. It was obvious she would accomplish nothing by brow beating the man. So, rather than answering him, she kicked the washtub. A stab of pain shot up her leg, and she barely stopped from grabbing her injured toe as tears gathered in her eyes.

"Listen lassie. This here washtub will just have to do. This is all there is and I'll not be arguing with ya about the subject anymore. It's all ya be getting from Old Sullivan." He walked around the offensive object, pulled a couple of clean towels from the dresser, and thrust them at her.

Letting out a resigned sigh, Elizabeth snatched the towels out of his hands, knowing she has been beaten.

Then, slamming the door shut, Sullivan locked it firmly behind him.

"Unlock this door immediately, do you hear?" She bellowed behind him.

Sullivan sighed and kept on walking. Out of reflex he ducked when a vase crashed against the door.

Maggie caught his eye and waved up at him. Now, that was a grand woman, his Maggie. Nothing like that pretty brunette banging on the door behind him.

49

"Those big hairy brutes. Those illiterate bullies, those...those..." Elizabeth muttered to herself, peeling off her muddy clothing with frustrated little jerks.

"The very idea of locking a lady in a saloon like a common criminal." She seethed, as angry tears ran unchecked down her face.

She peeled off the last muddy garment and took a deep gulp of air. There had to be a way out of this place. She studied the tub through blurry eyes. First, of course, there was the bath. Blowing her nose, she cautiously stretched out a big toe and tested the water before her.

She quickly jerked it right back out of the tub. Why that wasn't water, it was a block of ice in disguise. She shivered and clutched herself for warmth. A smirk crossed her face. What else had she expected from such a crude place? This water probably seemed warm to those thick skinned savages.

On the other hand, if she didn't attempt some sort of gesture in the area of cleanliness, she would soon be able to grow crops on her dirt covered body. She chewed her bottom lip indecisively. It looked like if she wanted a bath, this was it.

Closing her eyes as if in deep pain, and trying to keep her teeth from chattering, she stepped into the washtub. She slowly eased her objecting body down into its freezing depths. Then, before her body had a chance to develop frostbite, she quickly scoured her body and attempted to escape its numbing clutches.

It was then she realized a horrible thing. She was stuck. In reflex she pounded on the exterior of the tub and shoved hard against it. Nothing. No doubt about it, she was stuck tighter than a cork in a bottle.

To make matters worse, if she did not get out of this chilly water soon her body would very much resemble a shriveled up blueberry.

She tried once more to pry her body loose, and then sank down in defeat. Quite a dilemma you have here Elizabeth, she scolded. You certainly can't scream for help.

She couldn't bear the humiliation of having a roomful of people observe her being pried from a tub, naked as the day she was born. They already thought her crazy; she didn't want them to consider her an idiot as well. Driven by seer panic, she pushed against the tub's sides once more. The tub only seemed to become more tightly bound around her.

She heaved a sigh of defeat. She supposed eventually Adam would come to fetch her like some bone, and find her frozen to death, imbedded in a block of ice, a permanent reminder of his callousness. She could read it now in the newspapers, "Woman freezes to death while stuck in saloon tub."

In fact, the more she thought of it, the angrier she became. It wouldn't surprise her in the least to discover that awful man thought up this whole thing as some sort of practical joke. Her temperature rose higher as her thoughts raced on. She just bet at this very moment he was laughing at how well she had fallen for his vile plans. Visions of Adam's laughing face brought a frown to her brow.

Well, he would just think of some other method to get rid of her, she refused to die in such an embarrassing way. Spurred on by these thoughts she fought the tub with a vengeance. This time her struggles produced results, freeing her from its icy bondage. Shivering uncontrollably, she grabbed a huge towel from the bed where she had laid it, and began briskly rubbing her body with it, hoping to generate some form of heat to her unfeeling limbs.

Rubbing her hair dry, she glanced out of the window, and then moaned. They would have to put her on the second floor—without a balcony. It seemed the only way out of this room was if she sprouted wings and flew.

She slipped on her camisole and looked out from behind the curtain. No need to panic yet she consoled herself. After all, she had been through a lot worse than this and managed fine. She grimaced, rolling her eyes. Somehow, getting oneself married to a complete stranger who couldn't talk without yelling at her and being kept prisoner in a saloon didn't seem to fall into the realm of managing fine.

No, more than likely she would break both her legs if she attempted to escape out that window.

She plopped down on the feather mattress and dug out her spare underskirt from a frayed tapestry bag. She thoughtfully fingered its thin soft fabric. There had to be a way out of here. She slowly began tugging her clothing on while going over her options.

She couldn't get out the door, or the window, and she had already tried reasoning with the people in this bunch of lean-tos they called a town. That left only one thing, brute force. So far though, all that had gotten her was a sore foot and married.

Her fingers tapped impatiently on the quilt cover in an erratic rhythm. If only she could find a way back to the ship before it sailed, and stowaway on board. Then the Captain would have no other choice, but to take her with him. It was certain that once she reached Galveston where people actually recognized the law, the authorities would help.

The more she thought about the idea, the better it sounded. Her brain refused to listen to arguments such as Rawlings managing to kidnap her in Galveston to begin with. No, right now it was quite enough to find a means of escape.

She glanced down at the rumpled covers underneath her and for the first time that day, an idea caused a slow conniving smile to surface. The answer was right at her fingertips all along, the sheets.

A heroine in a book she had read by the name of "Lucy Largrove" escaped her wicked step-father by tying the ends of her sheets together and climbing out a window. If some fictional character could do it, she certainly could. Without a moment's hesitation she jumped off the bed and began pulling the bed sheets off.

Ten minutes later, dangling from the second story window Elizabeth wondered if perhaps this as not such a good idea, after all. She could feel the knots in her hastily fastened rope slipping and she had little doubt what the outcome would be. However, before she could decide exactly what to do about the situation, one of the knots became unraveled and sent her plummeting the short space to the ground, landing with a smack on her unprotected backside.

"This really is the worst day imaginable," she muttered to herself as she rubbed her sore bottom.

She glanced around for curious eyes and struggled to her feet. Dusting off the sleeves of her last remaining clean dress, she admitted the truth. Actually, she was having an awful lot of those kinds of days lately.

She looked worriedly about her once more, afraid someone might have seen or heard her fall. Still finding no evidence she had been caught, she allowed herself to relax. So far, so good. She peeked around the corner reminding her self she wasn't home free yet. The sun was bursting forth now in its farewell before nightfall, brightening up the town as if a gas lamp had been lit. She would have to be extremely careful.

The cracked mud road was clear, except for a drunken old man spitting a disgusting stream of tobacco, not too accurately, to the side as he walked. Elizabeth wrinkled up her nose in distaste.

Thank heavens she would not have to tolerate these people much longer. She silently watched the drunk make his way across the street, weaving back and forth, with each halting step. At last he managed to stumble into the store across the street.

With one last look, she hiked up her skirts, sprinted around the building, and headed towards the ship waiting in the harbor. She didn't dare chance a look back till safely reaching a pile of unloaded cargo strung in heaps upon the dock. She ducked behind the first group of crates she came to, placing a steadying hand out against one of their rough sides. For a moment she allowed herself the luxury of catching her breath.

Almost afraid to look, she twisted around and faced the still empty street. She sunk down in relief. So far, no one even seemed to notice she was missing. Just a little farther and she would be safely aboard and headed home.

Making sure the coast was clear, she smoothly made her way to the long wooden pier where the sailors were finishing loading supplies from the row boats. Elizabeth could see the ship anchored in the distance. She made sure to stay low, weaving through the unloaded boxes. If she could just make it to one of the small boats and hide under the tarp, she could sneak back onto the ship. Elizabeth felt her heart flutter at the taste of freedom. The Captain, who had just made his way back to the pier after getting a long soothing drink of whiskey, watched in disbelief as the crazed woman zigzagged between the crates. A fierce scowl accompanied her little jump of joy when she made it onto one of the small rowboats unnoticed. It deepened even further when he saw her crawl up under one of the wooden benches, and neatly arrange the weatherproof tarp around her. "Oh no you don't." he said, hurrying to catch her in the act.

Elizabeth reminded herself that all she had to do was stay quiet until she could find a place to hide on the ship. Once they were out to sea, it would be too late; the Captain would be forced to take her along. Simple and foolproof.

"And just what do you think you are doing?"

Elizabeth jumped clean out of her skin at the accusation in the Captain's booming voice. She hit her head on the bench above. Didn't anyone talk quietly around here?

As the Captain reached out and pulled the tarp away, she looked around for an escape route, but the Captain was too quick for her. He latched hold of her collar at the back of her dress and hauled her up before him.

"I believe I asked you a question, Missy. I'd thought I had gotten rid of you for good."

Elizabeth turned pleading eyes upon him. He had been her last hope of escaping and from the look in his eyes that hope was dashed.

"Captain, please, you have to help me," she begged, "I can't possibly stay here. I am being kept a virtual prisoner by that man. Even you couldn't allow such a thing to happen."

Seeing him start to object, she continued, "Do you know he actually locked me away in a room, with a guard to make sure we didn't escape. Tell me sir; is that the action of a sane man?"

The Captain's eyes flickered with surprise, and Elizabeth pressed her point, "Just allow me to go with you and I promise not to cause any more trouble." Now the Captain's eyes narrowed in suspicion, "Honestly. And you can drop me off at the first port you come to, as long as it's as far away from that man as possible."

She could read the obstinate look in the Captain's eyes at the mere mention of having her aboard again. Elizabeth was desperate now,

"Please Captain, you can't be so heartless. I'll do anything you say; scrub decks, stay in my cabin, give you all my money, anything. Just take me with you."

The Captain gave her an astonished look, "Mrs. Reed, I wouldn't so much as carry you across a puddle, much less an entire ocean again."

He pushed his cap to the back of his head, "I'll not subject myself to any more torture, thank you, by allowing you or any other bride to stowaway aboard my vessel."

Shaking his head at the stubborn glint in her eyes, he added. "As to why Mr. Reed wants to subject himself to that torture is beyond me, but I've never been one to look a gift horse in the mouth."

Elizabeth wasn't insulted in the least. She wasn't listening. Her mind was busying trying to come up with some other way to convince the Captain to help her.

"Have you no conscience whatsoever sir? How can you leave me here in this sham of a marriage? You know as well as I do that it can't possibly be legal. Why, the man had to literally carry me back slung over his shoulder, in order to bend me to his will. And now I've just told you he has had me locked up in some saloon all afternoon. There is no telling what manner of horrible plans he has for me. Knowing all this, can you still say you are willing to just leave me here?!"

The Captain raised an eyebrow.

She whispered urgently, "I simply cannot stay here one more day. There is no telling what may happen to me. I insist you do your duty and take me back home immediately."

"Mrs. Reed, the only home I'm escorting you back to, is the one you left."

"But," Elizabeth sputtered, "what about your duty?"

The Captain wasn't waiting to hear anymore, he firmly grabbed her arm and started pulling her down the long pier. She might as well be walking the plank. Elizabeth dug her heels in, true panic written on her face. Soon, she would be locked in that saloon again. She had to do something. Elizabeth quickly latched onto one of the wooden beams lining the pier, wrapping her arms and leaping around its rough surface.

55

She realized how ridiculous she must look but, desperate times call for desperate measures, as someone had once said, and right now she was pretty desperate.

The frustrated Captain tried to pry the stubborn female loose from the pier to no avail. He let go for a moment, spit in both hands in order to get a better grip and resumed tugging even harder. Exasperated, he wondered what it would take to get rid her, hadn't he suffered enough?

Elizabeth gritted her teeth and held on tighter, as she said between tugs, "Captain, wait. What if I promise to go back to the insufferable man and never bother you again?"

The Captain's eyes lit up at the mere suggestion. Never to have to deal with this crazy female again would be worth any price he had to pay.

She smiled charmingly up into his suspicious eyes, "I only ask that you do me one small favor."

Elizabeth hummed a victorious battle hymn as she hurried along the dirt road leading back into town feeling quite pleased with herself. A great burden had been lifted off her shoulders when the Captain finally agreed to post her hastily scrawled letter to Sister Agnes. In it she explained everything that had happened, and the life threatening situation she found herself in.

Yes, soon her mentor would come and rescue her from this purgatory. She realized it might take some time for her letter to actually reach its destination, but at least now all she had to do was wait. That is, if she didn't come up with a better idea between now and then.

Coming up on the town, Elizabeth felt the first twinge of dread. The sun was nearly down now, leaving the sky a soft pink hue with swirls of deep purple throughout.

Two words ran through her mind; sunset and Adam. Elizabeth just hoped Adam was extremely late. She shivered at the memory of his threatening words and picked up her pace. No, she didn't think she wanted him to find out she had left the room.

She raced with the sun's setting to the saloon. Once she reached her destination, a small groan escaped her insides. She stood in indecision below her window, sides heaving and out of breath. It appeared that getting out of a window was a whole lot easier than getting back in.

How in the world was she ever going to manage climbing back into that locked room? She didn't, however, have long to ponder her dilemma. As a matter of fact, she barely had time to gasp in shock as she was snatched up roughly from the ground and hauled, backside up, against an all too familiar shoulder. It appeared that Adam was back, and just as overbearing as ever.

She tried to get the breath to scream, but his shoulder was rammed unmercifully into her stomach and every time the enormous lout beneath her took a step, it caused the breath to be knocked out of her anew. She very much doubted she would have received help anyway from the bunch of ruffians gathering in the streets to watch the show. Her limited experience with the townspeople had more than proven that point.

Adam Reed really was the most irritating man she had ever met. Imagine treating a lady so shabbily. Why, no one with any sense of decency would carry his wife through the streets even once, much less twice, in the same day.

At last regaining her breath enough to speak, she shouted, "Put me down this instant. You can't keep picking me up and hauling me around in public. It…it isn't decent!"

She pushed herself up off his back and took in the crowd gathering in front of the saloon, "You insufferable brute, can't you see that half the town is watching us?"

Adam just continued walking steadily toward the buckboard across the street. "Who do you think you are anyway?" Elizabeth's indignant voice, muffled by the huge back she was lying against, demanded.

"Your husband, unfortunately," he said, plopping her, sore backside first, down in the carriage seat. His furious eyes dared her to try to run again. She decided that maybe later would be a better time to vent her self-righteous anger.

He went to the other side of the wagon and climbed in stating firmly, "Although I wish I could change the fact, fact it is. So, you might as well get it through that hard head of yours, lady."

57

He had spoken with such contempt and anger, that Elizabeth didn't know quite how to respond. But, since it wasn't in her nature to sit back quietly and take what she felt was a totally unfair accusation, she sputtered indignantly, "Well! It certainly wasn't my hard-headedness that got us into this predicament to begin with."

She chose to ignore his pointed look. There was simply no talking to the man sitting rigidly beside her. She huffed in response and turned slightly away from him. Then, crossing her arms over her chest and sticking her pert little nose in the air, she made up her mind then and there never to speak another word to the man.

Adam took one look at her high fluting attitude, and struck the horses hard across the rump, starting the wagon with a jerk that sent an unprepared Elizabeth tumbling over backwards into the wagon bed. Adam looked back over his shoulder at the heap of arms, and remarkably shapely legs, flailing around wildly and let his amusement show in unbridled laughter. Latching hold of the side, Elizabeth's auburn head shot up, glaring daggers at her amused husband. She'd just bet he did that on purpose.

Instead of attempting to climb back over the seat, Elizabeth righted herself and carefully spread her skirt around her.

"Aren't you going to say anything, wife? No accusations?"

She looked up at his grinning face; her own face, as cool as a cucumber, gave him a withering glare. If the truth be known, he was lucky she didn't push him under the wheels.

A puzzled frown crossed his features as he looked into the clearest green eyes he had ever seen. They were unsettling to say the least and he especially did not care for the way his body reacted to someone he didn't even like.

"Murder is against the law here, too," was all he said, as if reading her thoughts.

The way he kept studying her in hostile distaste made Elizabeth squirm uncomfortably on the hard boards. He acted as if she were some sorry trick life had played on him. Now what had she supposedly done? Was he always so disagreeable? What, after all, did he have to be mad about? She had been the one tossed in the back of this bouncing contraption.

Adam gave her one last disapproving look, before turning back around to tend to the horses. He appeared to have decided to ignore her completely.

Elizabeth stuck out her tongue at the back of his head and faced the road back to town. It was fine with her, she much preferred his silence. She settled back and took in the landscape around her. She just couldn't figure the man out. Apparently he regretted his hasty actions in making her his wife, so why put up such a fuss about keeping her?

Looking up at his strong handsome profile, Elizabeth shook her head in confusion. It wasn't as if his looks could send a woman running. So, why didn't he find someone better suited to him? Someone he had something in common with; say for instance, a stubborn mule. She gave a small ladylike sigh; she supposed even mules had their standards.

The more he sat there in silence, ignoring her, the more it grated on her nerves. After all, why should he be the one to decide to ignore her? If anyone was going to do the ignoring, she should be the one doing it. Changing her mind, Elizabeth gingerly climbed over the seat and perched herself beside him. She cleared her throat... nothing. Adam never even glanced her direction. He seemed determined to pretend she didn't exist. Elizabeth just itched to break his calm, arrogant manner.

Turning to him, the picture of innocence, she asked, "And so, Mr. Reed, just how old are you anyway?"

When he didn't respond, she continued, "Because, I really think I ought to be warned, just in case."

She peeked up at his expression, "You know, in case there's some, you know, bad heart or handicap I should be made aware of. Being raised in a boarding school, I haven't been exposed much to that many 'older' people. I would hate for you to wither away because of my ignorance on the subject." Elizabeth smiled sweetly at his aggravated expression. She was rather enjoying herself now.

Adam on the other hand was not. All he kept thinking of was the mess he had gotten himself into marrying her. She sure could get to him faster than a mountain storm. She certainly was a sassy little thing, and he hated how even the ugly brown dress couldn't hide her tempting curves. He had the feeling he was going to have a hard time trying to keep his hands off of her. So much for the peaceful existence he had envisioned.

Keeping his eyes straight ahead, he calmly remarked, "I don't think you have anything to fear, 'Mrs. Reed', since I happen to be the ripe old age of twenty-seven. I wouldn't dream of dying and upsetting you."

Elizabeth let out a feigned gasp of shock, "As old as that? I myself just turned eighteen this past May!"

If her aim was to make him feel uncomfortable, she had done a fine job of it. Adam shifted uncomfortably in his seat.

"My word. Why you're almost old enough to be my...." Adam shot her a heated look. "Uncle." She finished, smiling sweetly at his discomfort.

Adam narrowed his eyes at her insinuation. He forced himself to relax his strangle hold on the reins and eased over till his thigh was rested up against hers in casual intimacy. Elizabeth was very aware of the warmth his body, a strange feeling grew inside her. Oh dear, what had she started? Now she was wishing she would have stayed in the back of the wagon where it was safe. She couldn't retreat now though; she'd look like a coward.

Adam placed a sun-bronzed hand on her leg giving it an affectionate squeeze. Elizabeth gasped.

"Don't you worry none, Sugar. I'll be well enough to perform **all** a husband's duties."

Elizabeth sputtered in shock. The man was past enduring. She moved quickly to the edge of the bench, becoming so pale, Adam was afraid she would feint dead away. He chuckled to himself when he noticed her white knuckles clutching the edge of the worn wagon seat in apprehension.

Adam flicked the reins and didn't try to hide the satisfied smirk. Yep, that sure took the wind out of her sails. For some reason, he'd just bet his dear little wife wouldn't be giving him anymore trouble for quite a while yet.

Chapter 4

He was wrong. Even now, as they pulled onto the dirt leading to the house, he suspected she was working up the courage to speak to him again. His blue eyes danced with mischief when she wrinkled her brow and bit her full lower lip in indecision. She cautiously peeked up at him through thick, sable lashes and opened her mouth to speak. Then just as quickly snapped it back shut.

Adam tried hard not to grin at the obvious fear in her light green eyes. He could even understand her apprehension, though she tried hiding it by raising her chin a notch when she caught him watching her. He supposed he should try and ease her mind a little.

He leaned forward and ran a hand through his black hair. In response, his trusting wife firmly placed her right foot on the wagon's side. No doubt in case he attacked her, and she was forced to jump. He grinned. Nope, on second thought, he would just let her stew awhile. That crack about his age didn't put him in a very generous mood at the moment. Besides, he was enjoying the quiet.

Elizabeth let out a small sigh of relief when they rounded the corner and came to a stop before the lovely, two story frame house nestled in a thick circle of trees. The vegetable patch off towards the right was full of healthy growing things, with a sturdy fence to keep out any intruders who might be tempted to help themselves. Although no flowers brightened the outside, or pretty curtains graced the windows, it was infinitely better than what she had expected to find.

She released her death grip on the wagon seat. Maybe this would be bearable, after all. She cast a worried glance Adam's direction. That is, providing, Mr. Reed would be reasonable when she explained this arrangement was only temporary. She looked doubtfully at his hard lean features and huge muscular frame.

Of course, if past experiences were any indication, that hope was as farfetched as the hope she would sprout wings and fly away. She sighed. Unfortunately, all their conversations so far seemed to end up being extremely one-sided...his.

Adam pulled back on the reins, wrapping them around the brake, and then hopped down. She twisted her hands in aggravation and avoided his eyes when he lifted her effortlessly out of the wagon. Deep in thought, neither one spoke as they made their way to the porch.

What kind of a fool would bring a perfect stranger into his home and life? The finality of his actions hit him like a dunk into an icy river. Not only was he married, which was bad enough, but to an impractical and ill-tempered girl.

This was not at all what he had envisioned those long months ago, when he decided to send for a bride. What he expected was a nice pliable wife. Someone to cook, clean, and run things around the house while he spent his days at the mill. No personal involvement, no emotional upheaval, just a nice predictable business arrangement. What he had gotten was—Bootsie. He should have been more careful and less in a hurry about this whole thing. Unfortunately, time was an option he didn't have, then or now.

He glared accusingly at her. Did she have to be so…so good looking? How was he supposed to remain cool and unattached, when his body reacted as if struck by lightning every time he touched her? What really irked him was her innocence. She absolutely had no idea how much restraint it took to resist kissing that pouting bottom lip of hers.

Elizabeth bristled under his intense glare. "Now what?"

Adam shoved the door open, "Nothing, just wondering what kind of mess I got myself into, that's all."

Elizabeth brushed him muttering; "Now you're worried? Couldn't possibly have considered your actions while I was in the process of being tackled to the ground, or forced…"

"Stop that muttering woman."

Elizabeth huffed in exasperation. He was beginning to get on her nerves. Did he always have to shout orders at her as if she were a child?

He reached out and dragged her unceremoniously into a large open room that was apparently used as the parlor. It contained a handmade rocker, a clock on the mantle, a skin from some poor animal lying on the floor, and a sofa. Apparently the only source of light in the room came from a well-used kerosene lamp resting on a rough pine table in the corner. Without special pictures or mementos gracing the mantel and walls, the place seemed barren and empty.

Noticing her look of disappointment, Adam leaned a broad shoulder against the door frame, "So, sweetheart, what do you think of your new home?"

Elizabeth flinched at the word home and turned away from the piercing look in his eyes. She gingerly reached out and tested the rocker, before placing her aching backside on its quilted cushion.

"I think," She remarked casually, "that you only call me sweetheart to irritate me."

He winked and gave her a slow sexy smile that made her stomach feel as if she'd just swallowed a dozen butterflies.

"Does it?"

She studied him a long moment, "Very much so. But knowing the extreme pleasure you receive from accomplishing that feat, I suppose there is little hope you will stop."

He shrugged his massive shoulders, "Probably not."

Elizabeth responded to the twinkle in his eye with an amazed, "You really are an awful man, did you know that?"

Adam didn't feel as if that statement deserved a response. Besides, he was too busy trying to imagine what it would be like to run his fingers through her wonderful mass of soft Auburn curls.

Their eyes met. Lightening hit him broadside. Yeah, Adam, he admonished, very cool and unattached.

He asked rather gruffly, "Would you like to see the rest of the house, or meet Nicholas and Chelsea?"

She gripped the arms of the rocker, "Oh my, I quite forgot about the children."

She whispered the word 'children' with such impending doom, that even Adam wondered if they were something other than his niece and nephew.

Helping her to rise, he smiled reassuringly, "Come on sweetheart, I promise they won't bite. Besides, I only allow them to do away with one

63

mother a year, and you're in luck, they finished the last one off a month ago."

Elizabeth was not amused.

She solemnly shook her head and explained, "Oh, but you don't understand, children hate me."

Adam sighed, "I am sure you are exaggerating."

Elizabeth tried once more to warn him, when a rather small streak came tearing around the corner and straight for her. She meant to move, but somehow the message didn't reach her limbs fast enough. She barely had time to let out one horrified scream, before the streak collided with full force and sent her flying backward. A minute later she was moaning in pain from her position on the hardwood floor, and trying to resist the urge to rub her now throbbing backside.

Adam tried not to grin at her unladylike stance. Her skirt was twisted immodestly underneath her and showed him a fair amount of sexy limbs. Her wavy hair meanwhile took the opportunity to spring free of its pins and half cover her face. From the heated look she was giving him, he didn't think now was the time to introduce her to Nicholas. Dazed, Elizabeth parted her hair out of the way and wondered what had attacked her. Looking up, she noted the only new occupant in the room. One, rather pleased with himself, little boy of about eight years old.

He studied her through mischievous brown eyes, much like Adam's. After rudely sizing her up, he frowned. Obviously, she was sadly lacking in his eyes. He then tried to intimidate her with a mean scowl.

Elizabeth scowled back.

"Nicholas," Adam admonished.

The small boy tore his gaze from Elizabeth, "Yes, sir?"

"How many times have I told you not to run in the house?"

Nicholas looked down guiltily, kicking at an imaginary rock with the end of his toe, "Sorry, Uncle Adam."

Adam ruffled his nephew's head affectionately. Turning to his wife still sprawled out on the floor, he made introductions. "Bootsie, this is my nephew, Nicholas."

"Your nephew?" She looked from the big overgrown man to the diminutive obstinate boy, "But I thought..."

Adam seemed to dismiss her confusion as unimportant and turned to his nephew. "Nicholas, where is Becky?"

The boy indicated a door to his right, "She's in the kitchen, getting Chelsea a cookie or something."

He then turned a puzzled and unfriendly face to Elizabeth, "Hey lady, are you gonna sit on that floor all day, or what?"

Elizabeth struggled to her feet and pulled her skirt back around properly. She continued to mumble the whole time to herself, "I guess he forgot to mention that his children were dangerous as well as rude."

Adam held back a grin and suggested, "Why don't the two of you get better acquainted, while I fetch Chelsea?"

Elizabeth's head shot up. The last thing that she wanted to be was left alone with the tow-headed boy glaring a hole in her.

"But," she sputtered.

Adam gave her a sounding whack on the back and an encouraging grin, "Don't worry, sweetheart, I checked him for weapons."

Elizabeth's eyes pleaded for mercy, but Adam just laughed and deserted her anyway. The unfeeling brute.

Nicholas eyed Elizabeth. She awkwardly wiped a clammy hand on her dress. She wasn't sure exactly what one said to children. "How very nice to meet you, Nicholas."

Nicholas, his hands clenched tight against his sides, announced, "Don't think you can come in here and be my ma, understand?"

She immediately decided boorishness must run in their family. For not only did he look like Adam, he sounded like him as well.

"Oh, and I hate that ugly old dress you're wearing. Even my sheep look better covered in dirty matted wool."

Elizabeth raised her eyebrows at his unsolicited attack, "I beg your pardon?"

"I said," Nicholas repeated as he scrunched up his face for extra emphasis, "that's an ugly old dress."

"Nicholas, cut that out," reprimanded Adam from the doorway.

Nicholas threw her another hateful look; as if it were her fault he had gotten in trouble, and then ducked around his uncle before leaving the room.

"Well," breathed Elizabeth, "I must say I certainly feel better about children."

Adam's troubled expression followed his nephew up the stairs. "Sorry about that. I should have warned you. His mother died two years ago giving birth to Chelsea, and he took it pretty hard." His blue eyes were stormy with the remembered pain.

Elizabeth instantly felt sympathy for the boy and something else for the man with the love still lingering from his eyes. She wondered at the slight twinge of jealousy rising in her breast. Maybe, it was because no one had ever loved her with that kind of intensity her whole life. Uncomfortable, she looked down at the rocker knob in her hand.

Adam turned and looked off through the window, "Then, when my brother dies six months ago of yellow fever, it tore the little fellow up pretty badly. Never the less, it still doesn't excuse rudeness, and I apologize."

Elizabeth was surprised by the protective urge rising within her. Whether to comfort the huge brute confiding in her and to erase the confusion and hurt from the little boy who had just insulted her, she didn't know. At a loss for words, she simply twisted the knob on the back of the rocker, before saying quietly, "No need to apologize, I had no idea. How very awful," she met his cloudy eyes over the back of the worn chair, "for both of you."

Adam was taken aback by the sincerity of her words. He stared at her a long moment, not quite understanding why he felt so drawn to this one particular woman. One minute she was deliberately riling him and the next comforting him. He started to say something, but a plump, dark-haired pixie, in her mid-thirties came striding into the room.

Unaware of the fragile bond she had broken by walking into the room, she stopped just short of Elizabeth and stuck out a friendly hand. "Hello, you must be Bootsie, pleased to meet you."

Elizabeth's hand was taken in an enthusiastic hand shake, "Why you scoundrel," Becky addressed Adam without turning around, "you didn't tell me, you snatched the prettiest one there. I bet the other men are just green with envy."

"Yeah, well envy might not be the word for it," Adam responded sarcastically.

Elizabeth ignored his veiled insult. Instead, she responded to Becky's enthusiastic welcome with real relief.

Becky smiled warmly at Elizabeth out of coffee colored eyes. But it was the small two-year-old on her hip that captured Elizabeth's attention. She was beautiful, with light curly blonde hair and violet eyes; she looked more like a small cherub than a little girl. The only thing she lacked was wings.

"And you must be the children's nanny. You cannot imagine how glad I am to meet **you**!"

Adam decided this might be a good time to exit before his new wife learned the truth, "Excuse me ladies, I believe I'll just go check on the horses." Then shoving himself off the wall, he left shaking his head in disbelief. Nanny, of all the hair brained ideas.

Becky glared at Adam's retreating back, chicken, she thought.

Then with a nervous giggle she explained, "Oh, Mrs. Reed, I won't be staying now that you are here."

Confusion marred Elizabeth's lovely features, "You won't?"

"That is, I ain't no nanny or nothing. I was just helping out Adam until you could get here. Me and my husband, Jim, live up the road a ways, and we are expecting a little one of our own soon." She switched Chelsea to the other hip, her protruding middle giving evidence of the fact.

Realizing that only meant one thing, Elizabeth's frightened gaze locked on the small child in Becky's arms. She took a step backward, shaking her head, "But, I don't know the first thing about taking care of a two year old," as if that would settle the matter right there.

Noting Elizabeth's pale face, Becky feared the worse. If she didn't act quickly the young girl would surely pass out. She practically threw the toddler into Elizabeth's arms, hoping to keep her mind off fainting.

"Now, don't you worry none, Bootsie. May I call you Bootsie?"

"Well, actually I…"

"Like I said, Bootsie," Becky rattled on, "Don't you worry none. 'Cause this one's a real little angel, straight from heaven she is. Hardly ever cries and she just about likes everyone."

"Yes, but…"

Becky untied the apron on her waist, "I left some fresh milk in the cellar, and there are some warm cookies, hot out of the oven on the table."

Elizabeth stood dazed for a moment watching the departing woman with a feeling of dread. Her eyes narrowed in suspicion at the beautiful baby with long golden curls, and pink chubby cheeks. Well, she certainly looked harmless enough.

Chelsea took one look at the departing Becky and the strange woman attached to her, before sticking out her lower lip in warning. Elizabeth duly noted the warning and tried to gain Becky's attention, but it was too late. Chelsea let out such a high pitched wail that it deafened her on the spot.

Frantically, Elizabeth clutched the sleeve of Becky's dress, "She hates me. Please don't leave me here alone!"

Becky looked uneasily from Elizabeth to the wailing Chelsea. "Now nonsense, she…ah…she's just getting used to you, is all."

Adam ran up the porch steps, shouting, "What on Earth are you two doing to my niece?"

Becky shifted uncomfortably, "Why, nothing Adam. Chelsea is just getting used to Bootsie, that's all."

Before Adam could ask her exactly what that was supposed to mean, Becky turned to Elizabeth. A guilty blush rose to her full cheeks, "I'm sorry I can't stay and chat, but you know how a man gets if supper ain't waiting on him when he gets in."

Elizabeth was so deafened by Chelsea's roaring, that she barely caught the tail end of Becky's statement. Something about—deserting her!

In a panic filled voice, Elizabeth shouted in order to be heard over the child's screaming, "You can't possibly mean to leave me here alone with, 'angel,' can you?"

Becky tried to sound convincing, "Look honey, you'll be alright. She'll calm down in any minute now."

Before she could begin groveling, Becky quickly walked out the front door and left Elizabeth with the wailing child perched on her hip. Then to Elizabeth's absolute horror, Adam headed for the same door Becky had just exited.

"Oh no you don't!" Elizabeth drew herself up to her full five foot two inches and blocked the doorway.

"I have to take Becky home. I'll be back shortly."

"You can't seriously be considering leaving me here, even for a second. What am I supposed to do with this?" She thrust a screaming Chelsea in his face.

Adam cocked an eyebrow, reached out, and took the crying baby into his arms. Once reaching the safety of her uncle's arms, immediately her crying stopped.

"Papa," she said before laying her corn silk head against his chest and plopping a chubby thumb into her mouth.

Elizabeth, her nerves shot, rubbed her aching head. "As you can so plainly see, I am not good with children. I wish you would listen to me just once. Now maybe you'll finally believe me when I say I am not..."

Out of the corner of her eye, she watched Nicholas bound down the stairs, and then begin running circles in the hall. Panic filled her voice, "Won't you please try and be reasonable for once?"

An amused Adam handed Chelsea back to Elizabeth, causing the upset child to open her mouth in a protesting wail, "Well, Mrs. Reed, I feel I am being reasonable. I am sorry if you don't feel the same."

She shot him an exasperated look.

"No? Well then, sweetheart, if you'll just give me a goodbye kiss, I'll be on my way."

He leaned dangerously close to her lips. Elizabeth gasped and nearly fell over her own feet trying to get out of the way.

Accomplishing what he set out to do, he smiled and tipped his hat her direction. "I guess we will just have to get around to that little chore later on tonight, now won't we sweetheart?"

With that fearful prediction to dwell on, he walked out of the door callously, leaving her to her fate. Elizabeth heard the door slam with the finality of nails being driven into her coffin. Chelsea continued her slow tortuous method of killing her, with little pause for one of the basics of life, breathing.

To top it off, Nicholas was now beginning to imaginary shooting sounds as he ran around the room, ever so often checking to make sure he was bothering her. Elizabeth grasped for ideas as she started upstairs, hoping for a miracle in the form of a toy.

Checking the rooms upstairs, one bedroom and the other, the children's bedroom. Elizabeth chose the messiest one for her quest. Toys lurked in every corner, but none seemed to be the answer to her problem. If anything Chelsea's cries became louder. After a few more halfhearted attempts to pacify the child, a defeated Elizabeth sunk down in the middle of the room and seriously thought about crying herself.

"Foo," hiccupped Chelsea between sobs.

Elizabeth spun the child around. Finally real words, well, close to real words anyway. "Did you say something Chelsea?" Elizabeth asked with a faint glow of hope.

"Foo," she demanded, now more angry than upset.

Elizabeth racked her brain for the elusive meaning of 'foo'. She picked up several more toys, thinking it was a name of some sort, but Chelsea only slapped them away. Elizabeth was desperate now. "Foo, foo…" she chanted, reverently, "I have to find 'foo' in order to make Chelsea cease her bellowing."

Gathering up Chelsea, she headed back down the stairs, but stopped dead in her tracks when she noticed Nicholas waiting at the bottom. There was no mistaking the challenge in his dark brown eyes. Great, thought Elizabeth. She wondered which was worse, Chelsea's screaming or Nicholas' attempt to aggravate her.

"Where'd you get an ugly, old name like Bootsie, anyway?" He threw out like a gauntlet.

Grimacing, Elizabeth tried not to imagine horrible ways to rid oneself of troublesome little boys. Instead, she descended the stairs, a fixed smile on her face. "I couldn't possibly agree with you more Nicholas. It is a dreadful name."

Nicholas looked up suspiciously at her.

"In fact, why don't you call me…say…Elizabeth, instead?"

Nicholas rubbed his chin as if carefully considering the suggestion and after a long pause, smiled and replied, "Nope."

"Why ever not?" she asked in exasperation.

"Cause you want me to."

Elizabeth's smile faded. Oh, how she hated it here. Everyone was thoroughly disagreeable. Gliding past the grinning thorn in her side, Elizabeth took Chelsea back into the parlor.

Her eyes locked instantly on the rocking chair. Didn't people rock a baby to sooth them? She seized the rocker, as if it were a life ring, and she drowning. Sitting down she rocked furiously for several minutes before realizing it was hopeless. The angel would never stop.

With sagging shoulders she gave up.

The baby turned big, blue and red eyes on Elizabeth and let out an even more outraged fit of bawling.

"Oh dear," muttered Elizabeth, as she regained strength and proceeded to bounce the child on her knee.

Chelsea stopped crying. Probably because it is extremely hard to cry while your teeth clattered together in a steady rhythm. She gave Elizabeth a deeply offended look, then turned up for a fresh bout of bawling.

Elizabeth shut her eyes and prayed for relief.

When none came and Chelsea's lungs seemed stronger than ever, she assumed the Lord was busy at the moment. Continuing to bounce she looked desperately around for a clock. Surely Adam couldn't be much longer. Surely he wouldn't leave her alone with…her eyes rested on Nicholas. Nicholas. He would know how to end her persecution. He was

71

her brother after all. She brushed the stray hair out of her face and ventured a tentative, "Nicholas."

He didn't even look up, long since losing interest in the strange woman torturing his sister. With a bored expression on his face, he sat absentmindedly throwing twigs into the cold fireplace.

When she failed to gain his attention she resorted to a rude bellow, "Nicholas!!"

The boy jumped in fright and turned around to see if he were on fire or something. "What?"

Elizabeth took a deep breath to calm herself, "Could you possibly try and help me here? Your sister refuses to stop making that awful noise."

Nicholas, in irritation, threw a stick to the floor. "What is the matter with you anyway? Anyone knows how to take care of a baby. She's starving, I'm starving, and Uncle Adam's gonna be madder than a hornet too when he comes home and finds you ain't done nothing about it."

She blinked in surprise, "She's hungry?"

Nicholas shook his head, "Where did he find you anyhow? How come you came all this way if'n you don't know how to do nothing?"

She frowned in disapproval at his poor grammar. "I don't know how to do anything," she corrected.

Nicholas threw his hands in the air. "Shoot lady, I already knew that. That's what I just said. Don't you hear good neither?"

She rolled her eyes heavenward, but resisted the urge to correct his grammar again.

Chelsea by this time was just plain mad and looked pointedly at the dense woman holding her, "Me want foo!"

Elizabeth looked questionably at Nicholas who sighed, "Food."

"Oh!" Elizabeth slapped a hand to her forehead, "of course, food."

With a crying baby perched on her hip, Elizabeth did what any other desperate person would do under the circumstances—she accepted the inevitable. She, Elizabeth Brown, would be forced to prepare a meal.

Spurred on by the thought of blessed quiet, she headed for the kitchen. After all, how difficult could this cooking thing be? "Come along Nicholas," she spoke bravely, "Let's make supper."

When she reached the kitchen door, she swung it wide, a smile planted firmly on her lips. The same smile that froze immobile on her face when she looked into the spotless kitchen. Her green eyes traveled to the one thing that dominated the room. There lying on the table was a stiff, bloody object, its sightless eyes staring up at her.

Both children peered in curiosity at her, she wasn't breathing and she was turning a funny shade of green. It was then she started screaming. So loud, in fact, that it even put Chelsea to shame.

A startled Chelsea stared in open mouth in surprise at the grown-up jumping up and down and screaming in her ear. Nicholas barely had time to do much of anything, because he was being yanked off his feet and drug to the front door. Elizabeth ran blindly for the door and safety. She had just reached for the knob when it burst open nearly knocking her to the floor.

There stood Adam with a loaded shotgun in hand and the remains of his front door all about him. Elizabeth overcome with relief, shoved Chelsea into Nicholas' grasp and lunged for her protector. Adam's fierce look was soon replaced by one of confusion when the young woman that had been screaming hysterically flung herself into his arms. In the process, she somehow managed in one movement to securely wedge the gun between their bodies.

Adam struggled to pry her arms loose from around his neck, "Would you cut that out, Bootsie. I can't get my gun."

She was sobbing hysterically into his shirt, "Oh, Adam, it was awful. All bloody. Its beady eyes staring right at me."

Adam ceased trying to free his gun as comprehension slowly dawned on him. "This bloody thing," he asked suspiciously, "it couldn't be lying on the kitchen table, now could it?"

She only managed a nod, before clinging to his broad shoulders and bursting out in a fresh bout of tears.

He wrapped a resigned arm around her and remarked dryly, "Bootsie, that bloody pulp happens to be our supper." He shook his head at the horrified look she gave him. How could she possibly be so naïve?

Elizabeth pulled back to get a better look at the daft man, "What?"

He sighed, "I said, that bloody pulp..."

She turned a ghastly shade of green and covered his mouth with a trembling hand, "Oh please, don't repeat it." Horrified she stared at him in disbelief, "You mean **that** is our supper?"

Adam only managed a nod, because for the first time that night he noticed the woman in his arms. He found himself temporarily distracted by her softness and the way she smelled. Like lye soap and fresh air. He liked the feel of her too, slender as a willow and curvy in all the right places. He pulled her closer.

Elizabeth's repulsion was slowly being replaced by something she could not even put a name to, when she finally realized how tightly he held her. Much too close, in fact, to be deemed proper behavior, why; she could barely catch her breath. Embarrassed, she attempted to dislodge herself from the warmth of his strong arms.

He pulled her in even tighter, whether to aggravate her or because he was reluctant to let go, he didn't choose to examine. She pushed harder against him. Breathless, she watched his dark head bend down to meet her soft, full lips; his blue eyes turning dark with desire.

She in turn stomped down hard on his foot.

He released her instantly. "Are you off your rocker, woman?" He bellowed, his face contorting in pain as he hopped on one foot.

"No, I most assuredly am not, but I warn you I won't allow any unseemly advances either."

"Unseemly?" He was fuming. "You happen to be my wife!"

Both children watched in fascination as their usually calm uncle turned purple with rage.

"I most certainly am not. That marriage was not legal." Then she remembered an important detail, "Oh, and I refuse to cook any longer, especially if it involves dealing with dead things."

Adam stared at her in stunned silence for a moment. Then, slamming the broken door shut behind him with a bang, he shouted, "You haven't even cooked one meal yet, how can you stop doing what you never started?"

Elizabeth huffed indignantly, "Well, there is no need to be rude."

Adam advanced on her until she found herself backed up against a wall. "Let me explain a few things to you sweetheart. Number one, you are my wife." She opened her mouth to argue, he stared her into silence, "And not only are you going to learn how to cook, but anything else I may so desire of you as well, is that understood?"

From her plastered position on the wall she glared a hole in him. She really hated that word, 'understood'. The man used it obsessively.

Not really expecting the fiery tempered woman to answer, he latched hold of her wrist and pulled her back toward the kitchen. Elizabeth groaned as if in agony. She had no illusions left as to what would occur next. Obviously, she would be forced to endure the cooking ritual. And most likely, humiliate herself further by becoming sick all over their supper.

Chapter 5

She did not get sick after all, she fainted.

Adam shook his head in wonder. The woman was a walking catastrophe. Never would he have imagined one human being could cause so much havoc in his life.

First, there was the business of refusing to marry him, which forced him to act like a complete idiot. He grimaced. Then, of all things, spouting off some fool story about being kidnapped. Not to mention, her climbing expedition out of a two story window in broad daylight.

The Captain had explained to him, after he dropped her off at the saloon, that her uncle had recited the sad story about Bootsie becoming ill. Apparently she had run a high fever for several days, soon after she'd accepted Adam's letter. Her body recovered, but her mind seemed to have been affected. She began making up stories, claimed she was someone else. The doctor said her memory would come back soon enough and the best thing for her was to reinforce reality. Her uncle felt the best thing was to go ahead with Bootsie's original plan, hoping it would jar her back to reality. Adam scoffed at the thought; he was probably just trying to get rid of himself a troublemaker. Other than sassing him every chance she got, and becoming hysterical over a couple of dead squirrels, he supposed she'd reacted like…he couldn't think what she'd reacted like. The only person he knew of who could cause that much commotion without even trying was Smitty.

He remembered back to when the cantankerous old soul was building a house and insisted his walls were being invaded by ghosts. He had gotten himself so worked up, that even the widow, Mrs. Edwards, who he had a hankering for, couldn't convince him otherwise. So, finally just to get some peace, Matthew and Adam pulled down one of the walls, and tore apart every last board. Proving beyond a shadow of a doubt, there were no ghosts.

As all three men stood looking at the empty space where a wall had once stood, Smitty had sniffed indignantly, "That don't prove a dang thing! Everybody knows them ghosts is invisible." With that stubborn observation, he had stalked into his three walled house, mumbling something about ghosts being easier to get along with than fool lumberjacks.

Well, this woman was even more hard-headed than Smitty. He stopped to listen, hearing her footsteps downstairs he continued putting the children to bed. After all, he had left her not ten minutes ago pacing a permanent path on his hardwood floor. No telling what fool notion she was working herself up over now.

"Uncle Adam," Nicholas remarked seriously from the middle of his bed, "I think we're headed for trouble."

Adam pulled his thoughts back from their wandering. Pulling the covers up to Nicholas' chin, he calmly asked, "What kind of trouble is that, Nicholas?"

Nicholas gave him an incredulous look, "Well, it's that lady you brung home. She seems to be just about as useful as a one-legged mule. I think maybe you better see if'n you can get your money back or somethin'." He pointed emphatically to his own head, as he leaned over to whisper, "If you ask me, I don't think she's got all the apples on her tree. If'n you know what I mean."

Oddly enough Adam had come to the same conclusion himself. Yep, his beautiful wife was as crazy as a drunken Indian and he wasn't too sure about Bootsie ever coming to her senses again. He also knew that because of his stubborn pride, it was too late to do anything about it. Seeing Nicholas' worried frown, he squeezed his nephew's shoulder.

"Don't you worry about it; everything will work out just fine."

"Chelsea hates her," Nicholas remarked matter of fact.

Adam's smile wavered as he tried to convince him otherwise, "Well, they just need to get adjusted, that's all."

"She can't cook."

Adam's hand tightened on Nicholas' shoulder.

"She can learn," he stated patiently.

"Not if'n she's passed out on the floor she can't."

Adam rose off the bed, trying to lighten both their moods, "Maybe not, but she sure does have powerful lungs. I bet she scared off Indians from here to California."

Nicholas rolled over on his side, grumbling, "Well, I just hope you know what you're doing cause she sure don't."

Adam tousled his hair affectionately before blowing out the light. He didn't have the heart to tell him the truth that his normally sane uncle didn't have the foggiest notion of what he was doing either.

Her heart hammering nervously, and her stomach in knots, Elizabeth tried to prepare for the confrontation sure to come. She shivered and looked down once more at the list in her hands. Maybe if she practiced a little, she wouldn't get so terribly tongue tied when Adam began shouting at her.

Spotting a small mirror over the fireplace, she stood studying her smudged reflection before sighing. Well, enticing him with her charm and beauty were definitely out. That settled, she poked a stray hair behind one ear and began 'rehearsing'.

She was just getting into her no nonsense speech, when a familiar voice startled her.

"Is there some particular reason you're speaking with a mirror?" Adam asked while comfortably leaning on the door jam.

Elizabeth whirled around, her face a bright pink, and wished the floor would just swallow her up and be done with it. Oh dear, now she felt all awkward and jittery again. How would she ever be able to convince him of anything if she continued stammering and falling to pieces every time he spoke to her?

"But I wasn't speaking to the mirror, I was talking to myself." Adam cocked an eyebrow, "I mean, I wasn't talking to myself, I was...," exasperated she gave up trying to explain, "Oh never mind. Was there something you wanted to speak to me about?"

Adam grinned, "Well, actually no there wasn't. I'm pretty worn out from all the other talks that we have had. As a matter of fact, I can't remember talking so much in my entire life. Why don't we just hit the sack, I am sure that whatever is bothering you can wait till morning."

Elizabeth's mouth suddenly went dry. Stammering she finally managed to get out a few coherent words, "Bed? ...Why, no I...I mean...That is..."

Adam watched her discomfort with twinkling eyes. So, that was what this was all about. He strode toward her with slow, purposeful steps and smiled to himself when she took two steps back for every one of his. Her green eyes never left the huge man stalking her, till he had expertly backed her up against the wall with a thud. "What's the matter sweetheart? You're not afraid of me are you?" He planted both hands on the wall, efficiently trapping her, an involuntary gasp escaping her lips.

Afraid? No, she wasn't afraid... terrified was a much better word to describe how she felt. She didn't know anything about being married, but she did know that having a towering man so close she couldn't breathe was not something she wanted to experience for very long.

Unbidden thoughts of Libby, the school flirt, confiding in several girls about what exactly marital 'duties' were, crossed her frantic mind. Unfortunately, Elizabeth never did find out the whole story. The little bit of jumbled information she possessed did nothing to ease her mind; rather, it only intensified her feelings of terror. Nor did it help matters any that the man she found herself married to was three times her size.

She gulped down the fear rising in her throat. What scared her most, she realized were the strange feelings this man's nearness caused inside of her. And, why she constantly found herself thinking all manner of totally un-nun-like things. Like right now for instance, she was wondering what it would feel like if he did bend down and kiss her. Why was it she actually enjoyed the way he smelled, of sawdust and sweat? She must really be going insane.

Forcing herself to concentrate on his eyes, and not his strong square hands that imprisoned her or his broad chest at eye level. She took another gulp of air before saying, "Now Mr. Reed, I am afraid what I have to say will not wait until morning. You see, it concerns our arrangement."

She was pleased to find that her voice sounded much more confident than she actually felt. He, however, didn't seem to be paying any attention to a word she said, because he only pressed his forearms against the wall, bringing his body even closer.

His heat engulfed her. Her chest tightened uncomfortably.

"Did anyone ever tell you that you have the greenest eyes? Why I just bet they would put a redwood in the springtime to shame." He definitely was not helping. Elizabeth felt his warm breath on her lips, and her heart skipped a beat. She was really panicking now. She had to get a hold of the situation, or she didn't know what might happen. "Now Mr. Reed, I really think we should talk about…"

A slow sexy smile crossed his features, "Yes?"

She licked her lips nervously, "About, well, about," she closed her eyes in mortification, whispering, "Things."

Adam was having a hard time keeping a straight face. Apparently, there was a lot more his wife didn't know about. "What kind of things, Darling?"

She let out a deep sigh. The man was determined to make her say it, "Things like, cooking, for instance, and then there are the children," he waited for her to continue. She gulped, "and well, things like, say, sleeping arrangements." There, she had said it.

He couldn't help but be touched by the slip of a girl before him. Yet, she looked awfully young. He remembered Bootsie's letter clearly stating that she was twenty-three years old, his girl couldn't be more than nineteen. Why had she lied? Was she worried he might reject her? There she stood; outweighed and out maneuvered by a husband she didn't want, and she still faced her problems head on. For some reason, that pleased him. However, he still wasn't ready to let her off the hook just yet. Putting on an angelic expression he asked, "Sleeping arrangements?"
She could just die. She dared a quick peek up at him, the awful man was grinning from ear to ear. Furious, she quickly ducked under his arm and put a good ten feet between them. She stomped an angry foot at him and replied, "You know perfectly well what I'm referring to Mr. Reed."

He faced her and crossed his arms over his broad chest, "I do?"

She glared at him, deciding to ignore the question. Moving with purposeful strides, she plopped down in the rocking chair. Pulling out the carefully folded piece of paper stuffed in her pocket, she looked up at him, "I think you will find the conditions to my proposal most fair."

Seeing his chin stubbornly jut out, a sure sign of his unwillingness to cooperate, she hurried on, "If you notice, I've stated here that I am more than willing to care for your niece and nephew, clean house, and even learn to cook." She decided to press her luck by adding, "But of course, I will not touch dead things. You will simply have to hack them up yourself, I just couldn't bear it."

She looked over at him as she continued, as if she really believed she was making a supreme sacrifice. "All I request from you, until this horrible mistake can be remedied, is my own room, and the use of my real name, Elizabeth. Elizabeth – not Bootsie, Darling, Sweetheart, or anything else that pops into your head. "

Lost in her purpose she failed to notice the color of Adam's eyes changing from a cool sky blue to a steel gray. "Perhaps you could move in with Chelsea and Nicholas, or chop down some more of those trees and build another room." She added helpfully.

Feeling fairly confident that he agreed with her suggestions, since she hadn't heard a peep out of him, she smiled warmly. During the delivery of her speech, she had failed to notice the now furious man fuming in the middle of the room. She neatly folded the piece of paper. Now that she had her life back in control, everything would be just fine, why any sensible man…

The paper was snatched from her hands and she watched in stunned disbelief, Adam's big hands crumbled her list into a wadded ball and threw it across the room.

This was positively the most unreasonable, impossible member of the male gender she had ever met. Facing her opponent, she said icily, "I had almost forgotten, you sir, are a barbarian."
Adam's hands clenched tightly into fists. His voice practically roared, "And you lady, are the most infuriating female I have ever had the misfortune to meet and if that weren't bad enough, you have to be crazy to boot!"

Elizabeth's mouth gapped open; her eyes glittered with sparks of rage. She quickly looked about her, for something to throw at his head. Finding a book, she picked it up without even thinking of the consequences and flung it at him, hitting him square in the head with an accurate thump. Horrified, she placed a hand over her mouth. Oops, thought Elizabeth, taking in the reddening imprint the book left on his forehead. Perhaps that was not the best avenue to take in trying to reason with the man. He was, after all, terribly large. Sister Agnes had warned her time and again that her temper would be her downfall, looks like she was right.

Seeing that she too recognized her mistake, Adam made his way purposely toward her. His barely restrained anger was evident on his face, and he no doubt intended to kill her.

Elizabeth quickly scrambled over the back of the sofa, placing the furniture between them. "I couldn't help it; you won't even listen to reason." She threw out as if it were a rational explanation for whopping him on the head.

"Reason?!" he bellowed so loud now that her ears rang. "Reason! You wouldn't even know reason if it walked into the room and introduced itself!"

Jumping over the sofa as easily as a panther, he tackled her to the floor and pinned her beneath his large body. Speaking through clenched teeth, he ground out, "Now you listen to me for a change. I have a few 'conditions' of my own."

"Why you overgrown…" Elizabeth pushed vainly against him. I was like trying to move a fallen tree.

"I'm talking now, and you are listening." He ordered.

Biting back the retort on her tongue, she simply glared at the dark haired man who was practically breaking every bone in her body.

"You will care for the kids, clean the house, cook my meals, including I might add, any cleaning of dead things I deem necessary," when she started to protest again, he finished, "And you will also sleep in my bed, because you Sweetheart, are my wife, regardless of how much we both regret the decision. I warn you Bootsie, I will not be made a fool in my own home."

Never mind that he was the one to blame for marrying her in the first place. "As for touching you," she flushed with embarrassment, "believe me that is the farthest thing from my mind. Your virtue could not be any safer if you were in the imaginary convent you so desperately long for."

If at all possible, he became even angrier when he realized how untrue his words had been. He fought hard against the urge to kiss the woman beneath him senseless and added, "Lady, I find you about as desirable as a case of smallpox," he lied, "What makes you think any man with an ounce of sense could possibly want an immature, prudish little girl, who is beyond a doubt, the most useless woman on God's green Earth!?"

Elizabeth flinched as if actually struck. She didn't understand why anything he said should bother her, but it did. Unwanted tears sprang to her eyes.

"Furthermore, I refuse; I repeat, refuse to call you some ridiculous name you made up and be constantly reminded of what an idiot I am for marrying a crazy woman in the first place! So Darling, you will act like a loving, dutiful, sane wife if it kills you, do I make myself perfectly clear?"

Rebellion screamed in her brain, as his angry face swam before her. "If you find this too difficult to accomplish, my dear wife," he added with feigned regret, "I may find myself having an uncontrollable urge to exercise my husbandly rights by forcing you to do certain things, you seem to find unappealing."

Horror filled her eyes, "Even you wouldn't dare blackmail me with something like that."

He looked down at her shocked face and smirked, "Bootsie, dear, I just did. Don't ever underestimate me, sweetheart. I am after all a Barbarian, remember?"

With that fateful statement he angrily lifted himself off of her as if he couldn't get away fast enough. She was still in shock, so it wasn't until he rudely yanked her to her feet, that she finally got a hold of herself.

She only wanted to escape; anywhere would do, just as long as it was as far away from this awful man as possible. Before she could, he hauled her up against him so hard that she could feel every finely developed muscle through her worn clothing. "Do we understand each other?"

She held her bruised feelings in check, a practice familiar to her, and replied, "Perfectly."

Releasing her, he headed for the bedroom, fully expecting her to follow. "Good, now come to bed. This has been the longest day of my life."

When she hesitated, still standing obstinately where he had left her, he growled, "Now what is the matter?"

She suddenly looked embarrassed, unconsciously rubbing her upper arms, "I…I haven't a gown to wear," she whispered. It was like torture having to admit such an intimate thing to a perfect stranger. She could feel tears welling up in her eyes again and she choked them back.

He didn't even give her the decency of a response, just came back, picked her up in his arms and carried her protesting form into the bedroom, dropping her unceremoniously in the middle of the bed. She quickly scrambled up against the headboard, watching as he dug a giant green shirt out of the dresser and silently handed it to her.

She looked from the shirt in front of her to the man holding it. "I really couldn't, I mean, it isn't proper."

He gritted his teeth, "Would you stop saying that? I told you we are married, everything we do is proper."

"We are not married and you know it," she added.

Adam slammed the drawer shut. "It is up to you, either wear the shirt or not, in exactly five minutes, I am coming back in here and I warn you I do not intend to sleep with petticoats taking up half of the bed, the choice is yours."

With that warning, he left the room.

Elizabeth shot up off the bed as if it were on fire. It was amazing how quickly one could disrobe, when under duress. Once on, the shirt reached well below her knees. It still was terribly indecent, but seeing as she had little choice in the matter, she supposed she should be thankful that at least it was clean. She hurriedly took down her hair and was almost in bed when Adam barged in, without the decency of a knock for a warning.

Time seemed suspended as Adam took in her scanty clothing and thick loose hair framing her body. It only seemed to further enhance her beauty, just as a picture frame enhances the artist's work. She froze, held in place by his intense stare. With great effort he tore his eyes away and turned his back to her. When he did, Elizabeth dove for the bed and yanked the covers up around her. She could feel the heat off her face as he blew out the light and wondered what could possibly go wrong next.

In the semi darkness Adam looked down at the strange woman lying in his bed. Nothing was clear any longer, he thought, running a hand through his thick brown hair. Closing his eyes, he hoped to shut out the vision of Bootsie, standing next to the bed with her waist long hair, and shapely legs poking out from beneath his oversized shirt.

Yes sir, Adam Reed, you are a very sick man, he thought, as he climbed into bed with a disgusted groan. Any man, who is attracted to a stubborn, crazy woman, has a definite problem.

Elizabeth stiffened like a poker when she felt his weight settle on the much too small bed. Nervously, she rolled over and scooted to the edge of the bed, gripping it tightly to avoid falling off. She squeezed her eyes tight and wished that he would change his mind and sleep in the parlor.

Adam turned over, closing the distance between them. Her throat constricted with fear and she inched over a little further.

Unfortunately, there was no more edge for her to inch to. She landed with a loud thump, face first on the cold hardwood floor. From the warm bed overhead, she could hear a deep rumble of laughter. Her fear and embarrassment forgotten, anger swelled once again in her breast. She sat up, mumbling to herself. Did the loathsome man think everything she did humorous?

"It looks like we need a bigger bed, Darling, especially if you're going to continue jumping off of it every time I get near you."

She grumbled under her breath once more, "Two."

"What was that Sweetheart?" he asked wiping the tears of laughter from his eyes.

She wasn't afraid any longer, just put out, "I said, two. We need two beds."

He turned his back and stuck his hands beneath his head. "Afraid not, Sweetheart, one will have to do."

She absolutely refused to say another word to the man. Climbing back in the bed, she tossed her hair back, accidentally slapping him in the face with it. "I really don't like you, did you know that?"

Adam grinned, "I believe you said that much earlier. And I think I told you, it didn't matter what you thought of me, or how scared you were, I intend to make sure you live up to your part of the bargain."

Silence met his statement, and he thought maybe for once she was wisely admitting defeat. Instead, she surprised him by turning back around and saying, "For your information, I was not jumping off the bed, I fell," she stated with much more bravo then she felt, "Furthermore, I am not in the least frightened of you Adam Reed, nor shall I ever be."

Adam stopped smiling. One look at those light green eyes shining in the moonlight and the sound of his name on her tempting lips had just about made him forget everything else except making her his wife in every sense of the word. Instead, he forced himself to keep his hands off her. Rolling over and taking a good amount of the covers with him, he warned, "You should be, Darling, you sure should be."

Elizabeth frowned at his manly back. There he went ignoring her again. She yanked on the covers and settled down to sleep. Adam yanked back and ended up with an even greater amount of the covers than before. She wrinkled her nose at him, before giving up and settling down to sleep. Yawning, she remarked sleepily, "In case I forgot to mention it, you Mr. Reed, are not the least bit pleasant."

Adam's voice sounded groggy with sleep, "You didn't."

Chapter 6

Not only was Adam Reed exceedingly unpleasant, but a tyrant as well.

As she vigorously pounded on the dough that Becky had shown her how to make, she tried to envision Adam in the sticky mass, or better yet, Mr. Rawlings. Her eyes narrowed in concentration as the frown line on her forehead deepened. She couldn't quite decide which of the two had caused the most upheaval in her life.

Carefully setting the dough aside and covering it with a clean kitchen towel, she brushed her flour covered hands off on the apron around her waist. Now, if all went well, by suppertime the bread would be browning in the oven.

She smiled in satisfaction down on the small white lumps of dough pushing up through the towel. One long whiff of the yeasty smell convinced her that this time nothing would go wrong. So help her, if Adam made one more snide remark about using her bread for ammunition, she just might hit him over the head with a loaf. Personally, she herself felt this cooking thing was going rather well. Especially considering the massive amounts of information she was forced to sort through and memorize.

If it wasn't Becky giving her suggestions, it was Adam and those aggravating lists of his driving her crazy. She wiped at the bead of perspiration gathering on her brow.

"Speaking of lists." She remarked to herself, drawing a crinkled piece of paper from her apron, "Let's see. That takes care of bread-making."

Her eyes scanned the rest of the long list and her brief feeling of accomplishment waned. "That only leaves; washing, ironing, jelly making, and mending socks."

She slumped against the rough pine table. Which meant that between fighting with Nicholas and chasing after Chelsea it should take her about...say three days, to finish.

She groaned and stuffed the list back into her pocket along with the urge to tell Adam exactly what she thought about his precious lists. Just this morning she literally gripped the bedpost until her knuckles turned ghost white to keep from snatching the list he was making right out of his hands and tearing it into tiny pieces. Only one thing stood in the way of her doing just that—blackmail. Of the worst sort, too. Imagine! The very idea of threatening her with…well, it was blackmail. Pure and simple.

Elizabeth grudgingly bent down and picked up the woven laundry basket. Surely being kidnapped and blackmailed all in the same year had to be some sort of record. She shoved open the door with her shoulder. Regardless, she didn't feel much like testing Adam's threat. Goodness knows the man could easily have his way with her if he set out to do so. Although, to be honest, he certainly didn't act as if he were consumed by desire. If the truth be known, he avoided her like the plague. In fact, since her arrival that first day, he hadn't made as much as one improper advance.

For some reason, that bothered her. She didn't know, of course, but she felt fairly certain from the way that Hannah had talked that that type of behavior was not normal. Especially, between a man and his wife. He closed the door with her foot and headed for the clothesline.

Those first few nights of sleeping together in the same bed had made her so nervous she couldn't even sleep. She would lay stock still with fingers apprehensively clutching the side of the bed and one foot planted firmly on the floor, (just in case) but Adam had never even looked in her direction.

To make matters worse, she even caught herself looking in the mirror lately every time she passed. Wondering what exactly it was about her appearance that Adam found so unappealing. The whole thing was so confusing. She had started to ask Becky about married life the last time she had come over, but lost her courage and somehow they ended up talking about pickles instead. But she wanted him to ignore her, didn't she?

Blowing a stray curl out of her face, she plopped the basket down beneath the clothesline. What was wrong with her? Of course she was relieved to be left alone. It was what she wanted. If it weren't for those lists of his, everything would settle down into a routine of sorts.

Her day always began with the breakfast lesson. Every morning Adam dragged her weary, half-awake body to the kitchen and gave a cooking lesson. As if any sane person would want to eat in the middle of the night. Why, it was still black as pitch outside when they stoked up the stove.

To top it off, the man actually whistled chorus after chorus of "Sweet Betsy from Pike", while she walked around trying to pry her eyelids open. No wonder she burnt everything, my word, she couldn't even see it. Besides she couldn't help the fact that all though she'd grown up in a convent school, her family had always been quite wealthy. She wasn't used to darning socks, making jelly, or raising children.

Growing up as an only child, her mother was always busy planning parties or hosting luncheons. Her father, on the other hand, was hardly ever at home. On the rare occasions that he was, he completely ignored her. Elizabeth had tried to win the attention and affection of her father for years, to no avail. Yes, this life as unlike any she had known. She'd been only twelve years old when her parents were killed in a carriage accident. All of her father's estate had gone to her uncle, including her. She'd only met her Uncle Benson twice in her life and much like her father he was too wrapped up in his busy law practice to worry about raising a young girl. He quickly packed her off to a school for girls in Pennsylvania. The nuns had run the school where Elizabeth spent the last six years of her life. They had been kind but distant, all that is except, Sister Agnes. Elizabeth had been well educated in all the normal studies, as well as etiquette for young ladies, but she could not manage for the life of her, a single task on Adam's infernal lists.

She placed a hand at the small of her back and stretched backward to ease the dull ache gathering there. Her eyes closed with pleasure as the seldom felt sunshine warmed her face. She couldn't remember the last time she caught a glimpse of the sun. Surely God must hate Oregon nearly as much as she did since he sent rain on their heads practically every day.

She gave the basket of clothes her best glare. And what was she, Elizabeth Brown, doing on such a fine day as this? Hanging out clothes. She sighed at her useless rebellion and attempted to throw Adam's dripping wet long John's onto the clothesline. She missed.

"Oops," she exclaimed, retrieving them. She picked them up and hung the dirt splotched article right on top of the clean white sheet already drying. She then untangled a small nightgown of Chelsea's before slinging it sloppily sideways onto the line, and pinning a tangled sleeve to the still dripping underwear. Deep in thought, Elizabeth hung up two more garments and was reaching down to get another, when she frowned. Honestly, this happened every single time she hung clothes.

With hands on her slim hips, she shook her head in aggravation. The clothesline was completely full and she still had a whole basket of clothes. Perplexed she tilted her head sideways, studying the clothing slung over the sagging line. One garment lay sideways, one was folded over in a heap, and every one of them still so thick with water that the line drooped in the middle.

No doubt about it—she needed a bigger line. Gathering the remaining clothes, she turned around and stopped dead in her tracks when a familiar screech assaulted her ears. Wincing in pain, she dropped the basket and covered her ears.

The angel.

"Bitsee!"

Elizabeth cringed at the mangled version of that name.

"Me thirstee Bitsee!" demanded the two year old as she stomped a chubby foot on the back porch.

Elizabeth pried her hands away from her ears and walked over to the frowning toddler. Where was Nicholas anyway, he was supposed to be watching her. Bending down until she was nose to nose with the little girl, she scolded, "Now I ask you, is that any way for a proper young lady to ask for something, Chelsea? If you desire a drink, then you must ask politely."

Not that the child needed reminding, the two of them had reached this impasse many times over the past two weeks. Scowling, Chelsea stuck out a bottom lip in obvious defiance. She turned light blue eyes on the stubborn grown up and looked as though she was debating whether or not it was worth it to throw a fit.

Elizabeth waited patiently.

Chelsea gritted her teeth as if in pain and pursed her lips as if biting into a sour apple. In the end, Chelsea's thirst won over the fit. With obvious forced effort she spit out the word, "Peese," like it was a mouth full of Castor oil and dared Elizabeth to find fault with it.

That was as sincere as a gunfighter at his own hanging, thought Elizabeth, but it was a start. She patted Chelsea's curly head, "See that wasn't so terrible, now was it?"

Chelsea appeared to disagree and refused to answer. She led the way into the kitchen with Elizabeth in tow. Reaching the sink, she waited patiently to be lifted onto the table.

Elizabeth smiled at the strong willed angel and pumped a glass full of fresh spring water. Then taking her own time about the matter, she helped Chelsea up onto the table before handing her the glass.

Still holding onto the glass, Elizabeth asked, "Now what do you say Chelsea?"

Enough was enough and a mutinous expression came to Chelsea's light blue eyes. She sealed her lips shut, her small hand still clinging to the glass like a vice.

Raising an eyebrow, Elizabeth wondered if a 'thank you' was worth getting drenched over. It only took a second to decide. She let go of the glass with a sarcastic, "You're welcome, Angel."

"Aren't you supposed to wait for Chelsea's line?" Came a familiar deep voice.

Whirling around Elizabeth gasped, "Adam, what are you doing here?"

"I live here, remember?'

How could she forget? His tall frame practically filled the small kitchen. Elizabeth felt as if he'd sucked every bit of air out of the room. Flustered, she unconsciously wiped a dirt smudged hand across her brow leaving a long muddy streak in its wake. "Of course I remember, it's just that…well…you usually don't…"

She groaned inwardly at her stammering. Why was it anytime he came near, this horrible feeling of plummeting down a cliff came over her? She might as well hang a sign around her neck that said 'Stammering Idiot" and be done with it.

She took a long steady breath, "I meant I am surprised you're here in the middle of the day, that's all. Don't you have trees to chop on or something?"

Adam raised an eyebrow at her description of his work and gave her a long appraising look. When he noted her worried dirt streaked face, he tried to hide a grin. No doubt about it, he had her spooked and he liked it.

"Papa Adam, swing me, swing me," interrupted an excited Chelsea.

Adam gave her a broad wink before grabbing and throwing her up over his head till she squealed for mercy. Elizabeth's exasperated tapping of her foot caught his eye, but he continued playing with Chelsea.

Trying to shout above the laughter and still appear vaguely interested was not an easy feat. "Well, surely it isn't your lunch…" her voice trailed off as horror filled her eyes. "Oh, dear."

Adam stopped in mid throw, asking suspiciously, "My lunch?"

The color drained from her face, "I was going to explain about the chicken."

"Explain what?"

Elizabeth smiled meekly at him, "Goodness knows, red pepper and black pepper certainly sound the same."

His voice erupted like a dormant volcano from deep within his chest, "Are you trying to tell me you covered my entire lunch in red pepper?!"

She shouted back purely in self-defense, "There's no reason to shout at me like that, it was an honest mistake."

Placing Chelsea on the floor, he faced her, "Honest mistake? Woman, I am beginning to believe you are an honest mistake. However, your failed attempt at poisoning me is not why I'm here."

She visibly relaxed, but not quite trusting her ears she verified, "You're positive you didn't come to shout at me about the chicken?"

"No." He ground out with a low roar, "And I don't shout at you. I came to see if you wanted to go on a picnic. It was Becky's brilliant idea."

"A picnic?"

The idea was not lost on Chelsea who began jumping up and down, "I wanna go, peese!"

Adam gave Elizabeth an irritated look, "Are you coming or not?"

"I wouldn't go with you if you were the last decent man on Earth, which you wouldn't be, because you're not. Not even if that picnic basket contained the very last morsels of food and I was starving to death," then remembering her manners, she added stiffly, "but thank you for the offer anyway."

Chelsea tugged on her uncle's pant leg, trying to regain his attention, "I wanna go."

He rolled his eyes at Elizabeth and gently pushed his niece out of the way and refocused on the petite auburn-haired vixen refusing him.

"And why not?" he demanded, while crossing his arms. "Becky went to a lot of trouble to make this stupid lunch, the least you could do is go."

Elizabeth refused to even look his direction as she angrily jerked the berries off the table to wash them. "You sir, have the manners of a two year old."

Chelsea waddled up and scowled at the two of them, pouching out her lower lip, "I said, I wanna go!"

Elizabeth moved her out of the way so she could yell at Adam. "For your information, a gentleman asks a lady out, not demands that she go."

Adam's mouth tightened in anger, "Is that so?"

"Yes, it is," she pushed her disheveled hair out of her eyes, "first he comes courting, then after a period of polite conversation, he asks permission."

Chelsea pushed her way between them, "Papa Adam…"

Adam finally looked down on his niece's upturned face and lifted her up, before turning around and placing her on the table behind him. She wrinkled up her button nose at him.

He then moved in closer to his prey.

Elizabeth began backing up. She didn't care one bit for the dangerous light in his eyes. Her knees hit the back of a stray chair, but she reached behind and moved it swiftly out of the way, the whole time making sure the bowl of berries were kept safely between the two of them.

"Well, here in Oregon we do things a little differently."

She swallowed, "Oh?"

He grabbed her upper arms and hauled her up against him, spilling the bowl full of berries in the process, "Here, we marry the woman first. Then, we proceed to the second level, which is—telling her what we want. It cuts out all the wasted time and effort."

"And what if your wife refuses?" she asked, a little breathless.

Chelsea bored with the whole grown-up conversation, found a much more interesting lump of dough on the floured table beside her.

Adam smiled disarmingly. "Well, we just find a way to persuade her, that's all."

Elizabeth's chest rose and fell as she tried to take in more air. Her frightened green eyes never left his, "Persuade her…in what way?" She croaked.

Adam tilted her face up to his, an angry glint in his eyes, "By kissing her into submission."

A clump of dough landed at their feet.

Elizabeth tried to stomp on his foot. He lifted her off the ground. She was now pulled so close against him; she could feel the very heat of his body where it touched hers. For a moment she felt warm and light headed. The thought crossed her mind that it was a very real possibility

94

she might faint. In fact, she wished she could, and then maybe Adam would release the crushing grip he had on her arms.

Another clump of dough landed on the floor beside them.

Adam reached up to hold her twisting head still with a gentleness that surprised her. In wonder, she ceased struggling and watched in fascination as he bent down towards her lips. Suddenly, she was caught up in some sort of magic spell his touch created.

But, just before his mouth touched hers, a blood curdling scream jerked his head up and away from her.

"Chelsea, what on earth?" Adam groaned for both of them as they looked on at the doughy mess that a mere moment before had been his scrubbed clean niece. She was covered from head to toe in flour and bread dough. The grey sticky mass was everywhere. It hung in ugly thick clumps in her hair, long stringy strands dripped from her nose, and she was frantically trying to spit out the gooey mass in her mouth.

Dazed until now, Elizabeth realized Adam had released her and they both hurried over to the Angel's side. Neither one of them anxious to touch the gooey mess she had become. Grabbing up a wet towel Elizabeth wiped at the flour and dough covering Chelsea's face while Adam started work on her hands.

Pleased to have their undivided attention at last, Chelsea turned big blue eyes on them. Elizabeth couldn't help the soft giggle that escaped at the sight of her. She looked like a ghost with spectacles.

With an indignant scowl, Chelsea scolded them back to the issue at hand, "I wanna go."

"Go where?" Nicholas came down the stairs carrying a brand spanking new kitten in his hands. "Look Mr. Miles just had kittens. He's not a boy, after all."

Adam opened his mouth to scold him about bringing animals in the house, but he was stopped short when Chelsea reached up and gave him a doughy kiss. Then before he could react, she straightened her small flour covered shoulders, neatly folding her sticky hands demurely in her lap, saying with all the grace of a true lady, "Peese, Papa Adam?"

There was no helping it. They all burst out in laughter. Leave it to Chelsea to pick a time like this to remember her manners.

Chapter 7

An hour later, stretched out on a worn quilt with his head propped up in one hand, Adam watched as his wife tried prying a jar of butter pickles open with her bare hands. The jar was proving to be the better opponent.

He shook his head in wonder. It never ceased to amaze him how any woman could be so beautiful and not even be aware of the fact. Her every movement was totally feminine. Take right now for instance, while wrestling with a jar of pickles her brushed mahogany hair hung loose down her back catching the sun in such a way that it literally burst in an array of auburn highlights.

She looked up and caught him staring at her. She wrinkled her nose at him and strained even harder against the sealed lid, determined to prove her independence. Adam sat up and reached out a hand for the jar.

She hugged it to her body and doubled her efforts. A slow grin came to his face. Shoot, he even liked her obstinacies. That as the problem, his smile faded. He was beginning to feel more than a simple grudging attraction. The fact that she could affect him so completely and not be affected herself was a blow to his male ego.

"Here give me that." He said matter of fact, once more reaching for the jar.

'No thank you," she said defensively, hugging the jar even closer to her faded cotton dress. "I can manage perfectly well without your help."

The muscle in his jaw tightened, "Blast it, do you always have to be so stubborn?"

"I am not stubborn," she argued, tugging unsuccessfully at the small jar.

Adam rested one arm casually on his bent leg and waited, "All right, suit yourself."

After several loud groans and one very sore arm, Elizabeth grudgingly realized he might be right. The lid was not coming off. How to admit the fact and still retain her pride was the dilemma.

She peeked out at him from under long dark lashes. He was ignoring her while nonchalantly twirling a blade of grass between two stocky fingers. She shook her head and placed the offending jar back into the basket. Deciding then and there no jar of pickles was worth humiliation.

"I have decided against cream pickles for lunch."

"Funny, I suspected you might," he looked up at her and flicked the blade of grass her direction.

Elizabeth met his twinkling eyes just before he winked. She blushed a becoming pink and fumbled with the picnic basket.

"And its butter pickles, not cream pickles."

Something in the manner he corrected her, his voice all warm and caressing, made her look up in surprise.

His eyes were hooded and glazed over like when he... she shook the thought from her mind. Surely she just imagined he wanted to kiss her. They were fighting after all, which was fairly common when it came to the two of them.

So instead, she decided to ignore his comment, curling her legs up under her chin, watching the children play chase through the trees. "We don't suit very well, do we?"

With a slight grin at her bluntness, he answered honestly, "It does appear that way."

"It's rather strange, don't you think?"

Adam followed her eyes to Nicholas who was pouncing on his chubby sister, tackling her to the ground then showering her with leaves. "What's strange?"

"I don't know, me being here instead of the convent. You stuck with me, when what you really need is someone like Becky. I wonder why God gets our orders all mixed up sometimes."

"Maybe he didn't."

Elizabeth cocked her head sideways casing a shimmering waterfall of warm brown hair to cascade over her left shoulder, "What do you mean?"

Adam shifted over to one hip, plucked another blade of grass and studied it seriously before answering, "I mean, maybe that's the trouble with us humans sometimes. We tell God what we want, when all along he knows that what we need is something totally different."

Elizabeth stared at him, whispering almost to herself, "That's exactly what Sister Agnes said."

"What?"

She studied the man she found herself married to in wonder. Taking in the lean hard muscles of a strong body with a face so devilishly handsome that it took her breath away; and for the first time, past all that, to the man he was beneath.

And it scared her senseless.

Oh, not because she thought he meant to harm her in any way. No, it was the way he seemed to see into her soul. Or maybe, it was the way he forced her to feel things that frightened her.

"Do you mean to say that you honestly believe I need you?"

He shrugged, and then boldly met her eyes, "Could be."

"But…that's ridiculous."

Adam didn't particularly like being called 'ridiculous'. He straightened a little and frowned. "And what's so ridiculous about it? You are married to me aren't you, that should be proof enough God liked the idea."

"The only thing our marriage proves is how stubborn you are."

He felt himself losing control. She could get to him quicker than any human being he had ever met, especially when she could be right, "Lady you're a fine one to talk about being stubborn. I think God has made it pretty obvious what he thinks, you just refuse to listen."

She gave him a dirty look and clamped her mouth shut in order to refrain from arguing with him again.

He ran a tired hand through his hair, leaving it looking rumpled and boyish, "Look, I'm sorry. I don't usually lose my temper this way. I don't know what is going on with me lately. Even if you are right and I jumped the gun," his voice sounded strained, "The fact is—you're my wife. If you're so worried about doing the right thing, what about Nicholas and Chelsea? How do you think it makes those kids feel when every other word you speak is about leaving them?"

Elizabeth bit her bottom lip to keep from crying, his words touching her own doubts, "You don't understand. It isn't that simple."

"Isn't it?"

Elizabeth swiped at her tear filled eyes, her voice hoarse with confused anger, "You don't understand anything about me."

Adam rose to his feet, tightening his hands into fists to keep from pulling her into his arms. He hated how much he wanted her, when all she ever talked of was leaving, "Maybe not, but I never will, either, as long as you continue pushing me away."

Confused and uncertain what he wanted from her she fought back, "Why are you always ranting at me? I didn't ask to come here. I was kidnapped and…"

"When are you going to start accepting what is. I didn't ask for my brother to die either, but he did. All the reasons why you don't want to be my wife hardly matter, because you are. Even if what you believed happened is true, can't you see there are other ways to serve God than becoming a nun? Maybe he wants you to serve him here, with us."

It was the closest he came to actually asking her to stay. Trembling, she shook her head, mentally trying to rebuild the wall Adam was so deftly penetrating, "I can't."

Adam took a ragged breath, "Then, Sweetheart, I suppose there is nothing left to talk about."

His eyes bore into hers, "Nicholas, it's time for lunch get over here."

He was barely civil to her throughout their short lunch. She thought maybe his silence caused the unbelievable consumption of six pieces of chicken in a matter of minutes. However, it did little for her own appetite. She pushed her food around with a fork and watched the seemingly civilized people around her stuff the entire remains of the

100

picnic, lick their fingers in ecstasy, and suck every morsel off the scattered bones. Right at the moment, Adam was running a sticky finger along the inside of an empty pie pan to catch any stray drop of filling.

Tired of being ignored, Elizabeth cleared her voice and tried to make conversation, "I didn't know you all loved fried chicken so much. Maybe I could try to fix it for supper tomorrow night."

"No!" Adam and Nicholas shouted as if she'd just announced a murderous plan.

"Why ever not?" she asked truly perplexed by their horrified expressions.

Both man and boy exchanged knowing looks. It would be a crime to let Bootsie get a hold of their favorite dish. She had already ruined nearly every other favorite of theirs with her attempts at cooking. Some things like fried chicken were sacred!

"Maybe some other time, Bootsie," Adam hedged, "Chelsea, why not give the birds some scraps, while Nicholas and I hitch up the wagon?"

Elizabeth raised an eyebrow at the platters licked clean and the pile of stripped chicken bones.

Chelsea lifted up her plate and fished out a piece of crumpled biscuit. Struggling to her legs, with the biscuit mashed within a chubby fist, she toddled off after the birds.

With a slight grin at her tottering form, Elizabeth decided maybe she'd better follow the little imp and make sure nothing happened—to the birds.

A short time later, Chelsea called back over her shoulder, "Look Papa."

Grinning impishly, she ran straight for the unsuspecting birds. Elizabeth was caught by surprise and since she had been crouched down where Chelsea was she barely had time to reach out a hand in reaction. Unfortunately, she was too late. Chelsea barreled through the mass of birds causing them to burst in a flurry of black feathers. Chelsea's giggling voice accompanied her body as she twirled around and around before collapsing in a fit of laughter onto the grassy slope.

Adam, who had hurried over to see what she was up to, burst out laughing, "Great running, Angel, you almost had one!"

Always awed by his easy way with the children Elizabeth wondered what her own father would have said if she had taken off after the birds.

"Why the serious frown? Don't tell me you never chased a bunch of birds before?" The ice broken by Chelsea's mishap, Adam gave her one of his heart stopping grins, as if he knew better.

She accepted the truce and smiled back at him, waving a sun-browned arm Chelsea's direction, "Oh, I did much worse than chase birds, I'm afraid," she replied with a twinkle in her eyes, trying to make up for their harsh words earlier.

"Like what, for instance?" Adam asked, pretending to be shocked at the very idea of her misbehaving and helping her stand.

"Like talking a bird to death, I bet," Nicholas remarked, as he walked up behind them. Elizabeth sighed. Nicholas's sarcasm seemed to possess no end of cutting remarks. "No, it was more like crawling around in the bushes with turkey feathers tied to my head."

"You're foolin'?"

"Not all the time though, sometimes I borrowed the groom's eye patch and became a pirate. I even swiped a rusty old hoe and limped along for effect."

Nicholas gave his uncle a dubious look, finding it hard to imagine her doing such a thing. Adam raised an eyebrow.

"Anyway, my father might have put up with those mild, if somewhat unseemly antics, but when I kept crawling out of the bushes and scaring the wits out of poor Mr. Ledbetter, our gardener, Papa put his foot down."

Nicholas was impressed. Adam was enchanted by the keep she must have been.

"So's how come your ma let you crawl around like an injun? I mean, you being a girl and all."

Elizabeth gave him a sly look, "Oh, I imagine up in heaven they had daily conferences about my disobedience. Or at least that is what my governess assured me was taking place, but since my mother died when I was very little I can't swear to the fact."

"Oh," For the first time since her arrival Elizabeth thought she detected sympathy on his young face.

"Anyway, the unhappy chore of reprimanding me fell to my reluctant father, who was much too busy for my antics."

Chelsea came running back and jumped into her uncle's arms. Slowly the group headed back to the spread blanket.

"Surely anyone could handle one mischievous girl," Adam teased.

Remembering her father's exasperation, she shook her head, "Well, according to my father I was worse than ten children. Besides, after that disastrous birthday party I gave him, I don't think even a saint would have forgiven me."

"What happened?" asked an extremely interested Nicholas.

She settled down on the blanket and waited for the others to join her before continuing. Her eyes took on a dreamy faraway look, but Adam could still see from the sadness in their green depths the story hurt her more than she was letting on. "Well, let's see, I guess I was about nine at the time. No, I must have just turned ten, because it was April and my birthday is in March. Anyway, my best friend Sam's golden retriever had this adorable new batch of puppies that I absolutely fell in love with. I especially fell head over heels with Saunders."

Adam wished he could have seen her wrestling with the rambunctious puppy. Somehow, the little girl he pictured must have gotten lost along the way. He could tell that the woman she had become tried too hard to do the right thing and wondered how long it had been since she let herself enjoy something like a new fat puppy. His eyes fell on her soft full lips again. Or, a kiss.

Elizabeth looked up and noticed the heat in Adam's eyes. She blushed and cleared her voice, although she now directed her story to him rather than the little boy at her side. "I was crazy about that silly puppy. He was deep yellow, except for the white hair outlining his eyes and front paw. We called him Saunders, as a joke. He was a constant wiggle. Well, nothing would do except that I possess that bundle of trouble."

103

Chelsea crawled over and tugged on Elizabeth's hand. She gracefully settled a squirming Chelsea onto her lap. Nicholas kept trying to imagine the lady in question falling in love with a puppy, but failed.

Adam didn't understand the surge of protectiveness that caused him to lay a comforting hand over hers as she nervously twisted the corner of Chelsea's dress, "I take it your father was not too pleased?"

"To tell the truth," she admitted sheepishly, "I didn't ask him. You see, I knew my father would never agree so I came up with the perfect plan. I would give the puppy to him for his birthday. Surely then, he would have to keep it. It is, after all, extremely rude to return a gift. Since my own father drilled this into me, I felt fairly safe in my assumption."

"Did it work?" Nicholas asked eagerly.

Elizabeth's green eyes twinkled with mischief, "It might have, except I failed to take into account that my father positively hated dogs."

She absentmindedly smoothed Chelsea's tousled curls, "But I was determined, so I began preparing for the big day. I asked cook to make a three-tiered cake with thick creamy icing. Even my governess helped with the decorations, and she hardly ever lifted a finger to do anything. The puppy sported a red satin ribbon around his neck and an eager look that I was sure even my father couldn't resist. To make sure it was perfect, I invited all of my friends."

Adam laughed, leaning back comfortably on one arm, "Your friends?"

"Certainly," she winked, "his were much too stuffy."

That innocent wink was nearly his undoing, "Then what happened?"

"Well, actually it was Edward Wilkerson's toad that spoilt the party, and I certainly didn't invite him."

Nicholas stretched out on his stomach with his face propped up by his hands, "Was he one of those huge bull frogs?"

"Yes, he was. And can you believe he actually jumped out of Edwards pocket and landed with a thump right on top of Cook's beautiful cake. I was so angry with Edward that I swung at him and missed. Unfortunately I didn't miss the flower filled vase behind him. It crashed

104

to the floor, scattering wilted flowers everywhere. Meanwhile the frog decided to have some punch before hopping across my mother's best linen tablecloth."

Nicholas' eyes were alight with excitement, "Did ya catch him?"

"Oh no, It went from bad to worse. Between chasing the frog, Edward, and the now barking puppy, the house was a total wreck. It rather resembled the aftermath of one of those Texas Twisters one is always hearing so much about."

She untangled her hair from Chelsea's fingers and kissed the top of her head. Seemingly unaware of it being the first time she had ever been comfortable and openly affectionate with the little girl. Adam noticed right away and tried not to break the spell by mentioning it.

Elizabeth herself was actually enjoying all of the attention. She widened her eyes for emphasis, "You should have seen how awful I looked with my frog printed dress and lopsided bow."

She wagged a finger at them, "let me tell you, when my father finally walked into the room I thought my life was over."

"I bet he was madder than a wild boar!"

She shivered, "I think I would have preferred a wild boar, but at least one good thing came out of that party…"

"What was that?" replied Nicholas.

"I certainly surprised him!" She admitted with a shrug.

Everyone burst out laughing and Elizabeth beamed, feeling all warm and accepted inside. She especially liked the way Adam studied her, as if seeing her for the first time. It was the only way she could open up with him without revealing too much of herself and he seemed to understand what she was trying to do.

Adam snatched Nicholas to his chest and started wrestling him to the ground, while teasing his knuckles across the top of his head. "Let that be a warning to you nephew, beware of inviting puppies and frogs to birthday parties."

When a short time later the children left in search of their own frogs, a kind of comradeship grew between the two adults. Adam lost in thought helped Elizabeth finish packing up their picnic. They picked up the log cabin quilt at the same time.

Elizabeth shyly dropped her end as if the electricity between them transmitted over the quilt they held.

"I could use some help folding this thing." Adam teased, trying to lighten the moment. While being affected in the same way, he wanted to touch her.

Again they fell silent. A wealth of emotion passing between them each time their hands met when folding the large quilt.

"So," Adam broke their silence, "did you get to keep the puppy?"

Surprised at the question, Elizabeth answered honestly, "Well, no, but I hardly deserved to keep it, did I? My father was…well, he was an extremely reserved and practical sort of man. I think it was the first and only time I ever actually heard my father shout in front of the servants. Hardly the sort of man to be very tolerant of puppies and wayward little girls."

Adam, in his anger over the callous way she had been treated, shook the quilt a little too hard, jerking it out of her hands. At her puzzled look, he asked gruffly, "Then, what did he do?"

She felt all shaken up inside, remembering the hurt; she answered a little too brightly, "What else do you do with unruly children, but send them away to school. I can't say as I blame him, I don't seem to be able to get along with children either."

A fierce need to shield her from past hurts caused his gentle reply, "Maybe that is because you never had a chance to be a child yourself."

"Perhaps," she lifted her eyes to his, searching for and believing, if only for a moment, that he held the answer to the loneliness inside her, "or maybe I'm not that easy to love."

Her breath came out in a surprised rush. She had never told anyone that before. It made her feel vulnerable and frightened. Trying to lessen the importance of her words she shrugged, picking up her end of the quilt once more and handing him the final fold. "Heavens, I practically told you my whole life's story. I guess we had better see about the kids.

A big bull frog might have recognized Chelsea for the pest she is and sucked her right down."

Adam picked up on her unspoken plea to change the subject. The whole time he couldn't help wondering about the story the Captain had told him concerning her background. Knowing her better, he realized the story did not match up with the woman he knew. It bothered him.

He followed her back to the picnic basket and seeing her struggle with the same jar of pickles, he took it out of her hands.

"Adam," Elizabeth pointed out cautiously.

"Not now Bootsie, I need to get back to the mill and can't argue with you about how stubborn you are. How in the world did you get this lid so messed up?" He growled, struggling with the bent pickle lid.

"I didn't, you did. But, Adam I am trying to tell you that the horse…"

"I said not now!"

Crossing her arms and plopping down on a fallen log, she remarked smugly, "Fine, just let that old horse run away with the wagon, I certainly don't care, it isn't my horse."

"Run away with the…," he shot up just in time to see the tail end of his wagon disappearing into the woods.

He threw his hat down on the ground, "Of all the… Why didn't you say something?"

Insulted, she yelled right back at him, "I tried. As I recall you said something about being too busy to listen, which isn't the least surprising."

Glaring at her, he picked his hat up and jammed it back down on his head, "Is it too much to ask that you stay put till I get back? All I need is to spend another hour looking for you after chasing that fool horse down."

"And what is that supposed to mean? I'll have you know I could find my way home without you. As a matter of fact, I managed fine all the way from Pennsylvania and you were nowhere around." She huffed.

Sometimes he wanted to shake her, "Yeah, and from what I hear that went real well."

Embarrassed she blushed a bright red, "You are impossibly rude, and your horse is getting away."

"I want your word that you won't leave this spot, or I am dragging you with me."

She knew he meant every word. Refusing to look at him, she said, "I won't leave."

"Your word?"

"Honestly," she ground out, "I promise. There... are you satisfied?"

"Immensely. If you need anything Nicholas should be within shouting distance." She wondered why he considered an eight year old more responsible than she, but to ask would require speaking to him.

Exasperated, Adam headed after the sorriest excuse for a horse he ever saw. Mumbling some very choice words to himself, he stormed off in the direction of the run-away wagon.

After several minutes passed and still no Adam, Elizabeth decided to take matters into her own hands. She intended on going home. Remembering Adam's words about Nicholas, she cupped her hands around her mouth calling, "Nicholas!" Never believing for one minute he would appear.

To her utter amazement, he broke through the trees at a dead run. She looked down at her hands in astonishment, then back at the small boy running straight for her. My stars, she thought, it worked.

"Bootsie, where's Uncle Adam?" Nicholas demanded between breaths when he finally reached her, "I have to find him."

Elizabeth patted his shoulder, "It's all right Nicholas, I called because it is time to go home," she gave him a determined glare. "He can just chase that horse all the way into tomorrow if he wants, but I refuse to wait on him a minute longer. If he thinks an eight year old is responsible, then fine. You're responsible."

Nicholas rubbed his head in confusion, "What are ya talking about? Please, Bootsie, pay attention. I have to find Uncle Adam before it's too late!"

His words finally sunk in. Something was terribly wrong. She looked behind him for his sister. She was nowhere in sight. Elizabeth's stomach knotted up in fear, "Nicholas, where is Chelsea?"

His frightened look told her all she needed to know. "What happened?"

On the verge of tears he was still gulping air into his lungs, "Honest, Bootsie, I thought she was right beside me…"

Panic rose in her throat until she thought it would choke her, "Do what, Nicholas?"

"We were chasing lizards near that old haunted cave. I didn't mean it, but she was buggin' me. Then, when I turned around she was gone and…I called and called, but I couldn't find her. There must be a million tunnels and I might have gotten lost too…I have to find Uncle Adam!"

The hair on her head stood up at the mention of the dark, looming place. She shivered as a familiar cold fear assaulted her. A cave, she hated caves, any dark place for that matter. Many times in the newspaper, she had read stories of victims being hopelessly lost in the depths of the Earth. Such stories only intensified her already strong paranoia.

Nicholas touched her arm, silently beseeching her to do something. Unfortunately, without Adam there, only one option was available.

A determined glint came into her eyes, filling them with the one thing Nicholas needed—hope.

"Nicholas, listen to me. There's no time to get your uncle. There is only me. I will just have to go into the cave and…" she swallowed, "find Chelsea."

"But you can't, that's plum crazy!"

"Then what do you suggest we do? Wait around until your uncle decides to show up? What if she gets hurt, or hopelessly lost, what then? Nicholas, you know this is the only way," she stepped back from him. "I am going in, with or without your help."

Nicholas hesitated, uncertain whether to trust her judgment or not. In the end, he knew she was right. They both had no other choice. Making up his mind, he gave her a short nod.

Then grabbing up her hand in a surprisingly strong grip, he pulled her toward the woods. Behind him, he heard her pray.

"Please God, just this once, help me do something right."

Chapter 8

It seemed like an eternity before the cave finally came into sight. It stood before them, its dark mouth waiting and silent. Elizabeth didn't know what she had expected, but certainly not this solemn, small hole with sparse bushes covering the entrance. It seemed harmless and unassuming, but she knew from past experiences it couldn't be. The thought of voluntarily entering its depths shook her to the very core of her being.

Clasping her trembling hands together, she turned to a very solemn Nicholas at her side. "Nicholas, I need you to go find Adam while I..." Go to my death, thought Elizabeth. She fought the wave of nausea that was slipping over her.

She could feel Nicholas' eyes on her waiting, and she continued, "See if I can get to Chelsea."

Nicholas bit his bottom lip in indecision, "Bootsie, I don't reckon that's a very good idea, it's awfully dark in there. Why, there are spiders and snakes and..."

"It doesn't matter if the devil himself is in there. I have no other choice. Are you going to get your uncle or not?" Elizabeth's voice sounded strained with near hysteria. His mention of slimy creatures crawling around in there was not helping. If only he would go before she lost her nerve.

Nicholas looked from Bootsie toward the dark opening, as if contemplating whether or not to trust Bootsie to save his sister. With no other options, and no one else to trust, he finally looked up at her worried expression and nodded, "I'll find him all right." Then he turned to leave.

"Nicholas!"

He stopped short, looking back over one shoulder, "Yeah?"

"Umm...Does Chelsea have a favorite song?"

"The Old Grey Mare," he answered soberly. Then a spark came into his eyes as he said, "Find something to mark your trail with Bootsie, something you can feel in the dark."

111

Elizabeth gave a weak smile, "Thanks. Now hurry, we are depending on you."

Watching him fade into the trees, she straightened her shoulders and prayed for courage. Before she backed out, she forced herself to turn around and walk over to the opening. Cupping her hands around her mouth she shouted into the cave, "Chelsea, hold on sweetheart, I'm coming!"

I can do this, thought Elizabeth, as she stepped into the dim opening. After all, there is nothing in the dark that can't be found in the light of day. Except, she gulped, one could avoid stepping on a snake in the light. She shook herself mentally. It would help nothing to become hysterical. She had to remain calm. She simply would think about something else. Like for instance…how much she wished Adam was here.

She inched down the slightly sloping path until it divided into two dark holes, one veering to the left, the other to the right. Pale light filtered in from the opening behind her. She knew that once she moved further away from its source the paths would continue to divide, and soon she would never be able to tell the difference. It was the most alone anyone could ever feel.

Which way should she go? The light behind her only seemed to make the dark before her that much blacker. Dust was dancing in the dim light around her. She tried to take a gulp of air, fearing she surely would suffocate if she had to stay there much longer.

Feeling weak with fear, she gripped the damp wall, leaning her head against its cool surface. How easy it would be to just stay here. Visions of Chelsea inside one of those dark tunnels, forced her to fight this overwhelming need for flight.

With one hand holding fast to the cold rock, she leaned into the tunnel on her right, "Chelsea, can you hear me? Answer me Angel."

Deafening silence was her only reply. Ignoring the pounding of her heart, she tried the other tunnel. Still nothing, she slumped against the dirt wall, now what? Tears of frustration clogged her throat as she went over and yelled again and again hoping for some response from the two year old.

Then just when she had decided to chance the tunnel on her right, she heard a faint whimper coming from the left.

Relief washed over her as she called loudly, "It's okay Angel, I'll be right there. Don't move."

Trembling hands grabbed the blue folds of the dress Becky had given her. She walked trembling forward, letting the dark void swallow her up. It was as if she had stepped into nothingness. There were no walls, ceiling or floors in this cool damp place and she felt her heart racing wildly in response to the fear welling up inside her. Her confidence slipping, she reached out to touch the moist dirt walls, only to have something wriggle beneath her fingers. A small scream escaped her lips as she jerked her hand away.

"I really hate dark, wet places," she whispered to no one in particular, as if some misunderstanding made her an unwilling participant in this experience.

Memories of another time entered her mind as she made slow progress through the cave, making sure to stop and place piles of stones along the wall with a torn piece of fabric from her dress beneath. She tried not to think about what she would do if she missed one on the way out.

Once more she was a small child of seven, not afraid of anything, except perhaps her father. It was ironic too that because of another dare years ago, she found herself so terrified now.

She had known better than to trust Callie. She was known for her cruelty. Her brother had stood there as well, watching her through handsome brown eyes, to see if she were brave enough to be shut into old Mrs. Anderson's cellar for two whole minutes. Even back then Elizabeth couldn't resist a dare. So, stupidly, she had walked down the steep steps to the dirt floor at the bottom. Never once uttering a word of protest as the heavy door slammed shut above her with a sickening sense of finality.

That is, she didn't utter a word until the two minutes were up and Callie refused to let her out. A shiver of remembered panic went over her body. She had frantically climbed up and pounded on the door overhead for what seemed like hours. She pleaded, threatened and sobbed to be let out. To this day, she could hear their cruel laughter, as they left her there alone in her dark prison.

At last realizing the futility of her efforts, she had given up and waited in deafening silence for a rescuer. With her hands aching, and her throat parched, she had promised herself then and there she would never enter any dark place again. That thought alone helped carry her through her long three hour imprisonment with quiet dignity until Mrs. Anderson discovered her.

Tears of remembered helplessness gathered in her eyes. She closed her eyes and drew in a deep breath to calm herself. She was not seven any longer. More importantly, she was not helpless or alone. A lot had happened since that day long ago. Her 'calling', her kidnap, and finally her marriage, she had survived them all and she would survive this too.

It was strange what thoughts pop into one's brain when faced with certain death. Well, maybe not certain, but as close as she cared to come. A ghost of a smile touched her lips as she forced herself to focus on taking one step at a time. Soon Adam would come and he knew so much about wilderness things that even if she managed to bungle this up he would save them both. He had to.

She soon came to another fork in the path, she could tell by the draft coming in from the right. There was a certain amount of pride she felt in realizing so small a victory, but it was short lived when she stood indecisively between the two options.

Her instinct told her to remain straight, but if Chelsea had turned…Chelsea's quiet sobs answered the question for her. They rose and fell from somewhere straight ahead. At least she thought it was straight ahead. As she walked deeper into the cave, the sounds were becoming more confusing. More ghostlike. Did she dare trust her ears?

Determinedly she tore off another much larger piece of her dress and felt around the damp floor for stones. Finding three large enough for her purpose, she laid the cloth under one end facing the direction she needed to go.

That accomplished, she entered the seemingly small chamber. Now there was no mistaking Chelsea's whimper of fear. Elizabeth had never heard anything so wonderful in all her life.

"Chelsea! Angel! It's me, Bitsee!"

Chelsea's loud sobs echoed all around them.

Trying to soothe her, Elizabeth spoke softly, "My, what a big girl you are. I bet Nicholas wishes he could come exploring with us. However, now that I have seen the inside of one, I don't much care for caves, do you?"

Chelsea's sobs died down for a moment and Elizabeth suddenly realized that for the past few minutes she had been solely relying on sound to lead her. She sent a prayer of thanks up to heaven and tried not to let the panic in her voice betray her, "Angel, can you hear me?"

For a long time silence filled the cave, and then it was sweet music indeed when Chelsea answered, "I wanna go home. I don't like 'ploring."

Elizabeth laughed, tears of relief running down her face. Chelsea sounded perfectly fine to her. It only took a few minutes of Chelsea answering inane questions before Elizabeth realized she couldn't pinpoint exactly where Chelsea's voice was coming from. She wiped a grimy hand across her face in a fruitless effort to see better. If she hadn't been so anxious she would have collapsed by now. Her legs were trembling and bruised from falling numerous times and crawling through small passages during the last twenty minutes.

Just a little longer she told herself, she had long since given up listening and resorted to feeling blindly around on the dirt floor. Surely the chamber could not be that big. At last she touched something soft that let out a terrified scream in response, almost deafening Elizabeth on the spot.

"Chelsea?" breathed Elizabeth.

Her heart full, she gathered up the frightened child, touching the springy curls, the small tear streaked cheeks and the wonderfully whole little body. "Chelsea, what do you say we get out of here?"

Chelsea's arms tightened around Elizabeth's neck before burying her head in her shoulder, nodding in agreement. Lifting the small child in

115

her arms, she began inching her way around the wall until her hands found the precious scrap of material she had left at the opening.

"So far, so good," she spoke to no one in particular. "Only one opening at a time."

Both woman and child were silent, heading along the narrow passageway. Chelsea clung to Elizabeth as if she were her only salvation. Meanwhile, Elizabeth concentrated on keeping one hand outstretched along the wall, in an effort not to lose the only real thing in the empty void around them.

Coughing, Elizabeth's lungs tried to expel the dust invading them. She could barely breathe, not to mention the fact that Chelsea had begun crying again and the sound of her voice echoed throughout the darkness.

Shaking her head, Elizabeth tried to shut out everything, except concentrating on where the next pile of stones was, but Chelsea was making it impossible to concentrate on anything.

Exasperated, Elizabeth got down on scraped knees and groped around searching for a pile of stones. It had been too long since she had come across one. What if she had missed it? What if she took a wrong turn somewhere? She pounded the ground in frustration. Everything was so black it was impossible to tell.

She sank the rest of the way to the ground, leaning her head back against the hard stone wall. Hopelessness filled her heart. It was no use; she didn't know where to go from here. Tears slid down her cheeks and dropped from her face. She was too frightened to move. Besides, she was supposed to be in a nice safe nunnery somewhere, not crawling around in this horrible cave.

Chelsea cried even harder, as tears raked Elizabeth's body, "Please God, help me," she sobbed.

It was at that moment Chelsea's hysterical sobs reached through Elizabeth's frightened haze. The child needed her strength. She didn't have time for self-pity now, but definitely later when this was all over she was going to have one good long cry.

"Chelsea," Elizabeth wiped at her eyes with a corner of her dress. "Let's sing a song until Uncle Adam comes, okay?"

The little girl shook her head no, giving a little hiccup.

"Oh, please Angel? I am a little afraid and it would help me feel so much better."

Chelsea lifted her head up off Elizabeth's chest. "I scared too."

"Then, let's sing about that old blue horse."

Chelsea giggled, "Old Grey Mare, Bitsee."

"I believe you are right," she said with pretended surprise, "it is an old red bull."

They burst out in laughter at her attempt at humor. Then, with both their voices a little shaky, they began to sing, "The Old Grey Mare". It was slightly off key and loud enough to cause an avalanche, but it did much to lift the spirits of two very frightened girls.

Ending the song in a fit of giggles, Elizabeth lifted Chelsea's finger up, "Okay Angel, let's sing one more time."

It was at that moment Adam's strong clear voice interrupted, "Bootsie! Can you hear me honey?"

Not only could she hear him, she would have kissed him were he close enough. So relieved was she to hear his familiar voice that she gave Chelsea a squeeze.

In a joyful voice she called out, "Adam! Thank goodness you're here! We can't find our way out."

"So I gathered, Darling."

She frowned at his attempted humor. Didn't that man ever take anything seriously? She could be killed crawling around in here and he cracks jokes. She scrambled to her feet retorting, "If you are well aware of the fact, then why are you out there instead of in here rescuing us, like any other respectable gentleman?"

Adam's voice betrayed a slight chuckle, "Because Sweetheart, if I were, we'd both be lost. I'll just get some rope. Hang on a minute longer, okay Sweetheart?"

"No!"

"What do you mean no?"

"I mean, I can't stay here, please can't you come and get me now?"

Silence met her plea, and then Adam sensing her panic, answered truthfully, "I can't Sweetheart. I wish I could."

Elizabeth sank to that ground weeping softly, rocking the child in her arms for comfort.

"Honey, can you hear me?"

Elizabeth wiped her eyes, answering softly, "Yes."

"It will be alright, I promise, but you will have to do what I say, understand?"

She was crying softly now.

After what seemed forever, she at last heard his voice coming from everywhere and nowhere around her, "Okay, Sweetheart, I have the rope now. It will just be a few minutes more, but you have to stay put. It's important."

"But," this wasn't exactly what she had in mind, "maybe I could come to you? If I followed your voice…"

"Absolutely not! Adam replied, and then catching himself his voice became soothing again. Although he sounded short of breathe, no doubt tying the rope to something or other while he talked. "Listen, the sound of my voice is deceptive. There is a good chance you could get even more lost than you already are." Silence. "Okay, the rope is tied; now just let me get the lantern."

Elizabeth gave a barely conscious nod, as she began to concentrate on the sound of his voice. Although Adam couldn't see her, he took her silence as agreement, and then ever so patiently he began talking. Making her laugh with his endearments, yet all the while very steadily coming closer with his voice and the safety of his arms.

Time and again, Elizabeth had to force herself to stay put. She swore something was crawling up her leg once and screamed. Fully prepared to run, she was commanded to stay put or else.

What would be worse, she couldn't imagine. His slow progress was only interrupted once by unbridled laughter. "Hey Sweetheart, are you wearing anything in there?"

Shock made her momentarily forget the imaginary walls closing in on her. "What?!"

"Well, I found another piece of your dress, and it makes me wonder what else you took off in here."

"Very funny." She shifted Chelsea to her right leg, trying to get the feeling back in the other one. Suddenly she heard a sound behind her, "Please Adam hurry. I can't…" Fear clogged her voice and throat.

"Don't lose it, sweetheart," came Adam's voice strong and full of confidence, "I'm nearly there."

Unbelievably, the light that was beginning to grow stronger stopped just short of them.

"What's wrong? Why aren't you coming?"

She could sense his hesitation as the light dimmed even more. Finally he answered, "I can't fit. It's too tight; you're going to have to crawl to me."

"But you said you'd come get me. There are…things in here and Chelsea won't let go of me and…"

"Stop it."

Once more, the authoritative sound in his voice broke through her panic. "You have to do this. The lantern won't last much longer, so get moving, Sweetheart."

Aggravation at his tone momentarily erased the paralyzing fear in her stomach. She came to her feet eyeing the tight space before her. "Fine, I'm coming, but I am not happy about it."

His sigh of relief was the only way she could tell how worried he really must be, "Me neither, Sweetheart, but what do you say we get out here before it is too dark to see?"

Knowing she had no other options, she entered the crumpled space. However, getting Chelsea out was proving harder than she imagined. For one thing she obstinately refused to let go of the stranglehold she had around Elizabeth's neck. Then to top it off Elizabeth was constantly walking into spider webs. Every time she was just about to give up, Adam's strong confident voice would urge her on.

Finally, she reached the smaller part of the tunnel. Since Chelsea refused to release her, she was forced to carry her on her back and crawl through, bruising and scratching her already sore knees and hands.

119

After what had seemed like hours, Elizabeth caught her first glimpse of the pale light. As she advanced on toward the lantern light, she felt an overwhelming urge to kiss the ground at her feet. Her hand went up involuntarily to shade her eyes when light flooded the entrance before her. Then, when her eyes had adjusted to the faint light she got her first welcoming glance of Adam. He had a rope tied around his waist and a lantern held high.

She had never seen anyone who resembled a guardian angel more than the man standing there with a worried expression on his face. Stumbling out in her anxiousness to reach him, she flung herself weeping into his waiting arms. Adam. She wrapped a grimy scratched arm around the big man's shoulders and took in the comfort of his presence. For the first time, she allowed herself to enjoy the sound of his soothing voice and the soft kisses he was placing all over her dirt covered face.

"It's all right, Darlin' go ahead and cry."

Adam held Elizabeth tightly, arms wrapped in comfort around her, and the now sobbing Chelsea wedged between them. He patiently held them, whispering words of comfort until their tears were spent. The whole time all Elizabeth could think of was how very wonderful, how sensitive, how caring…that is until the meaning behind his soft words actually sunk in.

"I swear, Sweetheart, if you ever do anything that stupid again, I'll make sure you don't sit down for weeks. You scared me to death."

Elizabeth's confused look went from his stormy eyes above her, to the small child still clutched in her arms and back. It was then she realized, much to her utter amazement, that he was speaking to her. Not Chelsea and he looked mad enough to carry out his threat that very moment. Why, the last time she had seen him this angry was…well…when he had forced her into marriage. That had been no more her fault than this incident.

Her sodden eyebrows narrowed in anger. For just a moment there she had almost forgotten what an obstinate, egotistical…

"Are you referring to me, Mr. Reed? Because if you are, then I have only one thing left to say to you…" she pushed away from him and

120

searched for a word to express just how angry she was. Finding none, she sputtered, "Ughhh. Never mind, because I am too much of a lady to repeat anything that remotely describes what I am feeling right now.

She shifted Chelsea in order to free her right hand then pointed at his broad chest, "Since you are so superior, maybe you could suggest just what I should have done instead. Leave Chelsea in that awful place alone? Or maybe send Nicholas in after her? If you could have heard how scared she was, and how alone you feel in the dark. Besides, I had no idea how long it would take to find you. All I could think of was, what if she ran deeper into that cave, or fell, or..." She started crying again.

Adam let out a long deep sigh. "Are you going to start that infernal weeping again? I just meant you should have waited for me, instead of going in half-cocked as usual."

"Half-Cocked?" Was that supposed to be an apology?

"Bootsie, do you have any idea how deep underground this cave goes? It has literally hundreds of tunnels in it. What if both of you had become hopelessly lost, then what?"

Elizabeth could not believe that he stood there lecturing her on caves when she had risked her life to save his sweet little niece.

"I refuse to speak another word to you. But if I were going to speak to you, which I am not, I would tell you how absolutely wonderful it sounds to be hopelessly lost right now. For then I should never have to listen to your constant orders, or deal with your insane reasoning."

She gave him one last wilting look before brushing past him on her way out of the cave. She took a few steps and stopped suddenly. Slowly she sighed and turned around to face him, an embarrassed flush on her cheeks, "Maybe you had better go first?"

He simply raised an eyebrow at her and pulled in more rope before taking the lead.

She closed her eyes for a second, too upset to even look at him. It didn't matter that all she could see of him, as she followed from a distance, was more ghost like than human. She swore she could see the look of accusation on his face, which made her very...well...aggravated.

Meanwhile, the object of her anger was not too happy either. Something deep inside of him snapped as well. Who would have thought she would have the guts to go into the cave after a little girl who made her life miserable? Like it or not, he found himself attracted to her again, and the simple truth was it made him edgy. She was right, he was being unreasonable. He turned around to face her.

"Bootsie?"

Elizabeth looked at him her green eyes flashing, "Now what?"

Adam gave her one of those rare heart-stopping smiles that caused a riot on her insides, "You're right. I guess when I thought about what could have happened I overreacted. Anyway, thanks for going in after Chelsea. Even if it was a stupid thing to do." He added with a grin.

Elizabeth shook her head in confusion. Would she never understand the man? "You're welcome, but be warned," She added with the baby perched on one sassy hip, "If you are ever stuck in a cave, I am leaving you there."

Adam threw back his head in laughter, "Okay Sweetheart. Just do me one favor if you do change your mind and come after me."

She gave him a suspicious glare, "What?"

"Whatever you do, don't try and comfort me by singing. It just might bring the walls down on top of me."

"Are you insulting my singing now?"

He gave her a wink to soften the blow, "Sweetheart, you couldn't carry a tune if someone gave you a bucket."

She drew in a breath to argue with him, but realized how ridiculous that would be since, after all, it was the truth. So instead she let out a resigned sigh and surprised him with a slow sexy wink in return, "For your information, Chelsea thinks I sing extremely well, don't you Angel?"

Chelsea smiled, hugging her tightly, "Uh huh." Elizabeth gave Adam a smug look, "when I'm lost." She finished.

Smiling, Elizabeth whispered, "Traitor."

Adam laughed. That is, before Elizabeth looked up at him with dancing emerald eyes, then he was lost. He fell silent, drowning in their depths. In shock, he realized just how fast he was falling for the bewitching beauty looking up at him with a teasing glint in her eye. He barely refrained from grabbing a hand full of soft wavy hair and kissing her thoroughly for the scare she had caused him.

Unfortunately, they still had a cave to get out of and they were moving too slowly. Tenderly he touched her face, "Follow me okay?"

Sometime during their exchange Elizabeth had forgotten how to breathe, so she nodded in compliance, however deep inside she found herself whispering, "Anywhere." While following her unexpected husband out of the cave.

Within a few minutes they found themselves at the mouth of the cave and at a loss for words.

Finally, Adam broke the silence by handing her one of the now coiled up ropes. "Nicholas must be worried sick about the two of you, why don't you head down to the wagon and let him know you're okay. I will finish gathering the ropes and be down in a minute."

Once more, Elizabeth found that the thought of leaving him here, even for a moment, was something she would prefer to put off. What was happening to her? Surely it was simply because he had been her lifeline throughout a terrible time. She cleared her throat and ignored the pulling on her hand by Chelsea.

"Thank you Adam."

He looked up surprised, "For what?"

Her eyes watered in response, but her smile was genuine, "For coming to get us."

For a moment time stood still as he looked deeply into her eyes. "You're my family, Sweetheart; I will always come for you."

A warm glow spread over Elizabeth and she ducked her head in confusion. Adam noticed how sun kissed her cream colored skin was becoming, her soft blush only adding more color to her already pretty face. In response, he felt an overwhelming desire to trace a finger along her bottom lip. Who was he kidding; her lips were not the only thing he wanted to touch.

She lifted innocent eyes to his. He could tell the current between them was affecting her just as strongly, as she began to nervously shift her feet and brush at the soot that was imbedded in her clothes.

"I think it is pretty hopeless, Darlin," Adam teased tenderly, "That dress is ruined."

Elizabeth blushed at his endearment, "When you stare at me that way, it makes me nervous."

"Not half as nervous as this probably will." He said as he leaned over to kiss her.

Her eyes became big and round, as she half-heartily put out a hand to stop him. "Adam," she stammered, caught between the desire flickering within her and the resolved feeling that she had chosen for herself long ago.

Bored with the grown-ups, Chelsea tried to wiggle free of Elizabeth's hand. "Race, I wanna race."

Elizabeth gratefully placed the rope on the ground while trying to avoid Adam's intense stare. Undaunted, Chelsea latched hold of Elizabeth's hand and began tugging her into a race down the hill.

"Aren't you a little curious?" he asked in the deep rich voice she was beginning to know so well.

She took one look at what his steel blue eyes were promising before she squeaked out, "Actually, scared is more the word I would use." Then, she gave in to Chelsea's whim and began running down the slope with the little girl's hand wrapped securely in her own.

Adam's mouth twitched at the corner. He wasn't sure if she was giving into Chelsea or fleeing for safety, he suspected the latter. Adam stood at the top of the hill watching them play. When she reached the wagon and slowed to a gentle swaying walk, Adam clicked his tongue in appreciation. No doubt about it, the lady definitely had a nice walk, and this situation was not getting any easier for him. He was still lost in thought as he gathered up the rest of the rope and lantern watching as Nicholas came up the hill to help him.

"Uncle Adam," Nicholas asked, coming up beside him.

"What is it Nephew?"

124

Nicholas kicked a stray stone, "She's kind of growing on you, huh?"

Frowning Adam placed his hat on the back of his head wondering if that were true. Was there just a physical attraction? All he knew for sure was that it was becoming more important to him that she stay.

Perplexed, he turned and answered truthfully, "I guess she is Nicholas, it sure doesn't make a lot of sense does it?"

Nicholas reached up and placed a consoling hand on his shoulder. "That's all right; I reckon girls do that to a fellow. Even the crazy ones."

"I suppose they do, but can't say as I care for it much."

Both man and boy watched as the object of their conversation, looked up and waved. Nicholas buried his hands in his pockets to keep from waving back, "Me neither." He added.

Chapter 9

"Well, I am waiting," Elizabeth said impatiently, her dainty foot tapping with each swish of the mama cow's tail.

Mabel cut her large brown eyes back at the exasperated girl. After studying her for a few minutes, the contented cow turned back around and continued chewing her cud. Obviously she was not concerned in the least with the still empty milk pail sitting beneath her. Nicholas was usually the one who milked the cow and gathered the eggs, but Becky had taken him and Chelsea to town with her.

"It'll give you some peace and quiet for a change." She had explained with a warm smile. She truly liked Becky, but she constantly had to 'teach' Elizabeth how to do things. She was always patient and kind. It was just that Elizabeth wanted to do something all on her own and how hard could it be to milk a cow? Once more Mabel kicked over the empty pail, and with a sigh Elizabeth replaced it. She leaned in determined to learn this particular chore on her own. Surely, she could handle one stupid cow.

She bit her lip indecisively, and then scooted the rickety old stool in closer to the cow. She wiped her sweaty hands on the skirt of her dress. There was no helping it, Adam was right, in order to milk her she would have to…she took one look at the udders before her and shivered. She would have to touch Mabel in a most embarrassing manner.

"Pardon me, Mabel, but there seems to be no other way of going about this."

Mabel replied by kicking the pail backwards into a dirty pile of hay.

"Oh!" Elizabeth spat out around a clump of dusty hay, "that was extremely rude. Especially since I have…"

Elizabeth's lecture was cut short as Mabel's whip of a tail swung again in her direction. A tad wiser since she first began this tasteless endeavor, she quickly ducked. The dangerous weapon whizzed past her head, "See here, you overgrown piece of steak! If you think for one moment I intend to put up with—Ouch!" Elizabeth exclaimed when Mabel's next attack hit her square in the ear.

Rubbing her now ringing ear, she eyed the deceptively innocent-looking cow. If she didn't know better, she would have sworn that cow winked at her! She scrambled to her feet, a determined look in her eyes. "Two can play at that game."

She surveyed the barn around her until her eyes lit on the perfect solution, a nice sturdy piece of rope. She tugged it down from the wall and proceeded to make a large loop in one end. Her sewing lessons were coming in handy, after all. However, she doubted Sister Mary imagined the art being used on a hard-headed cow.

Ever so slowly, she snuck up on her victim and eased the rope over the swishing tail. Mabel stopped chewing. Careful not to tug too hard, she was about to tie the other end to the post behind her, when she heard a deep chuckle.

"Oh, I wouldn't do that if I were you," came a stranger's warning.

Elizabeth whirled around, hesitating and squinting, to see who was there.

"You wouldn't?"

"Nope."

A handsome man with light blonde hair stepped out of the shadows. "You must be Adam's wife."

Elizabeth wondered why his words made her feel like a cherished possession, when she should still be feeling irritated.

"And you are?"

The man stuck out a hand in greeting, but Elizabeth gave him an apologetic shrug since it took both hands to manage the rope.

"Sorry about that, I'm Michael, Adam's foreman. I've been out of town for the past couple of weeks, so I haven't had the pleasure of meeting you."

"Oh, well, then nice to meet you." Elizabeth responded absently still struggling with the rope, "And I appreciate your concern, Michael, however since Adam insists that I get more from this cow than a knot on my head, I'd better tie this tail."

Michael did not seem the least insulted that she choose not to take his advice. He watched her tie the tail and position herself lady-like on the stool.

"I tied a cow's tail once," he remarked casually, pulling a homemade pipe out of his pocket.

Elizabeth wished the man would find something else to do. The last thing she wanted was a witness to what she was about to do. She took a deep breath, trying to work up the courage and pretended interest in what he had to say. "To a post?" she asked.

"Nope. To another cow." He replied.

Now, he had gained her attention. Shocked, she completely forgot about her task, "To another cow? How awful, what happened?"

Michael leaned one arm on the stall, and drew on his pipe to get it going before answering her, "Caused quite a ruckus. My brother and I laughed till our sides ached. That is until Pa got a hold of us."

"Oh dear, was he extremely angry?"

"Yep, after he dusted our britches, he made us milk those fool cows for over a month before he finally sold them to old man Hammon for butchering." He took a long drag on his pipe, "You see, when those cows finally broke loose, they stripped all that hair off their tails, and without the sound of air whistling through, those tails can be somewhat dangerous. I was black and blue all over by the time he sold those cows."

Elizabeth's eyes shot to Mabel's tail trying to tug loose from the rope. "Perhaps it would be wiser if I untied her tail."

Michael shrugged, "Suit yourself."

Elizabeth hurried over and freed Mabel. Only breathing easier when she heard the beautiful sound of a hair covered tail cutting through the air.

Embarrassed at her near fatal error, she offered up a shy smile of friendship. "I guess you must think I haven't any sense, but, you see, they don't give milking classes at finishing school."

"Then, I would be honored to teach a beautiful woman the art of milking."

Elizabeth looked leery, "I don't know, Adam is a bit testy lately. I think he expects me to do this on my own."

"Now, I ask you, does that make any sense? How can you do something without being taught?"

Elizabeth straightened her shoulders, "Exactly what I asked him."

"What did he say?"

"He growled something about if he wanted to teach me something it wouldn't be milking. Which… makes absolutely no sense."

Michael threw his head back in laughter, "Oh, I think it makes perfect sense."

Elizabeth scowled at him. Did all men think alike?

Still chuckling, Michael maneuvered her over to the stool and pushed her down onto it. "Trust me, Bootsie, he won't mind."

A short time later, Elizabeth leaned back and gave Michael a tired but proud smile. The pail was nearly full of warm frothy milk. A definite sign of what she could accomplish, or rather, what she could accomplish with a few little instructions and the help of someone who talked in a normal tone of voice instead of bellowing at her.

"Michael can you believe it? I think I am getting the hang of it!"

"Getting the hang of what sweetheart? Flirting?" asked a familiar sarcastic voice.

Elizabeth and Michael jumped guiltily apart. When she nearly fell backwards, Michael instinctively reached out a hand to steady her.

"And I suggest you take your hands off my wife, Michael, before I break them."

Elizabeth raised a knowing eyebrow at Michael, "I warned you. Testy."

"Yep, just a little," he whispered back, before winking at her and standing to his feet.

"Hello, Adam, I have been looking all over for you."

"So, I see." Adam remarked in a voice that would have turned a lesser man to jelly.

Bootsie came quickly to her feet, refusing to be intimidated despite the accusing glare Adam was bestowing on her. "I know you wanted me

129

to manage by myself, but my stars, Adam, can't you be just a little reasonable for once?"

"I'll be reasonable all right," he turned to Michael who stood there grinning at him. "Get out."

"Well," huffed Elizabeth, an embarrassed blush staining her cheeks, "that certainly wasn't reasonable."

Michael reached out to pat her shoulder, but then thought better of it when Adam looked ready to commit murder. He slowly lowered his arm, "I think I'll head up to the mill, we can go over the supply list later." He tipped his hat at Elizabeth, "Nice meeting you, Mrs. Reed."

His farewell brought a sinking feeling in the pit of her stomach. The last thing she wanted right now was to be alone with her coldly quiet husband.

"See you later, Adam."

Adam didn't bother to answer. He was too busy giving Elizabeth a look loaded with promise. By his stance, not one she relished him to keep.

Michael gave up trying to calm Adam down, but just before he left, he got Bootsie's attention behind Adam's back and pointed to the shovel leaned up against the wall.

Elizabeth barely stifled a nervous giggle at the suggestion. Adam's head snapped suspiciously back around. In mock innocence, Michael broke out whistling as he strolled lazily from the barn, not worried in the least about his friend's temper.

With Michael gone, the barn was so full of tension; Elizabeth wondered why she did not buckle beneath it. She cleared her throat.

"How long do you intend to glare a hole in me like that?"

Adam appeared to relax his angry stance, but the fire in his eyes betrayed him, "I suppose, until I can stop from strangling you."

"Oh!"

Still Adam said nothing, which was making her extremely nervous.

She put her hands on her his hoping to intimidate him. It didn't work.

"Adam, for crying out loud! What is the matter with you? We were milking a cow, for Pete's sake."

"Funny that's not what I would call it."

She blushed a fiery red. "For your information, Michael was simply trying to help."

"Remind me to thank him later." He answered in a dangerously low voice.

He unfolded his crossed arms. She gulped.

"You…stop that." She ordered as he began to advance on her, "if you would just let me explain about the stupid cow," she raised up a hand to ward him off, stumbling two steps backward.

"See, I couldn't get the thing to stop flailing the devil out of me and thought maybe I could tie her tail…"

He stopped one corner of his mouth twitched just a little at her admission.

"This is not the least bit funny, Adam Reed."

He did smile then, but his piercing blue eyes held her rooted to the spot. "You were saying?"

Did he have to make her feel so nervous? She licked her lips and swallowed. "I have nothing to feel guilty about. I was just…just…" she wondered why if she had nothing to feel guilty about, she felt so –guilty. She frantically searched for something profound to say. Something that would make him realize what a complete fool he was making of himself.

Adam's only movement was the quirk of an eyebrow.

"Excuse me, I need…," she began, once more flustered by his nearness.

Sensing the passion growing between them, Adam reached for her. "You need what, Sweet heart?"

The flutter of her pulse leapt at the base of her throat. "I need to…take the milk inside. You know Nicholas and Chelsea will be home any minute…" she ended dramatically, quickly slipping past him as if he were a hunter and she the deer.

Puzzled by his own reactions to her, he looked off in order to compose his own erratic heartbeat. "Bootsie," he called out without turning around, "we need to talk. You can't keep running way every time this happens between us."

131

She forced herself to slow down a bit, but didn't bother to turn around, "I am sure I don't know what you mean. Besides I was not running, it's just the milk will spoil and I need to gather some eggs."

Then with head held high and patched skirt swishing, she picked up the pail from under Mabel and left the barn as regally as a queen. The sound of a slamming door ruining the entire picture of aloofness she tried to create.

"Well, Elizabeth, I guess you certainly told him," she mumbled to herself. "Fetch the eggs?" Never once in all the books she had read, did she ever hear a heroine say at an important moment. "Excuse me dear, while I fetch the eggs." Honestly, the man was making her into a raving idiot.

She stormed to the porch and set down the milk and then made her way to the chicken coop where she slammed the weathered door with a bang. Chickens exploded around her, clucking and flapping in terror. Chicken feathers rained down on her like leaves in a wind storm. Before long she found herself covered in them. She blew a stray one off of her nose.

The sound of a squawking chicken drew her attention as one of the frenzied creatures flew straight for her. Elizabeth swatted at it in self-defense, and then stifled a scream. The hysterical hen landed dazed at her feet. She feared she had killed the thing. "Oh dear," she mumbled before poking it cautiously with her foot. Nothing.

It was at that precise moment she realized there was one more thing she despised here besides cows and husbands. Chickens. She definitely hated chickens.

She had had enough for one day. She spun around and chicken feathers filled the air. In response, she let out a very unladylike sneeze.

"Oh honestly….ah ah choo."

"I take it chickens don't agree with you either?" Observed an amused Adam from the doorway.

Elizabeth's eyes began to water as another sneeze fought its way up her nose. "Would you just leave me…ah choo."

Adam held up his hands in mock surrender, trying not to laugh at the chicken feathers that still clung to her hair, "Slow down, I came to apologize."

Elizabeth cocked her head suspiciously at him, "Why?"

"Why what?"

"Why are you apologizing? You always act like that and you never have apologized before."

Aggravated, Adam strode up to the fence. "Well I am apologizing this time, is that all right with you?"

"See, there you go yelling at me again."

"I was not yelling," he pointed out, "THIS," he roared, "happens to be yelling."

"See why I can't have a normal conversation with you," she stated in a superior voice that belied her surrounds, "I think its better not to talk right now until you…"

"Well that'll be a change for you." Adam stated sarcastically. "Not talking that is."

"Why you…" Elizabeth instinctively picked up an egg from one of the deserted nests.

"Don't even think it, Bootsie," he warned.

He hadn't even finished his warning when an egg went flying through the air and burst all over his light brown shirt. A pair of shocked eyes watched it's slowing decent down the front of his shirt.

Elizabeth started backing up, trying to explain, "You made me do it. If you wouldn't shout at me all the time, I wouldn't lose my temper."

"Temper?" he remarked almost casually. "That, Darling, was mild compared to what I am about to demonstrate."

Elizabeth crossed herself when he looked up in cold fury. Without a moment's hesitation she flew past him and ran for the safety of the house. She just prayed someone was there to stop him. There was no doubt in her mind she had provoked him past reason. From the look in his eyes, whatever he had planned would not be pleasant.

She barely managed to clear the kitchen threshold before he was upon her. He grabbed her arm and spun her up against him, his chest heaving from chasing her down.

"I think, Darling, I will teach you something after all. A lesson in manners is in order." He instructed silkily.

Panicking, Elizabeth pushed against him. She recognized that look, and she thought maybe dying would be better. Adam crushed her against his hard frame, knocking the small amount of air from her struggling lungs.

This time it wasn't a gentle kiss, which he took from her, but one full of unleashed passion. It was as if he were molding his very lips and body with hers.

Struggling, Elizabeth tried to break free, but he only tightened his hold, forcing her to accept his punishing kiss. She had never felt so many emotions at once; fear, excitement, and the hardest of all to bear, indifference. She started crying against his mouth, tears of heartbreak streaming down her face, yet he only yanked her head back, opening her to his kiss. Taking what she was unwilling to give.

"Please," she whispered, "please don't hate me."

At her tortured words, Adam realized what he was doing. He was past stopping the fire racing through his veins, but he couldn't control its direction. His kiss grew gentler, touching her wet cheeks, her closed eyes, saying soothingly. "Hush, Sweetheart, I could never hate you."

"But you do. I feel it." She was sobbing uncontrollably now.

Adam stoked her tenderly, his hands exploring, soaking up the warmth he had been resisting for weeks now. His mouth covered hers again, only this time not in anger, more as an invitation. Elizabeth clung to him as both her punisher and savior. Her body responded to his unspoken call. She melted against him, deepening their kiss. Soon, everything else disappeared in passion's haze.

"Bootsie, we have to stop." He half whispered against her mouth, as he forced himself to pull away. He closed his eyes willing his body into submission.

Her only answer was a soft cry of abandonment, as her response to him intensified. Her hands were touching him now, her breathing heavy, and her own passion out of control.

He groaned with defeat. "What am I saying?" he asked himself, pulling her even closer and gently bringing her with him to the floor. His head reeling, he touched every inch of her and still he wanted more, when a voice penetrated his fevered brain.

"Adam, I forgot…" Michael called, pushing open the door and stopping mid-sentence at the scene.
Elizabeth shrieked in surprise and Adam swore.

Yet it only took a moment for Michael to realize his mistake, quickly he began babbling, "Sorry about that, I thought…you were…I mean…" His face a bright crimson, he tried unsuccessfully to look anywhere but at them.

Elizabeth was frantically straightening her clothes, while Adam stood up blocking her from view. "Now's a good time to leave Michael." He advised fiercely.

"Sure thing, Adam," he said, then tipping his hat, "Mrs. Reed." Then realizing how absurd his attempt at politeness, Michael groaned, quickly shutting the door and disappearing.

The small room became deathly quiet. Embarrassed, Elizabeth buried her face in crossed arms as they rested on her drawn up knees. Adam quietly buttoned up his shirt. "I didn't mean for that to happen, Sweetheart, I lost control and I am sorry."

"I don't think nuns let people kiss them like that, at least I…" came her muffled tear-filled voice. "Oh Adam, what am I going to do? How will I ever explain this to Sister Agnes?"

She raised her head, a horrified expression on her face.

"I could never tell her. She would never understand how I could do such a thing. I don't think she has even been kissed before and certainly not like…" she burst into tears, "that."

Adam bent down, running his hand over her bent head, "Sweetheart, you didn't do anything to be ashamed of. You're my wife. I

135

admit the timing wasn't the greatest in the world, but what we felt was perfectly natural."

Elizabeth looked up into his concerned face, confusion and panic on hers. "Adam, I'm not legally married to you. I know you don't want to believe me, but I'm not who you think I am. Don't you see? I have to go back home." She looked down at her feet, fidgeting with a button on her boot. "And if I'm going to keep my sanity through all of this, you have to keep up your end of the bargain. You can't keep...kissing me like that. It's so confusing."

A look of pain flicked across his face as he studied her a long moment, "Do you mean that, Bootsie?"

Elizabeth wanted to burst into tears, but she managed to nod before she did.

Adam watched tears slip down her sun-kissed cheeks and came to a decision. "All right, Bootsie, if it means that much to you, I swear I won't kiss you again unless you ask me to," he slowly rose to his feet, towering over her with unyielding pride, "but I warn you, Sweetheart. When and if you do? Next time, I won't stop with just a kiss."

Chapter 10

By the time three long weeks had rolled around and things between him and Bootsie still lay unresolved, testy was a mild account when it came to describing Adam. Everyone at camp stayed clear of him. Everyone, that is, except Smitty.

"I told that fool Sullivan, the boss plans on cutting down them Firs first thing in the morning. But the hard-headed man goes ahead and cuts them down anyway. I was mad enough to spit nails." As if to emphasize his point, he spit a long stream of tobacco at Adam's feet.

Looking up and noticing for the first time that Smitty was still jabbering and complaining, Adam growled, "Don't you have trees to cut, or do you plan on talking them down."

Smitty bowed up and instantly shut his mouth, but not before mumbling something under his breath.

"What did you say?"

Smitty puckered up, clamped down on his tongue, then spit out, "I didn't say nothing Boss. Except that if'n I was you and planning on doing anything more dangerous than walking? I'd rethink my plans."

Adam shook his head at Smitty's odd reply. Why was it, he wondered, that everyone insisted on riling him lately?

Too busy to reprimand the man, Adam spun around and headed for the shoot. Once there he checked on the progress of the lumber being sent down the man-made slide to the river below, and then headed for the office.

There was a pile of paperwork on his desk from this morning, which needed finishing before he could go into town. Last week's shipment of supplies still hadn't come in, but a boat was due in today. He hoped to head back into town this afternoon to check on it.

Slowing his steps and crossing over the wooden planks laying across a large mud hole, his mind was lost in a sea of things left to do before the mill would finally be his, free and clear. He tipped his hat back on his head and looked up at the cloudy sky. "Soon, little brother, this will all be ours."

Sudden sadness filled his heart. The victory seemed shallow without his brother to share in it. Yet, the thought of Nicholas and Chelsea one day owning a piece of it, spurred him on to fulfill his dream. Through them, he would be able to keep his word to his brother.

Hearing a rumble of thunder, he hurried his steps. As soon as this shipment of lumber was paid for, he would need to head into Eugene. A frown furrowed his brow; it was something he had been putting off since the first of the month. A necessary evil, of sorts. It was a nuisance to make the long trip twice a year to pay on his loans, but if his luck held out, in another couple of years, he would have the capital to pay back all that he owed.

Unfortunately, it was a long backbreaking process between the cutting of trees and any actual profit seen from such a venture. Stopping to check the line on a pile of lumber outside his office, he felt a fat drop of rain land on his hat. More set-backs. Still, it shouldn't take more than three months, before all the lumber piling up around him should be on its way to California.

Long strides brought him up to the door of his office where he stopped short, snapping his fingers. Shoot. The North Section. He knew there was something he forgot. Michael made it a point to remind him several times yesterday about the new section of timber his crew needed approval on. Adam dreaded the ribbing he knew was sure to come. Lately every time he slipped up, Michael gave him that knowing smirk, as if there were some deep dark secret behind Adam's forgetfulness. Something other than he simply had too much on his mind.

Adam sighed deeply to himself. Who was he kidding? He was having more trouble concentrating lately. His thoughts kept straying to his physically frustrating marriage and the beautiful green-eyed girl responsible. Funny, three months ago he thought that a mail-order bride would be the easiest solution to his problems. He rubbed his forehead with tired slow motions. Little did he know that before Bootsie he had no problems.

An unbidden image of his wife, all fire and innocence rolled into one, made him wonder if things would ever return to some semblance of normal again. She was not at all what he had envisioned when he first thought of a mate. No. What he thought he wanted was someone to help raise his niece and nephew. Someone who would have supper waiting on him. Clean his house and keep him warm at night. No conflict, no emotional attachment. A clean-cut business deal.

He sneered at his naive thinking. How carefully he had thought about this whole marriage thing, before finally deciding it was the surest route to go. He shook his head over the hours spent reading every willing female's letter, until finding just the right one that suited his needs.

He groaned. Yeah, so far, only one of the children even liked his new wife. And let's face it; a two year old was not a reliable source. His house looked like a tornado ran havoc inside it. Then there was the food, which was only sometimes edible – when he cooked it himself. To top it off, he was married to a woman so beautiful his eyes hurt just looking at her, yet they might as well have been sleeping on separate planets the gulf between them was so wide.

Each night was one long endurance test. With her teetering on the edge of the mattress, no doubt in case he might suddenly become overwhelmed with desire for her. And him, clenching his teeth in pain, in order to stop from doing just that. The whole thing would be laughable where it not his life.

No, the best way to describe his carefully planned out marriage was – a fiasco. And as for his feigned cool detachment from his lovely wife? Even that was becoming harder and harder to manage. Maybe Michael was right. He needed to just admit the truth to himself. That, or else start sleeping in the barn in the hopes it might help him keep his hands off his temporary wife. At least, temporary according to her.

Not that she would have let him get close enough to worry about such a thing occurring. She'd been avoiding him like the pox ever since that day in the kitchen. And poor Michael. Every time he came over, she turned ten shades of red and started stammering like she didn't have a lick of sense. That is, when she talked at all, mostly she hid in the bedroom.

Michael finally suggested they meet at the mill instead of the house to cause her less embarrassment. Adam couldn't help but wonder what would have happened if Michael hadn't walked in on them. Even now the thought of how soft and vulnerable she felt in his arms, surrendering to his passion, affected him. Desire coursed through him. No, he hadn't imagined the attraction she felt for him or the conflict in her eyes when he teased her, or called her "sweetheart". She may not want to admit it, but she showed all the signs of a woman who needed to be loved.

So why did she fight him so hard? They were married after all. The memory of her tousled head and tear filled eyes insisting all she wanted in the world was to go home, invaded his thoughts. Those doubts she placed in his mind, were the reason for the conflict he was experiencing.

Hitting the door open, he let himself into the office. She was the most infuriating female he had ever run across. After he looked over his books for an hour so, he would head over to the North section and get the men started. Until then, he planned on having a nice strong cup of coffee and some peace and quiet.

Pulling off his Stetson, he hung it up on a nail in the wall. Then sitting down, he rubbed his blood-shot eyes wearily. It was only 10:30 in the morning and he was already getting a headache. "That woman is going to be the death of me. She'll probably worry me right into an early grave." Once voicing his frustration out loud, he reached for his ledgers in order to get down to some work.

So preoccupied with his thoughts was Adam that he didn't even notice the young woman sitting in the corner, nervously plucking at a faded blue dress. That is, until he heard her uncomfortably clear her throat. Adam's head snapped up in surprise. There, out of nowhere, sat a pretty blond woman, looking extremely embarrassed. Adam noticed his overstuffed leather chair seemed to swallow her slight frame in its depth. No wonder he hadn't seen her when he first came in.

Her corn silk hair was pulled back away from her face with a faded blue ribbon that matched the blue of her muslin dress, trimmed in soft cream velvet. She looked more than a little nervous, as she watched Adam scrutinizing her. In her hand she clutched a small carpet bag that had seen better days. She gave Adam a timid smile and he automatically

140

smiled in return. It was a nice change to actually have a woman smile at him.

"Is there something I can do for you Miss?" Adam asked in a friendly tone trying to ease her discomfort.

A hand fluttered to her throat, then back down again to rest on her bag.

"I really feel rather forward, coming here in the first place, but well...I had nowhere else to turn. I was so terribly frightened, you see. There is no telling what he might..." Her voice broke as tears filled her light blue eyes.

"Adam, we have to know about that North Section, Grady and crew are down..." Michael's voice drifted off as he entered the room and noticed the young woman sitting across from Adam. His face registered both surprise, as well as curiosity when Adam motioned for him to sit down.

Plopping down on the edge of the desk, he was overwhelmed by the heart-stopping beauty of the teary eyed girl before him. Where did Adam come up with all these women in distress anyway? Was he stockpiling them up somewhere?

Speaking patiently so as to not upset the girl further, Adam asked, "Miss, I don't believe you have told me your name."

The girl seemed to weigh her answer carefully before answering, "Miss Logan. Jana Logan."

"Well, Miss Logan, what can we do for you? Something tells me you are not in the market to buy lumber." Michael's eyes never left her, as he took out his pipe casually tapping a little tobacco into its bowl.

Blue eyes met Michael's for just a moment and there was no mistaking she resented his intrusion. Her hands were trembling, but Michael suspected it was more from anger than fright.

Rather than answer Michael, she turned her attention back to Adam, "I apologize for bothering you like this. I just didn't know where else to turn. To be honest, I still feel as if he could find out where I am somehow."

Michael struck a match against the sole of his boot. "Who might find out Miss Logan?"

"Smoke of any kind makes me terribly sick Mr...I am sorry, I can't recall your name", she dodged and pointedly leaned around him to address Adam once more.

He blew out the match and watched her. Something was not quite right here.

"Perhaps I should come back a little later when you are not so busy, Mr. Reed." The young woman came to her feet, but Adam signaled her to remain seated. "Nonsense, continue with what you were saying, Miss Logan. This is Mr. Warren, my foreman. But, he's also one of my deputy's and anything you say to me, you can say in front of him."

Giving Michael the barest of nods, she focused once more on the big man speaking to her. "Well, this is actually of a more personal matter, although the law is certainly involved. I would therefore prefer to keep my affairs - well, I don't wish to divulge them to just anyone." She nodded toward Michael, "No insult intended Sir."

"None taken I assure you Miss Logan", Michael answered smoothly; "However, since I am appointed deputy sheriff, I feel it is in Adam's best interest if I stay. No insult intended, ma'am."

Pursing her lips in anger, Jana gave a curt nod, "As you wish." Then seeing no way around it, continued, "As I said before, I have nowhere else to turn." Seeing Adam's perplexed look, she explained, "I suppose I should start at the beginning."

"That is usually where one starts, Miss Logan." Michael added, deliberately lighting his pipe in front of her.

She sent a withering look his direction. Sighing prettily, she focused instead on the more sympathetic Adam. "My grandfather died a few months ago, and I was left with several gambling debts of his. You see, he was a bit of a gambler and unfortunately, not a very good one. When his health started to decline, the creditors flocked to my door, hoping, no doubt, to receive even a small fraction of what was owed them."

Pulling out a handkerchief, she gently blew into it. "Oh, I don't blame them, but I'm afraid that by the time his dear soul passed from this world, there wasn't anything left. Not even enough for my own needs."

At these last words Jana broke down, burying her face in the white handkerchief, soft sobs shaking her body. Michael and Adam exchanged a look and then gave the distraught girl their attention. "Miss Logan, please continue," encouraged Adam.

Jana sniffed, nodding her head. "I'm sorry, it's just this is so painful." Drawing in a shaky breath she continued, "You can imagine how hopeless I felt. I had no one. That is until Mr. Otis Rodrick came to my grandfather's house asking after him. He was a traveling medicine man on his way through our small town in California." Big blue eyes brimming with tears looked up into Adam's. "He claimed to be an old friend of my grandfather's for many years."

Imploringly Jana leaned forward, "He seemed so sincere in his grief when I explained about my grandfather's death. I truly believed he wanted to help me. Anyway, he at once offered me a job working with his show. At first I resisted his offer, but he soon won me over by his kindness."

Michael wondered why she would take off with a perfect stranger. Or why, for that matter, she was putting on such a show for Adam right now.

"I was desperate, and I admit, a bit flattered by his attentions. For the first month or so after I began working for him, I was given my salary and we seemed to get along fairly well. You have to believe me; I only sought his help temporarily. I hoped that once I reached a large enough town, I would be able to find work and not be forced to rely on his generosity any longer."

Michael looked down at her hands, which were clutching the handles of her bag so tightly her knuckles were turning white. "A little over a month ago, Otis started drinking. It was just a little at first, but eventually he was drunk most of the time. I was so frightened I didn't know what to do."

143

"Then he began to..." she blushed, finishing quietly, "well...he was becoming increasingly forward. When I refused him, he threatened me. Then when that was not enough to convince me, he began...hitting me." Jana wept bitterly, unable to continue.

Just at the thought of the pretty young woman being treated so badly, drew Adam to his feet. With cold fury, he asked, "Where is he now?"

Automatically her voice filled with remorse, "I wish I knew, for I would love nothing better than to see the man jailed for his actions. Unfortunately, all I could think of when he fell into a drunken stupor was getting away. I didn't have any idea where I was until a day ago when I stumbled across a sign to your town. I don't think you know how lucky I am to be alive. You see," tears flowed freely down her cheeks now, "he said he would kill me if I tried to leave him."

Not wishing to frighten the young woman any further, Adam asked gently, "Miss Logan, I know how difficult this is for you, but if we are to help, you have to tell us everything. For instance, what was the last town you went through," coached Adam.

Her eyes cut frantically to the left, "Oh, I seem to have forgotten most everything that occurred that day except escaping. Please, you can't let him find me. There is no telling what he'd do."

To calm her, Adam walked over and bent down, looking directly into her eyes. Giving her a reassuring smile, he promised, "Don't worry Miss Logan. We will find him."

The girl's eyes widened in fear, as she quickly stood to her feet, nearly knocking him down in the process. "Oh, no. You mustn't."

Both men turned in surprise at the overwrought girl. Blushing, she stammered, "I mean he might be dangerous. I would hate to think someone became hurt because of me. I wouldn't be able to sleep nights."

Clutching at Adam's muscled arm, she pleaded, "I am certain if he knew the sheriff was protecting me, he would eventually move on. Surely, that would be a simpler and less violent answer to my problem. You see, ever since my dear grandfather was shot down in cold blood, I

144

can't endure the thought of another man brought down by such violent means."

Michael looked skeptical. "I thought your grandfather died after a long illness."

Jana turned around in shock, "Did I say grandfather? I meant father. My poor misguided father was a man prone to violence. I still have nightmares about that awful day when he was brutally murdered."

"But-"

Not allowing Michael the chance to speak again, she cut off his attempt, focusing instead on Adam. "I couldn't live with myself if I thought I caused another such tragedy."

Adam frowned and looked at Michael who shook his head. "No, it's better to deal with him now. He might come after you anyway sometime later. I promise there will be no bloodshed. Though why it should matter to you after being treated so badly, I can't begin to guess. But if it's that important to you, we will do it your way."

Jana licked her lips. "Thank you Mr. Reed. You have been more than kind. I won't trouble you any longer. I should be on my way if I am to find shelter for the night."

"Miss Logan, under the circumstances I think you should stay with us tonight," Adam offered, "for that matter, I insist you stay as long as it takes to rid yourself of this scoundrel and get back on your feet again."

Jana smiled warmly, her bottom lip trembling, "Oh, you are too kind, but I couldn't impose."

"Adam I don't think..." Michael broke in.

"No imposing about it. In fact, you would be doing us a favor. I know for certain Bootsie would appreciate the extra pair of hands with two youngsters running about."

The young woman only hesitated a moment before smiling and holding out a hand in agreement, "Well, if you are sure I wouldn't be a burden on your family. I know I would certainly sleep better with the sheriff himself protecting me."

"Then, it's settled?"

"How can I possibly argue with such logic? I appreciate your kind offer, Mr. Reed, and I accept."

"All my friends call me Adam.

"All right, Adam."

Michael watched the exchange, frowning. "Excuse me Miss Logan, but if I am to find this man, I will need a fairly accurate description. What does he look like?"

Irritated by his question, she answered shortly, "He looks, Mr. Warren, like a traveling medicine man. I don't believe you will have any trouble recognizing him. He has this huge painted wagon following him around."

He turned beat red and rose to his feet. Their eyes locked in combat for a moment. Then, Jana turned demurely towards Adam, "Forgive me that was unkind. I must admit that my temper is frayed after such an ordeal. Would you mind terribly if I sat down for a moment?"

"Of course not. Michael, why don't we leave Miss Logan alone for a bit while we take a look at the North section. Then, I'll bring back the wagon to pick up Miss Logan. Is that fine with you Miss?"

The smile she gave was one of gratefulness, although she suddenly leaned against the bookshelf. "Perfectly fine. I find this whole experience has taxed me more than I know. If you don't mind, I might lie down on your couch until you return."

"Of course. Let me help you."

Michael eyed the suddenly weak female being led away and smirked, "Are you sure you wouldn't be better served at the doctor's office, rather than my boss's home?"

Jana stiffened, and then seemed to think better of a confrontation. Instead, allowing Adam to gently lead her over to the sofa. Best if she ignore the taunting man; after all, she had gotten what she came for.

Chapter 11

Humming contentedly, Elizabeth picked up Chelsea and headed into the bedroom to change. Today, for the first time in weeks, she would get to see the other brides. Unbelievably, she actually was looking forward to the outing. Maybe it was living out here, totally isolated from everyone except Becky, or maybe it was the instinct to be around other wives much like her who found themselves thrown into a man's life they hardly knew.

Sighing, she shut the curtains on the endless sea of trees wondering if maybe she was changing in other ways too. Whatever had made her feel this sense of isolation also had caused her to drag a surprised Christina through her front door two days ago. She cringed remembering the desperate way she had practically shoved her friend down on the hard chair and started bombarding the poor woman with questions.

You could have knocked Christina over with a feather at Elizabeth's new found friendliness and welcoming smile. In an almost dazed fashion, she did her best to answer questions and not stare as Elizabeth maternally pulled Chelsea into her lap.

Finally, after retrieving a plate of raw cookies and odd colored tea from the kitchen, Elizabeth asked the one question closest to her heart.

"So, Christina" she ventured casually, edging forward and offering her friend a cookie, "Do you happen to know when the next ship is due to arrive?"

Christina watched as the small child in Elizabeth's lap grabbed a half-baked cookie and bit into it. Making a horrible face, she then proceeded to eat it anyway. Hesitating a moment, Christina picked up a cookie from the plate, answering casually, "Not for certain. Charles says it will be at least two weeks though, why?

Elizabeth couldn't help the disappoint that crept into her voice, "Oh, I had hopes a letter might have arrived for me."

Her friend seemed to eye her cookie warily. The outer edge was a crispy dark brown, while the middle drooped precariously, "A letter? From whom?"

Not wishing to jeopardize her new found friendship by bringing up Sister Agnes, she changed the subject, "Christina exactly why did you stop by?"

At that precise moment the young woman in question took a tentative bite into the cookie's doughy mass. From her face, too late she realized her mistake; for the large gooey mass had lodged securely in her throat, while the crunchy outer edge seemed to crumble and scatter its way down her windpipe. She began coughing and choking at the same time. Tears of pain were gathering in the corners of her eyes as she reached out a hand to Elizabeth for help.

Jumping up quickly, Elizabeth began whacking Christina on the back. This, of course, only succeeded in lodging the clump even more securely in place. Now her skin had turned from white to blue. Never a good sign.

Acting without thought, Elizabeth quickly tried to pour some tea down her friend, the whole time apologizing, "I'm so sorry. I should have warned you about the cookies. They take a little getting used to."

Christina looked at her incredulously and snatched the glass from her hands. Gratefully, she helped herself to a huge gulp of the strange colored tea. It was then she realized her mistake, but much too late. She held the awful stuff in her mouth in an indecisive moment. Then, with eyes slightly bulging, she forced herself to swallow down the foul tasting stuff. In fact, she was almost glad for the gritty texture of ground tea leaves, since it seemed partly responsible for dislodging the stuck cookie dough from her throat.

Elizabeth breathed a sigh of relief when Christina's color slowly returned to normal. Only then did she allow herself to give into embarrassment. To think, the first woman to stop by in weeks and she nearly murders her.

Trying not to think about her near death experience, Christina got up to leave. "Bootsie, I really must go."

"But…it wasn't the cookie incident was it?" Elizabeth rose with her, adding with a tentative smile, "what if I promise not to feed you ever again?"

The lovely blond woman couldn't resist laughing. "Believe me, wild horses couldn't drag me near your cooking again. Honestly though, I only came by to invite you to a quilting bee this Thursday."

Disappointment showed clearly on Elizabeth's face. "A Quilting Bee? Oh, Christina, I guess you probably never noticed, but I can't sew a stitch." She shrugged good-naturedly, "Now if you ever have a knot-tying bee I might be interested."

Taking in Elizabeth's much too large shirt and torn skirt, Christina answered kindly, "I am sure you are just being modest."

"Oh, no", Elizabeth admitted, scooting the tea leaves out of the way in order to sip her tea, "I actually paid Margaret Patrick to stitch all of my pieces in finishing school. Unfortunately, I had not thought it through carefully enough. Who would have thought there would be tests?" All her former guile gone, she confided, "Needless to say, I did not pass sewing."

It touched Elizabeth the way Christina drew her into a warm hug at her confession. However, instead of dwelling on her friends shortcomings, she responded, "Why don't I send over a couple of my dresses until you can manage to order some?"

It was the first time Elizabeth had felt kindness from anyone in a very long time. Her eyes filled with tears, "Oh, that is kind of you but –"

"Don't be a goose. I insist. Besides you will need something to wear Thursday."

"But I told you I don't sew."

"You don't need to." Seeing Bootsie's confusion, she explained, "It's not a real Quilting Bee, silly. It's a meeting. Now that we're settled in, we Brides decided it was time to do something about making this lumber camp into a real town."

Caught up in Christina's enthusiasm, Elizabeth paid little attention as she reached for a cookie bringing it dangerously close to her lips. Christina's eyes danced back at her, as realizing her mistake, she dropped it quickly back onto the plate.

"Do you really think you can do that? Make this into a real town? I mean, the men seem—"

149

"We will make them see reason. After all, with more children sure to come," she blushed becomingly, "well, we feel it is our duty to make sure they have a Christian upbringing and an education. Being so far from civilization, we felt it is time we got started."

Bodily taking a step back, Bootsie pointed out, "It sounds wonderful, but I don't think I should. After all, the other brides hardly consider me one of them."

"Nonsense", Christina interrupted, "we would be pleased to have you."

"But, Christina, I couldn't possibly" she was making it difficult not to bow out graciously. Finally she said with utmost honesty, "even if I were going to stay here, which I am not, the other brides don't even like me."

"Don't be a ninny. Of course they like you."

Elizabeth raised an auburn eyebrow at the obvious lie. "Oh, I see. Then Maggie wanting to throw me overboard was simply a friendly overture on her part?"

"Okay. Maybe Maggie dislikes you a little."

"A little?!"

Admitting defeat, she shrugged, "all right then, maybe more than a little. But I like you, and so does Hannah and the others. Or they will when they see how you've changed." She reached out clasping one of Elizabeth's hands in hers. "Bootsie, you really could help, being married to the Boss you have more influence than any of us. Will you come?"

Elizabeth blushed at the erroneous idea that she could ever influence anyone, especially Adam. Was it really only a few months ago she felt as if she had all the answers? Now what she wouldn't give to swallow her pride and ask this young mother's advice about children and dealing with a husband. Not to mention a yard full of stubborn animals. Instead, she quietly sat back and let herself be talked into a meeting she had absolutely no business attending.

Still, it might be a good opportunity to hear how other wives responded to their husband's advances. Ever since Adam had kissed her, well, she was worried something might be seriously wrong with her. For no matter how she tried, lately all she thought about was kissing. She even found herself watching Adam's every move. Mesmerized by such simple acts as washing up before supper and shaving. She shook her head at her own irrational behavior.

Blushing, she remembered how his eyes sometimes darkened with an emotion she didn't fully understand, yet caused havoc to her insides, even at the mere memory of it. Her reaction couldn't possibly be normal. In fact, she feared the opposite was true.

Feeling herself weaken, she asked sincerely, "Do you really think Maggie will agree to me being there?"

Laying a reassuring hand to Elizabeth's shoulder, she confided, "If you can get her to think of anyone else besides that big Irishman she is married to, I would be impressed."

"Maggie's in love?"

"It happens to the best of us, even you apparently."

Her breath caught in reaction to Christina's words. "I don't know what you mean."

"If you say so." Giving her an indulgent pat, she continued "you should see Maggie now. Why, you would think that man was on leave from heaven itself the way she talks."

So, with the understanding that she was not to confide in Adam, she agreed to go.

Brought back to the present by the sound of a slamming back door, she began braiding her rebellious locks with a thoughtful expression. It turned out to be harder than she thought. Not telling Adam that is. For that night at supper when she had casually mentioned the Quilting Bee, he had put down his fork and stared at her as if she had just announced she was sister to the Queen.

"You're what?"

Somehow between stuttering and looking off at the ugly dear head on the wall, she managed to say once more, "Christina invited me to a Quilting Bee this Thursday. I don't know why you are all so shocked by that."

Sitting back, he studied her a long moment before answering. Elizabeth gave him a nervous look, as she began pushing the food around on her plate. She hated that she was such a poor liar. Why she probably couldn't lie herself out of a feather bed.

Nicholas had not been as diplomatic as his uncle. "That's the dumbest thing I ever heard tell of." He dropped his fork dramatically, before reaching for a dark brown biscuit. "I ain't never even seen you pick up a needle, much less do anything with one. Shoot, if you sew as bad as you cook, they won't even let you through the door."

That said he attempted to bite into one of her biscuits hard exterior. Failing that, he rubbed his jaw which ached from the experience, before clamping his teeth down harder and screwing up his face. Somehow he managed to tear off a chunk, as if to prove his point.

She noticed Adam quietly laid his own biscuit aside. Deep in thought, he continued to chew instead on the leathery mouthful of venison he had mistakenly chosen to try before finally giving up and forcing it down with a swallow of fresh milk. "Did Becky leave a pie tonight?"

She frowned at him. Honestly, you would think they would starve to death without Becky's help. Chelsea seemed to be the only fan of her cooking. Grinning sweetly she banged her biscuit on the table before plopping the hard pieces into her milk. But then again, could you really count the opinion of someone who considered an empty corncob a delicacy?

He tapped his spoon thoughtfully against the metal plate and eyed his wife who continued to look anywhere but at him. Clearing his throat to get her attention he finally said, "I think it's a good idea."

The sound of the deep timbre of his voice caused her to jump, "What is?"

His sigh was full of impatience. "The Quilting Bee. I think if it means you gain some knowledge on the subject, why not?"

Instantly her shoulders relaxed. Unguarded she gave him a grateful smile. And it was then their eyes met. It was a mistake, of course. For suddenly his eyes turned that dark unfathomable blue that caused her to think on kissing again. Feeling her cheeks flush she quickly

152

looked away. Would she ever get used to the man looking at her like that? She hoped so, or else she would have to learn how to exist without breathing. He surely did take her breath away each and every time.

He seemed just as agitated as he pointed out rather briskly, "We have to get the north ridge thinned out, and those Douglas Firs stacked up before the rain starts up again, so I won't be home for supper anyway. Why don't you ask Becky to watch the kids for you? I'm sure she could use the extra money before the baby comes."

Elizabeth nodded, but her appetite was long gone. She almost wished he would have insisted she not go. It was pure instinct, but nonetheless she had a bad feeling about the whole thing.

So here she was dressing for a secret meeting, and feeling worse about it as each moment passed. Realizing her braid was not cooperating; she unbound her curls and made a low ponytail instead, simply tying a peach ribbon around it for color.

Hearing Nicholas outside her bedroom she went and fetched her sunbonnet. Tied it on, then untied it and finally flung it to the bed. No matter if the sun bronzed her skin, its large brim made seeing impossible. This would probably not be a bad thing, except on the off chance she might actually need to stop a horse from jumping off a cliff or some other mishap.

Nicholas entered the room with a fresh sheen of sweat on his forehead. "Now why ain't you taking the wagon? Pepper is worked up something awful today. Took me a good twenty minutes to saddle her. She doesn't like nobody riding her."

"Anyone" she corrected.

"Anyone what?"

"Never mind. I told you the… you know…that round thing is broken."

"You mean the wheel?" His sarcastic tone was not lost on her.

Narrowing eyes in on the young boy, she continued, "Believe me, I wish there were another way, but I am sure you and Becky can teach me how to ride one little horse. How difficult could it be?" Her gulp at the end caused Nicholas's eyes to dance in mischief.

"Sure. How difficult could it be?"

Landing on her backside for the third time since Becky's arrival, Elizabeth had learned two very important things about riding. One; there were some things an eight year old could do better than she could. And two; she hated horses.

Climbing back to her feet, Elizabeth caught a glimpse of her loyal supporters lining the corral. Nicholas shook his head, as Becky stared at her in stunned disbelief. Neither of which was extremely helpful at the moment. Then there was Chelsea, the traitor, who fell to the ground in a fit of giggles. Elizabeth eyed Pepper, a look of determination on her face. This time, she would mount that horse, even if it killed her. Which at this rate was a very real possibility.

Placing one foot in the stirrup, she hobbled around on the other, trying to swing her leg up high enough to mount. The saddle seemed to have a mind of its own as it kept moving. She thought it might be easier to use the fence as leverage. Pepper followed her to the gate. Then climbing up on the rail, she held on to the saddle horn and lunged for the saddle.

Within seconds, she found herself lying flat on the ground, breathless, dusty and feeling rather silly at being outsmarted by a dumb animal.

"Bootsie" Becky suggested, just as Elizabeth grabbed the reins yet again, "why, don't you take my horse instead?"

"Rufus?" Elizabeth looked cautiously over at the swaybacked old horse leaning against the barn. "I don't know..."

"Honestly, at this rate, the social will be over before you even mount that horse. I know he looks a little the worse for wear but he's so calm that he even walked right over a rattlesnake once and didn't even spook."

"Are you sure he even saw it? He looks blind in one eye."

Pepper jerked the reins out of her hands giving her a wild eyed look. For a moment she looked from half dead horse to very likely make you dead horse. Making her decision she dusted off her once peach colored borrowed dress and admitted defeat. "I suppose your right

154

Becky." As the dust began to settle, she searched around for her lost peach ribbon. "Besides, I wasn't sure what would have happened had I actually managed to stay on that animal."

Becky laughed as Elizabeth finally gave up her search for the elusive ribbon. They settled down on the porch swing and Becky poured them a cool glass of water. Meanwhile, Nicholas dragged the toothless old horse from the shade of the barn and saddled him up once more. Elizabeth laughed out loud, "Poor thing. He looks more dead than alive. I guess it's now or never."

Full of apprehension, she mounted the horse from the porch, her heart racing as she felt the horse shift beneath her. "Now what?"

After a quick refresher on steering the horse, Becky grabbed the bit and turned the horse towards town. "Just give him enough rein and he'll head straight for town." Elizabeth bit her lip till she tasted blood, but managed to nod. "Are you sure about this, Bootsie?" Becky repeated trying to hold back her uncertainty.

Once more Elizabeth gave a short nod, her eyes glued to Rufus' backside.

Grabbing her protruding middle, Becky slowly moved out of the way.

"Okay horse. Giddiup."

He didn't.

Elizabeth peeked out of one eye. She shook the loose reins a little harder, "giddy up. Go!"

He simply lowered is head and pulled out a large mouthful of wild grass.

Becky and Nicholas exchanged a look. Then, Becky seeing the young woman would likely still be sitting there come morning if she did not do anything about it, reached behind him and swatted Rufus' backside sending both horse and Bootsie towards town. She hoped.

As they watched her bounce out of sight, Becky asked worriedly, "Do you think I should remind her Rufus is going on twenty years and can't hear a blame thing?"

"Nah", Nicholas grinned slyly, "I bet she will figure it out soon enough on her own."

She sighed in relief when the old horse plodded into town. Just a little further and she could get off –"Stop. I mean Whoa!"

Unbelievably Rufus seemed to gain a new found burst of energy as he trotted right past the store heading for a horse trough at the edge of town and picking up speed. She watched in horror as Christina's hand raised in greeting, fell in confusion as Elizabeth bounced right past her. She reminded herself to stay calm; after all, she was a lady wasn't she?

"Help!!!!" Was that her scream she heard as she dropped the reins and grabbed the horse around the neck, closing her eyes in fear?

Suddenly she was jerked to a stop. Slowly she looked up to find Christina holding the abandoned reins in her hands, chest heaving, she grinned up at her. "First time on a horse?"

"How did you guess?"

Christina laughed out loud, as she deftly maneuvered the horse to the front of the store, tying the now complacent horse up front. She gave a questioning look up at Bootsie, who still sat up on the horse gripping the saddle horn in indecision.

"Is something wrong?"

Elizabeth glanced nervously at the store front where a crowd was gathering, "I don't know about this, Christina."

"I do. Now get down off that horse before he falls over."

Two bright spots appeared on Elizabeth's face, "Do you suppose the other brides noticed I missed the store?"

"Of course not", Christina lied, deftly blocking the faces pressed up against the store.

Climbing off the horse, she was still mumbling half to herself, "I can't understand it. I asked that horse to stop in every language I knew and some I didn't."

"Well since Rufus is deaf as a doornail, next time try pulling back on the reins instead. Didn't Adam warn you?"

156

"I suppose he just assumed I knew. " She blew a stray curl off her cheek. "Am I late?"

Putting an arm protectively through Bootsie's, the young blond smiled reassuringly, "Waiting on you. Now stop worrying."

Walking inside Elizabeth suddenly felt shy. It had been over two months since she had last seen any of the other women. The way they all stopped, needles in midair to stare at her was not helping put her more at ease either. Each bride looked up from a chair around the large quilting frame as if she were some strange creature dropped in their midst.

She gave them a wan smile.

Cornelia's eyes widened.

Although they were told Bootsie was a changed woman, they weren't prepared for the stunning beauty standing before them. From her golden skin, to sun lightened hair, she looked a complete stranger. The old Bootsie had been uppity and unbending. This woman, with loose disheveled hair hanging down the middle of her back was somehow softer and more approachable.

More noticeably than that, she glowed, as only a woman loved by a man could. Even Maggie noted the change, and found it hard to imagine this girl as the same crazy woman she last saw, kicking and screaming, backside up.

Hannah was the first to break the spell. She brought her ample frame over to Bootsie and caught her up in a fierce bear hug. "Why, honey, you look wonderful. That Adam of yours is one lucky man, and by the looks of it, knows how to take care of a woman." Elizabeth blushed becomingly. "Yes sir, one more ally, especially the boss's wife, is appreciated, isn't that right girls?"

Confused by all the attention, Elizabeth wondered what Hannah had meant by "taking care of" and "ally"? The only 'taking care of' Adam had been doing lately was 'taking care' to make up enough chores to keep her busy from sun up till past dark, not to mention the havoc he made out of her insides with words such as 'darling' or 'sweetheart'.

And she wasn't sure she wanted to become a part of anything, especially if it meant a confrontation with her not-so-understanding husband. Yes, arguing with a six foot, two hundred pound male made about as much sense as canning snow for the long hot summer.

Cornelia beamed at her from a rickety old chair. She clasped bony hands in delight as a giggle escaped her thin lips. "I think, I have figured out what is so different about you, dear."

Elizabeth returned her secret smile with a puzzled look of her own.

"You must be expecting, isn't that right dear?"

"What?!" asked a stunned and horrified Elizabeth.

"I know you probably wanted to tell us yourself, but one look at your radiant face speaks for itself."

Sputtering incoherently in response, "Oh, no, I couldn't be...I mean", Elizabeth lapsed into a shocked silence.

Cornelia waved her objections aside, "Now, now there is no need for you to say anything. It so happens, Hannah here is an excellent midwife, and as soon as our little 'meeting'" she giggled, "is over, I am sure she can answer all your questions. Just think, the first baby born in Reedsport. Isn't this wonderful? Why I can hardly wait to hear the details."

A gasp of horror escaped Elizabeth, "My stars! I most certainly am not...you know..." expectant eyes turned her direction.

She turned even a brighter pink as if that were possible. She felt at a loss for words. How did she explain there could not be anything further than the truth, much less details of a subject she knew nothing about? Short of explaining the bargain her and Adam had made, she couldn't think of a thing to say.

"Oh, never mind, couldn't we talk about something else?" Anything else would do.

"Of course dear" winked Cornelia, "we understand."

"Honestly", moaned Elizabeth, throwing her hands up in defeat. What did it matter anyway? Time would surely show the women how mistaken they were. Regardless, she noticed her face felt hot throughout their long meeting because of all the sly glances sent her direction. It was becoming increasingly apparent that everyone believed Cornelia's reasoning behind the changes in Elizabeth.

She on the other hand could not have been more embarrassed had she been sitting there in her camisole and nothing else. She didn't even know enough about the subject to defend herself. Instead she sat seething in silence, enduring their sly winks and understanding nods.

"So, it is settled." Alice said, finishing up the meeting. "We will ask our husbands to build a school and furnish a teacher for it as well."

It didn't sound settled to her. That is, unless their husbands were more cooperative than her's ever was. Reluctantly, she raised a hand, clearing her throat to gain their attention. When Alice sent a questioning glance her direction, she squirmed in the hard chair.

"Was there something else you wanted to add, Bootsie?"

The whole room became deathly quiet, waiting, and staring straight at her. Elizabeth took a deep breath to brace herself, "Well, actually – yes, there is. Do you honestly believe the men will just build you a school simply because you ask them to?"

Standing up to relieve her aching back, she held her sore index finger out of the way. This day had been a mistake. She didn't know which hurt worse, her finger, her back or her pride. She must be delirious from this long torturous day. That could be the only explanation for her interfering in something she shouldn't even care about.

"It seems obvious to me" she continued, "that what you need is a real plan. Some method in which to ensure that what you want is accomplished."

All the women began muttering amongst themselves.

"And tell me, lass", Maggie rose her intimidating frame up to meet her's, "exactly what kind of plan did you have in mind?"

Why was she becoming involved? This wasn't her problem; she could care less if this mill town ever had a school.

Seeming to read her mind, Maggie scoffed, "Just as I be thinking, lass. You don't have any ideas on the subject. No, you haven't changed your ways at all, have ya now? Still spouting out high-fluting ideas, but no backbone to carry them through."

What she should do is sit herself right back down and keep her mouth shut. For once, Maggie was right. But from somewhere deep inside herself, she shockingly heard her own voice ring out in confidence, "Well, Maggie, it seems the only one who hasn't changed, is you. Of course I have an idea. Would I be standing here if I didn't?"

Apparently she would. What was she possibly going to say next? She waited with everyone else to see what would come out of her mouth next. Her eyes shifted from side to side searching for an idea of some sort.

"Maggie cocked an eyebrow. "Well, out with it, lass, what is it?"

"Well, it's obvious isn't it?"

"Not to me."

"Me either" inquired a curious Cornelia leaning in closer.

All eyes were on Elizabeth as she gripped the back of the chair in front of her. "We make a trade."

Several women gasped. Christina looked stunned.

Hannah gave a reluctant nod of approval before motioning the others to silence. "Whatever is the matter with you girls?" she challenged. "Bootsie is right. We only have one weapon at our disposal."

One? Now Elizabeth was really confused. What did they think she said that was so shocking? After all, what was wrong with trading household chores for schools and churches? People bartered things all the time. Trying to appear confident despite the strange looks cast her direction, her smile wavered slightly.

Maggie seemed lost in thought. Finally, she pounded a fist into her other hand. "I hate to admit it, but the lass has a point. Although I'd be hard-pressed to see who would be punished more by the withholding of favors."

Now it was Elizabeth who was shocked. "But I meant -"

Several women reluctantly agreed with a sad shake of their heads. Elizabeth's innocent green eyes grew wider by the minute; surely they didn't mean those kinds of 'favors'?

Christina was the first to reach out and pat her on the shoulder in approval. "I agree with Bootsie. This is the only way we will ever get a school from our men. But, I suggest we get this over with as quickly as possible. First we try Alice's way. Who knows maybe we are wrong about our men. Then, if they don't agree we go to Plan B. No cooking,

160

cleaning, or sewing. If that fails? We will have no other choice, but go to Bootsie's Plan C."

Her plan? She watched the other women look down at their wedding rings then back up with determination. Their shoulders were pulled back with spines straight. They looked like an army going off to war.

Opening her mouth to object to whatever it was they thought she said; she quickly shut it again as the other women gathered up around her, placing their hands out in the middle. One wedding ring laden hand was placed on top of another in a silent pledge.

Oh, no! Adam would be furious. Never mind the fact that she hadn't meant to suggest any such thing. After all, what did she have to bargain with? She had already been 'withholding' cooking, sewing, cleaning – not to mention, favors.

Christina picked up Elizabeth's limp left hand, placing it on top of everyone else's. She gave a brave smile.

"Don't worry, Bootsie" she whispered, "with your help it will only be a matter of days before we have our school."

Worrying her bottom lip in indecision, Elizabeth tried to work up the courage to tell them all the truth. That it would be a lot longer than a few days, especially if they were relying on her help.

In fact, there might never be a school, or anything else because of her.

Because she, Elizabeth, had absolutely nothing to bargain with.

Chapter 12

"What do you suppose those women are doing in there?" Smitty asked the young lumberjack as they peered through the dirt smudged window of the local Mercantile.

Young Charles scratched his light brown head in confusion, "Don't rightly know Smitty, but it can't be much. I mean aren't they just a bunch of women? Maybe they're discussing," he pondered on what possible things women might discuss, "dresses or something."

"Does that look like their discussing dresses to you" Smitty asked in aggravation, just as a unified shout rose from within the store.

Charlie's eyes widened. "It doesn't matter. Adam said to get those nails and extra rope back in an hour. I, for one, don't aim to cross him." With that said, he headed for the door.

Smitty stretched out an arm to block his path.

One look at those excited, twittering women inside made him nervous and he wasn't about to enter that store till he had some real back up, and not some wet-behind-the-ears, love sick boy either. He pressed his face up against the glass, where it flattened and spread unbecomingly.

"I can tell you right now, that them women are up to no good." His eyes glowed with conviction, and Charles for the first time looked a little uncertain. He glanced from the dingy window to Smitty and back again.

"Just look at them cluttered up there, hands and mouths flapping like a sheet in the wind. Yes sir, that means trouble as sure as my name is Smitty Montgomery."

With that, he aimed a large brown stream of spittle at a spittoon by the door. It landed a good foot shy of its target. "Mark my words, boy; they're in a dither about something. There are only two things that get a female that riled… men and religion, and the preacher left town three weeks ago."

Charles could hold it in no longer and burst out laughing. He slapped old Smitty on the back and headed for the door. "What's a matter with you? Afraid those defenseless ladies in there are plotting your murder?"

The wiry older man looked over his shoulder in disgust. Yes sir, that boy was green as gourd. "Well, I'm sure old Samson said something just like that right before Delilah cut off them there locks of his." He responded in dooming tones.

That stopped the young man just shy of the door.

"Mark my words; there ain't nothing defenseless about a woman who's got her feathers ruffled. But, if you're positive those ladies in there are really quilting them a quilt, then just go ahead in there, but don't say I didn't warn ya."

A doubtful look came over Charles face. On the other hand, he felt plain silly standing outside the store afraid of a bunch of chattering women. It was getting downright embarrassing. "Aw, come on old timer, those women ain't doing nothin' except yakking like they always do."

"We'll just see about that, now won't we?"

Shoving a warning finger up against Smitty's chest, he pointed out, "Then you explain why we ain't got any supplies to the boss. I imagine he'll be real understanding when we explain we were attacked, no, just afraid some woman might light into us."

For the first time Smitty admitted to himself that it did sound pretty lame at that. Visions of his three-walled house came to mind. They still snickered about that behind his back.

Charles was through discussing the matter, apparently, as he turned on his heel and pushed through the store door muttering out loud, "Why am I even listening to you anyway? You ain't never been married."

The old man bowed up his scrawny chest before hollering back, "There is a reason for that boy, and it's because of what I know about women."

Pulling up to the store a short time later Adam found old Smitty pacing and peering through the front window and mumbling something fierce. His eyes met Michael's beside him who shrugged noncommittally.

163

Adam could feel his temper flare. He sent those men in after supplies well over an hour ago and there they were lally-gagging around on the porch.

To top it off, there was a witness to his men's foolishness, the petite blond sitting demurely between Michael and him. Glancing over in the hopes she hadn't noticed the crazy bald headed man talking to himself, he noticed her eyes kept straying over to the porch then back at him in confusion. Apparently luck was not on his side today.

"Doesn't that man work for you, Mr. Reed?"

"Unfortunately, yes. But I assure you, Miss Logan, my men don't usually carry on preaching services in front of the mercantile. It is just lately they…"Adam trailed off.

Lately what? Lately they were acting like a bunch of love sick school boys instead of the reasonable, hardworking men he hired? There were no excuses he could offer. Besides, this was all his fault in a way. If he hadn't sent for those women in the first place, none of this would be happening.

The young woman looked up at him from clear blue eyes. "I believe you Mr. Reed. I am sure they are normally very rational. And I can only hope as thoughtful as you have been. Especially, opening your home to me. I don't think I could go through another night in that cabin after last night."

"Did you ever find out who went through your stuff?"

"No, but I will sleep better knowing you're protecting me until that awful man is caught."

Michael rolled his eyes. The woman was about as genuine as a chuck of 'fool's gold. "Adam, isn't that Becky's horse over there? You don't think Bootsie actually rode it over here do you?"

"Now why would she do a fool thing like that?"

Hearing their voices, Smitty turned around and froze when he saw Adam.

Jumping down from the wagon, Adam asked sarcastically, "Smitty, having ghost problems again? I didn't know they took up haunting stores full of people. Surely that could be the only reason you haven't gotten those supplies I sent you after over an hour ago."

Running a bent finger along the inside of his collar, he tried to explain, "Boss, I know how foolish this looks, but I can explain."

The only response he got was a look that spoke volumes. He ducked his head sheepishly.

"You know what Smitty, I don't even care. Wait here with Michael, while I see if I can find Charles."

"Dadburn it, Adam. I'm trying to tell you those women..."

Jana opened her moth to protest being left behind, but Adam didn't seem in the mood for arguments. Seeing she had little choice, Jana scooted as far away from Michael as was humanly possible, trying her best to ignore the way he glared a hole through her.

Seeing Adam as he barreled into the store, slamming the door behind him, Charles threw the fourth pound of tobacco on top of the supplies on the counter and hurried over to explain. "Boss this ain't my fault. I told Smitty you were going to be mad enough to spit nails if we didn't get right back. He just wouldn't listen, even when I reminded him how touchy you are lately."

Adam glared him into silence.

"I didn't mean touchy, exactly...more like a Mountain Lion with a sore foot." Adam's glare intensified. "No, I mean, you know, more particular about things. Kind of like a mouse wanting that piece of cheese in a trap, but knowing if he takes it..."

"I am not touchy."

"Right Boss."

Shoving past Charles, he searched the store for his wife. He was getting just a little tired of people insinuating he had some sort of temper lately. Besides, right now he had a right to be a little "touchy" as the men called it. His camp was falling apart. If they didn't straighten up soon someone could get hurt. To top it all off, he had a woman out front who couldn't keep her hands off him, and a wife who could. If anyone had a right to be touchy, he certainly did.

Zeroing in on his wife, who seemed to be the center of attention at the back of the room, he mentally steeled himself in for a fight.

Convincing Bootsie to be reasonable in front of a crowd was usually a losing battle. A twinge of guilt caused him to take a deep breath. To be honest, he dreaded this whole confrontation. He never should have volunteered to let Miss Logan stay with them, but lately she didn't feel safe in the old foreman's cabin; and he was the Sherriff, after all. He had a duty. Besides, he was at his wit's end, between his wife's temper and Miss Logan's eye batting every time she barged into his office to "talk" he wasn't getting any work done?

Anyway, it was too late now. He'd given his word and it was just until he could find her a better place to stay or arrest that elusive medicine man of hers. His wife would just have to understand. Running a hand through dark hair, he headed straight for Bootsie with a determined look in his eye.

As Adam neared the small group, all chattering ceased. He suddenly grew more uncomfortable as, wide eyed and nervous, they scooted even closer together like hens surrounded by the fox. His stern expression grew even sterner.

With unspoken accord, they gently nudged Bootsie to the front. Their sacrificial offering no doubt, he thought. Elizabeth gulped, as a guilty blush stained her cheeks. Now what? He quirked a suspicious brow.

She gave a weak smile in return. It was ridiculous to think he actually knew anything about her newest little mistake, and didn't he always look like he had just taken a spoonful of castor oil when he was forced to talk with her about something?

Nervously she tucked a strand of hair behind one ear, looking off to avoid his eyes. If only he weren't so handsome which irked her, and intimidating like he was right now, then maybe she might think of something clever to say.

"Is something the matter, Darling?"

His frown deepened. Oh, she was up to something all right. She never called him darling, unless she was being sarcastic or up to something. But right at the moment all he seemed to be able to think about was how pretty she looked, and how much he wanted to kiss that defiance right out of her. That dress. He really liked the way it seemed to hug her slender frame. Yes Sir, it was making all clear thought fly out the window.

"Where did you get that dress?"

"Christina" she automatically answered, momentarily caught off guard, "is something wrong with it?"

Why did she always have to act as if she were some sort of indentured servant instead of his wife? Feeling irritated with her, even he heard the briskly authoritative tone in his voice. He cringed. The woman always got a reaction from him and never the one he wanted to give.

"No, nothing is wrong with it."

"Then why do you sound so irritated?"

"I think he likes it dear" Cornelia suggested, "men always sound gruff when they think we look nice. Isn't that so Mr. Reed?"

For the first time Elizabeth saw him blush, before changing the subject. "Bootsie, I need to talk to you in private for a moment."

She had absolutely no intention of doing anything of the sort. She was feeling nervous and ill at ease. To top it off, he sounded mad and something else she couldn't quite put her finger on.

"I can't right now, Darling" she stressed the endearment, "We are right in the middle of something. Maybe later."

She turned away as if to dismiss him. His steel grip turned her back around to face him. "I insist, Sweetheart."

Their eyes locked. She had no doubt he would carry her out if necessary.

"Now Mr. Reed, a girl in her condition should not be bullied" Hanna warned, putting a comforting arm around her, "Maybe later when you are not so, well, touchy, you could discuss whatever has you so upset."

"I'm not upset" he practically roared.

"Of course not dear" Cornelia broke in quickly, her thin hands clutching each other in fear.

"Now see, your bellowing has upset poor Cornelia" Elizabeth scolded.

167

"Bootsie, I'm warning you."

Hanna stepped in closer to Bootsie, wrapping a mothering arm around her. "Really, Mr. Reed, I will have to insist you stop upsetting the poor girl. Think of your child."

Bootsie shot a horrified look his direction, "I never…"

Confused, he asked in a dazed voice, "Child? What are you talking about woman?"

Prying Hanna off her, Bootsie rushed forward trying to explain, "Adam, this was all a mistake. See, I came here and someone said something about glowing and before you know it, they all just assumed I was…" Her voice trailed off in embarrassment.

Comprehension lit his eyes, then something else, a gleam of mischief in their blue depths, "Oh, that child."

"Adam you know perfectly well…"

"I apologize, ladies. I thought it was our little secret, but you know my wife. Never one to keep something quiet. Now when exactly is our babe coming sweetheart?"

She just wanted away from the women's sympatric looks and her husband's dark humor, as she brushed past him in frustration, "Ohhh. Never mind. Excuse me, I am feeling in need of some fresh air."

"Of course, dear. We understand." Murmured Cornelia.

Apparently they didn't, but there was no fixing that thanks to her husband.

"Ladies." Adam tipped his hat. "I had better check on her. You know how a woman gets in her condition."

As he left through the front door, several of the women were singing his praises on being a most understanding husband. His wife, on the other hand, was ready to kill him.

Reaching the porch, she swirled around so fast her skirts caused a miniature cloud of dust to circle their feet. "I hope you are satisfied. Now every woman in there thinks we are", the words got caught in her throat, "you know."

"Having a baby, by chance?" He ventured, in a voice loud enough half the town had to have heard.

Lowering her voice to a furious whisper, she admonished, "Hush. Someone might hear you."

"It's a little late for that, Sweetheart."

Following his eyes behind her, she slowly turned around in dread. Michael gave her an apologetic shrug as she noticed for the first time, the beautiful young woman perched up on the wagon with him. Her eyes narrowed. Who was she? And why was she looking at Adam with such familiarity? Surely, she didn't ride all the way over here saddled up against her husband? As if in answer, the pretty blond looked to Adam, and then demurely cast her eyes to her lap.

Elizabeth turned a shocked expression on Adam, as he turned up his hands. "Bootsie, you have the wrong idea. Miss Logan here needs a place to lay low for a while and I said she could stay with us, that's all."

That's all? She felt like she had been hit in the stomach for the innocent looking woman watching them so intently out of cornflower blue eyes was much too beautiful. A powerful surge of jealousy hit her so strong, it shook her. She didn't know what was so shocking, that she felt so passionately about her husband or that she seemed unaware of the fact until this very moment? After all, she didn't even like Adam half the time, did she? So, where did this urge to protect what was hers come from? She pressed a palm to her forehead. It made no sense.

As people poured out of the store, she found herself between a rock and a hard place. If she refused Adam, she would appear churlish, but if she didn't, she would very likely be forced to compete for her own husband.

Obviously Adam had left her with little choice. She turned hurt angry eyes to his. "Of course, Adam. It is your home, after all."

He felt like a heel. What else could she say with half the town watching? He felt irritated with her. Why didn't she fight back?

"What do you mean by that?"

Stepping back, she glared at him, "Nothing. I'm simply stating a fact."

In response, he reached over and pulled her possessively up next to him. She struggled a moment, before resigning herself to his touch.

"Oh, Mr. Reed, have I created a problem" Jana's eyes clouded over with concern, "I wouldn't think of intruding. I will just have to find some other place to stay."

Adam responded quickly by letting go of Bootsie and walking over to help Jana down from the wagon. He did it so carefully you would have thought she was made of glass instead of flesh and blood. "Miss Logan, I assure you you're not intruding. Bootsie and I would like nothing better than to have you come stay with us. Isn't that right?"

Cornelia gasped behind her. The other women stared from her to the lovely blond and back again. No doubt fully expecting her to explode. Well, she wouldn't give any of them the satisfaction. Stiffening her spine, she held out a hand in greeting.

"Don't be silly. Of course, you are welcome to stay with us."

Jana clung to Adam's arm, looking uncertainly up at him. Several women covered their mouths in shock. Bootsie had changed. Christina frowned. Even Maggie let out an indignant snort. Hanna moved forward in support of Bootsie, standing so stiffly beside her.

Elizabeth herself felt torn between instant dislike of her rival and humiliation that that Adam should be so blatant about not caring for her. Tears of injured pride sprang to her eyes, but she bit her lip in order to not give in to them.

The other woman bowed her head shyly, but Elizabeth thought she detected a sly smile before Jana lifted adoring eyes to Adam. From the look on Michael's face he wanted to get down off that wagon and give Adam the whipping he deserved.

Loudly clearing his throat, Smitty stuck hands in his overall pockets and spit a stream of tobacco at the spittoon by the door. For once, Elizabeth knew just how he felt and couldn't agree more.

One glance at the betrayed look in his wife's eyes, told Adam he had made a mistake. Suddenly, it looked even to him as if he purposely meant to flaunt this woman in her face. Too late, he realized the last thing in the world he wanted was to hurt the proud beauty standing so stiffly beside Hanna. Her faded peach dress clung to her curves as a slight breeze caught at loose strands of auburn colored tresses, tossing them gently about. It always amazed him how he could possibly forget how truly beautiful she was from one time to the next.

Instinctively he removed Jan's hand from his arm and reached for his wife.

She stepped away as if his touch burned. He figured he deserved that. "Bootsie, you're taking this the wrong way."

"Am I?" She spoke so quietly he had to lean in to hear.

"Adam" Jana began, and then realizing her mistake, corrected, "I, Mr. and Mrs. Reed, thank you both. If there is anything I can do…"

"Miss Logan" Michael broke in sarcastically, "I think you've done quite enough already. We better get these supplies back to camp Adam. Bootsie, can Jana catch a ride home with you?"

Still dazed she answered shakily, "Oh, I rode Becky's horse. Maybe Christine could bring her out to the house."

Adam stopped in mid-swing dropping Jana's bag to the ground, "You what?!"

"I said I rode Becky's horse here."

"And how did you manage that? As of yesterday you could barely ride in the wagon without bouncing out. You could have been killed or worse. Sometimes, I think you lack the sense the Good Lord gave a horse."

She was truly mad now, which probably explained her poor use of words, "Well, at least I don't act like the back end of one."

Christina giggled, and Charles coughed in order to cover his smile. Adam's eyes narrowed in anger. Elizabeth gulped, as she quickly began backing up the two steps behind her. She didn't know what had gotten in to her lately. Her emotions were so raw that anger was a lot easier to deal with than what she really wanted to do, which was to sink on the step under her and cry for hours.

Adam surprised her by stopping just short of actually touching her. Calmly walking to the bottom step, he placed a booted foot on top, and then leaned in closer, to make certain she heard every word.

Instinctively, she clutched her skirts as if ready for flight.

In response, a grin surfaced briefly before he replaced it with a severe frown. "You forget yourself woman. Have Christina drive 'both' of you home." He gave her a pointed look before adding, "We'll talk about this later. In private."

"Ladies," Adam tipped his hat once more to the other women standing around gapping, "Smitty, Charles, load Miss Logan's trunks, and then see if you can manage to get the rest of those supplies loaded."

"Yes, sir", they answered in unison, fairly stumbling over themselves to get the job done.

Adam climbed back into the wagon and released the brake. "See you at home, Sweetheart" he added, before turning the wagon around and leaving in a cloud of dust and mixed emotions.

Smitty shoved his end of a trunk up on the back of the buckboard, muttering the whole time, "Yes, sir. Nothing but trouble. Sure as the world goes round. Nothing but trouble."

Chapter 13

Men were nothing but trouble, Elizabeth decided, as she blew a sticky strand of hair out of her eyes; especially when they came in small sizes like the one in front of her now.

"Nicholas hold still or I won't ever get you dressed in time for services."

"Good. 'Cause I don't have a hankering to go anyhow" he announced, slipping out of her hands like a lizard through a hole in the rocks.

She caught hold of a loose shirt tail and pulled him back in front of her, "Too bad, because you are going."

"But, I ain't never had to before."

"I can tell" she observed dryly trying to keep him still long enough to button the constantly moving object in front of her.

"I bet if Uncle Adam hitched up with Jana instead of you, she wouldn't make me go to some dumb old church service."

Jerking his shirt closer together, nearly yanking him off his feet, Elizabeth gritted her teeth. Jana again. If she heard one more person use the words, 'wonderful' and 'Jana' in the same sentence, she just might scream. Was she the only one who saw through that sweet act of hers?

"Well, Nicholas, since your uncle is already 'hitched up' with me, I guess we will never know" she pointed out, as she finished buttoning up his starched white shirt and hurriedly ran a comb through tousled hair.

"Besides, I don't understand why you are so upset. Think of how exciting it will be to have a whole church full of people singing and being together." She was so lost in her own excitement that she failed to notice the way Nicholas's eyes clouded over with pain.

He turned around and shoved his drawer shut.

"Well, churches only make me think about burying people and you can't make me go, you hear" he shouted, running out of the room and slamming the door shut behind him.

Shocked, Elizabeth whispered, "Burying?"

Slowly, understanding dawned and she sank down on the feather bed, her heart aching for the little boy. Of course. She should have remembered that the very last two times he went to church were for funerals; his mother and father's funerals.

Without a moment's hesitation, she jumped to her feet and ran out to the top of the stairs, "Nicholas!"

She barely caught him. He stopped on the very last step and began to run a finger along the wood grain of the banister, refusing to look up at her. "Yeah?" His voice sounded arrogant, but there was no mistaking the husky sound of unshed tears.

"Nicholas, I didn't think. Forgive me?"

Taken by surprise, he looked up in confusion, "For what? I'm the one that yelled at you."

The words she needed were stuck in her throat and refused to come out. How could she explain this overwhelming sadness she felt for him. Something he would neither accept nor believe she meant.

"I'm sorry because…" the look he bestowed on her was one of stubborn pride so like his uncle's that it stopped the flow of pity she nearly offered him. Instead she finished simply, "Because church isn't supposed to be about dying Nicholas. It's about living."

His stare penetrated her soul. Then, just as quickly, he dismissed her with a shrug. "I guess I gotta go to church. But I warn ya, I'm putting my foot down about that school."

"I beg your pardon?" Elizabeth responded as she slowly sank down on the top step. "How did you know about the school?"

Shoving hands deep down in his pockets, he stuck his small chest out in defiance, "I seen how you been wheedling Uncle Adam about things."

Guiltily she blushed in response, "I most certainly have not been wheedling anyone. Besides, you are mistaken Nicholas in thinking I am doing this for me. This is for you."

"Then you go to school."

Exasperated, Elizabeth tried to explain, "Having a school is one of the things that will help make this lumber camp into a real town. Don't you want to play with other children?"

Nicholas looked incredulously at the culprit before him; her eyes alight with a fiery passion for change. "I ain't going to no school, no matter if you tie me up and torture me to death."

Sighing, Elizabeth rolled her eyes, "My heavens, Nicholas, must you always be so dramatic?"

"If'n dramatic means I ain't going to school? Then I reckon I'm dramatic."

Coming to her feet, she faced the stubborn boy, "All right Nicholas. It is your decision. And since I haven't tortured anyone in such a long time, I am quite certain I have forgotten how."

"It is up to you after all. We can hardly force you to read now can we? And I am sure after your Uncle gets over the initial disappointment, he will understand entirely. He will just have to find someone else to help run the mill is all."

"What are you talking about? I want to be a lumber jack."

"Oh?" Elizabeth acted surprised, "I must have misunderstood. I thought you said you didn't want to go to school."

"I don't."

"Oh, really?" Now the little boy looked more confused than ever as he suspiciously eyed the grownup fixing his tie so casually. She smiled warmly. "Then I guess you must already know how to write out orders for shipments."

"Not yet, but…"

"Not? I see, well then, arithmetic must be your strong point. I assume you can add up columns of figures to keep track of all the money flowing in and out of a business."

His scowl darkening, she continued on cheerfully, "You see Nicholas, without an education, the very thing you want most is out of reach for you. I suppose you could work as one of the hands, however. Who knows you might turn out to be the next…say, Smitty."

Running a hand through his hair in aggravation, he mumbled more to himself than her, "Heck, I'd have to take up chewing tobacco. Last time it made me turn as green as gourds."

"What did you say?" She reached out to adjust his jacket. Deftly, he pulled away to glare at her.

"Nothing. I didn't say nothing."

Smiling sweetly, she rose to her feet. "That's what I thought."

Looking over at the clock on the wall, she gasped, "Oh, dear. The time. We are going to be late for church and the very first Sunday, too. Nicholas run and see if can find your sister, I'm sure she's escaped Jana by now."

"Oh, all right." Nicholas grumbled, and sped up to what could only be described as a stroll in search of his baby sister.

Whirling around, Elizabeth picked up her skirts and raced towards the bedroom. If Chelsea was her usual elusive self, she would barely have time to pin up her hair. No doubt Jana looked immaculate. She bet her best pair of garters that Jana was plying Adam with stories of her short comings this very minute, blue eyes batting demurely up at him.

Why was it that she seemed to be the only one aware of what Jana really wanted when she moved in with them? Adam. "Ow!" Elizabeth narrowed eyes on the pin in her hands as if it, not she, had angrily jabbed itself into her scalp.

Not that Jana would dare show her true nature by acting rudely in front of Adam. Even Jana knew better than to test his loyalty. No, she used subtle means to make Elizabeth look as bad as possible. Somehow managing to come out smelling like a rose, while Elizabeth more the wicked briar.

For example, there was that dreadful shirt incident last week. Looking in the mirror, she cringed at how easily she had played into Jana's calculating hands. It certainly started off innocent enough. Jana pulling out one of Adam's torn shirts and offering to mend it. Yet somehow before the incident was over, Elizabeth was so furious she actually threatened Jana bodily harm if she so much as laid a hand on the thing.

Her temper flaring once again, she quickly twisted her hair up and forcefully drove another pin into its soft depths. Maybe it was the way Jana implied she didn't take good care of Adam, sympathetically noting the sad shape of his clothes. Dropping her hands, for the first time she admitted the truth to herself.

No, what rankled her more than hurt pride…was jealousy. Pure and simple. She supposed because what Jana said was partly true. She wasn't a good wife. In fact, she wasn't a real wife at all.

She felt – inadequate.

This must have been why she acted so foolishly. What could she have been thinking insisting on mending it herself? They all knew she couldn't thread a needle in a pinch, much less actually sew something.

In response, Jana had simply shrugged prettily. Adam, on the other hand, had raised a questioning eyebrow at her show of possessiveness. It was then she realized, perhaps she'd over reacted just a tad bit. Nevertheless, it had been too late to back down. So needle in hand, she spent the better part of the evening trying to mend the stupid thing. All the while, Jana took a place opposite Adam in a game of checkers. Her musical laughter grating on Elizabeth's every nerve, until she had the thread in such a tangle that it took most of the night just correcting her mistakes.

Around midnight, with a tired yawn, she'd finally finished the impossible task. Proudly draping the shirt over the back of a chair, she crawled into bed beside Adam. Secure in the knowledge that for once she had beaten Jana at her own game.

Well, by the next morning it became all too apparent who exactly had won, and it wasn't her. For after a few minutes of struggling with the red cotton shirt, he burst out in hearty laughter, at her expense, of course.

Somehow she had managed to sew the front to the back. After seeing the embarrassed look on her face, Adam got ahold of himself enough that only a soft chuckle remained as he kissed the top of her head. Claiming he never really cared for the shirt anyway.

To which Elizabeth burst into tears.

And sewing was not the only thing Jana did better. She could ride, cut hair and cook, to name a few. Watching her family practically devour Jana's cooking, devastated her.

Later that night blowing out the kerosene lantern, Elizabeth sat up in bed twisting her hands in agitation.

"Adam?"

"Yes", came his muffled rely from the bed covers.

Drawing in a trembling breath, she asked, ""Do you think Jana cooks better than I do?"

Apparently even Adam knew better than to answer that one. He sat up on one elbow, opened his mouth to answer, and then got a thoughtful expression on his face. No doubt remembering the incident with the shirt.

"Well, I wouldn't say better... exactly."

She slumped down in defeat, looking down at her hands.

"I mean...for crying out loud Sweetheart, what has gotten into you lately? You don't even like to cook."

"That isn't the point," she replied in a huff, throwing herself down and punching her pillow.

"Well, what exactly is the point then?" he asked in a dull roar.

"If you don't know that, I'm certainly not going to tell you."

Adam's exasperation was obvious. He just sat there staring at her back for a long time. Finally, he seemed to calm down enough to speak. "Well, you're right about one thing, wife."

She refused to look his direction. "What?"

"I have absolutely no idea what you are talking about."

Elizabeth might have explained. That is...had she known herself.

"I bet Jana kisses better than I do too," she horrified herself by blurting out.

"That's it." Adam announced, throwing off the covers and putting his pants back on, "when you decide to act like a rational human being, come and get me. I'll be in the barn."

She had cried herself to sleep.

"Oh, there you are, Bootsie. Adam has been looking all over for you."

She glared over at the very woman in her thoughts. As usual, she looked like a blonde-haired angel, compared to Elizabeth's own disheveled appearance. Feeling Jana's eyes go over her wrinkled dress as she smiled falsely, Elizabeth was hardly surprised by her words.

"Oh, dear. I see you aren't ready yet, and you know how Adam hates to be late. The poor man puts up with enough without that, too."

Narrowing eyes as she blew a wisp of hair off her nose, Elizabeth challenged, "For your information, I am ready."

"Oh, how very thoughtless of me. I hope you don't think I meant you looked anything less than charming." She purred, patting at neat curls and ran a slender hand over her wrinkle-free gown. "Why, some men find it adorable when their women look un-kept."

Remembering Sister Agnes's advice, she looked down at her own rust colored dress with the braided brown trim and counted to ten. Sorely wishing she wasn't a lady, and could show Jana exactly what disheveled meant.

Instead, she coolly asked, "Weren't you supposed to be watching Chelsea?"

"Was I? Oh, you know how messy she is. No doubt she's keeping the pigs company by now."

A maternal instinct Elizabeth didn't know she possessed rose up with a vengeance. "Chelsea is just a baby. You're supposed to be watching her. I specifically remember asking you to dress her for services this morning."

Jana's response was a blank look, followed by one of pity, as she coyly played with the silver pin she had been about to place in her hat. "Of course you did Bootsie. If you say so."

Hardly believing Jana actually meant to lie about something so insignificant; her first reaction was one of stunned disbelief. "I beg your pardon?"

Their eyes met. It was then obvious exactly what Jana meant.

"Are you implying I made it up?"

Jana met the challenge by lifting her head and remarking coldly, "I'm not implying anything. I'm simply stating a fact."

She'd been playing this little game ever since moving in a week ago. The only thing that surprised Elizabeth was that Adam was not around for the show. Usually these 'performances' were entirely for his benefit. Now without Adam intervening, it was taking every ounce of strength Elizabeth had to keep from ripping Janna's perfect cornflower hat right off her perfectly pinned curls.

But it was Nicholas, not Adam who intervened this time.

Stunned, the two women watched as Chelsea was being dragged kicking and screaming into the room by an equally disheveled Nicholas. He somehow managed to plant both feet firmly, hanging onto the door frame with one hand, while trying to hang on to his squirming muddy sister with the other.

"You won't believe where I found her", he announced between bouts of trying to drag a resisting Chelsea into the room.

"Let me guess. The pig pen," Jana offered, with a pointed look Elizabeth's direction.

"Yeah. How'd you know?"

She shrugged. "Oh, just a lucky guess."

Chapter 14

Somehow they made it to church. Breathing a sigh of relief as they scooted into the back row during the last stanza of "Mansions over the Hilltop", Elizabeth felt at peace for the first time in a long time. It felt good to be in a church again, even if there were no elaborately decorated candles, or stained glass. Still, the warmth was there. The safety of being loved and accepted by a God that didn't seem to mind what a misfit she was.

As the young preacher had them stand for the final prayer, she offered a heartfelt one of her own. Of thanks. Because maybe Adam was right after all, perhaps she was making a difference since arriving here. True, it might only be to one hardheaded lumberjack and the two unruly children sitting beside her. But, whether they admitted it or not, they needed her.

Apparently, the other women needed her as well. Elizabeth sighed as she watched the other women make a determined bee line straight for her after church services were over. So much for peace and tranquility. Leave it to the other brides to abolish both in a manner of minutes. With a heavy sigh she turned away from the other families chattering warmly outside the church, her attention now on Cornelia, Christine, and Maggie as they came to a sudden stop in front of her.

"Are you going to let that hussy take your man?"

"What?" Elizabeth sputtered.

"Cornelia, of all the ridiculous things to say. Mind your manners." Christine patted Elizabeth's hand. "Never mind her dear, you know she has a flare for the dramatic."

Elizabeth instantly relaxed. Christina was right. There was nothing to worry about. After all, she was Adam's wife, not Jana. She gave her friend a grateful smile. It was hard to admit, but she had missed these women. All of them, even Cornelia with her love of the dramatic. Somehow, they had grown on her. She shook her head at her new found sentimentally.

"I hate to agree with Cornelia. You know, I think she is as daft as you lass, but that Jana woman is about as genuine as a one-legged leprechaun."

Instantly Elizabeth's gaze traveled to the object being discussed. She was as at that very moment clutching Adam's arm, pretending to adjust a button on her black boot.

Elizabeth bit her bottom lip in worry. "Do you really think so?"

"Aye, she's a crafty one that one." Maggie added with a sharp nod.

"Who's a crafty one?" Abigail asked, shoving up her sliding bun.

"Who else?" Maggie scoffed, pointing a finger at the pretty blond.

Abigail shuttered. "Oh, I can't say as I care for that one, Bootsie, she gives me the willies."

Giving an undignified huff, Cornelia commented sarcastically, "Everything gives you the willies."

"It does not!"

"Is that so? Why, let's see. Seems I recall that last full moon gave you the willies." Cornelia mimicked. "Before that, the old man that's always spitting gave you the willies. I suppose when you die, your tombstone will read – the willies finally got the best of her."

"Will you two stop that bickering? We are trying to help Bootsie keep her man." Maggie stated matter of fact.

Elizabeth blinked. "Have I lost him?"

Eyes wide, Cornelia piped in, "I've seen it all before. Unsuspecting wife generously helps a fellow woman down on her luck, then – BAM!" Cornelia slapped her hand against her thigh for emphasis making all four women jump in unison.

"Yep, then that poor woman finds herself penniless and abandoned. Their husband's run off into the night with that hussy…"

As usual it was Christina who was once again the voice of reason.

Hanna's large form appeared out of nowhere. "That's enough. Cornelia, your husband's been glaring this way for the past ten minutes. I think he's ready to go."

Without a moment's hesitation she took off in the direction of the tall skinny man, but not without giving Elizabeth a warning nod towards Jana.

Jana was laughing charmingly at something Adam and the preacher were discussing. Maybe, she was in trouble. Maybe, Adam was falling prey to that…what did Cornelia call her? Well… she was right. Something had to be done to save him, of course; not because it really concerned her. It was her wifely duty wasn't it?

"Well, I'm sure Bootsie can take care of her own affairs, girls. Can't you Bootsie?"

Could she? Until now she had no idea how serious things were.

Christina gave her a hug before parting, "See you at our next meeting, Bootsie. Remember to bring a few canned items."

"But I…" No one seemed to be listening as she finished mumbling more to herself than the others, "I don't know how to can." What did it matter anyway? According to the women, she would be left penniless and alone while Jana and Adam lived happily ever after. She glared over at her nemesis. On second thought, maybe there was something she could do about it.

After pulling the kids away from a game of chase, they all climbed back into the wagon and headed for home. Elizabeth glanced over at Jana beside her. Now that she had a plan she felt better and even the beautiful blonde ignoring her couldn't break her good mood.

Taking off her sunbonnet, she let the wind catch at her hair, tugging some mahogany strands loose. One upon a time, she might have worried about her skin. Somehow the worry seemed moot now that her skin was a light apricot color from hours outdoors. Feeling Adam's eyes on her, she felt herself blush, his look warmer than the sun's rays on her face. In so many ways her feelings about him were changing, much like her appearance. And that knowledge raised all sort of questions that she wasn't able, or willing to answer yet.

Pulling into the yard a short time later put an end to such thoughts. Watching as Adam wrapped the reins around the brake and climbed down, her eyes shifted to her new home. There it stood, solid and sturdy, like the man who built it. The kind of house that would gather her up and keep her always, if she let it. If she let him. A huge sigh escaped her chest. But that would mean staying here forever.

He looked up, curiosity in his eyes. She shrugged and put out her left hand so he could help her down. A mischievous glint was in his eyes, as he left her side and helped Jana down first. Ignoring his outstretched arms a moment later, she scooted past him and climbed down in a flounce of petticoats.

His laughter turned serious as he reached out, halting her exit into the house.

"Bootsie, we need to talk."

She tried her best to sound bored and indifferent, but his hand on her arm was making her stomach feel all tipsy-turvy again. "About what?"

"You know what", he motioned behind them, as Jana hurried the children inside the house.

"I am sure I don't have the faintest idea what you are talking about."

"Good. Then I'll explain."

Before she could stop him, he grabbed her hand and pulled her along with him as he led the horse back to the barn. He was making it hard for her to maintain any sort of dignity. Being dragged along with a horse hardly exemplified the trait after all. She tried to twist free. He clamped harder down on her aching wrist.

"I don't want to talk to you."

"Good. Then I'll talk. You listen."

She thought he sounded a little too sarcastic for any sort of real conversation to take place. This made her extremely nervous. Because for some reason, every time he started out sounding angry with her, she ended up being kissed, which made absolutely no sense.

Just the thought of being alone with him in a huge dark barn caused her stomach to tighten. It didn't help matters that it had been over a week since she had had the pleasure, unless you counted their bedroom. She didn't.

There, the only communicating he did was more commanding growl than talk. Demanding ridiculous things like insisting she wear the heavy flannel gown instead of her light cotton one in the heat of summer. Oh, and demanding she stay on her side of the bed. Really, what was he thinking? Of course, all that was before he started sleeping out here in the barn. Her plan was to change that. Well, in theory it had seemed like a good idea when she was talking to the other wives. That is... until this very moment. Now it looked like a very bad idea.

She dug her heels into the ground.

He jerked her forward and through the barn door.

Once inside, she pulled her wrist free and began rubbing the soreness out. No, she couldn't possibly talk to him when he was like this. Hadn't she tried to about the gown?

When she complained about being overly warm, he gave her a look so hot, that it made the flannel seem breezy in comparison.

Then all he said was, "better you, than me."

What his discomfort had to do with anything, she could not possibly imagine, but the matter did not seem up for debate. Nope, talking was definitely not a good idea. Then again, since he was ignoring her again, maybe there wouldn't be a discussion after all.

Out of the corner of her eye, she watched him unhitch the horse with a diligence that surprised her. "I don't think you should be flinging that big heavy object around like that."

He simply stared at her, before throwing the trace chains into the corner. Pepper whinnied in response.

She frowned back at him. For someone who wanted to talk, he certainly wasn't saying much. Well, except for the several unsavory expletives coming from his direction as he continued unhitching the wagon. She turned her back on him, pretending to study the latch on one of the stalls.

Moistening dry lips, and smoothing out the wrinkles in her dress, she tried her best not to notice the large muscles bulging under his sweat-

185

filled shirt as he struggled with Pepper. And she certainly wasn't aware of how his strong hands were gripping the… Straining to get a better look she leaned backwards just a little.

This was a mistake. The gate, unfortunately, leaned with her swinging wide and leaving her skirt hung underneath. She was trapped in a most embarrassing way. Acting out of reflex, she frantically clutched the gate to keep from falling. She didn't dare look Adam's direction. Praying beyond hope that he didn't notice her dilemma.

He did. Leaning in against the horse he had been struggling with, she commented casually. "Problem?"

She jumped. "I beg your pardon?"

"Didn't those nuns of yours teach you it was impolite to stare?"

Caught in the act and suspended somewhere between standing and falling, she could hardly deny it, but she tried. "For your information, I wasn't staring." He crossed his arms and grinned. She cleared her throat. "I was merely ahh…observing." She added, frantically trying to disentangle herself.

His sexy crooked grin only intensified; as he reached down to unhook the stubborn fabric. Out of necessity, she found herself forced to clutch his muscular shoulders in order to keep from falling right on top of him. She felt her face grow hotter.

Straightening, Adam remained directly in front of her, making the act of breathing extremely difficult. "Well frankly, darling, all that um…observing you're doing is a little distracting."

"Oh." Quickly looking down, she tried to disappear, to no avail. He tilted her head back with one finger, and as their eyes met she knew there was no way to hide her attraction to him. Or his to her.

Laughing to break the sexual tension, he turned away from her and retrieved the trace chains from the corner, placing them up on the wall. The heavy chains caused even more muscles to bulge forward. Her treacherous eyes refusing to obey her command, stayed transfixed on him. Apparently, she couldn't take her eyes off the man. What in the world was wrong with her anyway?

"Bootsie, why don't you come over and give me a hand", Adam winked, deftly unbuckling the heavy collar on Pepper.

"Oh, I don't think I'd better."

"Well", he noted playfully, "it's been my experience that observing is better from over here."

Closing her eyes in embarrassment, she slowly opened them to find him crooking a finger at her.

Giving up, she gave a shy smile and walked over. Ducking underneath the horse to the other side, she observed, "You're a hard man to understand, Mr. Reed."

Absentmindedly, she began stroking Pepper's soft mane. The horse tried to bite her in return. "I thought you wanted to discuss Jana, not flirt."

Adam reached over and removed the collar, laying it on the ground beside him. In silence he fingered the horse's mane, his hand accidently brushing against hers. Her heart skipped a beat in response.

"Could you pass me that brush?"

She simply stared into his eyes, mesmerized by the deep rumble of his voice. He raised an eyebrow at her.

"Oh, certainly", she sputtered, taking the brush and handing it to him.

When their hands touched again, this time he slowly rubbed a calloused thumb along the outside of hers. "In answer to your question, I do want to discuss Jana. I guess what I wanted to say is this", he brought her hand to his lips and laid a feather light kiss on the back. "You have nothing to worry about. I gave you my word to be faithful and," his eyes strayed to her lips. She moistened them. "I will be. See, you can trust me to keep my word. Even when it's difficult, like right now for instance. If I were less honorable, you would already be kissed."

Elizabeth blushed prettily before subconsciously moving away from the horse. "I guess I know that deep down inside, it's just that I..."

"It's just what?"

Her grin was sheepish. "Well, Jana makes me so mad sometimes."

Adam laughed out loud, his blue eyes dancing with her blunt honesty.

"Besides, I don't know what I am so worried about anyway", she answered with honest bewilderment, "I mean, it isn't as if we are really married."

Slamming a hand against the horse's side caused both Elizabeth and Pepper to jump in surprise. The horse reacted more violently by rearing up on two back feet and pawing the air. Forcing himself to calm down, Adam soothingly talked the horse back down on all fours.

Finally turning back around, his whole body was tense with suppressed anger. "I swear, Bootsie, you could make a saint lose his temper. When are you going to accept our marriage? What will it take to convince you this is for life," his chest heaved with frustration. "You don't want to be my wife, but you sure don't want Jana flirting with me, either. So, tell me. What do you want? Because, honestly, I don't have any idea."

Shaking her head in denial, even though she knew everything he said was true, she tried to explain. "It's not you. It's this place. I can't stay here."

"Why not? Don't deny you want me as badly as I do you. I can't be that wrong about the way you respond to my touch. So tell me, Bootsie, what is it you want from me?"

"I want to go home."

Adam's gut clenched in response to the bare honesty. Even he could not deny the confusion in her voice, or the scared pleading in her eyes.

Instinctively, he pulled her into his arms to comfort her. "Sweetheart, you are home."

Oddly enough this time she didn't resist his touch. In fact, she welcomed it. She needed his understanding, his arms holding her. They stayed wrapped in each other for several minutes both not wanting to spoil the moment with words that only seemed to get in the way of what they both needed.

Finally, slightly embarrassed, Elizabeth leaned away and gave a weak smile. "At least you didn't kiss me again."

Adam released her and remarked honestly, "Kiss you? Shoot, woman, I wanted to kill you."

They both had a laugh at that accurate statement. Reluctantly they slowly dropped hands. Shyly Elizabeth asked, "Friends then?"

A sexy look met her straight on, "For now."

Then in comfortable silence, Adam continued unhitching the wagon while Elizabeth 'observed'. Now all he had to do was lead Pepper into the stall. They exchanged a wary look. Pepper hated his stall.

Adam tugged on his bridle. In response, the horse dug his hooves into the ground and refused to budge. "Come on…you…sorry excuse…for a horse."

"Perhaps if we both pulled it might help", Elizabeth offered.

Letting the reins drop to the ground, Adam studied the horse in question. "Nothing would help. This horse is about as worthless as they come."

She couldn't agree more. The animal rarely obeyed anyone, except Nicholas, who seemed to have some sort of special bond with the thing. She frowned, tapping a thinking finger along the railing beside her.

Once more Adam began coaching the horse forward. His muscles bunching up in the never ending battle of man against beast. Out of the corner of her eye, Elizabeth noticed a glint of steal. There within reach lay the bright new pitch fork Adam bought at town two days ago.

Of course…the pitchfork! Hurrying over, she picked it up, but worried her bottom lip. Adam told her to stay out of it, but looking over at Adam still tugging on Pepper, she made her decision. Maybe he just needed a little help. No doubt he was too proud to ask. Besides, she saw no reason why she should just stand by and do nothing.

Adam looked up just in time to see a determined Bootsie coming straight at him and Pepper, wielding a shiny pointed object their direction. It took a second to realize the weapon in her hand was none other than his new pitchfork. As if in slow motion, he watched her head straight for him, pitchfork thrust before her like a bayonet, a determined glint shinning in

189

her clear green eyes. "No, Bootsie, don't. You'll spook…"Adam shouted, but it was too late.

The poor horse had about all he could stand of this whole experience. The female welding a large sharp object at him was the final straw. With the sun bouncing off the pitchfork and into his blood shot eyes, his fear intensified. To the horror of both humans, he commenced bucking in full-fledged panic. Throwing his head about and arching his back as all four feet left the ground.

"Bootsie, get out of the way!"

Adam's shout failed to move her. She stood rooted in terror as the horse pawed the air above her. She dropped the pitchfork.

Racing forward, Adam shoved her out of the way and into a hay covered stall. His shout of pain the only way she knew he hadn't made it out of the way himself. Stumbling to her feet, she raced back out in time to see Adam quickly roll out from under the spooked horse's hooves, barely missing getting his leg smashed.

Reacting quickly, she began tugging him into the safety of the deserted stall. Somehow, between the two of them, they managed to lock themselves in. Meanwhile, the still panicked horse ran kicking and bucking through the open doorway.

The barn got strangely quiet. The only sound was Adam's heavy breathing as the barn door swung to and fro, a reoccurring reminder of the near tragedy that only a moment before seemed unavoidable. At last, she forced herself to look down at her husband; afraid to see just how badly he was hurt. His eyes were closed tight against the agony he was no doubt trying to control.

"Adam?"

He opened his pain-filled eyes and bit his lip against the moan threatening to escape. His right hand reached down for his foot. Reluctantly, Elizabeth's eyes followed its path.

His foot was already swollen to twice its normal size.

"Your foot. I'll go get help."

His bruising grip on her arm stopped her. He looked about ready to pass out. Eyes round with terror, she tried to apologize, "I am so sorry.

I had no idea Pepper would react like that", her voice trailed off. When he failed to respond, panic hit. Running a hand worriedly over his body in search of more damage, she kept apologizing profusely the whole time. What if he died? It would be all her fault.

Once more Adam stilled her hands with a bone crushing grip. She forced a brave teary smile and waited for his last dying words. He pulled her in closer. She gulped back tears.

"Would you stop that infernal fluttering woman and leave me alone", he growled.

Sitting back on bent knees, she gave a strangled gasp. "I was only trying to help."

"It was your help that got me into this mess in the first place. You could have killed me."

That little remark earned him a hysterical woman. She burst into tears.

"Oh, for Pete's sake." Adam tried to sit up, but a fresh wave of pain shot through his foot when he tried to move. He sank back down, gritting his teeth against the pain.

"No, you're right", Elizabeth said through sobs "all I ever do is make a mess out of things. No wonder Sister Agnes said I wouldn't make a good nun. Why, I probably would have burnt down the convent while trying to make a meal for the poor defenseless widows and orphans." She covered her tear-stained face with her hands.

The word picture she created caused a reluctant grin to surface. Adam shook his head at himself. Here he was hurting mad, yet still she had the power to make him smile. Regardless of her belief that she was failure, he knew better. There was one area where she was most adapt, and that was at finding a way into his heart. "It's okay sweetheart, it wasn't your fault." A trembling smile came to her lips. Adam's finger traced her soft bottom lip, still quivering.

His touch seemed to soothe her. She suggested shyly, "Perhaps if you got up and walked around, your foot might start feeling a little better."

As his foot began throbbing, Adam knew he wouldn't be feeling better for a few days yet. "Beth, I can't even stand on it, much less walk.

191

Maybe you could catch Pepper and have him finish me off instead. Believe me it would be lot kinder in the long run."

Elizabeth looked down in wonderment from a face covered with dirt and tears, her wild hair falling half way down her back and smiled. Strange that even lying there in pain, he could still make jokes. The smile left her face, as she slowly realized what he had called her.

"You called me Beth." Her voice was a reverent whisper. She hadn't been called that since she was a little girl.

Adam shrugged. "It seems to fit you. After all, a grown man can't go around calling his wife 'Bootsie' all his life, now can he? Hate to hurt your feelings, sweetheart, but I really hate that name. Besides, the name Beth sounds more like you, soft and warm like a quilt on a cold winter's day."

Her eyes clouded over with emotion.

"Now what", he asked thoroughly exasperated, as beads of sweat gathered on his forehead and upper lip.

"That has to be the most beautiful thing anyone has ever said to me. And you said it after I nearly killed you."

"Sweetheart, you are killing me."

Jana stood in the doorway watching the touching scene, her dainty light brown brows meeting together in a scowl. She gripped the frame a moment before plastering on a false look of sympathy as her lilting voice carried across to the two of them, "Adam are you all right? I thought I heard shouting?"

The warmth Elizabeth felt fled at the sound of Jana's voice. Adam noticed the change in his wife and took a long, hard look at the young woman gliding into the barn, her voice filled with sympathy. To the naked eye she appeared genuinely worried about him, yet somehow she lacked the sincerity of Beth's heartfelt sobs. Of course, in all fairness, Jana wasn't the one who nearly caused him to meet his Maker earlier than planned, either.

"I'm fine, Jana" Adam lied, grimacing as a fresh wave of pain shot through his foot. "I just had a little accident that's all."

Gracefully sinking down beside him, Jana deftly pushed Elizabeth out of the way. "Oh Adam, how awful."

Bristling as she watched her rival ease her husband up to a better sitting position, she felt flush with anger as one massive arm wrapped around her slender shoulder. "Now take a deep breath, I will try to get you on your feet. Bootsie, grab his other arm."

Elizabeth thought about ignoring her, but in all reality she was right. It would take the two of them to help get him inside. So, reluctantly, she grabbed her husband's arm and jerked it over her shoulder. His deep inhale reminded her that she was supposed to be helping him, not playing tug of war with Jana.

"Sorry."

He looked like he didn't believe her half-hearted apology, and was it her imagination that he leaned more Jana's direction?

"Oh Adam, your foot looks terrible." Jana cooed, "Are you in awful pain? When I think about a good man like you nearly losing his life because of a stupid mistake" she looked pointedly over at Elizabeth, "I mean, horse. Why, it just breaks my heart. Don't you worry about a thing. Did I mention I did some volunteer work at the Santa Fe Hospital once?"

Of course she did. No doubt she flew with the angels on her time off.

"What did you say, Beth?" Adam asked, as if reading her thoughts.

"Nothing." She mumbled. Although, she had just about had enough of this performance thank you very much. "I just think. Jana. That if my husband needs any sort of help? I'll be the one giving it." She ordered over his head on the way out the door.

Jana blushed prettily. Adam's brows drew together at Elizabeth's unprovoked attack. "Beth, would you mind being jealous later, I have a splitting headache and your yelling at Jana is not helping."

Turning on him, she demanded, "And since when did you become on a first name basis with Miss Logan here?" Adam groaned in pain, and had to lean against the door frame to stop from falling.

"Beth, not now."

"Please Bootsie, can't you see the poor man is about to pass out?"

That did it. Letting go of Adam, she shoved her fists into her gown. He barely managed to grab onto the door, sinking his head down on his arm as fresh waves of dizziness took him by surprise.

"What I see is that you're making the most out of touching my husband."

Jana huffed indignantly, "I beg your pardon?"

Finally managing to focus his pain-racked brain on her words, Adam ground out warningly, "Beth don't you think you are being a little harsh with Miss Logan here? She only offered to help."

He wished his head would just explode and be done with it.

As if to hurry the process, his wife grabbed up his arm propping him against the door. He fell against her and the movement sent a sharp pain up his body. If he would have had any stamina left he would have died right there.

"Fine, let her help then. Forget all about your marriage vows."

"Woman, the girl is only helping me inside. Do I look in the mood for flirting to you?" He demanded between clenched teeth.

Well actually, no – he didn't.

His foot was now turning a bluish color. To top it off he was as white as a sheet. Instantly contrite, she admonished herself for yelling at him at a time like this. What was she thinking? Why was she being so irrational? For the remainder of the time it took to get him inside, she would behave herself. Act like the lady Sister Agnes taught her to be.

Jana tsk, tsked her behind Adam's sagging shoulders.

That was it.

"Either take your hands off my husband, or I do it for you", she demanded.

Adam felt Jana stiffen beside him. Then after a moment's hesitation, she gently eased his weight from her to Beth. Which must have been considerable for she barely caught herself in time, before sinking to the ground. He felt her tremble beneath his arm.

"Adam, I apologize if my offer of help was inappropriate," Jana's voice broke just a little, as if trying to hide how upset she was by the accusation.

Elizabeth didn't have to see Adam's face, she could feel his disapproval. They shuffled along in silence until they were just out of ear shot of Jana, before he said gruffly, "I think you owe Miss Logan an apology. Your censure of her was both irrational and uncalled for."

"I think Miss Logan can take care of herself."

Reaching the house, Adam pushed himself up the stairs using the posts on the front porch. "It seems to me Beth, that by now you would realize that temper of yours causes nothing but trouble."

She blushed angrily, "This fight is not about my temper and we both know it." He stopped, slowly turning to face to her, confusion on his face. She continued irrationally, "This is really about mending my minding abilities."

"Your what?"

"Don't pretend you don't know what I am talking about", she said accusingly.

"I'm not pretending," Adam answered truthfully, "I haven't a clue what you're talking about."

Once more, Elizabeth could feel the all too common feelings of inadequacies threatening to surface. Didn't he see how badly she paled in comparison to Jana? Yes from sewing to cooking and even temperament, Jana was apparently a better wife than the one he had.

"Why doesn't that surprise me? Lately all you think about is Jana. As far as I am concerned you can have each other." She raised her chin a notch, choking back tears. "Now if you will excuse me I am leaving and you can find your own way into the house. Or then again, maybe 'Jana the perfect' will help you."

Adam was more confused than ever and just as furious.

"Beth!" He roared at her retreating form.

She just kept walking, head held high, too mad to think straight.

"Woman, you get your shapely backside back here this instant or the bargain's off."

That stopped her. A worried look replaced her angry one. He wouldn't dare blackmail her this way, and in broad daylight. Land's sake, God and everyone else could surely hear every word he said.

"I mean it. Shall I describe to you just how I intend to go about breaking it?"

She spun around fire shooting out her eyes, fully prepared to give him a piece of her mind. However, before she could begin, to her horror he crumbled to the ground. Running over, she knelt down, afraid to touch his deathly pale face. Horror darkened her normally clear green eyes to a cloudy hazel color.

Heaven help her. She had killed him.

Chapter 15

Well, unfortunately, she hadn't killed him.

Not that she wouldn't enjoy killing him at this precise moment. Adam had to be the worst patient in history. He not only was demanding and rude, but true to his word was making Elizabeth rue the day she spouted out those dooming words, "I can take care of him, myself."

"Beth, would you mind fetching me another piece of that fresh blackberry pie Jana made?"

Balking at yet another insignificant order, she jerked the pie off the shelf and slammed it down on the table.

"Oh, and while you're at it, would hand me that ledger over there?"

Her fiery gaze shot to where the object lay on the floor beside him, not an arm's length away. Catching the rebellion in her eyes, Adam raised a dark eyebrow, asking innocently, "Do you wish to renege on our bargain sweetheart?"

Fuming she answered tightly, "I wouldn't dream of it. Darling."

This whole last week had truly been a test of her patience. For one thing, there was her guilt over causing Adam's accident. Then to top it off, Jana acted like a beat pup every time their paths crossed. She even flinched when Elizabeth handed her a knife the other day, as if she would really use it on her. Of course, the thought was becoming more and more appealing.

Jana, of course, could not appear more the picture of innocence and helpfulness. She was literally driving Elizabeth crazy. For instance, there was the newest way she found for tormenting her by moving things around, making them impossible to find. When confronted, she would stand quietly with a look of pity on her insincere face, before showing Adam that the item was exactly where Elizabeth swore she had looked. Even Elizabeth was beginning to wonder if it were her mind playing tricks on her.

At first, Adam reprimanded Elizabeth for assuming the worst of Jana. Which might have been bearable, but lately his anger was being replaced by a worried frown and real concern. As if he too were starting to believe that something was really wrong with her.

She wasn't crazy. Ill-tempered? Maybe. Stubborn and unreasonable? Probably. But, not crazy.

The only bright spots during the entire week were Michael's nightly visits. Every evening after he and Adam finished discussing business, Elizabeth would insist he stay for dinner. In truth, it was more from fear of being alone with Jana's subtle accusations and Adam's growing doubts. Anything that postponed those nerve wracking moments when she doubted her own sanity, were a relief.

And to be honest, the fact that Jana absolutely hated Michael had its benefits too. She had no idea what had caused Jana's obvious animosity, but it was refreshing to see her less than angelic. Yes, anything that caused her halo to slip, if only a little, pleased Elizabeth. However, she did feel somewhat guilty for subjecting Michael to Jana's cooking. It was becoming more and more obvious that Michael's life was in jeopardy with each and every meal he consumed.

Oddly enough, it was always Michael's glass that somehow accidently tipped over into his lap. Or his piece of venison steak that was burnt to a crisp, while everyone else's was done to perfection. And after a week of dinners, he had yet to receive a single piece of Jana's homemade pie, his piece always managing to end up on the floor somehow.

Ironically, instead of becoming angry Michael made it a point to stay an extra hour after supper and to return back again the very next evening with a smile on his face. Needless to say, as the week wore on, everyone's nerves were stretched tight as a drum and even the children picked up on the tension and were bickering constantly.

Just yesterday, poor Christina showed up for a visit, but left in a hurry. And who could blame her? She was met by a forced smile on Jana's lips, a growl coming from the direction of the sofa and Elizabeth's breathless greeting that she couldn't possibly talk right now, because Adam's glass of water was only half full. From the look on her friend's face, she surely thought Elizabeth had taken leave of her senses. Either

that, or was taking her own advice too seriously when it came to
bargaining with Adam for a new school.

"Beth, what are you doing over there?"

"I'm poisoning your pie, of course," she answered mumbling
under her breath.

"For Pete's sake Beth, I wish you would stop that infernal
mumbling. I can't understand a word you are saying half the time."

Coming up behind him, she held the pie dangerously overhead,
hovering in indecision.

A knock sounded at the door, and Adam looked back to discover
how close he was to wearing his blackberry pie. He gave a cocky grin,
full of promise, "Sweetheart, I warn you, what you are thinking is a big
mistake."

Their eyes locked in combat. Adam didn't even flinch, as she
raised the pie again…before carefully reaching over and placing it into his
waiting lap.

"You are probably right, but honestly, sometimes I think it just
might be worth it. Don't bother to get off that sofa. As usual, I'll get the
door." Her voice brightened. "Besides, maybe it's Michael."

Adam glared down at the innocent piece of pie resting on his lap,
then back at the door. Apparently, he needed to have a little talk with
Michael about other men's wives. Oblivious, Michael cheerfully accepted
Elizabeth's shy offer of supper once again, sticking his hand out in
friendship to Adam, despite the fierce look he was impaled with.

"Don't you have a home of your own?" Adam ground out. He was
getting just a little tired of Beth's eyes straying to his handsome friend as
if he were her only lifeline.

Giving his out of sorts friend a cocky grin, he answered easily,
"sure, but mine doesn't have the scenery yours does."

He was tempted to knock that grin right off his face could he have
reached him. Fortunately for Michael, he couldn't. Instead, Adam sent
his foreman a murderous look, motioning to the chair in front of him. "If
you are through admiring the scenery, perhaps we could get down to what
I pay you for."

Michael responded with a good natured shrug, before getting down to business, "Smitty and George said they lack half an acre to be done with the east side."

Strolling over, Elizabeth bent to retrieve Adam's ledgers, before ceremoniously slamming it against his chest. "There you go, Your Highness." Before leaving, she turned to Michael giving him a warm smile.

Adam leaned back and glared.

Michael ignored him, continuing on slightly ill at ease, "As I was saying, the men are nearly done felling those firs. Still I am worried…"

They were interrupted once more as Beth sailed back into the room, and removed his uneaten pie. He watched her out of hungry eyes, as she wiped the crumbs from around him. But, it wasn't the pie he wanted.

Noticing he was being ignored by the two people in front of him, Michael cleared his throat, muffling a smile. "About Sullivan… Seems he ran off with the cash box yesterday."

Elizabeth managed to shake off the strange spell Adam had on her, remarking over one shoulder, "That's nice Michael." Then breathlessly adding, "I'd better see about breakfast – I mean dinner."

Adam's eyes followed her out the doorway. Michael's words fell on deaf ears. "This wouldn't have been that bad except Smitty rigged it with dynamite. Blew up the whole mill."

Michael's words finally penetrated his mind, Adam exploded, "Blew up the Mill?!"

"You have it bad, don't you, Boss?"

"I don't know what you're talking about." Clearing his throat, Adam began again. "Now if you are done fooling around, is there something more important you wanted to add?"

"As a matter of fact, there is." He leaned in, resting elbows on his knees, "we found that medicine man."

With all that had been going on at home, he had nearly forgotten about the elusive medicine man. "About time. I'm surprised he didn't have the sense to leave the country. Did you convince him otherwise?"

Eyeing Jana through the open doorway, as she expertly sliced the potatoes for supper, he admitted, "I planned on doing just that, but I have to admit, he had some mighty interesting things to say about our Miss Logan."

"Such as?"

He sat up, clasping his hands together, then leaned in closer so as to not be overheard, "Such as that he has never heard of a Miss Logan. The only girl he knew of who fit that description was a young actress he picked up in San Francisco. Annie Stokes. Claimed she needed a ride to Reedsport, Oregon. Even offered to cook and clean for the man till they arrived here."

Again his eyes went to Jana, as she seasoned the slabs of ham before placing them in the skillet, "Said she was one wonderful cook, and pretty enough to put any sunset to shame."

Adam looked interested now, his own eyes following the direction of his friend's, "And, you think he was telling the truth? Miss Logan warned us he was an accomplished liar."

"Well," Michael drawled, pulling out his pipe from front pocket and twirling it around in his hands, "It wasn't what he said that convinced me."

A suspicious gleam came into Adam's eyes, as he asked calmly, "No?"

"No. I'm afraid I have an aversion to hitting a seventy year old man."

Elizabeth walked in to set the table. Hesitating for just an instant at the cold anger in her husband's eyes, her first instinct was he and Michael were in some sort of argument. However, her husband's anger seemed paradox to the lazy grin that came easily to Michael's face.

If they were fighting it was extremely one sided.

Ill at ease, Elizabeth said softly, "Adam. Michael. Supper is just about ready, why don't you two go wash up."

Adam nodded and waved her towards the kitchen. "Give us a minute, Sweetheart."

She hesitated. Adam as usual seemed to read her mind. He gave a reassuring wink. "I promise there is nothing to worry about. Besides, all Michael has to do is out run me, remember."

Her shoulders relaxed at his teasing. "Oh, I wasn't worried about Michael," she assured him sweetly. "After all, he wasn't the one who couldn't unhitch a simple horse."

Adam grabbed the hand towel in her hands and twisted it up in warning. She decided not to wait around to see how good his aim was.

Watching the obvious attraction to each other, Michael cleared his throat uncomfortably. "So what do you plan to do now? Jana, or Annie, apparently isn't telling us the whole truth here. It even looks as if she actually planned on moving in here with you for some reason." Michel grinned. "And we know it isn't your fine physic she's after. You never even met until that day in your office."

Reaching for the crutch made of smooth pine, Adam's mouth set in a grim line. What was going on here? If Beth was just Bootsie, crazy mail order bride, then why would someone like Jana come all this way to discredit her? His frown deepened. And if Beth wasn't Bootsie, then he had no right to hold her here against her will.

His stomach tightened in a knot.

If only he hadn't been so hard-headed in the first place and had listened to the woman, maybe she would be safe in a convent somewhere instead of in some sort of danger. Cringing, his hand tightened on the crutch. If what his wife said was true, then he was honor bound to straighten this mess out. And if it wasn't - well, he still needed to find out just exactly what Miss Jana Logan was up to.

Michael noticed Adam's hand clinch up in a fist, then slowly open back up again, "I think, for now, we act like Miss Logan is exactly who she says she is. If she doesn't get suspicious, she might answer a lot more questions for us. Like for instance, who sent her here. And why."

Nodding, Michael dropped his cold pipe back in his pocket and rose to his feet. "Sounds good to me. In fact, I might throw her off the track a little by continuing to make myself an ever present burr in her saddle."

Oblivious to the serious conversation between her husband and Michael, Elizabeth peeked under a cup towel at the fried potato cakes. She could smell the cooked onion rising off them. Her stomach growled in response. Surely the men were finished talking by now. She would just poke her head in and hurry them along. As she neared the open doorway to the dining room, the men's words brought her to an abrupt halt.

"I'll make a trip into Portland next week and stop by Sam's office. He'll take care of all the legalities involved."

Michael's voice sounded doubtful. "I hate to see you do it, but I think you're right. It's the only way. When do you tell Beth?"

"I don't think I should for a while. Not until I see how long it will take to untangle this whole mess. You know her temper and with Jana living with us right now – well, it wouldn't be a good idea."

Elizabeth stifled her gasp with the back of a hand. Adam meant to get an annulment in all likelihood to marry Jana. Stunned, she pulled back into the kitchen and leaned against the wall.

He was letting her go.

She should be ecstatic, instead she was devastated. He was breaking his promise to her. The illogical reasoning behind such a thought totally escaped her, especially since it was the very thing she had said she wanted.

Behind her, she heard the soft rustling of clothing. Looking over her shoulder, her eyes caught Jana's smug smile. The importance of Adam's words not lost on her either apparently. Everyone must have been aware of Adam's plans, but her. With all the strength she possessed, she fought down the ache in her heart and somehow managed to straighten up away from the wall.

"If you will excuse me, I just remembered something I left in my room" My heart, she added to herself, before running past Jana for the safety of the bedroom.

Jana nodded in satisfaction, as a slow smile came to her lips.

"Where did you say Beth went?" Adam asked again.
Supper was nearly over and still his wife hadn't shown up.

203

Pouring him another cup of coffee, Jana ignored Michael's outstretched empty one before answering. "I hate to sound unkind, Adam, but you know how irrational she's been lately. She said something about going back to her room, and then she ran off."

Throwing his napkin down, Adam pushed away from the table. "Well, something must have happened to make her run off like that. I better go check on her."

He was already reaching for his crutch when a puffy eyed Elizabeth slid into an empty chair beside him. "I'm sorry I'm late, but I forgot Chelsea's bib."

Adam took in her red rimmed eyes, the delicately crocheted bib dangling from her hand and frowned. The time for bibs was long past.

Apparently Chelsea didn't think so as she reached out for her bib with greasy fingers.

As if in a daze, Beth gave it to her. Happily, the two year old began to use it to playfully scoot around the remains of her food. Beth simply gave them all a shaky smile. She looked a mess.

Michael sent a worried look her direction before saying a little too loudly, "Adam and I were just discussing that school you women are determined to have."

Adam raised an eyebrow. "We were?"

The blonde man smiled easily, as he crossed one booted foot over the opposite knee. "Yep. We decided to turn that old trading post near the river into a school. All it needs is a fresh coat of white wash and it will be good as new."

He had gained Elizabeth's attention along with everyone else's in the room.

"Aren't you forgetting the roof? That is, unless you plan on teaching weather firsthand," Adam reminded.

Undaunted, he continued, "Oh, the men can fix that in no time next Saturday. So, Bootsie what do you think?"

She thought he was wonderful. But it still didn't change the fact that Jana or no Jana, her marriage was over. Looking down at her lap in order not to cry, she responded woodenly, "It sounds fine."

Concerned, Adam reached over, covering her cold hands protectively with his. She never even moved. "Beth…"

Nicholas groaned. "Great. There goes trout fishing."

"Didn't you forget one minor detail, Mr. Know-it-all?" Jana scoffed, taking up Michael's half full plate just as he was about to take a bite.

His fork hovered in the air a moment, before coming to rest on the empty spot where his plate had been. Sighing, he casually wiped off his mouth and asked, "And what would that be Miss Logan?"

"How about someone to teach this school? Say, a teacher, for instance."

Adam had to admit he had been wondering the same thing himself.

Elizabeth just wished he would stop caressing her hand. It made her want to weep.

Thoughtfully, Michael began picking his teeth, "It's simple really. The answer is standing right beside me. Jana can be the new teacher."

"What!?" The usually poised young woman in question became livid, the pie plate dropping to the floor.

Even Elizabeth was shocked, lifting her head in confusion. "Jana?" Why, he might as well have said Jana could lead the church choir.

"Michael, that has to be the worst idea I have heard in a long time."

"No, it isn't," Michael explained to his doubting boss, "Actually, I have to admit it is one of my best. Think about it. Jana would have a place of her own and be able to earn a living at the same time."

He purposely ignored Jana's furious motions, as she shoved the pie back onto the plate.

Adam finally understood what Michael was trying to do. Get Jana out of his house. The man deserved a raise. He gave Elizabeth's hand a reassuring squeeze.

"Well, Beth, what do you think?"

She honestly didn't know what to think. If Adam was in love with Jana, why was he looking up over at her with such tenderness? By the looks of things Jana had no idea this was coming.

Then a thought struck her. A beautiful smile broke out on Elizabeth's pretty features. Maybe Adam wasn't in love with Jana, after all. Maybe what she heard was some horrible misunderstanding. And just maybe, he intended to keep her prisoner here with him for the rest of her life.

Wasn't that wonderful?!

She met his twinkling blue eyes and gave a sigh of contentment. "I think" she shyly squeezed his hand in return, "that Jana would be perfect."

Apparently Jana felt differently. Too furious to speak, she simply dumped the full plate of smashed blackberry pie straight onto Michael's unsuspecting lap.

Automatically leaping out of his chair with a yelp that sent pie sliding down his leg to the floor he roared, "What did you do that for?"

Nicholas's eyes got round as saucers, "Wow. I never saw anyone dump a whole pie on someone before. That was great!"

Michael's glare silenced him.

"Well?" He demanded of the small blonde as he towered over her.

"Well, what! I think that is the stupidest idea I have ever heard of. Furthermore," Jana stuck her hands on her slender hips, blue eyes blazing, ""Only you could come up with such a lame-brained, idiotic idea. As if I would even consider such a thing."

Turning on her heels, pale hair swaying in time with her walk, she stormed from the room and slammed the door for emphasis.

Relaxing his angry stance once Jana left the room, Michael began licking the blackberry off his index finger, "I think she took that fairly well, don't you?"

Adam took one look at an extremely pleased Michael with blackberry pie dripping off his lap and burst out laughing.

To Elizabeth, Michael was a wounded hero who had given up his lap for her happiness. Without another moment's hesitation, she hurried over to give him a hug, whispering, "Thanks, Michael."

"I think you better let go of me before Adam forgets I did him a favor."

As if to prove him right, Adam gently but firmly removed Elizabeth's arms from around Michael's neck and possessively pulled her up beside him.

"Well, there is one good thing that came out of this evening, Michael."

"Yeah, like what?" Michael groaned, swiping at his sticky pants.

"At least you finally got a piece of Jana's pie."

Chapter 16

Heading into Portland three days later, Elizabeth wondered what had gone wrong. She thought that once Jana was set up in the old foreman house that they decided to make into the new school, her troubles would be over. She couldn't have been more wrong.

In frustration, she kicked at the wooden plank in front of her.

"Do you have a particular problem with that footboard?"

Stiffening at his sarcasm, she answered a little too quickly, "Of course not, I was simply trying to knock some mud off my shoe."

"Beth, it hasn't rained in three days."

She opened her mouth to argue, but didn't see the point. The truth of the matter being - she was kicking the daylights out of the footboard. Clutching her wool cloak around her for warmth she buried herself into its scratchy interior. It was now near the end of October and the weather was becoming colder especially in the early morning hours. If not for the trees blocking some of the wind, it would be miserable. She yawned sleepily.

"Tell me again why we had to leave so early?"

Instead of answering, he reached back behind the seat, pulling out a couple of hard biscuits and offering her one. Shaking her head, she waited for him to decide to answer. After all she was a little surprised he actually followed through with his invitation to her. Now that Jana was gone, she wasn't exactly sure why they were going in the first place.

"It's a long hard trip, and I wanted to get back before too late. It gets pretty cold out here at night."

She huffed. So, he meant to stick to his story. This could mean only one thing that he actually intended to go through with the annulment. She looked out over the side of the wagon as if searching for answers in the dawn's early light. The news should have made her happy, instead she felt miserable. Everything was so terribly confusing lately.

"Okay, Beth. Out with it."

Drawing out a handkerchief, she blew into it before retorting, "Nothing. Why would you think something is wrong?"

He rolled his eyes and pulled her up against him. "Beth, are you going to tell me what the problem is or not? You've been acting strange all morning."

Shaking her head, she leaned into his warm side. Absentmindedly brushing a stray wisp of hair from her cheek, his look turned protective before pulling her back into his arms. She stayed there a moment breathing him in, then with a resigned sigh admitted, "I know all about why you are going into Portland. I heard you and Michael talking."

Instead on arguing with her logic, he asked calmly, "Just what is it you think you overheard?"

"Ha! As if you don't know."

So much for hoping they could have a rational discussion. Her shout woke Nicholas and Chelsea in the back. The sleepy little girl pulled a doll filled hand out from under the quilt and rubbed the sleep out of her big blue eyes.

"Well, humor me and explain anyway."

"I don't want to talk about it."

Immediately jerking back the reins, he pulled the wagon to a halt, "Too bad sweetheart, you brought it up, so we are talking about it."

"Oh, it's not that I blame you," she continued, as if he hadn't spoken, "why, I even welcome it. Believe me..." She forcefully jerked her cloak up tighter around her, "I couldn't be happier."

Frustrated beyond belief, he interrupted, "Why don't you quit tugging on that coat and start making sense for once."

Wide awake and all ears by now, Chelsea clutched her doll tighter, as if to keep someone from snatching it from her. Nicholas, on the other hand, edged closer up front, excitement making his eyes grow larger.

Her tears forgotten, Elizabeth narrowed green eyes in on him and huffed indignantly, "You know perfectly well what the problem is, and it just shows your lack of manners by making me voice such a scandalous thing. If you think convents take fallen women, you are very much mistaken. My whole life will be ruined and just because you suddenly realize what a horrible mistake your stubbornness caused. A mistake, mind you, that I tried to talk you out of. After all this time no one will ever believe that we haven't –you know," she blushed furiously.

"My word, half the town thinks I am expecting. The very idea of an annulment would be humiliating. If you have to cast me away," she added dramatically, throwing an arm wide for emphasis, "couldn't you at least leave me some dignity by divorcing me?"

The whole time she was getting herself worked up; Adam was resting his forehead against a hand, propped up by a knee. When she paused to take a breath, he interrupted almost calmly. "Let me get this straight. You want me to divorce you?"

"I most certainly do. I would become the laughing stock of the whole town if we got an annulment. It would seem like our marriage was a lie."

"But you just told me it was a…"

Her glare stopped him.

"This hasn't, by the way, got something to do with mending does it?"

Now Elizabeth looked perplexed, "Of course not."

"Good. For a minute there I was afraid this was one of those one-sided arguments of yours, where I don't have a clue what you are talking about."

Nicholas leaned in over the back seat between them, not a bit intimidated by the anger in his uncle's voice. "Are ya gonna punch her lights out, Uncle Adam?"

Giving his nephew an exasperated look, he jumped down from the wagon. "You kids stay right here. Beth and I are going to have a little discussion…without an audience."

Nicholas looked disappointed. "Ah, come on, Uncle Adam. I never get to see nothing."

Ignoring his nephew, he reached up to pull his wife down from her perch. Seeing his intent, she quickly scooted clear to the other side. He put both hands against the wagon and demanded, "Get back over here and stop acting childish."

Looking straight ahead, she ignored him.

"All right then. We do it your way."

"Are ya going to punch her now?" Nicholas asked hopefully.

Chelsea scurried under the quilt when her Uncle jumped up and dragged his loudly protesting wife off the wagon and towards the trees.

"Shucks, I bet he does punch her and I'm gonna miss it all," Nicholas remarked, slapping a hand against his leg.

Reaching a small clearing, yet still within sight of the wagon, Adam let Elizabeth go and spun around to face her. "I'm not even going to ask where you came up with this crazy idea of yours."

She opened her mouth to speak, but he cut her off, "It doesn't matter. I just want you to pay close attention to what I'm about to say, because if I ever have to repeat it again, maybe I will punch you."

He reached out and gripped both her shoulders, forcing her to look at him. This wasn't easy. His eyes were blazing. Maybe it would be better if he did punch her and get it over with.

"I am not, repeat not, going into Portland for some imaginary annulment. Which I might add, is practically impossible to obtain after living with a woman for nearly two months. I am, however, going to see my lawyer on business about my brother's will. I want to set up a trust fund for the kids."

"Oh." Elizabeth breathed, shock and relief hitting her all at once.

Tenderly, he raised her chin up, his warm sweet breath brushing against her lips like a caress. "Like it or not Beth, you are stuck with me. Nun or Nut, it doesn't matter. I am your husband till death do us part. Do I make myself perfectly clear?"

There was a catch in her throat, so the only thing she could manage was a relieved nod. Although she did feel tears in her eyes, and a certain disappointment as he let go of her.

"Good." He brushed his hands together as if dispensing with the subject entirely. "Now if you haven't any more imagined reasons for our trip, could we get on with it?"

"So if you're not in love with Jana, why don't you try to kiss me anymore," she blurted out before she could stop herself.

His groan was loud enough to make her take a step back. "Beth, you certainly don't beat around the bush do you?"

Shoving both hands in his pockets, he looked down at the ground, as if searching for an answer to her question. Finally he raised eyes filled with such desire that it literally took her breath away. Without any warning whatsoever, he pulled her into his arms and kissed her with all the pent up passion of a starving man.

Caught off guard, she barely managed to hold on for dear life. She felt so alive, so wanted that she was very near bursting with all the new feelings exploding inside her. When he did finally release her, she stumbled back, dazed from his kiss. Adam was not faring well either, his breathing as uneven as hers. And his beautiful blue eyes? Well they were full of promise. A promise she found herself wanting to accept.

She blushed clear down to her toes.

Adam, his voice harsh with emotion, explained, "That's why I don't kiss you, Beth. I can't. At least not until you ask me to, because kissing leads to other things. We have a bargain, remember?"

Elizabeth gulped, "Oh."

"Now can we go?"

She nodded, a warm feeling growing inside her. Adam wasn't going to get an annulment and marry Jana. She was stuck with him. A satisfied smile crept up, taking hold as she strived to keep up with Adam's long legged stride. But more importantly, he liked kissing her. She shook her head in wonder. For some reason, that knowledge especially pleased her. Yes, it did indeed.

Three hours and a numb backside later, Elizabeth wished he had taken a switch to her backside after all. Any feeling in her lower portion would be welcomed. Chelsea let out another high pitched scream jostling Elizabeth's last nerve.

"Nicholas, give Chelsea back Clara this instant. That is, unless you want me to hang you over the side of the wagon as well."

Just when it appeared she might have to make good her threat, Nicholas snatched the doll back inside and threw it at his bawling sister. "Cry baby."

In response, she reared back, punching him in the stomach. Nicholas stared in disbelief at his little sister's attack. He was very surprised she had actually hit him. To add further insult, she stuck her tongue out at him. His face turned a fiery red just before he proceeded to tackle her to the floor of the wagon, kicking and screaming.

"Oh, for Pete's sake!" Turning to Adam for help, she narrowed her eyes as he seemed not only blind but deaf as well. He was suspiciously engrossed by the same dirt road they had been traveling on for over an hour. Gracious, did she have to do everything? Then as the brawl in the back intensified, she reminded her now grinning husband, "Did I happen to mention I don't particularly like small children?"

Finally gaining his attention, he propped a foot on the board in front, casually laying an elbow across a knee and winked, "Sweetheart, I already told you. You are stuck with us."

Apparently no help coming from his direction, she glanced back at the two rolling about in the back. Well, as usual, she would have to do something. So, heaving a resigned sigh, she began climbing over the seat to the back. Adam watched her struggle, her cute little backside flung up in the air with one extremely shapely leg hiked up over the seat.

He pushed his hat back on his head and grinned. It would take a better man than him to resist the temptation. With a practiced hand, he headed straight for the large pothole in the road.

She must have bounced a good twelve feet into the air before landing in a heap of petticoats. Her legs were flailing frantically over her head right at his feet. His grin deepened. Yep, it was worth it.

"Sorry about that, Sweetheart, I must not have been paying attention to where I was going."

A gasp came from the tangled mess before him, as she frantically tried to cover herself and get in a position to give him the set down he deserved. "I just bet. One can only hope that in the last few moments you have developed some manners, and are averting your eyes right now."

213

His long meaningful whistle answered her question.

Untangling herself at last, she came face to face with her tormentor, "I think you did that on purpose."

He burst out laughing, because if she would have been just a mite taller he would be in trouble. Her eyes were blazing at him. He grinned back at her. Then as if nothing could be further from the truth, turned his attention back to the road and began whistling a ballad.

She closed her eyes in mortification. She didn't suppose she would ever get use to his outlandish familiarity. A new tussle broke out in back, but this time she chose to ignore it. She was not about to believe her innocent husband would not manage to find another 'pothole' if she didn't.

A swinging pine sign with the word 'Portland' carved in rough letters came into sight, causing a flood of relief and cheers from the back.

Elizabeth sat up and straightened her dress, a genuine smile on her face.

At last, civilization.

Chapter 17

As two men came sailing through the Saloon's huge glass window landing at her feet, bloody and smelling of liquor, Elizabeth had only one thought; maybe civilization had changed since the last time she experienced it.

Quickly picking up Chelsea as she yanked an ogling Nicholas away from the two limp forms, she only wanted to make it to the general store before something worse happened. Wrinkling up her nose as she headed for the general store, she managed to weave past four piles of horse droppings and one drunk. She had to admit the drunk did possess some manners. He at least took off his hat, before smiling and belching in her face.

Yes, civilization was not all it was cracked up to be.

Daring to look up, she noticed one lone bank and a few scattered stores away from all the commotion at the edge of town. Now, that was more like it. First, she went to the mercantile and purchased the things on Adam's list with the exception of one dress. She would pay him back, of course, as soon as she got her life back.

She nearly made it to the bank when she spotted it. It was the most beautiful thing she had ever seen, and she found herself staring blissfully into one particular dress shop's polished window biting at her lower lip in indecision.

She loved that hat.

With a look of longing, she imagined how perfectly it would match the cheerful green and yellow dress she had bought only moments ago at the mercantile. Its saucy tilt and bright green feathers stuck on a cream yellow background, seemed to call out to her.

It seemed like a lifetime ago since she had worn anything so feminine.

Looking down at her soft blue calico dress and ugly old wool hat she clutched in her hand, she frowned. A glint of rebellion rose in her eyes. She deserved that hat.

"I don't wanna go in another store, Bootsie." Nicholas' aggravated voice broke into her thoughts. She sighed and turned around. Leave it to Nicholas to bring her back to reality.

"You're still upset about that rock game, aren't you? I told you, we have to find your Uncle first."

"It is marbles, not rocks", he shouted in irritation, kicking at the dirt around him, "That tall skinny kid had a tiger's eye that I would have given my best shooter for. Besides, last time I checked Uncle Adam wouldn't be caught dead in some hat store."

Not really paying attention, her eyes kept straying to the beautiful hat, "What is wrong with your other marbles?"

He dug out a huge round marble of green glass. "Nothing is wrong with them. I just want to win more of them. For your information, this is my lucky marble. Just last month, Jimmy Cole lost three to me because of this."

He held it out almost reverently.

Perplexed by what could be so special about a round piece of glass, she picked it up, turning it around in hands as if looking for the magic Nicholas claimed it had. Finding none, she shrugged and dropped it back into his palm. "It looks very glass-like."

"Girls." Nicholas stuffed it back into his pants pocket, thoroughly disgusted.

Chelsea tugged one hand, shifting from one leg to the other. "Bitsee. I wanna..." her small eyebrows knitted together in agony, "I gotta potty."

Ignoring her, Elizabeth leaned in closer to the window, "In just a moment, Chelsea." She bit her lip in indecision. Surely, it wouldn't hurt to just try it on.

The little girl tugged harder, asking pointedly, "Can I potty on the road then?"

That got her attention.

"Absolutely not." Elizabeth exclaimed, as she began searching for the nearest outhouse.

Spotting one across the street, she began pulling the small girl towards it. "Hold on darling, there is one right behind the band. See that clump of trees?"

But her words were small comfort to the little one dancing on the end of her arm.

They barely made it and as Elizabeth waited outside, she thought more and more about that perky yellow hat. It drew her to it, like a cat to cream.

"Are you through, Chelsea?"

"Yes Ma'am."

Good girl, try to hurry okay? It is nearly lunch, and I still have to buy that lovely hat across the street."

Cupping a hand over a huge green grasshopper he had been chasing, Nicholas readjusted his fingers before stating matter of fact. "I didn't see no hat on Uncle Adam's list."

"Well, not everything I needed was on that list." Chelsea came out all smiles as Elizabeth tried to ignore Nicholas' suspicious glare on her back as she retied her sash. Standing up she strode purposely towards the store's direction. "Come along children."

Apparently Nicholas was calling her bluff.

Sighing, she turned back around, "Are you coming?"

The grasshopper poked his head up between Nicholas's fingers. He pushed him back down, never missing a beat, as he stated the obvious. "I'm coming. But I bet you money that Uncle Adam didn't put a hat on his list, because he didn't want you to buy some stupid looking hat in the first place."

Exasperated, she picked up Chelsea, remarking just as confidently, "For your information, the hat happens to be a surprise for your Uncle."

"He doesn't like surprises, and he sure won't like that hat."

"I guess we will see, won't we?"

It took only a moment to sign Adam's name for the purchase of one yellow hat, despite the fact that Nicholas was frowning disapprovingly at her the whole time. Ignoring him, she paused a second to tie Chelsea's bonnet as they exited the shop, hat box swinging from one arm.

Not being able to ignore his accusing stare, she blushed guiltily, "You can stop frowning like I committed some sort of sin Nicholas. It's only a hat."

"All I got to say is last time I did something like that; I got a lickin' for it." As if to punctuate his point, he let go of the grasshopper, which chose Elizabeth's hair to fly into.

Screaming and dancing around like she was being attacked, she finally noticed Nicholas standing there. He was smiling.

"Nicholas Reed, one of these days…" her voice trailed off in confusion. For across the street was someone far more frightening than any grasshopper.

Rawlings.

Shocked into silence, she watched as the familiar figure left the bank, stopping not three feet away from where her trembling hands clutched the hat box. Glancing quickly both ways before crossing the street, he never even noticed her as he continued on towards the center of town.

She froze in horrified indecision, the color draining from her face.

"Are ya all right, Bootsie? The grasshopper was just a joke." When she turned confused eyes to his, he took a step back. "Bootsie?"

"It can't be possible," she whispered to herself.

Looking around in confusion, Chelsea confided in a whisper, "Nicky is Bitsee going to cry?"

He put a finger to his mouth, before asking Elizabeth, "What's impossible?"

It was then he found himself jerked off his feet and pulled along with Chelsea straight past 'Nell's Place'. "Hey, where are we going? What about lunch?"

Distracted, she didn't bother with an in-depth explanation. She kept moving, skirts billowing out behind her, "I have to check on something."

Seeming to enjoy her feet barely touching the ground, Chelsea giggled. "Look, Bitsee, I'm flying."

Nicholas on the other hand was not enjoying this mad flight of hers, as he dragged his heels in order to slow her down. "Come on Bootsie, you just knocked a lady off the sidewalk."

She didn't even glance back, or slow, despite the dust flying up around them. She just kept going, like a hound with the scent of coon in his nostrils. Rounding a corner, she stood helplessly in the middle of an empty alley. He was gone. She didn't know if she was relieved or disappointed. Maybe it wasn't even him. Wondering what to do next, she rubbed a trembling hand over her face.

"Nicholas, where did your Uncle Adam say he was?"

"The Wild Rose, but I don't think he wants us to go barging in there."

"This is an emergency."

"I don't see no emergency," observed Nicholas logically.

"Nicholas didn't you see that man leaving the bank a moment ago?"

"What man? I saw lots of people there."

Exasperated, Elizabeth explained, "the dark one with the mustache. No, that's what was different about him," she reminded herself, "He had shaved it off."

"I didn't see no man shaving."

"He wasn't shaving. I said...oh, never mind. Will you take me to your Uncle, or do I ask a perfect stranger to do it?"

He looked panicky. Knowing his Uncle would not be happy with either idea, he seemed to decide it was best to keep crazy in the family. "I'll do it, but I'm telling you he ain't going to like it."

"So you keep saying. Let's go."

Elizabeth didn't have time for this, Rawlings could be anywhere by now. Giving Nicholas a stern look she pushed him in the direction of the street. Walking swiftly, high buttoned shoes clicking against the wooden sidewalk, she frantically sought a reason for Rawling's presence here.

There could be only one. She broke out in a cold sweat. His last words to her left a bad taste in her mouth. Didn't he promise to finish her off if she caused any trouble? The letters. Somehow he must have found out about the letters to Sister Agnes, but how?

How didn't really matter anymore. No, right now she had bigger concerns. There was only one reason he would travel all this way.

He meant to kill her.

After an hour with Sam, his attorney, he felt easier about the whole situation. There was something about Sam that promoted confidence. Maybe it was his firm handshake, or the way clear brown eyes looked straight at you when speaking. Whatever it was, Adam trusted him.

There was no doubt in Adam's mind that if the information was out there, Sam Wheeler would find it. This was precisely why Adam chose him to handle the legal end of his business five years ago and he had never regretted it.

"So, can you clear this up for me?"

"It shouldn't be too difficult. However, I have to warn you it might take a while. Travel is still pretty slow across the Oregon Trail. We're talking a month, maybe two."

A groan slipped out at the mention of two long months. He just hoped he could keep away from Beth that long. Forcing a smile he shook hands with his old friend, "Well, do the best you can."

Leaving Sam's office, Adam headed for the Wild Rose. It was just after eleven. He should have plenty of time to ask Rose about Annie Stokes. She gathered more information at her place than a bee gathers honey. Stepping up his pace, Sam's words came back to haunt him. Two months was an awful long time to wait.

Coming to a sudden stop behind Nicholas, she looked up at the saloon and knew Nicholas was right.

Adam would not be happy to see her.

Still, all she could think of was reaching him. Somehow he would know what to do. Acting purely out of instinct, she pushed open the saloon doors and pulled the children inside with her.

The smell of hard liquor and smoke caused her to cover her nose, as a shocked hush fell over the rough crowd. She stepped forward, searching for Adam's familiar face in those staring up at her. She nearly lost her nerve as the last cords of a banging piano lingered in the air, reminding her she was not welcome.

Finally, the scarred bartender spoke up, "Are you lost lady?"

Suddenly unsure, she protectively pulled the children in closer, "No. I'm looking for my husband. Adam Reed."

The bartender clamped down on his cigar in obvious displeasure at her intrusion. "He's upstairs with Rose. You want to fetch him yourself, or can I give him a message?"

Elizabeth turned ten shades of red. For the first time she took a good look around her and noticed the scantily clad women and drunken men. What in world had she been thinking, to waltz into a saloon with two children in tow? She was about as wanted as an ant at a picnic.

Awkwardly, she held out a hand in greeting, which the bartender ignored. She snatched it back before unconsciously wiping it on her skirt, "No, thank you. I guess this was a mistake."

Embarrassed beyond belief she turned to go when the bartender's words hit home. Did he say Rose? If she wasn't mistaken, that was a woman's name the last time she checked.

Whirling around, she asked in a choked voice, "Rose?"

Letting out a chuckle, the bartender answered clearly, "Yeah, Rose, the owner."

Elizabeth felt her temperature rise from somewhere deep inside her. Of all the two timing, rude, and barbaric things to do. She glared at the messenger, "I've changed my mind."

"Ma'am?" asked the bartender, wiping the back of a beefy hand across his bulbous nose.

"I believe I will 'fetch' my husband. If you would be so good as to point me in the right direction."

The piano player slammed the lid down on the keys.

One of the barmaids, a curvy dark-haired girl of about eighteen stepped up. "It's on the second floor. The last door on your right."

221

Was that a look of sympathy in her light gray eyes?

"Thanks. Would you mind watching the children for me? I should only be a minute."

"Sure, Honey."

Their polite exchange sounded strange in the rough room. Nicholas blushed, a worried look on his face as all eyes watched Bootsie head to the top of the stairs and turn left. Everyone seemed to be waiting. And the response was what they all expected to hear.

The sound of Adam's loud bellows before two voices were literally raising the rafters in anger. Then just as suddenly, the voices became so quiet everyone leaned in to catch snatches of words, like scandal and hot tempered.

The Bartender took a hesitant step forward just as a door upstairs slammed shut. Within seconds Bootsie stormed back down the stairs, her head held high and skirts swishing. She barley nodded her thanks to the saloon girl before grabbing Chelsea and leaving the saloon. Nicholas ran to catch up.

"I told you he wouldn't like it," Nicholas reminded.

Elizabeth was too mad to speak at the moment. Adam's look of pure shock when she opened the door to find her standing there was still on her mind. Served him right, to be caught red handed. Maybe she wasn't a true wife, but to humiliate her further by denying anything happened. To actually expect her to believe he was there on 'business'.

Some business. And just what kind of business was it exactly with that...that painted woman having to do with it? That he thought her such a fool was past enduring.

She stormed through the restaurant's door, mumbling furiously, "Well, he can think again if he thinks I'll wait in any old wagon. I happen to be hungry."

"What?" Nicholas strained to hear her.

She ignored him, taking a seat at the back of the room.

"Did you tell him about the man with the invisible mustache?"

Barely glancing his direction because she was too busy watching the front door, she asked, "Invisible mustache?"

222

"Ya know," he sounded exasperated with her, "the man at the bank."

Instantly she sank back in the chair, admitting sheepishly, "I forgot." She had been so angry, she completely forgot all about Maxwell Rawlings.

"You forgot?! How could a person drag two kids all over tarnation, make a scene in a Saloon of all places, and then forget what they wanted to say." He sounded disgusted, as he shook his head in wonder.

She had to admit. He had a point.

Their waiter came over just as a furious Adam stormed into the restaurant and slammed the door shut behind him. His blazing eyes searching the crowd for her face.

Not feeling quite as self-righteous as a moment ago, Elizabeth shifted over to her right, trying desperately to disappear behind the waiter. He politely moved out of the way. They played dodge for a few more seconds, before she snatched the menu from him to hide behind it instead. Maybe Adam wouldn't notice her. After all, it was one thing to face him when she was furious and quite another when he was.

It only took a second for Adam to spot her cowering behind a menu and head with a determined stride straight for her.

"So much for lunch," predicted Nicholas with a sigh.

Elizabeth, on the other hand, vainly tried to ignore her imposing husband who was glaring down at the back of her head. Instead she focused intently on the menu until her eyes blurred from concentration.

He snatched it out of her hands, "Perhaps ignoring me would work better if the menu was right side up."

She bit her lip in nervous laughter. Now what?

"I thought I told you to wait in the wagon."

She straightened in her chair, bravely picking up a fork in defiance, "And I told you I had things to do. As you can see, I happen to be hungry and am preparing to eat lunch."

"You should have thought of that before you embarrassed me in front of half the town."

"Ha," snorted Elizabeth, throwing her fork to the table, "I'm certainly not the one who should be embarrassed. For your information, I could have been killed while you were attending to 'business' with Rose there. Why, I wouldn't have even had a decent burial with everyone snickering behind their hands the whole time."

The waiter tried to sneak off.

She snaked out a hand and stopped him. "I would like to order now."

"I told you, we are leaving."

The waiter looked down worriedly at the small hand gripping his coat. "Ignore him. I would like two bowls…"

Adam slapped his hat against a leg to keep from strangling her. Suddenly, he reached over, jerking her out of the chair, while Nicholas knowingly stuffed his pockets full of bread and cheese. "Like I said, we're leaving."

Customers watched in amusement as the obviously furious man dragged his sputtering wife from the restaurant. Then with the show over and because occurrences like these were fairly common in their still rough frontier town, they picked up their forks and commenced eating.

Elizabeth was past angry at his high handedness as he dragged her down the street. And she only got angrier as they loaded up the supplies and packages from the general store and headed home. His silence only intensifying as they the town faded in the background. Even Chelsea and Nicholas were quiet, waiting for the confrontation that was sure to come. It didn't. Both grownups now chose instead to stew in silence.

It was just after dark when they finally pulled up to the house. Without saying a word, Elizabeth climbed down as Adam lifted a sleeping Chelsea into her arms. Nicholas was nudged awake, and Elizabeth took them both up to bed while Adam unhitched the wagon.

As she finished tucking the children in, her nerves were strung tighter than a barbwire fence. With slow steady steps she made her way to the cold and empty bedroom downstairs. The waiting for him was the hardest.

Upset and tearful, Elizabeth finally managed to light the oil lamp then slip a cotton nightgown over her head. Once in bed she began removing the pins from her hair, wondering why she had overreacted like that at the saloon. Why should it matter who he chose to be with.

Threading a hand through tangled hair, she sighed when a broken nail hung in its mass. Pretending to study it, she nervously fumbled around for something to smooth its rough edge. Breathing deeply the whole time in order to stifle the tears welling up in her throat, she wondered why one broken nail seemed to be so important to her. Maybe it was what it represented. Nothing was the same anymore. Her husband was not really her husband and her hands? She looked down at the unfamiliar chapped, work roughened hands…were not her hands. No, her hands were smooth and well kept. Pretty.

And Adam?

It wasn't as if he were a real husband and being unfaithful. After all, she could care less what he did or with whom. A single tear splashed on the back of her hand. She wiped it away. She hated crying.

She hiccupped. It was this awful temper of hers. She was just angry because of the embarrassment of the whole thing that was all. If only this once, she would have curbed her tendency to act first and ask questions later. Restless, she pushed back the covers from her legs and climbed back out of bed to brush her hair. It swished softly across her back as she plopped down in front of the dresser, staring at her reflection. With slow deliberate strokes, she pulled a brush slowly through its thick mass. What was wrong with her lately? She felt so terribly mixed up all the time.

Adam stood in the doorway, his anger quickly being replaced with desire. Beth was one beautiful woman. If he had his way, her hair would always lay soft and loose like that... But then again, what he really wanted was to love her as only a man could love a woman. A sad regret about this afternoon made him speak softly so as to not startle her. "You misunderstood about this afternoon, you know."

Elizabeth's hand tightened on the brush, "I don't think so."

"Rose owns a portion of the mill. Regardless of how it looked, it was business," he seemed to hesitate, debating how much to tell her. "I also needed to ask her a few personal questions that I did not want overheard; that's why we were in her office upstairs."

Elizabeth closed her eyes. She wanted to believe him. More than anything else she wanted to trust him. She felt so alone at times. Opening searching eyes to his, she whispered, "Do you remember when I first told you about my kidnapping in Galveston?"

At his silent nod, she quietly continued, "I know you don't believe me, but that is why I went to find you. I saw Rawlings today. Or at least I think I did. Regardless, I was so terribly afraid." She turned to face him, "and all I could think of was reaching you. But when I saw you with that woman," she shrugged in helpless confusion, "Honestly, I don't know what came over me."

Adam could feel his heart hammering inside his chest, "Jealousy, maybe?"

She turned green eyes up to his as if he had the answer somewhere in their depths. Then, he watched her expression change to something that took his breath away.

"I've been thinking. I...I've decided to release you of our bargain."

Slowly he straightened away from the wall, his voice husky with emotion. "What did you say?"

"I said," she gulped, "I am releasing you from your word. I want to be a wife to you."

"Beth, I think..."

"I realize I haven't been fulfilling my duty towards you and I want to remedy that. You see, I think I am jealous. I don't know exactly what of, but I know I don't want you going to Rose again for whatever it is...people, I mean men need from their wives." She blushed. "Oh, this is so embarrassing." Closing her eyes and bracing herself, she added, "You may proceed."

Adam nearly laughed at her martyr pose, but stopped himself just in time. For one crazy moment there he almost took her up on it. But she looked so innocent standing there with her eyes wrinkled shut, and mouth puckered up waiting for his kiss, that whatever desire he felt was drowned out by common sense. "Beth, as inviting as your sacrifice is, I think we should wait awhile before we finalize our agreement."

She frowned, opening one eye, then the other. Did he always have to sound so business-like?

"You do?"

"One month." He must have taken leave of his senses. Before him stood a beautiful woman offering herself to him and because of his fool honor he was turning her down. He cleared his throat. "If you still feel the same way, I guarantee I'll take you up on your offer."

Confused but relieved, Elizabeth studied him for a long moment. "You're sure?"

Reaching out and touching the side of her face, he answered honestly, "No, I'm not sure, but I think it would be best for now."

"Oh," uncomfortable and embarrassed, Elizabeth turned and slowly crawled back into bed to wait for Adam to change. However, instead of joining her, he began pulling a few things from the dresser.

"I think I'll sleep in the parlor."

"I see." But she really didn't. What she did see was that he was rejecting her yet again. She fought back tears, as she looked down at her hands.

Placing a hand on the door frame on his way out, Adam cocked his head sideways, "Beth, look at me."

She lifted her head, giving him a quivering smile.

"I can't sleep in the same bed with you anymore and not touch you. Do you understand?"

Her heart skipped a beat. "Is this like the kissing thing?"

His grin was contagious. "Yep, only worse. Now just one more thing before I go. Are you sure it was Rawlings you saw in town today?"

Knowing logically she should deny it because it only made her appear crazier than usual, she found herself nodding instead. She could never prove it was Rawlings she saw today, but as she looked up into her husband's face, she found she couldn't lie to him.

"Yes, I believe it was."

" We'll get to the bottom of this mess. I promise you."

She could barely breathe. Her eyes searching his for any sign he was just humoring her. She found nothing but a protectiveness that comforted her. He actually believed her. For some reason this only made his leaving her tonight worse. Hesitantly she whispered, "Adam?"

"Yes?"

"Thanks."

"For what?"

"For believing me." Tears of gratefulness welled up in her eyes.

She was making leaving impossible for him. Did she even realize how beautiful she was sitting there cross legged under the covers, her big green eyes full of unbelievable trust? He sighed, more than likely not. She was an innocent. This was why he had to get out of this bedroom before he lost all semblance of control. With a wry grin, he spoke the truth before pushing away from the door frame to leave.

"Sweetheart, you don't know how badly I wish I didn't believe you right now."

Chapter 18

After one entire week of Adam sleeping on the sofa, Elizabeth was more miserable than ever. Never did she imagine she would miss his unsettling presence beside her, but she did. Badly. So badly in fact, that she hardly slept a wink. Most nights she found herself tossing and turning, wondering if Adam even noticed her absence.

Gathering up a bar of lye soap, Elizabeth headed for the warm springs a short walk away. She was very much in need of a bath. Before leaving she checked on Chelsea playing quietly on the floor beside her bed. Tossing her curly head on her way to the window, she peeked out to make sure Nicholas was still out back helping Becky gather pears. A contented sigh escaped her. Letting the curtain fall back into place, she wondered if Rawlings was the cause of this new found protectiveness of the children. This was the feeling of family.

After picking up Chelsea and taking her out to Becky, she began the rather long walk to the springs. This time though she found herself scanning the trees for some unknown presence. But all she noticed was a stray skunk rooting through the leaves on the ground. Reaching the bank of the warm spring, she paused yet again as a shiver passed down her spine. Despite her fear, she began slipping out of her clothes, trying to ignore the feeling of being watched.

Submerging herself into the soothing pool of water, her troubles seemed to melt away. The peacefulness of her surroundings as the earth heated water warmed the chill from her body made her almost forget all about Rawlings and her marriage woes. She reached over to the bank to retrieve the square slab of lye soap, wetting it before beginning the tiresome chore of scrubbing her mass of long auburn hair. Finishing at last, she tilted her head back into the water, rinsing out the soap as she tried to analyze once more exactly what was happening to her from a purely logical point of view.

One. The man she saw yesterday had to have been Rawlings. There was no other explanation for the gut reaction she experienced when seeing him. Two. Jana was for some reason, deliberately and with cold calculation, trying to make her seem unstable. But, why? To steal her husband? She hardly thought so. No, instinctively she knew somehow the two things were connected, but how?

Ducking under the water one last time she held her breath, enjoying the feel of being submerged in the water's relaxing embrace. She came up shaking off the warm cocoon. The chill of the air only intensified the Goosebumps on her upper body as she rose out of the water. Forcing herself to exit the spring, she quickly began drying off, rubbing her hair and dressing in the sun warmed clothes she had left on a rock. The feel of soft cotton against her skin made her sigh with longing. She missed Adam. The strength of him as his arms held her and his bold laughter that seemed to fill up a room. But more than anything else, she missed that intensely passionate look he gave her when she dared to meet his eyes.

She closed her eyes. "Stop it Elizabeth. You are only complicating things." She whispered out loud.

The deep yearning inside refused to lessen despite her words. Still, Adam was right. After all, she was leaving – wasn't she? It wasn't fair to either one of them to go back and forth like this. Running a slim hand across her face, she refused to admit to the seed of doubt growing in her heart. Which forced her to admit that there was the very real possibility that when it came time to go, she wouldn't be able to.

She was so confused and frightened.

Not to mention that things continued to show up missing. And since Jana had left to live at the old Trading Post by the river, she could no longer blame her for trying to drive her crazy. Without Jana to blame, Elizabeth had to face the very real possibility, that maybe it was her own forgetfulness that caused the occurrences. Even the determined confidence that carried her through most of life's problems somehow had deserted her.

Looking heavenward, she pleaded "What am I going to do?"

She stood there humbly waiting for some great revelation, but nothing happened. The sun still shone. The birds still sang. The whole earth seemed unperturbed that her life was in such turmoil. Heaving a deep sigh, she headed home. Maybe the problem was that she knew the answer. She just didn't like it.

Becky greeted her cheerfully as she walked into the already warm kitchen. "Well, Bootsie, you look a sight better. Although why any human being would prefer to take a bath outside this time of year is beyond me."

Elizabeth's smile was troubled, "I needed time alone to think. Besides the hot springs are especially nice this time of year."

"But the walk home wet will be the death of you."

Becky's easy laughter lightened Elizabeth's mood. That is, until she noticed the bushel of pears on the floor at her feet. There were pears piled sky high. How Becky had managed to pick so many in such a short time was beyond her. And what she intended for her to do with them was another problem she didn't intend to deal with.

"Surely you don't expect me to do something with that massive amount of pears."

"Oh, now" she laughed good-naturedly, "it's not as bad as that. Just thought you might like to make some pear preserves before the freeze. Nothing tastes as good as pear preserves on a cold winter's day. It's like a taste of sunshine when the cold is seeping into your bones."

She eyed the basket warily. "I am sure I don't need that much sunshine. But thank you anyhow." Becky was helping her right into an early grave.

Giving a quick hug, Becky jerked back as a 'practice' pain, as she called them, caught her by surprise. She clutched at her protruding middle.

Worrying her bottom lip, Elizabeth asked, "Are you sure you are all right?"

Waving away the look concern, she grinned, "Nothing to worry about. That one just took my breath away."

Elizabeth was very much afraid that one of these days Becky was going to 'practice' her way right into delivering a baby, the whole time swearing it was a false alarm. A fresh wave of guilt caused Elizabeth to

231

feel awful, if not for her, Becky would be home right now not picking pears trying to help. This was rather sweet, if not slightly misdirected.

"Well, we'd better get a start on this mountain of Pears before they sprout trees of their own. After we're done, we can cut Nicholas's hair. It's beginning to be hard telling him and Chelsea apart."

Elizabeth smiled to herself at the word 'we'.

"Thanks for your offer Becky, but I think I can handle everything here myself. Adam isn't coming for lunch, so I have all day to get caught up on things." Pleased that for once she was thinking of someone else, she shoved Becky towards the door. "Besides," she teased, "you left the recipe remember? Anyone can read a recipe, even me."

"That's true Bootsie, but them pears…"

"No buts, I insist you go home and rest. I can handle everything myself."

"Well, all right. I am a little tired. But make sure and send Nicholas over if you need any help, okay?"

Smiling confidently, Elizabeth handed Becky her shawl, "I won't need any help, now stop worrying."

Still looking doubtful as she was hurried out the door, she gave a hesitant wave back to Elizabeth from the porch. "If you're sure?"

"I'm sure."

That decided, Elizabeth shut the door and turned towards the mound of pears. She frowned. "I believe I will cut Nicholas's hair first. That shouldn't take too long."

Anything to avoid those pears.

The last time Becky cut Nicholas's hair, she had used a bowl for the pattern. So, digging through the cupboard, she pulled a large earthen one from the shelf. Then retrieving the scissors from the sewing room she placed them on the table. Feeling more and more confident, she dragged a protesting Nicholas into the room, pushing him down into the chair. Plopping the bowl on his head, she stepped back to have a look.

Perhaps she should have picked a smaller bowl. He looked like a giant toad stool. She frowned. This might be more difficult than she thought.

"Hey", echoed Nicholas inside the large bowl, "I can't see a blame thing under here." Her sense of humor surfaced, causing a slight giggle to escape. Perhaps it was better if she couldn't see what she was doing as well.

"You don't know a darned thing about cutting hair do you Bootsie?" Nicholas accused, squirming in his chair.

She patted his shoulder. "Just relax. I know what I'm doing."

"Like that time you burnt up our clothes in the washing kettle?"

"Well, that wasn't exactly my fault. How was I to know it would boil dry?"

"After six hours?"

He sounded a little sarcastic to her ears. But he did have a point. Maybe she should wait for Adam? But if she did he would just be aware of how inept she was at everything. Feeling that stubborn pride of her surfacing she picked up the scissors. Hadn't she watched Becky cut his hair just last week? It didn't look that difficult.

Nicholas tried to sneak off his chair. She pushed him firmly back down. "Now sit still and stop acting like a baby."

He bowed up at the insult, "I ain't afraid," he said indignantly. Then like a victim awaiting a hanging, he stiffened in the chair and took his punishment.

The torture began. His Aunt hacked away at his hair; lifting the bowl to get underneath it, but never taking it completely off. She did ask him if he wanted a mirror once during the long ordeal. He refused it. Why watch your own execution.

He did manage to console himself on one account. Even if she did mess up his hair, it would grow. She nipped at an ear with scissors once, which caused a yelp of pain, but that was the only time he cried out. It was just that he had grown rather found of having two of them.

Once her task was complete, she lifted off the bowl to admire her work.

Her gasp was not a good sign. Nicholas glared at her.

"Oh, my," Elizabeth's hand flew to her mouth.

Nicholas's hair hung in uneven clumps all over his head in no particular pattern whatsoever.

"What did you do to my hair?" he asked, snatching the mirror away from her.

One look and he had his answer. She waited for the storm. She didn't have long to wait.

"I look like I've been chewed on by an angry bear and lived to tell about it," he yelled at the top of his voice. Even Chelsea's eyes widened at how goofy he looked.

"Now, Nicholas. I know you are a little angry, but it's not quite that bad," she consoled, feeling guiltier by the minute.

"A little mad! I am so mad I could chew you up and spit you out, then stomp on you for good measure. That's how mad I am," he stormed, slipping out of her hands and racing for the door. "If Uncle Adam asks, tell him I'm in the storm cellar…for the rest of my life!" He ended dramatically, slamming the door for emphasis.

Chelsea and Elizabeth exchanged a worried look at the shut door, then back at each other. "Maybe the pears would have been the wiser choice," she admitted truthfully.

She was wrong. Pears were worse. Much worse. Yep, after three long hours and one pitiful bowlful later she learned one very important lesson. She despised pears. And unless she was dying of starvation, she would never eat another one. With a heavy sigh, she placed the half-filled pan on the stove top and stoked the fire.

Putting a sticky hand to her aching back, she tried to stretch the kinks out to no avail. Nicholas still had not emerged from the cellar and to be honest, she was getting a little worried. Maybe once Adam came home and fixed his hair…oh, she sincerely hoped he could or else Nicholas would never go to the new school. At least not till his hair grew some.

Leaving the sugared pears beginning to simmer, she decided to go ahead and dress Chelsea. At least she could do that without incident. Pausing to check her hair in the mirror at the bottom of the stairs, she reached up then shrugged in defeat. She looked nearly as bad as Nicholas but with more hair. If someone saw her now they would think she never even heard of a brush, much less used one. Her long brown hair lay in a tangled mess down her back. Not to mention the flour and sticky pear remains she wore all down the front of her dress.

"Good thing I'm by myself today", she thought as she plucked off a slice of pear from her bodice. This morning Jana had brought by a note from Adam saying he needed to catch up on some paperwork so he would not be home for lunch. She had thought it odd to send Jana all the way out here for that, but was so grateful for the extra time it allowed her that she never even questioned it. If she was lucky she could finish those stupid pears and change before he made it home.

Turning from her reflection in disgust, she searched around for Chelsea when the front door swung wide and the very object of her thoughts filled the doorway. Adam. A confused question rose to her lips then froze there.

To her horror he was not alone. No, as she watched in disbelief the new part-time preacher walked in, pretty as you please, right behind him with Jana bringing up the rear. The resounding thud of the closing door sent a queasy feeling through her that started in her throat, worked its way down, until finally settling in the pit of her stomach.

Whatever in the world was Adam thinking? Imagine bringing the new preacher here without so much as a warning, and her looking like she'd gotten too close to an exploding giant pear. Horrified, she tried to squeeze behind the hall tree and hide. Frantically, she whispered a promise to God never to ask another thing of Him her entire life if He would just do her this one last favor. Make her disappear.

Adam stopped, hat in hand, right before her shadowy hiding place. He paused, "Beth. Honey, where are you?"

Elizabeth flattened herself against the wall.

He turned away to the pair waiting expectedly behind him, "Why don't you two head into the parlor, I'll see if I can locate her."

She thought about making a dash for the bedroom, but Adam's big frame was blocking her exit. Her only hope lay in that Adam escorted them there himself. Then, she just might have enough time to bolt inside the bedroom and change

He reached up to place his hat on a peg and dropped it. Landing at her feet she didn't even dare breathe, as he bent over to retrieve it. He paused. Slowly, he rose till he was looking straight into her sheepish eyes.

"I take it you have a valid reason for hiding from the new preacher?"

He blocked her flight with a deftly placed hand to the wall beside her, "Let me guess. He found out you're an escaped nun and threatened to take you away from me. Don't worry, Sweetheart, after today they will probably make me a saint for keeping you." He leaned in closer to whisper furiously, "What in the world are you doing and where is Becky?"

"What am I doing," she asked full of justifiable anger?

"Quiet down before someone hears you." For the first time he seemed to take in her shabby stained dress and loose hair. Sighing he waved her explanation away. "Never mind. Just try and get cleaned up before someone sees you. I'll stall for a while, but Beth I warn you any more games and I will be forced to lose my temper."

"Excuse me? You will be forced to lose your temper?!" She poked at his massive chest for emphasis. "First of all, I couldn't care less if you lost your temper. Although I strongly doubt that is possible since it keeps reappearing every time you claim to have lost it. Secondly," She poked him once more for good measure, "I am certainly not the one who brought a houseful of company home unannounced, now am I?"

Clearly frustrated, he stuck his hands on his hips and glared at her, "What are you talking about woman? Didn't you get my note?"

"Of course I did," she bit back in an exasperated tone, "and it only makes it worse."

Adam was just about to question her as to the logic of that statement when his nephew or something that looked a lot like him went shooting into the parlor.

"Uncle Adam! Look what Bootsie did to me. I'm nearly scalped bald headed!"

His eyes shot a questioning look at his big eyed wife. She shrugged guiltily. "I can explain."

He warded off her explanation with a raised hand. Then with a sense of dread, spun away and headed for the parlor. His long legs covered the ground in a manner of moments. Elizabeth ran to catch up. She had a feeling she'd better be there to explain.

Elizabeth collided with his back when he stopped suddenly and bellowed, "What in the Sam hill happened to your hair?"

Nicholas pointed an accusing finger at her retreating form, "That awful woman you married did this to me. I tried to stop her, Uncle Adam, but she almost cut both my ears clean off."

She cringed and began inching backwards. She would explain later.

Unfortunately, the new preacher heard Nicholas's words clearly for he turned horrified eyes on her. My word, you would think she just grew another head. "If you would only let me explain…"

Adam's voice was suspiciously calm, "Is it true Beth? Did you butcher his hair like this?"

What could she say? The evidence looked pretty compelling. Placing a trembling hand to her brow she sunk down to the rumbled coverings still on the couch, and tried. "Well, yes I did. But I didn't mean to, honest. See, Becky was having these contractions and…" her voice trailed off as everyone turned accusing stares on her. "Nicholas, tell them. Tell them the truth. That I never meant to cut your ears off."

Nicholas's mutinous look answered louder than words. She would get no sympathy from that direction. Searching the room for one understanding person, she noticed Jana's eyes fell to the couch Elizabeth sat on, then calculatingly over to Adam. For the first time, Elizabeth noticed the crumpled sheets and lone pillow she sat on. Jana's assumption was easy to read. Apparently, Adam noticed the same thing. He strode over and jerked Elizabeth up off the sofa, gripping her arm so tightly that she only managed a grimace instead of the embarrassing smile she started off with.

Surely now, she thought, Adam would ask them all to leave so he could kill her in private. Instead, he motioned their guests to have a seat. His jaw clenched tight, with one muscle twitching under the strain, he tried to regain some of the pride this whole incident had cost him. "Reverend, I don't believe you've ever met my wife, Beth."

Feeling as ridiculous as the situation she found herself, she held out a hand politely still dazed that he could be so brazen as to actually claim her. She tried to speak, but it came out rather strangled. "I am pleased to meet you, Father – I mean..." her voice trailed off once again in embarrassed silence.

The preacher's eyes moved to the make shift bed sympathetically, "Perhaps I should discuss marriage vows next Sunday." He cleared his throat. "Seeing as there are so many new brides, that is."

Jana blushed becomingly. Elizabeth was doing her level best to keep her eyes averted from the object behind her, dutifully waiting for the ground to just swallow her up and be done with it. Adam on the other hand looked like he would like to choke something, or someone, namely her. Was she the only one who saw how hopeless this effort at polite conversation was?

Chelsea chose just that moment to toddle in, dressed in bed clothes, her face smeared with pear preserves. "Bitsee, I drew a pretty picture for you," she said proudly holding up a jelly smeared slate.

Adam groaned, closing his eyes. Unfortunately, it looked like this fiasco was past saving. It was time to just leave before anything worse happened. "Beth, since it is obvious there is no lunch; I think we should be going. Jana, Reverend, I want to apologize for-"

Wrinkling his nose, the new reverend asked suspiciously, "Is something burning?"

Jana sniffed distastefully then spied the black smoke billowing in from the kitchen. "Adam, Fire!"

All four adults reacted quickly. In unspoken accord, they ran through the smoke filled hallway and into the kitchen, where Elizabeth's Pear preserves were fast becoming a permanent part of the cast iron pot they were burning in.

Reacting instantly, Adam waved everyone out of the way and headed straight for the burning mess on the stove. Not wasting any more precious time, he quickly lifted the smoking pot from the stove with a large cloth and heaved it out the back door and into the yard. He at once motioned them out the door and for several minutes the woods filled with black smoke and lung-searing coughing.

Throughout the long ordeal, Elizabeth's eyes kept straying to Adam, unconsciously picking up Chelsea as a shield. He would never forgive her and who could blame him? All in one day she had scalped his nephew, let Chelsea take a bath in Pear jelly and announced to the new preacher he slept on the couch. Then to top it all off, she had tried to burn down his house.

She hid her face in Chelsea's pear scented hair.

Yes, no doubt about it, her life was over.

"Don't' feel too badly, Bootsie, I'm sure it could have happened to anyone," Jana remarked coolly, before wiping a trail of soot across one eye. "Not that I have ever heard of anyone doing such a thing, but surely it's possible."

The preacher nodded his thinly covered scalp in sympathy. She gritted her teeth in annoyance. Were all men blind to Jana's ways? Did she only hear the sarcasm in the woman's voice? All thoughts of Jana soon fled as Elizabeth's heart hammered in fear. The time to face Adam had come. His blue eyes were stormy as he walked up to the small group. Instantly he zeroed in on Elizabeth, who squirmed in response.

"Jana, you and the reverend go wait for me in the wagon. It seems my wife and I have a little matter we need to discuss in private."

Elizabeth was just thankful he wasn't going to kill her in front of strangers. When he didn't speak right away, she hesitantly looked up at him, trying to put on a brave front. Yet, at any moment she knew it was a very real possibility she might burst into tears.

After one come hither look, Adam headed towards the house, assuming no doubt she would follow. Which made it especially hard to do so seeing as even now smoke was coming from the windows in weak dying whiffs every now and again, a reminder of her crimes.

"Well?" He demanded as she reached him on the porch.

"Well what?" She retorted, with more bravery than she felt.

"You know what."

Elizabeth pushed back a tangled mass which at one time had been her hair and simply glared back at him. "This is really your fault, you know."

He blinked once as if he hadn't heard her correctly. "My fault?"

"Of course. After all, you were the one who surprised me with a houseful of company."

"I hardly think sending a note over this morning is considered surprising you," he responded a little too sarcastically for Elizabeth's taste.

Truly baffled now, she asked "Then why in the world didn't you mention coming home with guests?"

He studied her for a long moment, and when he did finally speak it was roughly and to the point. "Do you still have that note?"

Taken by surprise, she nodded, "I believe so. It was on the lamp stand in the parlor."

In a cold voice, he stated, "Show me."

Uncertain as to his mood, she preceded him into the smoky parlor and retrieved the note from the mantle. "Here it is, but why…"

"Read it."

Her hands trembling in uncertainty, with flickers of past occurrences crossing her mind, she cleared her throat before reading softly;

"Beth,

Jana stopped by this morning and said she and the reverend wanted to discuss the opening of the new school with us. I invited them to lunch. Try not to burn anything.

See you later green eyes,
Adam"

Elizabeth paled. She felt as if someone had kicked her in the stomach. This couldn't be the same note. Her shocked eyes flew to Adam's. "Adam, this isn't the same note. You have to believe me."

Adam no longer looked angry, he looked worried. He never said a word, just turned away to walk over to the window. He stood there in accusatory silence for a long time before finally turning to her. With brutal honesty, he said, "Beth, I don't know what to believe anymore."

Chapter 19

The next morning when Elizabeth awoke, Adam's words still lingered in the air between them. Her green eyes clouded over with sadness as she watched him methodically run the dull razor over the leather strap. The hardest part of all was that she badly needed him to believe her.

Hugging knees tight against her, she tried desperately to still the longing inside her. Lifting her head to watch him lather his face and slowly run the razor across its hard planes she actually smiled. This was her favorite part of the morning, watching him shave.

Something about the familiar sight caused a dull ache to settle in her heart. Who was she kidding? Despite how much she wished otherwise, she cared very much what he thought of her. Groaning she threw back the covers and started to exit the bed.

The sound drew his attention as he finished wiping off the razor before cocking a soap spattered brow at her. "Beth?"

"Yes?" Breath held, she waited; wishing so badly to heal the widening gap between them.

He studied the razor in his hand, and then seemed to change his mind about something. Instead he remarked casually, "I won't be home for supper tonight. It's getting close to shipment and we still need to finish pushing the logs down river."

Her heart instantly sank. But what had she expected him to say? Words of undying devotion? Would she even believe him if he said them? Smoothing the bed covers beside her, she never even looked up. "Should I wait up?"

Something in her voice made him pause. Slowly he wiped his face clean. "No, it might be pretty late."

When she didn't respond, he walked over and sat down on the bed, resisting the urge to touch her. There were so many things left unanswered between them that it would be wrong to take her as his wife no matter how desperately he wanted that. Especially if she was this Elizabeth person she claimed, then she deserved her freedom.

"I've been thinking. You have been under a lot of stress lately." She looked up as if ready to deny it. "We both have. Maybe you should invite Becky or Christina over for the afternoon and just relax today."

Frustrated tears gathered in her eyes. He didn't want her alone. Was he afraid she would do something crazier than burn his house down? She sat up a little straighter. "Maybe I will."

He sighed at her rebellious tone, kissing her on top of the head, "No, you won't. But at least promise me something Green Eyes."

Her soul soared at the endearment. Almost breathless, she asked, "What?"

Dead serious, he looked her straight in the eye, "Promise you won't go anywhere alone today."

"But…"

"I want your promise, Beth."

Her heart skipped a beat a beat at the urgency in his voice. For the first time, she realized he was actually worried about her. Which meant, he must care, right? Well at least a little. "All right", she whispered, their faces mere inches apart.

Suddenly they both became still, afraid to move and afraid not to. Instinctively she leaned forward, inviting his kiss. As if in answer to her unspoken need and before he could stop himself, he brushed his lips softly across hers.

The shock such a simple action caused made him pull quickly away. Afraid if he didn't, he might never stop.

"I have to go", he said huskily, trying to ignore the bewildered look in her eyes. Then, stopping only to get a clean shirt, he left her sitting alone and confused in the middle of the bed.

"Heaven help me," she whispered to the empty room, "I've fallen in love with you Adam Reed."

When Becky never showed up to fix Nicholas's hair, Elizabeth became worried. And when two hours had past and still nothing, she became even more so. It wasn't like Becky to forget anything. That is unless for once her practice pains weren't practice after all.

243

Christina's knock ended all doubt.

Leading a frazzled Christina into the parlor, Elizabeth tried to make out key words in the exited jabber, "Oh, Bootsie, isn't it wonderful? A baby, I mean. You should have seen how clam Becky was. She even thought to send me over as soon as soon as she delivered the baby. Said she knew you would be worried sick."

Relief washed over her. "Is everything all right?" She didn't know much about the process of having babies but she did understand that sometimes there were complications. The thought of anything happening to Becky caused a stab of pain to her heart.

Quickly reassuring her, Christina added, "More than all right. She had a precious baby girl. No complications. Agatha use to be a midwife, you know, and knew exactly what to do. And to watch her, you would have thought Becky had babies every day."

Elizabeth smiled. It certainly sounded like the Becky she knew. After a pause, Christina looked uncomfortably down at the homemade knotted rag rug on the floor. "By the way, she also told us about yesterday. She's really worried about you."

Uncomfortable with the subject, she tried humor, "Well, to be honest, I was a little worried about me too."

Not taken in, Christina continued, "I think there is something you should know. I wasn't sure if I should mention it, but Maggie insisted I tell you."

"Tell me what?"

"Well, Jana was in the store yesterday and she mentioned what happened about the note Adam sent you."

"She did, did she?"

How well she could imagine the picture Jana painted to her friends. Poor, confused Bootsie couldn't even manage to handle one little message without messing it up. No wonder they were worried about her.

Clearing her throat, Christina repeated what she heard. "She said you were...um..."

"Unstable? Unbalanced? Am I getting warm?"

Caught off guard by Bootsie's honesty, she admitted, "As a matter of fact, unstable is the word she used. Of course none of us believed her, except Cornelia. You know how dramatic she is. Anyway, she said you claimed that the note was not the same one as the one Adam found later. He told her all about it. How you claimed the original one had disappeared. Only there it was plain as day, and still you insisted the words changed somehow."

In stunned silence, only one thought kept entering Elizabeth's mind. How could Adam tell Jana a thing like that? Unless he didn't and she exchanged the note herself, which was a very real possibility and one she clung to.

"You know, I have been a little overwhelmed lately," Elizabeth spoke up as a plan began forming in her mind, "Would you mind doing me a favor?"

Taken aback at the change in subject and the eagerness in her voice, Christina hesitated, "No, of course not."

"Could you watch Nicholas and Chelsea for me? Just for a little while."

"You know I don't mind. In fact, why don't they stay over, Edward would love that. Not to mention, it would give you and Adam a chance to be alone for a change. To tell you the truth, Bootsie, I don't like the gleam in Jana's eye every time Adam's name is mentioned."

Grateful for Christina's support Elizabeth reached over and squeezed her hand, "Don't worry. I think tonight is just what we both need."

Chapter 20

She pulled back the curtains, looking into the dark night for signs of Adam. Seeing none she let them fall back into place. Just the thought of what she was about to do unnerved her. She tried to ignore her rapid heartbeat and sweaty palms. Instead, trying to concentrate on what she planned to do tonight. The thought petrified her, but the way she saw it she had little choice. Without some kind of proof, who would believe her?

It was getting late. Pulling the pale pink shawl down from the top of the dresser, she headed out into the chilly fall evening. Her nerves were on end. Every hoot of an owl, every windswept leaf made her jump in response. Till at last she reached the barn. Sifting through the tool box in the semi darkness, her hands found at last what she needed; a small iron bar.

True it wasn't much, but it would serve two purposes if she needed it. Tucking it underneath her shawl she quickly took the path that ran along the creek. It was a little faster and she could avoid detection easier. She didn't have much time. If she hurried she just might make it back home before Adam did. If not? She shivered. Well, she would deal with that if necessary.

Less than an hour later, Elizabeth watched from her vantage point among a huge circle of Douglas firs, as two shadows played back and forth in front of the soft warm light of an oil lamp. Jana was not alone. Now what? If she waited much longer Adam would beat her home, and if she didn't, this might be her only chance to find out what Jana was up to. As if in answer to her question, the light in the back room went out. And a few minutes later, two people emerged from the front, a man and a woman.

A shiver of anticipation shot through Elizabeth. They were leaving. It seemed to take forever for the two to leave in the wagon and even longer to wait for them to roll out of sight. Somehow the night seemed stiller without the soft glow of the lamp, as if it too were holding its breath in anticipation.

Reluctantly, she left the safety of her position in the woods and crept up to the front of the temporary school house. The night seemed to swallow her up, and she rubbed her arms for warmth. Somehow the prospect of what she planned to do seemed a whole lot simpler when decided on in the light of day. Tonight, it just seemed terribly dangerous. Unfortunately, the thought of living one more day like yesterday seemed worse. She wasn't crazy, but she needed proof of her sanity. Hopefully what she needed was inside, like that original note that seemed to disappear for instance. If not that, then maybe something else.

Reaching the door, she wedged the iron bar into the door frame and shoved with all her weight against it. It didn't budge. Looking for another entrance, she began trying the windows. The first two were locked. She ran a trembling hand through the stray bangs in her a face. Who locked their windows in the middle of nowhere? Frustrated she tried another and it budged an inch. Finally. And as luck would have it, it opened into the bedroom. Determined now, she grabbed the bottom and jerked it towards her. After several more tries she managed to make just enough room for her to climb through. Struggling through the narrow opening, her slender legs kicking for momentum, she landed in a noisy heap upon the floor. Dazed, Elizabeth sat perfectly still; fearful someone might have heard her. After several minutes of undisturbed silence, she rose on wobbly legs.

First, she searched the dresser. Nothing. Of course it would have helped tremendously could she have lit the oil lamp, or even a candle but she dare not take the chance. Just about as she was uncertain what to do next her eyes caught the faint glow of white coming from the moons reflection off several papers scattered on the dresser to the right. Quickly before she lost her nerve, she gathered them up, straining her eyes against the blurry images.

It was no use. Without light of some kind she would never be able to tell which papers, if any, were of use to her. Frustrated, she felt along the desk's surface until at last locating a match box. With hands shaking she lit the candle before her. The harsh light seemed to scream out her existence. Forcing herself not to blow it out, she lifted the papers one by one under the flickering light.

Disappointment filled her heart. There was nothing there except orders for new slates, supplies and some letters that were addressed to some woman by the name of Annie Stokes. Elizabeth's shoulder slumped in response. She hadn't realized until this moment how badly she had banked on finding that note. A wolf howled eerily in the distance as Elizabeth leaned over to blow out the candle then stopped. For her eyes caught a glint of something. Pulling the slender desk drawer out further, she slowly reached inside.

It was a ring. But something about it caused her to draw in a ragged breath. Hesitantly she lifted it up to the feeble light to get a better look. There was something vaguely familiar about its design. Something...her heart constricted in her chest. It was her father's.

But how could it be? Was she going crazy after all?

With almost a reverence for the dead, she slowly turned the ring till at last the inscription inside was readable. The words seeming to leap out at her, daring her to deny its authenticity for the words read, "For our beloved son, Edgar". Why now that her eyes were not so blurred with shock, she could even make out the family crest engraved artfully around the large green emerald that seemed to wink at her in mock gaiety. She released the ring as if burnt by it. She heard it bounce twice before rolling to a stop at her feet. What was Jana doing with her father's ring?

She remembered distinctly seeing it on his finger the day of his funeral. Knowing she couldn't possibly leave it here, she forced herself to pick it up and place it on her right thumb. There was only one thing left to do, tell Adam. Bending over, she blew out the candle. She wasn't certain how much time had passed, but she knew time was running out. So hurriedly climbing back through the window, she paused only long enough to retrieve the iron bar lying on the ground before running straight for the woods and home.

A million thoughts were tumbling through her mind as she raced for home. One thought however surfaced above them all – at last she could prove who she was. She knew it was flimsy evidence, but it was evidence. There had to be records somewhere back home with a picture of her family crest on them. The one her father bragged that her ancestors brought over from Ireland.

It seemed to take forever before she at last recognized her house in the distance. She didn't stop to wonder at the lamps being lit this late at night, so intent was she on her own thoughts. It wasn't until she stood outside her own back door that her senses returned and her heart sank. Adam was back. What would she say to him? Would he believe her?

Hesitatingly, she entered the softly lit kitchen, weighing her options on how best to proceed, when a large shadow fell over her. She instantly stopped breathing.

The booming voice did nothing to calm her nerves. "Where have you been? I've been worried sick."

Feigning innocence as she gingerly stepped around him, she tried to remain calm. For the first time, she took in his shirt that was partially buttoned and only halfway tucked into his pants. No doubt he had been about to go in search of her. And as he stood with booted feet planted firmly before her like some vengeful god ready to swoop down on her to deliver punishment, she found her voice sounded more guilty than confident.

"I'm surprised you're even home. Usually you're working late every night, or so you say." Swallowing the lump in her throat, she tried to appear casual as she walked past him and hung her shawl over a hook by the back door.

"What is that supposed to mean? And just where were you anyway?"

"I went for a walk. The children went to spend the night with Christina, and it was such a nice night, I decided to go for a stroll." She finished filling the tea kettle. "Would you like a cup?"

"You expect me to believe you went walking this late? It must be forty degrees out." He finished accusingly, pulling her up against him, their faces mere inches apart. "I think, Sweetheart, you had better come up with a more plausible answer than that. Do you realize that I have been pacing this floor for over an hour? I was half out of mind with worry. I had no idea where you or the kids were and no idea where to begin to look."

Struggling to pull free of his steel grip, she fumed, "Let go. You're hurting me."

"Beth," he growled, "I want some answers and not any more of your inept lies either. I want the truth."

"I told you the truth" she insisted, pushing harder against his partially bare chest.

She was genuinely frightened now. Truth be told, she had never seen him so angry. Still she tried to maintain some sort of composure and confidence, as she stamped her small foot for emphasis. "Adam, let go of me this instant. You cannot..."

Adam's hold only tightened as he bent down, picked her up into his arms and strode purposely toward the stairs. Eyes wide, she struggled in earnest now.

"Where are you taking me," she sputtered, real panic in her voice.

"To bed."

She dare not think about the implications of that remark. Instead, she resorted to changing tactics. "Adam, listen, I realize you are angry. And you're right, I should have left a note, but honestly don't you think you are overreacting just a little?"

Ignoring her, he kicked open their bedroom door.

"Wait. I can explain."

He dropped her unceremoniously down onto the middle of the mattress. All she could think of was escape. Quickly scooting away from him, she tried reaching the other side and the window behind it. He grabbed a foot and pulled her back across. "Bargain's over."

Shocked, she ceased struggling. Surely, he couldn't actually mean what she thought he meant. It was barbaric. In stunned horror, she watched as he slowly began removing the rest of his shirt, one button at a time, his eyes never leaving hers.

"What do you think you are doing," she asked in a thread whisper.

"I'm taking you up on your offer," he answered smoothly.

250

Elizabeth's eyes widened as her stomach clenched up in a hard knot. Frantically, she groped for something that would stop him.

"Wait, I…Adam, all right, I admit it. You are right. I didn't go for a walk." If only he would stop pulling off his boots, she might be able to speak a coherent sentence. "I went to the school."

His movements stilled. Checking her for signs of lying and finding none, he nodded. "What for?"

"Because," she sighed, he would never believe her now, "well, I went to spy on Jana. I wanted to find some sort of proof she has been setting me up. Adam, I swear to you, there was another note."

Adam's smoky eyes were returning to normal, although he dare not get too near her at the moment. He couldn't seem to concentrate on much else except her full lips and the way her hair lay in sweet disarray about her shoulders. Forcing himself to listen, he asked in a clipped tone, "Did you find anything?"

Her long sooty lashes fell softly against her flushed face, "Not exactly."

"Well, what exactly did you find," he asked impatiently.

"This." She held out a hand, showing him the ring on her thumb.

"What does that prove?"

Sitting up straighter, she was eager to explain, "Don't you see? It belonged to my father. It can be traced back to him. This proves," she drew in a satisfied breath, "that I am Elizabeth Brown."

Running a hand tiredly through chestnut hair, he pointed out, "Beth, all this proves is that you are a thief. That or either you are as crazy as Jana claims. Is that really what you want?"

"But it's true. Look."

Climbing out of bed, she trustingly placed the ring in his palm. "See,' she said pointing out its design, "it has our family crest on it."

He slowly gave it back to her. "No one will believe your father owned this ring and especially if you claim you stole it from Jana."

Defeated, Elizabeth knew he was right. She couldn't prove any of it. Still for some reason she couldn't stop herself from asking, "I know you have no reason to believe me, but couldn't you at least ask your lawyer friend to check it out? See if I'm telling the truth?"

Agitated by her nearness and the pleading in her eyes, he took a step back to distance himself from her. "I'll think about it. But on one condition."

She automatically wanted to argue with him, but realized she was in no position to make demands. Dropping her head in resignation, she whispered, "I really don't have a choice do I?"

"No you don't. So from now on I don't want you doing anymore stupid stunts like tonight. If what you say is true, do you really think getting yourself killed will prove anything?"

Looking down at her dejected pose, he felt an overwhelming urge to comfort her in the only way he knew how. Even now he couldn't help noticing how innocently seductive she was. Nor could he deny any longer how much he wanted her. Unfortunately, he also knew that if he did act on his feelings for her, he would never be able to let her go. Not without losing a part of himself along with her.

Trembling, she forced herself to look up into his searching face. "Are you still angry?"

Stormy blue eyes looked her up and down, as a shiver crossed her spine.

"No, it's not my anger I'm having a problem with right now."

Her questioning eyes told him that she clearly did not understand his meaning. Reacting matter of fact, he stated plainly, "Beth, I think it is time we talked."

"About what?"

Her tentative step back, caused his dimple to reappear. "About us."

"What about us?"

Now he was nervous. Thoughtfully he walked back and shut their bedroom door. Where did one begin to seduce one's wife? Especially since from the look of suspicion in her eyes it was not exactly a welcoming invitation at the moment. Holding out a hand, he gently invited, "Come here Beth."

A tingle of uncertainty caused her to stay rooted to the spot. "I'm fine here, thank you."

Slowly he approached her, lifting a silky curl and fingering it seductively, "Green eyes, I just don't think I can make it another night without touching you."

Her breath caught at his tender words.

Placing strong but gentle hands to both sides of her face, he looked deeply into her frightened eyes. "Beth, I want you as my wife…my real wife. Do you understand what I am asking you?"

"I think so, but…" A wave of nervous panic over took her, "I don't know anything about well, you know…being a wife. Did I mention I was raised by nuns?"

Her plea was cut off by his lips closing in on her trembling ones. After one drugging kiss, he turned his head to whisper in her ear, "I'll teach you."

She was afraid he might say something like that. Now he was kissing her ear, her neck and Elizabeth closed her eyes in pleasure, her body weakening under the assault. She barely found enough voice to protest one last time. "But you know how I have a way of bumbling the simplest tasks. I am sure you would not find it the least pleasant."

Grinning at her feeble attempt to discourage him, he shook his head at her. If she filled him with this much desire without even trying, heaven help him when she set her mind to it. Groaning, he admitted honestly, "Sweetheart, believe me, that won't be a problem."

Chapter 21

"Wake up sleepy head." Adam's husky voice penetrated her dreams.

Yawning sleepily, she stretched lazily against the still warm covers. A soft, satisfied smile came to her lips and a warm blush to her body as she thought of last night and the big man so casually smiling down on her.

Handing her a wild flower, he kissed the top of her head, "One more sexy stretch like that one and I'll never get out of here."

Quickly averting her eyes, the covers in her lap suddenly became extremely interesting, as she shyly admitted, "You're embarrassing me." When he didn't respond, she looked up just in time to catch his cocky grin, "and apparently you are not sorry in the least."

"Should I be?"

How could he seem so comfortable plopping down beside her on the bed as if everything was normal? After last night with him nothing would ever seem normal again. Why just the nearness of him, the casual way he gathered up his boots and began tugging them on made her breathless. And the need to touch him was overpowering.

Eyes twinkling he turned to her, "Sweetheart, there is nothing to be embarrassed about. People do this sort of thing all the time you know." He affectionately reached out and ran a calloused finger down the length of her nose.

Expressive green eyes widened in shock, "Do you really think everyone else does those things?"

Laughing, Adam got up and reached for his shirt. "Children are a pretty good indication that they are doing something other than reading at night."

Helpless to resist his teasing grin, she smiled timidly.

He winked.

She surprised him by boldly winking back.

Adam roared with laughter, "I think you are catching on fast to this side of marriage, Sweetheart. A little too fast. I'm having trouble keeping up with you."

She begged to differ, for she was having a hard time understanding how he could even joke about what occurred between them last night. Why she could barely think about it, without blushing clear down to her toes.

"Okay enough flirting. We're wasting good fishing time. The kids are dressed and delivered downstairs thanks to Christina. The lunch made. And all I need next is for one gorgeous female to get her sexy backside out of bed."

"Are we going somewhere?"

Pulling back the covers, he tugged her partially clad body out of bed and began throwing articles of clothing her direction. "Fishing." was all the explanation she got before a camisole came flying across the room, smacking her in the face.

Embarrassed, she fumbled the intimate garment, "Would you please stop doing that? Besides, I don't know anything about fishing."

"Good. I find I am enjoying teaching you things you've never done before." His smile was downright wicked.

Flustered, she pushed back tangled hair and groaned, "Oh, honestly."

Noticing her drawer now emptied of every garment she owned, he came over and gave her a quick kiss. "I'll give you ten minutes. After that if you're not dressed? Well, let's just say I will have the pleasure of assisting you."

She barely felt his kiss, "But what about your deadline?"

"I'm the boss remember? And this is my honeymoon. Now hurry Green Eyes. The fish are probably just starting to bite."

Listening to his whistling all the way out the front door, she sat back and sighed. Apparently men and women had different ideas about nearly everything. Including honeymoons, because fishing certainly wasn't what she considered romantic.

Before the sun was very high in the sky all four fishermen were plopped down on the side of the river, drowning defenseless worms. Elizabeth tried not to think about the object dangling at the end of her hook. Bored, she looked around for Adam. He was walking along the bank, periodically throwing in his line, then reeling it back. It had been over an hour and the only thing he had said to her was, "Make sure your line stays tight." As if she knew what in the world that meant. Oh, yes. This was her idea of romance all right.

Eyeing her still unmoving cork at the other end of her line, she sighed loudly. Turning longingly Adam's direction as he so freely walked down the bank with Chelsea tottering along behind him, she flung her pole to the ground. What rule said she had to just sit here if he didn't?

"I believe I'll just check my line", she announced to no one in particular.

Nicholas barely glanced her direction. She yanked up her pole and quickly began reeling in the line. Sneaking another glance at Adam as he whipped his line back and forth, she tried to immolate him. Sticking her own pole high above her head, she began welding it up and down until it resembled more chopping wood than fishing.

Nicholas eyes grew wide as the line hap-hazardly flew around his head in all directions. "What in tarnation are you doing?" He shouted, ducking swiftly out of the way.

"Oops. Sorry." Was her only reply, biting a lower lip in deep concentration.

It didn't seem very sincere and Nicholas didn't dare take his eyes off her, till she finally threw out her line one last time. It fell short of her destination, catching fast in the tree overhead. He slammed an open palm against his forehead. "Great. Now look what you've done."

"Well, it isn't as if I did it on purpose." Mumbling she began to yank viciously at the line overhead. "Besides, that was a perfectly stupid place to grow a tree anyway. It was right in my way."

After several minutes of being showered with pine needles, Nicholas shot to his feet and grabbed the pole from her surprised hands.

"Just let me do it before you yank the whole blame tree down on top of me."

Then expertly, he slacked up the line before giving it just the right jerk to send the hook sailing behind them. Not saying a word, he threw the line out in one smooth movement. It sailed through the air and back into the middle of the river where it belonged. With a superior air, he shoved the pole at her before sitting back down. The whole act took less than a minute.

Impressed, Elizabeth praised, "Nicholas, you are really quite good at this."

He shrugged off the compliment. "Oh, I reckon I'm all right. Are you going to fish or talk?"

"Actually, I hoped maybe we could talk."

"Only if you want to talk about fishing," he replied turning slightly away.

So much for that, she thought. Undecided about where to lay the pole down, she walked around in a circle looking for the stick Adam drove into the ground earlier as a prop. "Nicholas, did you see my stick?"

"That's it. I'm moving."

"But, I only asked about my stick."

Refusing to say another word to the dense female, he reeled in his line then picked up his tackle bucket and moved a few feet away. It was just enough, apparently, that maybe she would leave him alone.

At last finding the elusive stick, she sat back down. But then she noticed the line was sort of just floating around instead of taunt like Adam drilled into her.

Nicholas watched out of the corner of his eye as she reeled in the line yet again. Amazingly, this time she managed, after several unsuccessful tries, to maneuver it back into the water. However, this time the line scarcely got wet before she pulled it back out again. Time after time, he watched as she threw it into the river, developing a sort of predictable rhythm.

257

Shifting impatiently, he groaned in frustration before shooting to his feet. "For crying out loud! You have to leave it be, or you aren't never going to catch a fish."

Encouraged by his sudden interest, she responded warmly, "Are you sure? That's how Adam is doing it."

"He's fly fishing."

"Oh."

"Then how should I do it?"

"I guess that depends on if you're trying to catch a fish or just drag one up by accident."

Then as if to prove his point, his rod doubled over. Quickly jerking it up, he set the hook and pulled back till the line began to sing with tension. Whooping loudly, he headed up the bank in a tug of war with the fish on the other end.

"Hurry," he yelled out in excitement, "grab hold of him."

"I beg your pardon?"

Straining to hold the line tight, his small arms were trembling under the weight. Elizabeth watched in wonder as a rainbow trout shot out of the water, gracefully dancing on his tail fin before diving once more into the river's ice cold depths. The action only caused a fresh wave of hooting and hollering from Nicholas.

"Did you see that, Bootsie? I bet he's the biggest fish this side of Oregon. Quick, grab up that bucket and next time he starts showing off, scoop him up."

"Oh, I don't think…"

"Hurry. He's going to get away."

Frantically Elizabeth looked around for anything that resembled a fish scooper. Spying an old rusted tin bucket beside the tree, she picked it up and raced to the edge of the water, waiting. Just as Nicholas warned, the splendid specimen shot out of the water once more directly in front of her. She yelped in surprise, jumping back.

"Don't just stand there gawking, go get him."

Forgetting all else except the magnificent fish before her, Elizabeth waded into the water up to her knees and began wildly slinging the bucket in all directions, missing the fish entirely.

"I said catch him, not knock him out," hollered an exasperated Nicholas, still struggling with his pole.

The whole front of her dress was soaked now. She shouted back, "I'm trying! The thing won't be still."

No sooner had she spoken, then the obliging fish jumped right into her pail, causing her to shriek in surprise.

The fish, realizing his mistake, began frantically thrashing about thoroughly drenching every last dry part left on her body. Holding the pail at arm's length to avoid receiving anymore bombardments from her captive, she headed for the bank.

"He'll jump out for sure, if you don't stop fooling around."

Just like his uncle, she thought irritably as she pushed her way through the strong currant, finally reaching the edge of the water. He was constantly telling other people how to go about their own affairs. Her irritation was short lived when she looked down at her captive. He was the most splendid thing she had ever seen and she had been a part of his capture. His whole body shone silver with the streaks of the rainbow reflecting along his sleek body.

"Why, Nicholas, he's beautiful."

He beamed proudly at her. "He sure is."

Their eyes meeting over the bucket, an unexplainable bond began forming between the two fishermen. For a moment, he seemed to forget he didn't particularly like her. And she forgot he wasn't her greatest tormentor.

Breathless, she gave a timid smile.

Slowly, he answered her with one of his own.

"Well, Sweetheart, if you wanted to go swimming you should have told me. There's a better place down the river," Adam remarked teasingly as he came up behind them.

Nicholas beamed proudly at his uncle. "Just look at the fish we caught. You should have seen Bootsie, why, she scooped him right into that bucket. For a minute, I nearly forgot she was a useless girl."

Her eyes shining with pride at his inclusion of her, Elizabeth held up the pail so Adam could have a better look. Unfortunately he was occupied looking at something much more beautiful. Her.

Chelsea, refusing to be ignored any longer, tugged on Adam's hand, "I wanna go swimming like Bitsee."

He reached down sweeping the little girl into his arms and kissing her neck till she succumbed to a fit of giggles. "You better behave or I'll make you carry that fish all the way home."

Elizabeth felt warmed by the affectionate playfulness between them. Strange that today they actually felt like a family. Maybe Adam was right after all and this fishing thing wasn't such a bad idea. Moving in closer to Adam, she slipped a hand in his. "How about taking your freezing wife home?"

Feeling her shiver, he wrapped an arm around her, whispering in her ear, "On one condition."

She snuggled to his warmth, a little suspicious of the gleam in his eye. "Seems to me you have a lot of conditions."

He winked. "I think you'll like this one. Tell you what, when we get home, how about you let me choose how to warm you up."

Her stomach did a flip-flop as his words left her with a feeling of anticipation and longing. "I would like that."

Turning his head, his eyes met hers. Suddenly serious, he drew her closer in before kissing her so thoroughly that she soon forgot all about being cold.

"Aw, cut it out you two. Do you want to make everybody sick or something?"

Embarrassed they touched their heads together, smiling sheepishly. She wondered if she would ever get use to loving a man like him. So as day darkened into evening, casting its brilliant colors into the sky, the foursome headed for home. They reached their front porch just as stars appeared overhead, looking as if God Himself had gathered them up in His mighty hand and scattered them about just for them.

Not wanting the day to end, they sat on the front steps and before long their talk turned to stories, then more personal, to their own private thoughts and dreams. Chelsea laid her head on Adam's shoulder and slept. Her cherub features relaxed for the first time that day. In this strange peaceful existence, there were no conflicts, no Rawlings, not anyone else on the entire planet except the two of them. Nicholas kept drifting off, so to stay awake he went in search of frogs in the yard. They watched him dart about shouting in surprise every time one jumped up at him.

It was then that Adam broke the spell by saying, "The lumber party is next week."

The words spoken so quietly made Elizabeth wonder if she imagined them, "I know."

"There will be a lot of strangers milling around. I want you to stay close no matter what, understand?"

Instinctively he was tempted to call the whole thing off. There were still too many questions left unanswered. Jana for one.

She shivered. "Adam, why are you so worried?"

"Because," he answered turning to face her, "there is something I need to tell you about Jana."

Elizabeth braced herself. "What about Jana?"

To ease her, he caressed the side of her face with a strong square hand. "Sweetheart, I don't know why she lied, but her name is really Annie Stokes. She has lied about other things as well including needing a place to stay. It's almost as if she planned to stay with us."

Too stunned to reply at first, she slowly began thinking back to that bedroom. The name Annie stokes vaguely familiar. "Why didn't you tell me sooner? Don't you see? If she had my father's ring, she must be involved with Rawlings. That's the only other explanation of how she could have gotten it. We have to go over there and talk to her tonight."

"Beth," he spoke softly in order to calm her.

"No. Don't Beth me. I can't believe you knew all this and didn't tell me. We can't just wait around and do nothing. If Rawlings finds me..."

Grabbing her by the shoulders, he shook her gently. "Stop it. I won't let anything happen to you. Besides, without some sort of proof, how could I hold either one of them?"

"But the ring."

"By itself means nothing. This is why I told you I didn't want you running off and doing anything rash. I don't know exactly what is going on, but I don't want you hurt."

The tension between them filled the air, both determined and unmovable. It was Elizabeth who backed down first. Her sigh was heavy. "I'm not sure I can simply wait around to see what Rawlings will do next. All my life I have had to look out for myself." She searched Adam's face. Could she now trust him with what might turn out to be her life?

Seeing the wariness in her eyes, he pushed a soft curl away from the beautiful face he had grown to love. Affectionately, he asked of her something he knew was hard to give. "Beth, I need you to trust me on this. Nothing is going to happen as long as you don't go running off by yourself." He shifted the sleeping child to his other arm in order to move in closer. "I can't protect you if I don't know where you are."

Hearing the sincere worry in his voice and feeling the comfort of his touch soothed her more than the mere words. For now, she would do what he asked, "All right Adam."

His shoulders physically relaxed relieved he would not have to fight her on this. "Give me the ring and I'll make sure Sam has a look at it to see what he can find out. Meanwhile," he handed Chelsea over to her, "I think you should get this one off to bed. I'll round up Nicholas."

"Adam," she added, taking the little girl and feeling her nestle up against her, "Thank you for at least believing me. It means more than you will ever know."

"Beth, I'll always be here for you."

Once upstairs, she laid Chelsea on the rumpled covers. It made her heart swell at the way the little girl curled up instantly into a tight ball. Covering her up, Elizabeth looked around for the extra blanket usually kept at the end of the bed. Not finding it, she bent down, feeling underneath the edge of the bed. She touched a soft wool corner and smiled.

Tugging it out along with a rag doll of Chelsea's and Nicolas' sling shot, she shook her head in wonder. Not only was she feeling like a wife, but a mother as well. It amazed her how quickly her life had changed in just a matter of months. Placing the rag doll in Chelsea's arms, she tip toed over to the dresser to replace the sling. Opening the second drawer and reaching inside, she hesitated. Her hand brushing once more over the crumpled piece of paper, her curiosity won out as she pulled it out and smoothed its rough edges.

She had no intention of reading it of course, what she intended was to throw it away downstairs. Yet something drew her to it. Call it new found maternal instinct to understand the boy in her care or a gut feeling. Whatever it was, her eyes strayed casually over the words as she turned for the door. Her steps slowing, she came to a stop. Stunned, she looked up, her arm falling limp against her side.

It was the missing note.

Chapter 22

The day of the lumber party began with rain. It went downhill from there.

By the time Elizabeth reached the store that afternoon, it had settled down to a light mist. It never ceased to amaze her how a storm could conjure up the beauty of the mountains. Unfortunately, it failed to do the same for her. It did havoc on her naturally curly hair.

Not to mention, she had to get right out in the middle of it now, which was not helping her hair situation. She should have made the dessert she was bringing earlier, but going down into the cellar she found it empty of sugar, flour and apples. And she needed all three seeing as the only edible thing she managed to make was apple pie. This meant a trip to the mercantile.

She sighed heavily. Besides, she would use any excuse to get away from Nicholas for a while. She wasn't sure how to confront him about the note, or exactly what him having it meant. Since yesterday she caught him watching her closely with a look of confusion on his face. As if everything he thought he believed about her had changed.

A million miles away, she entered the store in a dreamy haze. Walking over to the busy counter, she waited for Cornelia to finish with a customer. The thin wiry woman smiled a welcome her direction before returning once more to the man's order. Deep in thought Elizabeth traced a finger lightly against the top of a peppermint jar. Watching it go round and round, her eyes following its path, she felt it represented the endless circle of questions that ran through her mind lately.

"Bootsie, is that you?"

Jana's unexpected voice called out to her from the stacks of material at the back of the store. Straightening away from the counter as the beautifully collected woman swooped down on her, she prepared herself for an insult. She didn't have long to wait.

"Adam didn't mention you were coming into town today. Does he know you are here by yourself?"

As opposed to with a caretaker? Oh, the woman really irritated her.

Placing a gloved hand paternally on Elizabeth's sleeve, her tsk, tsking contradicting the show of false compassion. "I really think you need to rest before venturing out again. You did have a…well, unfortunate day."

Pulling away none too gently, Elizabeth tried to ignore the insult, "I'm sure Adam is much too busy to bother about whether I go to the store or not. And I assure you, I feel perfectly fine."

"Really? Well that certainly isn't the impression he gave me this morning."

With that sentence hanging in the air between them, activity inside the store ceased as all attention became focused on their not so private conversation.

Caught off guard, Elizabeth whispered, "This morning?"

Jana pulled off a glove and fingered the spool of red ribbon on the counter, as if unaware of the havoc she was causing. "Well, certainly this morning. You knew of course that he comes by every day to check on me. I mean, how the school is progressing," she peeked out of one eye to watch for Elizabeth's reaction. "You look upset Bootsie. Didn't he mention coming by to see me?"

Shocked, Christina fumbled the jar of canned peaches she held, nearly dropping them to the floor. Cornelia, on the other hand, picked up a broom and under the pretense of sweeping, moved in closer. Her small beady eyes were magnified by the thick pair of glasses sliding to the end of her nose.

Jana frowned at the wiry woman who was practically breathing down her neck. "Do you mind doing that someplace else?"

Caught, Cornelia peevishly pushed her heavy spectacles up her nose. "Well," she humphed, "I suppose I could if I am truly bothering you."

"You are."

Huffing indignantly, Cornelia grabbed up her broom like a sword and started sweeping by the front door. The whole time, she was straining to hear what was said.

"As I was saying," Jana continued to a very much distracted Elizabeth, "he seemed genuinely worried about you. It seems he wanted to make sure I wouldn't press charges after you stole a ring form my things. But of course I could never prosecute someone who is so very – confused. Surely you don't actually believe it belonged to your dead father?"

A gasp was heard from the occupants of the store. When both women turned around, Cornelia once more began vigorously sweeping, working her way slowly towards them.

Reaching out to steady herself, with the taste of betrayal suffocating her voice, she barely found the strength to ask, "He told you that? That I was confused?"

Smugly pulling her glove back on, the petite blond smoothed out the wrinkles and shrugged, "What did you expect after the absurd things you have done lately?"

That was it. Elizabeth saw red.

All she could think of as Jana hovered over her, were the things Adam told her last night. The tender words. The laughter. Was it all a lie? She tried to focus on the face swimming before her.

"Bootsie, I don't mean to upset you, but I'm afraid Adam is right. You just can't go on making up these things."

Only wishing to get out of there before any more of Jana's maddening words could reach her, Elizabeth pushed past her on the way out the door. She never even heard the angry scream behind her. Caught off balance, Jana tumbled backside first into a big barrel of sorghum Molasses. Cornelia let out a horrified giggle and hurried over to the floundering young woman as Molasses oozed over the rim and trailed its way to the floor.

"Ohhh," Jana ground out, as she helplessly tried to push her way out of the barrel. Only it seemed as each time she came up and only sunk deeper and deeper into its sickening sweet depths. "Don't just stand there gawking, you little fool. Do something!"

Blinking at the irate woman, Cornelia reached out a hand –which went sailing past Jana's outstretched one to retrieve the dust pan from behind the counter.

"Why, I am doing something Jana dear," she answered sweetly, "I'm minding my own business."

Swiping at angry tears, Elizabeth flicked the reins more in reflex than anything else. Her mind raced blindly ahead, trying to understand why Adam would go behind her back and tell Jana about the ring. A fresh rush of humiliation hit her as she recalled the shocked faces in the store. Unconsciously she urged the horse on to a faster pace. She was so tired of all the lies. She didn't know what to believe anymore, or who. First the incident with Nicholas and now she didn't even know if she could trust her own husband.

The farther she got from town, the greater her temper. Yes, it seemed to grow with every step the horse took. How dare he confide in that horrible woman? She shook the reins with such force that Pepper looked back at her nervously.

"What are you looking at," she scolded, as her throat began to clog with tears, "haven't you ever seen a fool before?"

Apparently he had since he turned back around and trotted up the dirt road. When he reached the turn off for the mill, he automatically stopped and waited for direction out of habit.

Her driving forgotten, Elizabeth let go of the reins and burst into tears. Head thrown down across her knees she bawled like a baby, as all those feelings of insecurity came tumbling back on her.

Maybe Jana was telling the truth and Elizabeth was just too stupid to see it.

The treacherous thought took hold like a calf to its new mom. Slowly she lifted her tear stained face, drew herself together and tried to focus on the anger welling up inside her. Anything was better than the terrible sadness threatening the last defenses to her heart. Instead she thought of Adam. And Jana. The two of them together. She frowned and blew her nose on a kerchief from her purse.

She had to find out. Tugging on the left rein, she steered Pepper towards the mill. If Adam thought he could break her heart and then go to work like nothing happened – he was mistaken. By the time her wagon rolled past the lumber mill, Elizabeth was well past tears, she was downright furious. Reaching his office, she pulled back the reins and came to a complete stop before flinging them into the baseboard.

As she stormed past some workers, they gave her a look of mild curiosity. She never even slowed down. Caught up in righteous anger, she didn't pause to knock, but threw the door wide and barged right in with long skirts swishing angrily around her ankles.

A startled Adam looked up from the ledger in his hand, to find his wife glaring down at him, mad enough to spit nails. His chair creaked as he removed his booted feet from the desk and sat forward on all four legs. "Beth, is something the matter?"

"Hah!" she snorted, flinging a stray curl out of her face before impaling him with red-rimmed eyes.

Shifting uncomfortably, he tried to focus on what he possibly could have done to make her so angry? "What kind of response is that? Stop staring a hole through me and just tell me what is wrong."

Michael, who cleared his throat to announce his presence to the two lovebirds, was totally ignored. He ducked his head, pretending to be engrossed in the ledgers in his hands.

Without explanation, she pointed an accusing finger at her stunned husband, "How could you?" Her voice caught in her throat, "How could you do those beautiful things to me last night and then go to that…that…woman the very next morning."

Thoroughly uncomfortable now, Michael slid out of his chair and tried to exit quietly, but unfortunately there was nowhere to go without walking right past them. He hovered half out of his chair, uncertainty keeping him there.

"I thought," she choked, her voice full of unshed tears as she watched Adam leave his chair to come to her "No, don't. I couldn't take it if you touched me right now."

"Beth," he said so achingly that it tore her in two.

Warding him off with a raised hand, she ducked her head so she wouldn't remember how beautiful he was, "I guess you and Jana must have laughed at what a blind fool I am. To think, I actually thought I meant something to you." She was bawling heavily now, "I hate you. I never should have given myself to you. It was a terrible, awful mistake."

"That's enough Beth," he interrupted softly.

But she wasn't finished yet. She still hadn't told him she was leaving. Right after she shot him that is. "You're right Adam. It is enough. I am leaving. Leaving this wilderness. Leaving your lies. Leaving this nightmare. I want to go home," she pleaded. Every fiber of her being was in need of comfort. How she wished for just one person who truly cared about her.

Michael slowly let himself back down into the chair and tried not to listen.

Noticing for first time his friend slumped down in the chair, hat tipped forward to cover his face, Adam almost in reflex barked out, "Michael, it's a good time to leave. I am sure you have more pressing things to attend than listening in on my personal conversations."

The embarrassed man gave a wan smile, before rising quickly up from the chair he had been uncomfortably trapped in for what seemed hours. "Gladly." Then before anyone could change their minds, he hurried past them to blessed escape.

"You shouldn't have bothered," she retorted, gaining a little control when she realized Michael had heard everything. "I have said what I came to say, now I am leaving," she flung out. Whipping around she reached for the doorknob.

Adam never raised his voice, or moved a muscle, although she noticed the twitch in his clenched jaw out of the corner of her eye, "Beth if you dare walk out that door, I am coming after you and I can guarantee you won't like it if I do."

Her hand hovered uncertainly over the iron knob.

"I mean it Beth. I won't ever let you leave me."

Defeated, she dropped her head against the door. His words washed over her, cleansing the hurt deep inside. "Why? I only get in your way. I can't cook, sew or anything that matters out here." She turned back around tears still dangerously close. "I told you the first time we met the honest truth. I don't belong here."

He couldn't stay away any longer. Without thought he quickly crossed the room and gathered her up into his arms. By now even his own emotions were raw from the thought of losing her. "I couldn't let you go back then, and I can't now for the very same reason, Sweetheart. I happen to love you."

She looked up, wonder shining in her eyes, "What did you say?"

"I said, I love you. I guess I have since the moment I saw you step out of the middle of those brides, your large green eyes flashing fire at me. From somewhere deep inside, I found that I was determined to have you. Heaven help me, but I even love that stubborn pride of yours. And even if you are the worst cook I have ever met, you have to admit it is always an adventure to see what new concoction you come up with at night. Do you realize that when I walk through that door each and every day that I have absolutely no idea what is on the other side?"

"Maybe you should have stopped at I love you."

He brushed the back of a hand against her soft cheek and looked deeply into her eyes, "I love you Beth. Like it or not you are stuck with me. Do I make myself understood?"

She smiled and said simply, "I love you too." Then drawn to the warmth of his lips so close to her own, she reached up and pulled his head down to meet them.

Needing no further encouragement, Adam did what every part of him ached to do since she had walked in a few moments ago. He kissed her. Her lips. Her cute little nose. Her small slender neck. And he wanted more.

"Adam," her husky voice broke thought the haze.

"Yes," he whispered against her ear.

270

"Did you really go and see Jana this morning?"

He stopped, lifted his head and sighed. "What?"

Shakily pulling away, she repeated, "I asked if you visited Jana this morning."

"So," Adam began calmly, "let me see if I understand you correctly. You storm in here, announce our problems to every lumberjack within a five mile radius…and are prepared to leave me all because why? Because I went by the school house this morning! Do you realize how crazy that sounds?"

Eyes narrowing, she bristled at being called crazy. A faint blush came to her cheeks. No, she finally decided, he was just trying to push his guilt onto her and she had no intention of letting him avoid the question.

"So you admit it then."

Throwing his hands up, he stormed over to the desk and glared at her. "All right. I admit it. Now please explain to me since when did that become a crime?"

Refusing to be intimidated, she crossed her arms and glared right back. "Since Jana came into the store and announced to the entire town you visit her every single morning, that's when. Why she even said you actually apologized to her for your crazy wife stealing her things." She noticed her words hit their mark. Guilt was written all over his face. Or was that more the look he had when he wanted to throttle her?

"How could you confide in her about something so personal and dangerous? How could you tell her about my father's ring?"

Adam stood and slowly walked around the desk till it stood between them, then slammed his hands down, towering over her. "Think for a minute what you are saying. A woman, who is a known liar, comes to you and insinuates your husband is having an affair. Then tells you, no doubt in order to get you riled, that I apologize for a ring she must know you have."

She opened her mouth to defend herself. He dared her with furious eyes not to interrupt. She snapped it shut.

"But because I am your husband and live with you every day, I must be the one lying. Is that what you are telling me?"

She didn't feel half so brave with his large body only an arm's length away. Fighting to regain her shield of fury, she looked off to the side.

"Beth," he began, then seeing he wasn't getting through to her, sat down on the edge of the desk in an attempt to appear less intimidating. "Can't you see what she is trying to do?"

She hated it when he sounded so…so…reasonable.

Reaching up, he gently turned her face around to meet his. "I would never lie to you. I went over there to confront her. She must have gotten spooked, and when she saw you decided to get even."

Elizabeth's look of confusion twisted at his heart. "But it was the way she said it that sounded so convincing. If she knows I stole the ring and that you believe me, what happens now?"

His eyes met hers, "We wait."

Chapter 23

"I'm through arguing with you Beth, there is no way you are wearing that ridiculous hat anywhere."

So much for laying his life down for her.

"I most certainly am wearing this hat."

Watching as she limped across the room in search of a shoe, her hat bobbing on top of her head like some sort of circus act, he wondered what she could be thinking. Roughly stuffing in his starched white shirt, he shook his head in aggravation. Why on God's green earth would any woman want to wear such a contraption?

"Woman, you are trying my patience."

"What patience?"

His frown deepened. "I am being as patient as any man could be whose wife plans to wear a dead bird perched on top of her head. You're lucky I didn't mistake it for a live one and shoot it for you."

"Don't be silly." Exasperated and starting to feel a twinge of uneasiness about her choice in hats, she retorted, "For your information, this artistic creation in no way resembles a dead bird. Why, your reaction just shows how little you know about fashion. As a matter of fact, it is all the rage in Portland."

Dubiously Adam eyed the large hat in question. He looked it over from the large green feathers stuck with no apparent pattern in mind to the yellow lace threaded throughout before saying sarcastically, "And who told you that bunch of hogwash? The sales woman?"

Her angry blush answered his question.

"I rest my case."

Picking up a hair brush intending to throw it, she met his hard glare and thought better of it.

"Since you insist on going looking like that, I'll be waiting out in the wagon." He grabbed his jacket and string tie, "That is if you are still going in the wagon and not flying instead."

"Ohhh," now Elizabeth did fling the brush. It hit the door and slid down to rest serenely on the redwood floor.

The door popped open and Adam stuck his head inside, "Beth throwing things at me hardly changes the fact and is extremely childish." She picked up a hand mirror. Seeing he had pressed his luck, he quickly ducked back out and slammed the door behind him.

Elizabeth stomped her foot at his retreating form. Sometimes he really infuriated her. Why he had it in for her hat she couldn't fathom. Men.

Her eyes cut uneasily to the mirror.

Slowly tilting her hat a little to one side, she wrinkled up her nose. Moving in closer, she peered intently at her reflection.

"Oh, dear," she muttered. Horrified, she tried yet another angle; but nothing helped. Regardless of what she did her husband was right. It did resemble a big yellow bird flattened by a speeding wagon. For one sane moment she actually thought about taking the thing off but her pride wouldn't consent to such a treacherous idea. So resigned to her fate, she held her chin high and sincerely hoped it would get dark quickly. Like before they reached the dance quickly.

By the time their wagon pulled into the clearing alongside Christina's freshly painted one, Elizabeth was wishing badly for a way to remove her blame hat without Adam seeing her do it. And it certainly didn't help matters that all the way over Nicholas's eyes kept straying to her hat. She might have been able to endure that had it not been for the fighting off a pleading Chelsea, who only wanted, "to pet the birdie". A nervous wreck, Elizabeth let Adam lift her to the ground, her wide brim knocking him in the eye.

"Beth, what are you trying to do, blind me with that thing?"

"I'm not speaking to you."

Adam opened his mouth to reply, changed his mind, and then clamped it shut. "Fine."

"Fine." She retorted back, sailing past him.

Calmly watching the exchange, Nicholas commented, "Uncle Adam do you reckon she really likes that ugly ol' hat?"

Tipping his hat back in order to get a better view of his wife's angrily swaying backside, he shrugged, "There is no telling with that woman. But I imagine even if she doesn't, she'll split a gut convincing me otherwise."

Much as she feared, there was not one other woman there wearing a hat quite like hers. In fact, after facing a stammering Cornelia and flabbergasted Christina, Elizabeth knew beyond a doubt that the saleswoman in Portland must have been a con artist to have convinced her to buy the thing. Worrying her bottom lip, she felt conspicuous standing there with the bright yellow feathered article balanced on her head.

"Why, hello…Bootsie is that you?"

She would recognize that overly sweet voice anywhere. Jana.

Cornelia fluttered her hands in excitement, hoping for another confrontation. Christina on the other hand, inched in closer to Elizabeth for moral support. Or at least she tried to; the overly large hat prevented her from accomplishing her goal. Elizabeth swung her head around to face Jana and both women standing beside her dodged.

Jana looked lovely in a pale pink dress with delicate lace trimming along the modest bodice. Beside her Elizabeth felt gaudy and overdressed. Hannah who had been speaking to Maggie by the punch bowl took in Elizabeth's trapped expression and narrowed her eyes in displeasure. With a purposeful stride she headed straight for them coming up in time to hear Jana's insulting remark.

"Bootsie, how very – well, unusual you look tonight."

Instantly feeling a wave of irritation, Elizabeth clutched the cup in her trembling hand more tightly, turning to dismiss her. "Thank you."

Eyeing her nemesis's hat, Jana said pointedly, "Where ever did you find that hat?"

Stiffening at the obvious insult, she turned back around, an angry glint in her eye.

Hannah had seen enough. Pushing her way between them, she said rather gruffly, "What's wrong Jana? Wasn't that enough syrup to sweeten your disposition this morning?"

Instantly Christina choked on her lemonade, the image still fresh on her mind. Cornelia's eyes rounded in surprise, her thin hand reaching

275

up to cover her mouth. But the giggle she had been trying to stifle leaked out between bony fingers.

Whipping her head around, Jana said coldly, "I'm not certain, Hannah dear, but it sounds as if you just insulted me."

"Glad to know your hearing wasn't affected by your accident." Jana backed up a step as the big busted form towering over her demanded.

Elizabeth was too surprised to say anything. First, because she never thought she would live to see the day that Hannah of all people would actually come to her defense. And second because Jana for once seemed at a loss for words. If Hannah weren't so angry right now, Elizabeth might just be tempted to laugh at the whole unbelievable conversation. Was Hannah actually defending her hat?

"Well ladies, I hope I'm not interrupting anything."

All eyes turned his direction. Jana gave a disarming smile up at Adam. Her shoulders sagged in relief. "Of course not, we were just discussing fashion. I am sure it would bore you to no end. Is that the Virginia Reel they are playing?" Her smile broadened as her right foot began tapping in rhythm. "It's been years since I have tried my hand at one." Looking up at Adam expectantly, she waited for his invitation to dance.

Of all the nerve, thought Elizabeth. As if her husband would dance with someone else, especially... was he actually hesitating?

Taking in the watchful stares of the other women, not to mention the scorching one coming from his wife, he bent over the petite woman's hand, asking politely, "I would be more than happy to refresh your memory if you would allow me the pleasure."

His wife's green eyes were flashing with fury.

"That is unless my wife objects, of course."

From her furious look he assumed she did. Unperturbed, he smiled and winked at her.

She knew to refuse would make her appear jealous and petty. Who cared? She was jealous, and petty enough not to let that woman leave on her husband's arm.

Hannah held her breath. Cornelia twisted her handkerchief in a knot and waited expectedly for the explosion sure to come. Christina simply stared at the most dense man she'd ever met.

Elizabeth opened her mouth, perfectly prepared to explain exactly how much she minded. Unfortunately Adam didn't wait for her answer. Instead, he spun a pleased Jana toward the makeshift dancing floor.

She stomped her foot, before slamming her cup down on the long table holding the refreshments. Punch went everywhere. Taking in the shocked looks of sympathy on the other women's faces it was nearly her undoing. This night was going from bad to worse. If she stood there one more moment she was likely to burst into tears.

Reaching up, she tore the bothersome hat from her head, giving it a scathing look as if it alone were responsible for husband's treachery. Forcing herself to refrain from flinging it into the trees where it belonged, she managed to quell the look of murder still lurking in her eyes, remarking stiffly, "Excuse me. I believe I will go check on Chelsea."

The women watched in disbelief as the hottest tempered woman they had ever met, walked off from what amounted to nothing less than grounds for murder. Christina found her voice first. "Why didn't she do something?"

Hannah watched the spirited young woman in question walk towards the woods for some much needed privacy. In a voice filled with pity she replied, "I'm afraid the girl's too heartbroken."

Relieved that Bootsie had acted sensibly for a change, Cornelia confided, "Personally, I find it refreshing that Bootsie finally accepted what is common knowledge to the rest of us."

"And what," asked Hannah in a dangerous voice, "is common knowledge?"

Feeling flustered, Cornelia stuttered, ""Why, that Adam is quite taken with Jana of course. Not that I condone it you understand, but perhaps if Bootsie were not so…you know…unstable," she whispered, "I might find Adam's actions more disgraceful."

"You are nearly as big an idiot as he is," Hannah remarked, thoroughly disgusted with the tittering woman.

Turning to leave with Christina in search of their friend, neither woman gave Cornelia so much as a nod farewell. In response, the put upon woman sniffed irritably at being deserted. Apparently Christina and Hannah were becoming just as unreasonable as Bootsie lately. Tilting her head to get a better view of the dance floor, she slowly put her cup down beside Bootsie's. What were those two talking about out there? Maybe she should find Edward and see if he wanted to dance. It could prove interesting.

Trying to ignore Cornelia's penetrating stare, he failed to notice Jana moving her body in closer to him. In response, Cornelia's neck strained up over her husband's shoulder to get a better view. Feeling uncomfortable, Adam shifted, firmly placing Jana a safer distance away.

Out of the corner of his eye he noticed that busy body of a woman dragging her dance partner ever nearer their position on the floor. He cleared his throat, and tried to concentrate on his real purpose for dancing with Jana in the first place. Deftly turning them around until his back was to Cornelia's, he informed her, "I had a meeting with Michael the other day."

Cornelia blinked her eyes as if trying to hear better, "Edward, Edward, did Adam say something about a meeting in two days?"

"Cornelia, would you please stop dancing on my foot?"

Caught up in her mission, she spun around and bumped into Adam's back.

Exasperated, Adam ground out, "Is there a particular reason you are following me around on this dance floor?"

Cornelia huffed. "Don't be ridiculous. Fine. I'll move."

"Thank you."

Turning his attention back to Jana he continued, "It seems Michael thought you might know a lawyer by the name of Rawlings. Do you?"

"Never heard of him." From the way she stiffened in his arms, he knew she was lying.

Cornelia stopped dancing, her mouth hanging open. In a loud whisper, she demanded of her husband, "You heard it too didn't you? No use denying it. I know you did."

Edward only hoped it was the dance ending.

"Can you believe he actually said he was falling in love with her right her on the dance floor?"

Skeptical, her bone thin husband answered honestly, "As a matter of fact, no, Cornelia, I can't. Now let's get out of here and get a plate of food. I'm starving."

Not daunted in the least, she got a determined gleam in her eye. She couldn't wait to tell Hannah.

Glad to have the noisy woman out of the way, Adam continued, "He also seems to think you are not who you say you are."

Her laugh came out sounding rather strained, "Don't be ridiculous. You know how Michael loves to torment me. Now could we please talk about something else besides that awful man?"

He was getting nowhere.

Failing to accomplish anything this entire dance, except wishing it was Beth he held instead of the conniving blond, he wondered how much longer it would take a soused Smitty to realize he had repeated the same verse for the third time now.

"I have to admit, I'm becoming insulted Adam," pouted Jana prettily.

Adam worked on erasing the bored frown from his face, "Oh?"

"Apparently you aren't enjoying yourself. Whether it's me or this awful song, I haven't quite decided."

Not bothering to deny the truth of her words, he began looking around for his wife. Where did she take off to? The last time he remembered seeing her, she was talking to Michael.

"Jana, I hate to break off our dance, but...."

"Isn't that Bootsie dancing with Michael? I wonder whatever became of her lovely hat."

Following Jana's gaze till it rested on his much too radiant wife. He frowned. Then deftly steering Jana in the direction of the other couple, he seemed completely unaware they were playing a waltz, his long legs carrying them quickly across the dance floor.

Breathless from being dragged, Jana placed a hand to her racing heart. "Adam, I don't think...," she started to say.

He snatched up her hand and gave chase once again as the couple he was in pursuit of retreated farther away from them. By the time he finally caught up with blessedly ignorant couple, his eyes were literally boring a hole into Michael's back. It didn't take Jana long to realize Adam certainly wasn't acting like a man not in love with his wife, and two that he was a terrible dancer.

At last catching up with his prey, Adam tried to gain the attention of his wife.

She noticed him all right. But instead of stopping she moved in closer to Michael and did three graceful turns in a well thought out evasion.

Irritated now, Adam didn't even pretend to dance, but stood directly in her path demanding, "What do you think you're doing?"

Furious, Elizabeth tossed her head and purposely chose to ignore him. Michael on the other hand, tried to let go of her hand. She wasn't having it and clutched it to the point he actually flinched. When her husband refused to budge, she remarked coolly, "I am dancing if you don't mind."

"I know that," he gripped Jana's hand tighter, causing her to desperately try and remove it, "And I suppose you are unaware that dancing that closely to my ex foreman is creating a scene?"

Michael raised an eyebrow at the word "ex".

"The only one making a scene is you," she hissed back.

Jana started to object even before Adam picked her up, feet dangling in the air and marched over to his escaping wife. He then dropped her none too gently on the ground. Tapping Michael aggressively on the shoulder, he stated, "I believe this is my dance."

Shrugging confusedly, Michael fully intended to hand her over, but Elizabeth refused to let go of his hand. Stomping her foot in protest she practically shouted, "This is not your dance, I already have a partner, thank you."

"Well, you have the wrong one," ground out Adam as he smoothly removed her from Michael, before spinning Jana into the now vacant spot. Jana looked livid. While Elizabeth, on the other hand turned beat red sure that every eye in the place was looking their direction.

"I hope you are happy," she spat out, "you are embarrassing me."

"I'm downright ecstatic, I assure you."

She jerked at her hand, trying to pull away from her insane husband. He responded by slamming her up against his hard chest. Bending down, he whispered in her ear, "Cut it out Sweetheart, or I just might have to really embarrass you."

A shiver of pleasure went through her treacherous body, reacting at once to his warm breath in her ear. She couldn't believe that after being deserted for another woman, his touch still had the power to unnerve her. She was absolutely hopeless.

Smitty finally stopped singing, but only because he had to pause in order to stuff another wad of tobacco in his jaw. A sly grin on his face, Charles slapped Smitty heartily on the back. To which the scrawny old man commenced hacking and coughing in response. Fist turning a ghastly shade of green, then white as the wad he'd been chewing made its slow way down his tight windpipe and into his protesting stomach.

With Smitty out of the picture, Charles lifted his fiddle and commenced playing a livelier tune, starting boots stomping and skirts swirling.

"Adam, I want to go home now."

Adam curled a finger affectionately under her chin, trying to make amends for ruining her evening. "Now sweetheart, it can't be as bad as all that. If you promise not to drive your husband insane with jealously, I'll try to curb the urge to knock out any man who comes near you, senseless. Feel better?"

A tiny glimmer of a smile touched her lips, "Not particularly."

"No?"

"The only thing that would make me feel better is if Jana choked on some of Smitty's tobacco," she said sweetly.

"You, my love, are not very understanding."

281

Looking into her twinkling green eyes, he gently reached up and cradled her face in his hands. Ever so slowly, he bent his lips towards hers.

"Log Rolling Contest," bellowed a stout logger behind them.

The spell broken, Adam looked down and grinned, "Why is it now that we are truly man and wife, everyone is determined to interrupt our kissing? Yet, when I have a crazy woman to contend with, there isn't a soul in sight?"

Shrugging with false sympathy, she advised, "I'm sure I couldn't tell you."

"Yet, all I can think about right now is how much I wish it were more than kissing we were doing at the moment. On second thought, maybe going home isn't such a bad idea."

She answered by interrupting his complaining by wrapping her arms around him and finishing the kiss he had begun.

Chapter 24

A short time later, Adam and Elizabeth, hand in hand, headed towards the large crowd gathering at the river. Chelsea was running in front of them giggling with excitement. They were nearly too late, for already the men known as 'river pigs' were perched in pairs on thick logs scattered out haphazardly in the river.

Elizabeth edged in closer as Adam picked up his squealing niece and commented, "This should be some contest. You should see them at the job, Beth. Separating the logs as they are tossed into the river, and then sending them on their way as if it weren't very possible that they could be crushed in the process. One misstep could mean their lives, or at the very least maiming."

"But they look so confident."

"They have to be."

Observing they two men ribbing each other, it was hard to imagine the daily danger they put themselves in. Just in the short time she had been here one man, Dugger, had found himself crippled. Another nearly drowned just two days ago.

A gun went off beside her. Now laughing and joking, they pitched this life depending skill against each other for less serious purposes. The men began their graceful execution of spinning the log as quickly as possible, without losing their footing and getting drenched in the process. One by one the men toppled off their logs, until only two remained still running an endless race with an invisible foe.

Jackson she recognized, only because she knew Michael cared little for the man. If it weren't for his expertise, she felt certain they would be one man short in the river come spring. Yet, even now his rough face was beaded up in concentration, his legs working up to a constant rhythm. Then in a manner of minutes, he seemed to actually become part of the log itself.

Awed, Elizabeth noticed the other remaining man as he looked up for just an instant with a cocky grin at the admiring crowd. Just as a man could easily lose his life in a split second, the young man's eyes widened in disbelief, as arms shooting wide in a vain attempt to regain his balance he started to fall. Grabbing only air on his way down, his log's momentum sent him flying backwards into the waiting river.

The crowd cheered.

The other man gone, Jackson expertly slowed down the log's spinning to a slow roll. With more grace than a ballerina, he then began to show off his skill. Turning front first, then back, he proved it was no stroke luck that had won him the victory. Elizabeth wondered what her friends back East would think of such a talent. She was certain very little.

Feeling Adam's warm hand give hers a squeeze, she turned and studied the handsome man who was her husband now. He belonged here in this untamed land. This was his place in the world, anywhere else and he would just be one ordinary man among hundreds. Here, he shone. She on the other hand, couldn't even choose a sensible hat here.

The rest of the evening was so full of sack races, horseshoes and laughter, so that even her doubts about belonging here could not compete. But she did feel better about one thing. Since deserting her on the dance floor, Adam ignored Jana completely. This would have suited Elizabeth fine except for Jana's looks of hatred which were starting to make her uncomfortable.

Nevertheless, Elizabeth happily basked in Adam's strong teasing presence the rest of the day. In fact, many a time she found herself removing his straying hand from its roving. Evening quickly rolled in as a tired and contented Elizabeth put a cranky Chelsea to sleep in the makeshift bed the other women had made for the smaller children. Since her time to watch them was still an hour away, she strolled outside in the cold crisp night with the stars overhead glowing with a gentle light, as music drifted towards her. It had been a nice day. Peacefully humming the music, she climbed into the wagon to get an extra blanket for Chelsea.

"Hey, Beautiful, how about a dance under the stars?"

Love shining in her eyes at the huge man leaning against the wagon, she answered with a heartfelt, "I would like that very much."

Standing as she waited expectantly for Adam to lift her out of the wagon, her heart skipped a beat as his strong hands circled her waist.

Lifting her out, he slid her seductively down his hard lean body. Instantly a spark of desire ignited between them. Elizabeth physically shook in response to it. He stilled her descent, and eyes meeting in mutual understanding, her lips shyly touched his.

His eyes darkened, "I want you, Beth."

She certainly didn't need more of an invitation that that. Her right hand coming up from its resting place on his arm gently caressed the strong line of his jaw.

"I want you, too," she admitted softly.

Taking her lips in a kiss that melted the world around them to some far off place, he skillfully continued to touch her in such a way that they were both left breathless. His efforts to take things slow disappeared with the reality that she wanted him as fiercely as he did her. Gathering a handful of silky hair, his mouth became even more insistent against her now swollen lips.

"Oh, there you two are."

Recognizing Jana's sarcastic tone, Elizabeth tried to pull away, but instead of releasing her, Adam calmly settled her next to his side. A causal arm wrapped possessively around her.

"Can we help you with something in particular?" Adam's voice still husky from their embrace caused Elizabeth to blush.

The young woman's big blue eyes widened in feigned innocence, "Oh, dear, I hope I haven't interrupted anything."

"What did you need," Adam asked again gruffly.

Appearing hurt by his brisk question, she blinked back invisible tears. "Why, I don't need anything. Nicholas asked me to find Bootsie for him. It seems…well…several of the boys decided to go…swimming." She hesitated in embarrassment before continuing, "Obviously because of a dare of some sort. Anyway, he seems to have misplaced his clothes. He wondered if Bootsie might have brought a change of clothes for him."

Elizabeth smiled to herself at the age old trick of taking off with someone's clothes and leaving them stranded. "Yes, I do, but maybe Adam should…"

"Oh, he specifically asked for you," she broke in, "I think he was embarrassed to face his Uncle. I imagine he feels rather foolish right now."

"I imagine he does. Regardless, I'll take him the clothes."

"No, Adam, I don't mind. Really."

He started to object, but Elizabeth was already digging out the clothing articles he needed, "Don't be silly. I'll just be a moment. Besides," she added, "don't you remember what it felt like to eight years old and having to be rescued by someone you admire?"

Adam looked mutinous, but held his tongue.

Reaching up to peck him on the cheek, she whispered, "Remember where we left off." Then receiving a swat on her backside, she went to rescue what she was sure to be, one shriveled up eight year old.

After walking for what seemed like the whole length of the river and still not finding Nicholas, she became worried. She was now far enough away from the party that the only music she heard came from frogs and crickets.

"Nicholas!" She called out yet again, her voice breaking the eerie stillness of the night.

Memories of Chelsea lost in the cave caused her voice to tremble with remembered panic. "Nicholas, where are you?"

"Here I am."

Confused why his voice would be overhead, she shouted up to him, "Whatever are you doing up there?"

Straining to pierce the darkness with her uncooperative eyes, she still couldn't make him out. The only thing visible was the steep hill before her looming dark and forbidding.

"Nicholas?"

A small shadowy form stepped out from behind a big pile of what must be cut timber. Put out that Nicholas apparently meant for her to climb up after him, she never even noticed the loud snap of a rope until it was too late.

"Bootsie, watch out!"

Elizabeth didn't hear anything else as the rumbling noise intensified to a loud roar and an avalanche of logs began thundering its way towards her at a breakneck speed. A scream froze solid in her throat. She tried to move her feet, only to find she could only stand there in transfixed fear as the logs, picking up speed, bore down on her. Their path of destruction sure, a million things went through her mind. Most important of all was that Nicholas was safe. She whispered a prayer for him and waited to die.

"Beth!" Adam practically roared her into life.

Gaining her senses, she turned towards his voice and was sent flying sideways by a heavy objet thrown against her. Her mind took a moment to register the fact that the object was Adam. The two of them rolled over and over coming to rest against a rock ledge.

Reacting quickly, Adam shoved her under it in order to use it for a shield. Then suddenly she felt the weight of his large body completely covering her own in a further effort to shield her from the logs forthcoming assault. It seemed like hours that she lay there underneath him, feeling his body jerk occasionally with the impact of a stray rock, or limb. Amazingly it was really all over in a manner of minutes.

Oddly enough, it was the total quiet that made her aware that the danger had past. Slowly Adam rolled off her shaking form. Without uttering a word to her, his hands went deftly over every inch of her. No doubt he was checking for cuts, broken ribs or other damage. She would have reassured him, had she been able to find her voice.

Finding no real damage, he searched the darkness around them, asking, "Are you all right?"

She was shaking like a leaf and the tears were starting to come. She bit her bottom lip and nodded.

"I'll be right back. Don't move from this spot." When she did not answer, he made her look at him, "Beth, do you hear me?"

"Yes, but Adam where…" her voice trailed off when she realized he wasn't listening. Already he was half way up the steep hill, and before she could realize why, he had disappeared into the darkness.

Michael was the first to reach her. She noted his worried expression, yet his voice was calm and soothing. "Are you all right? You could have been killed."

"Yes, but I'm worried about Adam. He could be hurt. Would you please go find him for me?"

"Which direction did he go?"

Shaking the cobwebs from her mind, she tried to remember, "Up towards where the logs were stacked. I think."

"Don't worry, I'll find him."

She gave a grateful look as he took off in search of her husband. In a manner of minutes the whole party descended on her. Christina ran up, embracing her. "Oh, Bootsie, you gave us all such a fright."

Then from out of nowhere a full glass appeared in her hand, "Drink that down lass, it'll calm your nerves a wee bit."

Obeying mindlessly, Elizabeth nearly choked on the burning liquid eating away at her insides. "What is this stuff?"

Maggie winked, "Just a wee bit of Smitty's moonshine."

Wrinkling up her nose, Elizabeth gingerly tasted it again, and then placed it on the ground as far away as possible. "No wonder he can't remember the words to a song."

Hannah roared with laughter. "Honey, truer words were never spoken."

The true reality of what happened didn't hit Elizabeth until the Michael came back and carried her to the clearing. She insisted she could walk, but was grateful he didn't listen to her. She was still shaking uncontrollably. She still couldn't believe that someone would try to kill her and very nearly did. She assumed it must have been Rawlings, but one memory kept creeping into her mind, that of Nicholas' shadowy form calling out a warning to her. Even now she noticed how he carefully avoided meeting her eyes, his face looking pale and drawn.

Adam soon found his way to the clearing and she wanted to burst out in tears of relief. He was okay. She noticed he kept his right arm cradled to his body but he looked as strong as ever. And he looked furious. Gaining her attention, he asked again, "Beth, are you certain you didn't see anything? No matter how insignificant it could be important."

Should she tell what she knew about Nicholas? It sounded crazy. Surely he didn't have anything to do with trying to kill her? She searched out Nicholas, whose panic stricken eyes shot over the crowd to Jana's face. Unbelievably, the beautiful woman sternly shook her head as he opened his mouth to speak. Then wiping at the sweat on his brow, he looked off, burying his hands in his pockets.

No doubt certain of his silence, she watched as Jana slipped quietly away into the shadows of the cool, dark night. Elizabeth watched the play of emotion on Nicholas' face. He was really frightened of something, or someone. She knew the right thing to do was to tell Adam what she knew, that Nicholas and Jana, not Rawlings tried to kill her tonight. Still, she couldn't make herself say the awful words. It was as if by not saying it, somehow kept it from being true.

Her chest tightened with pain. How he must hate her to do such a thing.

Still waiting for her answer, Adam was becoming increasingly suspicious of her long silence. "I asked you a question, Beth."

"No. Nothing. I told you, I was looking for Nicholas when I heard a noise overhead. By the time I realized what was happening, it was too late." Real tears gathered in her eyes. "I'm so sorry Adam. I wish I could help, but I can't."

Gruffly Adam hugged her to him, "It's okay, Sweetheart. It's not your fault and it's not you I am angry at. I promised to protect you and I failed. What's worse is whoever did this is warned and won't take any more chances. They won't care if it looks like an accident or not next time. I should never have let you go off like that alone."

Turning to Michael, he ordered, "Do me a favor and find our Miss Logan. There are a few things I'd like her to clear up for me. Like, for instance, who cut those ropes? I'll meet you and Jana at the schoolhouse after I take Beth and the kids home."

Elizabeth laid a trembling hand against his massive chest and asked shakily, "Adam, are you certain it wasn't an accident? I mean, suppose someone didn't mean to cause those logs to fall. Couldn't that be possible?"

Perplexed by her pleading tone, he studied her hopeful expression. It was then he knew the truth. She was protecting someone. His eyes narrowed in anger when he realized she must have lied about not seeing anything. And if she lied about that, what else was she not telling him?

He removed her hand with a punishing grip, answering her question in a clear, cold voice. "It wasn't an accident."

Then to make certain she heard every word, he drew her closer. So close that his words blew hot against her face. "Beth, those ropes were cut in two. Whoever cut them knew exactly what they were doing. They meant to kill you."

Chapter 25

They never found Jana.

To make matters worse Adam was withdrawn and angry. Although he had not questioned her further about the 'accident', his accusing eyes told her he knew she was lying. But how could she possibly confide the truth to him? How angry would he be to know that his own nephew wished her dead?

Quietly she poured the flapjacks onto the already hot griddle, watching them bubble. When would all this end? Did she have to live the rest of her life never knowing when the next 'accident' might occur? She flipped the flap jacks, stealing a glance at the somber boy seated at the wooden table. He sat with his chin propped in the palm of one hand, toying with the fork on the table.

Adam came up beside her, silently filling their plates. She watched his strong hands load the plates with the precision she had grown to love. When his hand accidentally brushed against hers, she felt an uncontrollable urge to beg him to hold her. Never before had Elizabeth felt so alone.

The tension between them was a bittersweet thing. On one hand, her heart ached from the blow of his indifference. Yet, on the other, it was a small price to pay. Anything was better if it meant one more moment with him. The object of her thoughts bent down to kiss Chelsea's curly head. She drank in the way his hair fell carelessly across his forehead, refusing to be tamed. The way his eyes lit up when Chelsea reached up grubby hands to hug him.

When he came to get Nicholas's plate, she unconsciously reached up to brush the lock of dark hair out of his eyes. His frown stilled her hand in midair. She brought it back down, hurt and confused.

"Beth, I have to go in this morning, but I'll be back by lunch." He heaved a sigh, turning around to face her, "I want you to pack a few things. I think it would be wiser if you stayed with Sullivan and Maggie for a couple of days."

Her heart in her throat, she managed, "Pack?"

"Stop looking at me like that. It's just till this whole thing blows over."

"But…"

"No buts, Beth," he interrupted, agitated by her nearness and the look of betrayal in her eyes. "You saw what happened last night. Do you think it will stop just because whoever tried to kill you failed?"

"Adam, listen to me." She was more frightened to be away from him right now than of dying. "Even you should realize what a mistake that would be, last night's accident happened while the whole town was just a few feet away. Please, I feel safer here with you," she added quietly.

He was barely managing to refrain himself from gathering her frightened, beautiful body into his arms. Instead he reached out, tenderly rubbing a thumb along her cheek. "You know I'm right about this. I can't protect you here. I have to work."

The sound of his deep voice consoled and comforted her. She closed her eyes in defeat. He was right. Alone out here she was an easy target.

"All right, Adam."

Seeing his spirited wife so beaten brought out all his protective instincts. He didn't know who he was angrier at, her for lying to him or himself for it not making a difference. He gave a grim smile. "Well, sweetheart, I'd better get going. Christina should be here any minute. Last night I asked Michael to send her over this morning. I just don't feel good about leaving you by yourself."

His words managed to chase away some of the gloom hovering over her. "To be honest, I will feel better having Christina here."

"Bye, Papa", called out Chelsea cheerfully, oblivious to the two grownups staring into each other's eyes.

Pulling his eyes away from hers, Adam answered gruffly, "Bye, angel. Be good today." Then passing Nicholas' chair on the way out, he placed a hand on his shoulder, "Nicholas."

The small boy jumped guiltily. "Yes, sir?"

"Would you hitch up the wagon and have it ready by lunch?"

292

Letting out a pent up breath, he sounded relieved when he said, "Oh, yeah, sure."

Still uneasy about leaving them, but unable to think of any more excuses, Adam took his hat off the wall.

"Adam?"

He turned back around.

"You forgot to kiss me goodbye."

Unable to resist the soft plea, he strode back and held her close. "Beth, I have to know the truth. Why won't you tell me sweetheart?"

She shook her head. She could never allow herself to betray Nicholas that way. Today she would find out what was going on and then she would confide the truth to him. In order to avoid it for now, she anxiously captured his lips to hers. Ending all talk of secrets. Silent demands that he trust her…love her.

Never able to withstand the desire her touch evoked, Adam answered her need. He kissed her in a way that left both of them weak and shaken from the emotion behind it. For a long time afterwards he held her against him enjoying the feel and the smell of her. Then reluctantly, he turned to go.

This time Elizabeth didn't call him back.

Elizabeth stopped to put the laundry basket in the wagon and was rewarded with a rear end collision. This was the second time in two minutes he had slammed into her.

"Nicholas, what are you doing?"

He shrugged and backed up a step.

She shook her head. Considering that it looked like he intended her bodily harm last night, his actions were somewhat confusing today. The boy had been dogging her steps all morning long. "Well, would you please stop hovering?"

Nicholas gave her an exasperated look and ran a hand through his hair, reminding her of Adam when he got frustrated. "Look, Bootsie, you don't understand."

Watching him closely, she hoped he would finally tell her what he was doing up on that hill. "What don't I understand, Nicholas?"

Nicholas looked about ready to confess when Chelsea let out a – "I'm little and I need some help" – scream. Refusing to be sidetracked, Elizabeth gripped Nicholas' shoulders. "I don't understand what?"

Unable to look her I the eye, he bit his bottom lip. Then, apparently deciding against confession, he shrugged, "Aw, nothing. I guess I just thought maybe you could use some company."

"I give up," she muttered. "Why don't you go do something useful, like save Christina from your sister?"

Inside the house a short time later, Elizabeth kept drifting off, lost in thought. Totally ignoring the young woman beside her and the mess she was making out of the handwork in her lap, she went over last night one last time. The more she thought about it, the more convinced she became that Nicholas had not meant to kill her. Why else would he have called out a warning? Or for that matter, why try to protect her so adamantly today? Putting the tangled knots down Christina tried to convince her were tatting, she got up to look out the window. It was drizzling again. She should go get the clothes from the line. But then again, the sun was doing battle with the clouds. Maybe she should wait a few minutes.

"Tatting is supposed to relax you." Christina remarked with a sigh, laying her own tatting down and joining her at the window.

Elizabeth barely nodded, her attention now caught to the small figure hurrying towards the barn. Nicholas was up to something.

"Bootsie, are you listening?"

She strained her eyes through the thick glass, trying to see what he was carrying. Her eyes widened before letting the curtain fall back into place. It was his squirrel gun.

Christina lay a hand on her shoulder, "Bootsie, is something wrong?"

She had to see what he was doing.

Turning to her worried friend, she ignored the question, "Christina, could you watch Chelsea for me? Just for a few minutes. I have to check on something in the barn."

"The barn? I don't know, Bootsie," Christina answered uncertainly. "Adam said not to let you take off anywhere."

"Honestly, Christina," she scoffed on her way out the door, "I'm only going to the barn. I hardly think that would be considered taking off, do you?"

"Well, no, but –"

"Thanks Christina. Don't worry, I'll be right back." Her promise was an afterthought, for the moment her feet touched the porch, she took off at a dead run.

"Wait! Bootsie, listen to me a minute."

The empty doorway ended any further appeals.

Moaning, Christina hurried over to the window, peering anxiously outside. Bootsie had just reached the barn. She paused only long enough to look back over one shoulder then she squeezed through the doors and disappeared inside.

Christina stomped her foot in frustration, "Oh, that girl never listens to a thing I say."

"Land sakes, Cornelia, would you slow down just one minute and listen to me."

The thin woman in question stopped dragging a protesting Hannah and began tapping her foot impatiently, "Okay, I'm listening."

Hannah barley had a chance to open her mouth, much less say what she wanted, before Cornelia jerked her forward and commenced dragging. "Now hurry up or we won't catch them in the act," she confided with a certain excited glee.

Fed up, Hannah stubbornly planted her feet on the ground just a few feet from the wagon. That's it, Cornelia. I refuse to go one step further until you explain yourself."

A stream of brown spittle nearly landed smack dab on Hanna's polished shoe.

She spun around to find the party responsible. Smitty sat propped up on a stool not far away, whittling away at a new pipe. He paused. Then bending over, he spit towards the street once again. Hannah's eyes narrowed in disgust, "Watch where you are spitting old man!"

Smitty raised bleary eyes to the heavy set woman yelling at him and spit a new stream, just missing her stocky frame. Hannah put hands on amble hips and started for him.

Cornelia turned her back around, "We don't have time for him. We have more important things to do. I told you, they are meeting today and we have to do something about it."

"Who is?"

Heaving a sigh, she explained, her eyes darting longingly towards the wagon, "Adam and Jana, who else?"

Smitty, only half listening before, perked up at the mention of Adam's name. Did she say something about a meeting?

Hannah shook her head in confusion, "Where are they supposed to meet Cornelia? You're not making any sense."

"The schoolhouse, of course," she huffed in frustration. Then noticing Smitty leaning in closer to listen in, she lowered her voice to a confiding whisper. "There is less of a chance for them to be found out there. Don't you see? We have to catch – I mean – stop them. For Bootsie's sake, of course."

Smitty scratched at the day old growth on his unshaven face then shook a finger in one ear. Did that old biddy say Adam's having a secret meeting today at the school house? He puffed her chest out with indignant pride. Well, if those interfering old woman could go to Adam's meeting, then he'd be hanged if he couldn't.

Within moments of his decision, he saw the women's wagon leave in a cloud of dust. Smitty shoved on a hat and followed. It only took a second to mount his sway backed mule and kick her into a trot. Yes siree, he was going to that there meeting come hail or high water.

Nicholas was leaving out the back when Elizabeth slipped into the barn, a grim but determined look on his young face. Curious, Elizabeth

296

followed, the whole time making sure to stay far enough back that he wouldn't see her. They crossed a stream behind the horse pen and found the familiar path through the woods grown over with briars and wild flowers. She shivered as the drizzle dampened her skin and her fragile hope that Nicolas wasn't a part of the attempt on her life. His small frame before her was soon swallowed up in the shadowy forest ahead. Clutching her arms for warmth, she didn't' immediately follow. There was no need, for she knew where he was going.

The schoolhouse.

Chapter 26

When she reached the clearing she noticed there were four horses tied up outside the school house. Too late she realized her mistake. Jana wasn't alone. In all likelihood had never been in this alone. For she now knew that the only logical explanation was that she and Rawlings were in this together. It explained so much; the note, Jan's sly insinuations and even Nicholas.

Speaking of which, where was he?

Nerves caused a tightening in her stomach as she raced for the edge of the meadow, making sure to stay low and hidden. What she saw once there, made her legs go weak. In froze horror she watched as Nicholas, gun in hand, and headed straight for the schoolhouse. He crouched under a window, peeked inside, then not finding what he was looking for, darted forward. She had to do something and quick.

Frantically her mind began searching for options. She didn't dare scream, or Rawlings might discover Nicholas. However, if she went for help, Nicholas might be dead by the time she got back. No, her only hope lay in reaching him first and trying to talk some sense into him.

So, with heart pounding in her ears, she raced forward. The whole time praying fervently that Rawlings was either blind or deaf. It seemed the only way they would ever get out of this alive.

"I suggest you cooperate, Miss Stokes. Believe me; I have nothing to lose in killing you."

Rawling's voice sent chills up Elizabeth's spine. Not able to stop herself, she eased up over the windowsill just in time to see Jana rise to her feet. A huge man, missing most of his front teeth, appeared out of nowhere and shoved her back down into the chair.

"I never wanted to be a partner to murder, you know that."

"Oh, yes, I almost forgot. Villainy with ethics, how quaint."

An unexpected gasp escaped Elizabeth. Rawlings stood with his back to her, lazily twirling a silver revolver in one hand. He was real after all. Dangerously so. "And now tell me, Miss Stokes, just what did you intend I do with the lady in question? Invite her to tea?"

His humorless chuckle sent chills down her spine. She had to get Nicholas away from here. Dropping to her knees, she crawled towards the front door. Praying she wasn't too late. However as she rounded the corner, she spotted him. His small gun cocked and shoved into his right shoulder, he was shakily reaching out to turn the handle of the door.

"Nicholas! No!"

Without thought, she ran forward to stop him. Both of them were so lost in possession of the gun that they never even noticed the door handle click open. Since they were shoved up against the door, they could only tumble forward as an unseen hand swung it wide. As they lay there from their helpless position on the floor, the sound of Nicholas' gun as it slide across polished wood was deafening.

Rawlings stepped out of the shadows, one corner of his mouth turned up in a pleased smirk. Slowly he bent down and picked up the gun at his feet. Without hesitation he threw it across the room to his partner. "Why, hello Miss Brown, it seems we meet again."

Her eyes remained glued to the shiny barrel pointed at her chest. Finally, she forced herself to look up at the man who had took everything from her and now threatened the only things left that mattered. He would not destroy her family. She wouldn't let him. Bravely, she glared back and lied through her teeth. "Adam will be here any minute. If you let us go now maybe you can still escape."

He raised an eyebrow along with the gun and tapped the barrel thoughtfully against his forehead. "Ah, yes. Isn't he that lumber jack who keeps getting in the way of my killing you? Tsk, tsk, Elizabeth. I am disappointed in your lack of imagination. After all, I hardly think he would send you and our young friend here ahead of him, now would he?"

Grabbing an arm, he jerked her to her feet and pushed her towards down into a chair next to Jana. "Martin, tie her up and the boy, too."

Nicholas scrambled to his feet, his fists swinging wildly. Rawlings placed a bored hand on top of Nicholas's head, holding him a safe distance away as his skinny arms kept making wide arcs through the air. "Martin, it seems our young friend here desires your services."

"Let us go mister or I'll let you have it."

"You really are a tedious little boy. First you change your mind about helping me and now these terrible threats. I ask you ladies, what are young people coming to these days?"

Her fury barely contained, Elizabeth lifted from her chair, "Take your hands off him this instant."

"My, my," he stared in mock shock, "Don't tell me you actually care what happens to this tiresome child, especially after he tried to kill you last night."

Nicholas struggled even harder, "That's a lie! I didn't know you were gonna cut that rope."

Avoiding Nicholas's eyes, Elizabeth's voice was more uncertain. "That doesn't change the fact that he is still only eight years old. If you let him go, I promise to do anything you say."

Rawlings shoved the boy towards his silent companion, "My dear misguided woman, and you seem to have forgotten who is in control here. You have nothing to bargain with. Now sit down."

Slowly she sank down, really frightened now. Martin, having finished tying Nicholas, pulled her arms painfully around behind the chair and wrapped a coarse piece of rope around her wrists. Disgusted he walked away, rubbing his bitten arm and limping slightly from the solid kick Nicholas landed to his shin. "All done, Boss."

"Good. Now see if there could possibly be any more people you overlooked out there."

Elizabeth tried to gain Jana's help with a silent plea. When their eyes met, she saw a trace of despair in the young woman's eyes. It was soon replaced by a resigned indifference as she raised her chin and looked away.

"What do you plan to do with us?" Elizabeth's voice was so choked with fear that it came out more a whisper.

He walked over and lifted her face up towards his, then said with false regret. "Why Elizabeth, I will be forced to kill you of course."

She jerked her head out of his hands. "And Nicholas?"

Studying her a moment, he took in her softened features, long thick hair and gentle curves. Sighing he admitted, "You've changed. It seems frontier life becomes you. Too bad." His eyes hardened. "He dies with you."

"It must be hard to sleep at night with a conscious like yours."

"The man has no conscious. Anyone can see that." Jana broke her silence with such obvious dislike that it saturated every word.

"You wound me Miss Stokes. And this coming from a woman prepared to steal another's husband."

Flushing, she nevertheless admitted, "At least I'm honest with myself. It has always been greed guiding my actions. But, murder? That takes something even I don't possess, Rawlings."

He placed his gun under one arm and started clapping, "How dramatic Miss Stokes. Only you seem to have forgotten, that it is you that made all this possible." Her angry blush caused a low chuckle to rumble in his chest. "How very disappointing you have turned out to be. I had such high hopes for you. I might even have taken you with me, but your attitude makes that quite impossible. And I think we know what that means, don't we 'Annie'?"

At mention of her fate Jana shrank away, her face drained of all color.

"I thought you might."

Unbelievably, at that moment, Elizabeth saw Smitty's head pop up outside the window. Hope exploded in her chest, and then quickly turned to panic when Smitty raised a hand to knock on the window pane. Frantically she shook her head at him. He squinted his eyes and rubbed a little harder on the glass, no doubt trying to see better. Finally with a frown and wrinkling up his already weathered face, he blessedly lowered his hand, moving out of sight just before Rawlings turned to sit down.

Resting a hip on one of the desks, Rawlings crossed his arms loosely in front of him. His calculating eyes missing nothing, including the skinny shadow dodging back and forth outside the window.

Elizabeth broke out in a cold sweat and desperately tried to divert Rawlings attention from the window. "I don't understand any of this Rawlings. Why come back for me at all. Why take the risk?"

Rising to his feet, the handsome man walked slowly around the desk, "Because my dear, too many loose ends. It saddened me to no end to learn you could not be trusted." Walking over to her, he lifted a coppery wave off her shoulder. When she shivered in response, he let it fall and continued, "Sending that letter was most unwise."

"How did you…"

"Your Sister Agnes. She came looking for you. Of course, I assured her you were fine, and even showed her a telegram from you to me saying how happy you were in Oregon and asking me to send the rest of your funds there." He glanced behind him at the door. "Then, I reminded her how dramatic you tended to be."

"Did she believe you?"

"Not at first."

Elizabeth was afraid to breathe. Stammering with fear, she asked, "You didn't harm her? She is just an old woman."

Tsk, tsking, he narrowed black eyes on her. "What do you take me for? I am a gentleman, after all. No, after I showed her the telegram, introduced her to the federal judge, who happens to be a good friend of mine, she seemed to accept me at my word. Why, I even insisted on paying her passage back home. Then to make sure she suffered no mishaps or change of heart, I saw that she made it safely on board the train. It was then I realized what I must do and got on the first boat to Oregon."

Leaving her side, he casually headed for the door. She shook the loose strands of hair from her face, desperate to see what he intended to do. She could literally hear her own heartbeat, as his slim hand circled the door knob behind him.

Nicholas spoke up defiantly, "Why? No one believed her. They still won't if you let us go. I'll make sure she doesn't tell anyone."

Rawling turned the knob slowly. "Really? I am not an idiot young man. Eventually someone will believe her. And in the short time I have been acquainted with Miss Brown, she rarely keeps her mouth shut."

302

With a sudden jerk, he opened the door and a wide eyed Smitty, floundering Cornelia, and a spitting mad Hannah, spilled into the room like a busted grain sack. "So glad you could all join us."

Martin ran up behind them, grinning stupidly. "Sorry about that Boss," then pointing at Smitty, "Guess I didn't see him, on account of his size and all."

"And what, pray tell," Rawlings voice practically oozed with sarcasm, "prevented you from seeing the other two? The Wagon?"

Stupefied, the huge man shrugged.

Shoving Smitty at him, he ordered with a sound of disgust, "Imbecile. Tie them up."

"Do you plan on tying up half the town? You know it is only a matter of time before Adam comes looking for us."

Noticing Rawling's finger slide casually over the lever of the gun, Cornelia shrieked, "Bootsie, please shut up before you get us all killed."

"He is already going to kill us, Cornelia."

"Oh, in that case I guess…" She trailed off, her bespeckled eyes first shooting to the cold blooded smile on Rawlings face then back to the two people already tied up in chairs. Instantly her mouth slammed shut, her throat moving with a huge gulp. "Never mind then."

Throwing her large chest out, Hannah looked down her nose at the man a good two inches shorter than she and said to her friend, "Yes, Cornelia, apparently this scum plans on murdering us along with everyone else in this room."

Nicholas squirmed in his seat, fighting against the ropes that bound him. "You just wait till Uncle Adam gets a hold of you. He's going to tear you limb from limb."

Rawling shook his head sadly, "I do hope you are not going to wear yourself out in the useless endeavor. I may need your help later with the horses."

"You are despicable."

"And you, my dear Elizabeth, are right."

"Take your blame hands off me, you overgrown tree stump." Smitty shouted as he was forcibly dragged over to an empty desk.

Rawling' eyebrow shot up as the little man slipped through Martin's arms and darted past him for the door. Casually he stuck out a booted foot. Smitty went sailing through the air and skid face first into the wall. Dazed, he didn't even resist when Martin lifted him back up and under a bulging arm, before throwing him into a chair.

Gaining a little of his wits, Smitty struggled to pull away from the sound grip on his bony shoulders. "I can't wait until Adam gets to this here secret meeting, cause' then I reckon one of us will be dancing on the other's grave."

He ended his tirade by spitting a long stream of dark brown tobacco all over Rawlings polished boot. The women gasped and everyone waited expectantly for Smitty to be shot. Even they knew he had crossed the line.

A muscle twitched in Rawling's jaw.

For the first time, Smitty noticed the gun pointed his direction. He tried to straighten his stance. Failing at that, he squinted his best evil eye at the well-dressed man. "Name's Smitty. Thought you oughta know if you plan on shooting me with that there gun."

Disgusted, Rawlings stepped over the brown spot on the floor and drawled, "Well, Spitty."

"Smitty!" The small man bellowed at him, nearly choking on his tobacco.

"Yes, well, Smitty. It is a good thing for you that I am not a rash man. You see, I have the gun. Therefore, I win. Perhaps you should remember that."

Martin chuckled.

"Martin, go bring that wagon up front that these two ladies were so kind to bring to us. Oh, you know, it's that huge thing out there with four wheels. Do try not to overlook it."

Even that insult the large man understood. A dangerous look crossed his scarred face as he rubbed his nose nervously and snorted, "Sure, Boss."

No one was fooled by his submissive response. The least of which was Rawlings. In thoughtful silence, he watched him leave.

304

While he was distracted, Elizabeth noticed Hannah inching her way towards a corner. Jana did too. Their eyes met and Jana mouthed "shovel". Nodding, Elizabeth broke the tension-filled silence by asking, "Tell me Rawlings. Just how did you steal my money?"

His smile never reached his eyes, "Now, Elizabeth, steal is such a harsh word. I like to think of it as an investment." He paused on the way past her to swipe Smitty's bandana from a pocket, "In my future that is."

She hated even speaking to him, but Hannah was so close. Just a little further. "All right then, how did you manage to invest my money? The bank would hardly give it over to just anyone."

"Let's see. I guess the simplest way to explain things would be to say I married you."

"What?!"

He sat back down on the large desk and placed his gun down beside him. Had she been untied she could have easily reached out and touched it.

"That's impossible," Elizabeth sputtered. "I never married you."

Cornelia, who had been shielding Hannah, suddenly perked up at the mention of marriage. She eagerly leaned forward, exposing Hannah who was just reaching for the shovel. "Married?" She yelped and sat up straight as Hannah kicked her in the calf, which put her back in Rawlings line of vision.

He turned.

Licking her lips nervously, she gave a trembling smile. "Excuse me –um – I must have choked on something."

Suspicious, he studied her for a moment before slowly and methodically he began cleaning off his boot with Smitty's bandana. "Where was I? Oh, yes, your money. Or, should I say *my* money?" He chuckled as if at some private joke. "Actually if you recall, on paper a woman named Bootsie Bottoms married Adam. The woman everyone believes to be you, she married me. Now I think you see where this becomes a bit problematic."

She shook her head.

Finishing his task, he said almost pleasantly, "My dear wife suffered an untimely death just last month. I am now left a grieving widower with lots and lots of money. I am most upset I can assure you."

She believed nothing he said could shock her anymore.

"So you can see that when your nun came looking for you, I had to think quickly. I realized two Elizabeth's were a bit of a problem. Especially since it might prove difficult to explain why my own dear wife committed suicide just a day after your nun came to see me. She was quite demented at the end, poor dear. Claimed even to be in love with me."

He looked almost apologetic. "Which is why you leave me no choice, but to kill you and all these nice people here, even poor Spitty."

"I tol' ya the name's Smitty!"

Rawling looked surprised by the man's interruption, "Yes, well, whatever. The fact still remains that no one would have had to die if you would have just heeded my warning and kept you mouth shut."

"Don't believe a word of it, Elizabeth," Jana responded to his harsh accusation. Once more she drew his attention as Hannah struggled with lifting the shovel while having hands tied together in front. "He meant to kill you anyway and anyone else who got in the way."

"Oh, please, all this heroism is sickening. If I meant to kill her I could have killed her in Galveston. If you ladies will excuse me. I can't imagine what is keeping Martin?"

He barely turned when Hannah, wielding a huge shovel and Cornelia, eyes wide with fright and clutching a thick walking stick, stood directly in his path. Instinctively, he raised a hand to ward off the determined Hannah who quickly knocked the gun from his hand and backed him into a corner.

"Cornelia," Hannah shouted.

Standing in the doorway, her knees knocking together in fright, the poor woman nearly jumped out of skin. "What?!"

"Get over here and untie Elizabeth and the others."

Trembling all over, Cornelia finally managed to move away from the doorway. She shifted her head from side to side, looking for any signs of danger. "Don't worry Hannah. I'll clobber whatever brute tries to stop me."

"Would you hurry up and stop acting the fool. That ugly man outside might come in at any moment."

Mention of Rawlings' partner made Cornelia quicken her step, muttering nervously, "Didn't I say this was none of our business. I tried to tell you, but did you listen? Nooo, you had to drag us out here, and now look at the mess you got us into."

"I dragged YOU!" Hannah waved the shovel wildly around in agitation. Rawlings had to duck in order not to be hit with it. "Just stop that mumbling and…why are you still fumbling with those ropes?"

"Would you stop yelling at me, Hannah? It's not as if I do this every day, now is it?" Cornelia bit back, trying to still her shaking hands by smoothing out her hair. This was impossible since her own hands were still tied as well in front of her. When Hannah continued glaring at her she sniffed in irritation and once again tackled the tightly knotted rope at the back of their chairs.

Rawlings was unusually calm. His eyes took in the Amazon in front of him, to the gun lying on the floor behind her. He glanced up and smiled.

"Martin, it's about time you chose to join us. Do get my gun for me, would you?"

Hanna clucked her tongue. "You don't expect me to fall for that old trick do you? You must be as stupid as you look."

"Hanna…" Elizabeth warned.

"Hush dear."

"Hanna," whispered a horrified Cornelia, dropping her hands limply in defeat.

"Not now, Cornelia, I plan on telling this gutter rat exactly what I think of him."

"Oh? And what is that?" His voice was especially soft as he leaned lazily against the wall behind him. To any outsider it would have appeared as if they were discussing the weather.

"That if you were my son, I would rue the day I gave birth."

"Hanna!" burst out Elizabeth in a strangled voice.

The large woman looked over one shoulder in aggravation, "I said, not until I've had my say." The words died in her throat, as two bloodshot yellow eyes belonging to the villain she had hoped not there – met hers. He lifted his rifle and pointed it straight at her.

"Oh, dear."

"I believe you were saying something about my dearly departed mother?" Without a moment hesitation, he reached out and jerked the shovel out of the frightened woman's hands.

For once Cornelia was the only sensible one in the group.

She fainted.

Chapter 27

Leaning across the desk, Adam's voice was filled with cold fury. "What?!"

Sam ran a finger around the inside of his shirt collar, "I said, that it appears as if a Mr. Rawlings does exist, and that he married a Miss Elizabeth Brown a little over three months ago."

Adam slammed the papers in his hands to the desk. "Is this marriage legal?"

Very uncomfortable now, Sam cleared his throat. He had never seen Adam this furious. "Well, all the records seem to indicate so, yes."

Adam felt as if someone had just hit him in the gut. She was married. Now her reluctance to believe Rawlings capable of murder became all too clear. He narrowed eyes at the idea of another man touching his wife. He shook it off and quickly got to his feet, grabbing his hat off the wall.

"Excuse me, Sam; there is a certain young woman I need to have a little chat with."

Perplexed by his friend's reaction, or why for that matter, he seemed so upset over this woman named Elizabeth. He ventured, "Don't you want to hear the rest of my report?"

"Later," Adam clipped before bellowing out the door, "Michael, get over here."

He meant to get to the bottom of this. Beth belonged to him and only him. "Sam?"

"Yes, Adam?"

"I want you to check out something else for me. Find out how easy it is to get a marriage annulled if it was never consummated."

"Sure Adam. But just out of curiosity, whose marriage are we talking about here?"

Michael ran up on the two men as they were talking, trying to make sense of their conversation.

"Elizabeth Brown's."

Sam's face paled in shock, "I'm afraid that's impossible."

Michael still looked confused. Adam looked prepared to kill someone, namely Sam.

"Perhaps I didn't make myself clear, Sam. Do it."

His longtime friend and lawyer backed up a couple of steps before saying slowly so his addled friend would understand what an unreasonable request he was making. "Adam, you don't understand. The reason I can't is because Elizabeth Brown died over a month ago."

"What did you say?"

Retrieving his report, he placed it in Adam's shaking hands, "She committed suicide about a month ago. It's all right here in my report."

It took Adam a second to understand the importance of what he had just been told. His body turned cold and a hard look came to his eyes. Slowly, he handed the papers back to Sam. Without saying a word, he went into the office and retrieved his gun, carefully strapping it on his leg.

Michael knew that look and it didn't bode well for Rawlings. "I'll get the horses, Adam."

Without saying a word, Adam strode out the door and past a confused Sam. Murder shone in his steel blue eyes. Reaching down to pick up the forgotten report, Sam noticed a shiny object on the desk. He picked it up, slowly closing his fist around the slightly tarnished tin star. It appeared that whatever his friend planned to do, he didn't want the law standing in his way.

Hannah's hands, now tied behind her were beginning to cramp. "Rawlings, even you can't be stupid enough to expect the disappearance of six people to go by unnoticed."

The wagon carrying them towards some unknown destination lurched forward, slamming Hannah up against Rawling's accomplice who simply grunted before shoving her away. Rawlings from his position at the reins ignored her completely

Perturbed, she pointed out, "If you ask me –"

"Which shows my good judgment in not asking you. Martin, can't you keep that woman quiet?"

Refusing to give in, she jutted out a double chin at him, "You mister are nothing but a low down snake in the grass, a rabid dog with the mind of a gutter rat."

Elizabeth's eyes widened at Rawling's menacing look. Hannah was annoying him to no end. How much longer he would put up with her snide remarks remained to be seen.

"For you information, dear," he interrupted, "in a manner of mere minutes you good people will die in a tragic accident. You will plunge 200 feet off this mountain and out of my life. Personally, I can't wait."

Seeing her try to rise to her feet, he advised coldly, "Do have a seat, madam." Then with a flick of the reins, Hannah went tumbling back down into the wagon. "Thank you."

"Please stop antagonizing him Hannah," Cornelia wailed.

Scooting protectively closer to Hannah, Elizabeth pointed out calmly, "Isn't it enough you are going to kill us? Must you go into detail about it?"

At the word 'kill', Cornelia burst into a loud fit of hysterics.

His head aching, Rawlings propped it up with a hand. "Would someone do something about that woman before I shoot her?"

Elizabeth shot him a hateful look and whispered consolingly, "You have to get a hold of yourself Cornelia. Think of the others."

"Oh, Bootsie, you are right of course." She sniffled. "I'm being such a coward. It's just I have never been murdered before and it's quite upsetting."

With a slight smile at the woman's strange wording, Elizabeth admitted, "It's all right Cornelia. I'm frightened, too. But we have to try and keep calm."

From his seat next to Elizabeth, Nicholas lifted suspiciously wet eyes to hers. "Do you think Uncle Adam will come, Bootsie? I...well...we're going to die because of me aren't we?" He burst out, as silent tears of regret began to fall down his cheeks.

"It's not your fault." Her voice softened with kindness. "If it's anyone's, it's mine. Believe me; I know how convincing Rawlings can be. Besides, we are not going to die. I have a plan."

A spark of hope lit his features as he closed in to hear. After a couple of whispered instructions, a genuine smile of gratitude erased the doom from his face. Nodding eagerly, he nudged Hannah.

Lost in her own regrets, Cornelia shook her head, clearly dismayed. "But, to think how we treated you, Bootsie. How we all actually thought about throwing you off the boat."

Hannah, distracted by what Nicholas told her, elbowed Cornelia in the ribs. "No sense in going into all that now." Then catching Elizabeth's attention, she winked, "We have work to do." With a grin of devilment she struggled to her knees in the swaying wagon until she was shoulder level with Smitty's back and waited.

Inching over to the other side of the foul smelling Martin, Nicholas waited for Elizabeth's nod. When it came, he pulled back his feet and shoved full force, catching the unsuspecting man off guard. He went sailing backwards into the back of the wagon.

The sound of wind being knocked out of his partner made Rawlings turn around in aggravation.

"What are you doing back there, Martin, wrestling?"

Smitty bent over to spit beside the wagon.

Rising a little higher, Hannah cocked one shoulder forward.

"That boy kicked me. Why can't I just kill him now?" The furious Martin growled as he began fingering the bone handled knife in his boot.

"Now, Hannah!" Elizabeth ordered.

Not wasting another moment Hannah shoved an unsuspecting Smitty off the side. His outraged, "Hey!" was cut off as his bony frame bounced off the hard ground, then rolled over and over in a cloud of dust for a good twenty feet behind them.

"Martin, I told you to watch those women," Rawlings roared as he pulled the wagon to a stop.

"You watch them. I'm sick of taking your orders," Martin yelled back. Jumping to his feet, he pushed the women out of the way and grabbed Rawlings up by his shirt front. Then, in one fluid movement the bone handled knife was jerked out and placed under Rawling's chin.

312

A drop of blood trickled down Rawlings throat. Instead of being afraid, he merely looked amused. "Oh, I see you have a mind of your own after all."

Wasting no more time, the women and Nicholas emptied out the back of the wagon scattering in the woods to hide. Unperturbed, Rawlings watched them leave. Rolling his eyes, he sighed at Martin. Leave it to the man not to tie their feet.

"Martin, couldn't we do this another time? Our captives are escaping."

He responded by pressing the knife deeper into the smiling man's throat. "Maybe, I'll just kill you."

"Fine." Rawlings' dark brown eyes no longer looked amused, but cold and empty. Martin heard the click of a hammer being pulled back before pressure from a gun pushed into his protruding gut. "But since I now know you have some thought process, let me explain something to you. If you don't get that knife away from me, I fully intend to shoot you."

The knife slowly lowered.

"I thought you were a sensible man." Rawlings voice was deceptively soft as he added, "Oh, Martin."

The large man sighed and rose up from replacing his knife. "What now?"

The gun went off in Rawlings hand, sending the large man to his knees, a shocked expression on his face. Not a hair out of place, the cold-blooded murderer shrugged, "I changed my mind. I guess I will shoot you after all."

As Rawlings dragged Martin's body into the woods, Elizabeth clamped down on her bottom lip to keep from screaming and exposing them. Nicholas continued to patiently saw away at the ropes binding her hands with his dull pocket knife. Lying back to back, it was a long tedious job. At last the ropes snapped free and Elizabeth rubbed her sore wrists. The way Rawlings hit at the bushes told her he wouldn't have any regrets about killing them now. They had to get out of there. Picking up the knife, she started on Nicholas's ropes.

His hands free, Nicholas pushed her to the ground as a pair of booted feet walked past their hiding place and back again.

"I have a friend of yours waiting at the wagon. At least I think it is him. It's hard to tell under all those layers of dirt and mud. You know? That disgusting little man who has an endless supply of spit?"

Smitty. She clutched the knife so tight her knuckles turned white.

"I am pleased to report that he is alive and well. I found him sniffing around the wagon a moment ago. No doubt in a valiant attempt to save you. Instead, I captured him. I must say he is not too happy with the rest of you disappearing like that. Now if you do not come out this minute, I will be forced to shoot him one appendage at a time. And you know how I hate to resort to such low behavior."

She closed her eyes in pain. She couldn't let another human being die because of her. When she opened her eyes Nichols seemed to read the intent in them for he shook his head furiously at her. Peeling off the strong hold on her arm, she rose from her hiding place, making sure to step far enough away that Nicholas would not be found.

Then moving forward, she faced his tailored back. With a bravery laced voice, she answered coolly, "Here I am. Now let everyone else go. It is me you want."

Their horses covered in frothy sweat when they reached the house, Adam and Michael jumped to the ground, running straight for the front door.

Bursting into the parlor, he shouted at a stunned Christina, "Where's Beth?"

She got to her feet, the mending falling in a scattered heap at her feet. "The Barn. But Adam, what is wrong?"

He didn't wait to answer her. Instead, once again the door slammed shut as the two men ran out the door. Sighing deeply, Christina bent to retrieve the socks, "I think this entire household is a little crazy."

Chelsea toddled over and gave her a kiss.

She hugged her in return, "Well, except for you of course, darling." To which the small girl looked up and smiled, the remains of a beetle between her front teeth. "Oh, well, I guess you can't fight heredity."

A worried Adam came back from the barn within a manner of minutes, jumping on back of the horse Michael was holding for him, "She's gone."

"Do you have any idea where," Michael asked scanning the woods in front of them.

Running a shaky hand through tousled hair, Adam seemed more upset than before. "It's a pretty safe bet the school house. That's the direction of their tracks anyway."

"Their?"

They exchanged a look.

"Nicholas is with her."

With a groan, Michael turned his horse around, "Great."

That was exactly Adam's sentiments as well. Those two hot-headed people were headed straight for the one place where Rawlings might be. Kicking his already tired horse into a run, Adam tried not think what could happen if he were right. Because everything he held dear was at stake.

He didn't feel any better when reaching the schoolhouse a short time later. They skidded to a halt, fear gripping Adam's chest. The front door was standing wide open. The quiet and muddled wagon tracks leading up the mountain told a story that only added to Adam's ediginess. "Go check the school house. I'll see if anyone else is around."

Michael swung from his horse, giving it a pat and letting the reins hang free. "Adam, look."

Without hesitation Adam turned back around and bent down on one knee to examine the prints around them.

"What do you make of these tracks? I count at least five, maybe more, separate shoe prints."

Pulling off his hat, Adam swiped at the sweat on his brow with the back of one hand. "I don't know, maybe Rawlings brought several men with him."

"I see ladies prints here."

"So, what is your point?"

Understanding Adam's impatience, he elaborated. "My point is, if it is Rawlings he must be a bigger fool than we thought. The man must have half the town with him."

Adam looked up to see a faint outline of dust on the upper horizon. He quickly grabbed the horn of his saddle and pulled himself up. "I'm going to check out that wagon. Maybe it's nothing, but just in case I want you to check out the school. If you don't find anything, then I'll meet you back at the house."

"What if I do find something? Or you?"

The mountain road ended at the highest point in town. Both men knew no one could survive a fall from that cliff. With a grim look of determination, Adam slid his rifle out of the scabbard. "I suggest you reach me first. Otherwise, Rawlings is dead."

The man mentioned was at that moment dusting off his coat. "Get in."

Still holding the small pocket knife in the folds of her skirt, she asked, "What happens to us now?"

"You know," Rawlings rubbed at his aching head. Nothing in this absurd kidnapping was going right. He supposed murdering a nearly nun put some sort of jinx on things. "I haven't decided yet and what's more I am through talking. Now, get in the wagon."

Smitty scowled at Elizabeth in annoyance. "Next time you women have a plan, you might let me in on it."

"You said you would let him go."

"I lied."

More aggravated than afraid, Smitty bowed up as he was being shoved into the blood soaked back of the wagon, "Mister, you're lucky my hands are tied or I'd whoop you upside that fancy haircut of yours."

Without a moment's hesitation Rawlings whipped out the nickel plated gun and pulled back the hammer. "You are really beginning to annoy me. And since I no longer need you…well." He shrugged and aimed straight at the now silent man.

"No!" Elizabeth's scream tore through the air, just about that time a furious Nicholas started racing for them, chunking rocks as fast as he could throw them.

Too surprised to react right away, Rawlings never knew what hit him as Cornelia and Hanna jumped out of the bushes and tackled him to the ground. His gun went off aimlessly before it was jerked out of his hands and flung into the road.

"You yellow bellied swine. You no good…" Hannah continued her tirade while pelting him with a stick. Cornelia, her hands still tied, gave him a good kick every once in a while for good measure.

Reacting quickly, Elizabeth climbed up in the wagon and began cutting Smitty free. "Come on, what do you say we get out here?"

"Sounds mighty good to me, Mrs. Reed."

From out of nowhere a huge rock sailed by Smitty's ear and landed with a resounding thump against the horse's rump. They both turned in unison and yelled, "The reins!"

Poor Jethro and Geraldine took off running as the two people in the wagon behind them grappled along the floorboard in a frantic attempt to capture the reins before it was too late. Finally managing to get hold of one rein, Elizabeth hung on for dear life as she was flung sideways into the seat. Unfortunately, it was knocked out of her hands and went sailing to the ground in between the two horses pounding hooves.

"Shoot."

"Don't worry, Mrs. Reed, I've got the other one," Smitty proudly called out, holding the rein triumphantly over his head.

"Smitty, watch out!"

He looked at her in mild confusion just as a branch overhead knocked him across the seat and into the back of the wagon. Reaching out to catch the falling rein, Elizabeth fell over the side of the wagon and nearly toppled out off after it.

A dazed Smitty's bouncing head came up over the seat, a big purple knot growing on his forehead. "Sorry about that ma'am."

She felt like crying when things went from bad to worse. The wagon was now beginning to veer off the road, heading straight across the greenish yellow meadow. In just a few minutes they would reach the cliff. And unless a miracle happened, they would go over.

By the time Adam reached the small group of two women, one boy and Rawlings, he began to wonder just who he had come to rescue. Rawlings looked like he'd been drug through a rocky outback after being whooped by a cougar. Shaking his head, he grinned down at the poor defenseless women still whacking the man with a stick every time they took the notion. Nicholas noticed him first.

"Uncle Adam!" He ran over, barely waiting for Adam to dismount before starting to talk a mile a minute. "You should have seen us get him. And Bootsie, boy was she brave. There he was fixing to shoot Smitty and she just ran at him."

"Speaking of Beth, where is she?"

For the first time a perplexed and worried look crossed Nicholas' face as he pointed behind Adam. "Where is the wagon?"

"What wagon?"

Their eyes followed the new tracks to its faint outline heading across the meadow and straight for Dead Man's Bluff. He had his answer. Shoving his rifle at Nicholas, Adam ordered, "Watch Rawlings until Michael gets here. I'm going to try and stop that wagon."

Between being tossed around and Smitty falling on her every time he attempted to climb up into the seat, there wasn't much time for completing her task.

"Smitty, we have to try the brake," she yelled over the roaring of the wagon wheels.

The poor old timer's knuckles were white as they gripped the wagon seat, his body bouncing wildly through the air, his small eyes round with fright. He nodded but never moved.

She grabbed the front of his shirt and yelled into his face, "Smitty! The brake."

This time her words penetrated the paralyzing fear that had a hold of him. Trying to hold on to the seat as he grabbed the brake, they hit a

318

pot hole and his scrawny body tumbled over the side. Elizabeth screamed and covered her eyes.

Tears streaming down her face, she looked behind her fully expecting to see Smitty's broken and bloody body sprawled out on the road. He wasn't there. They hit a large rock and she flew into the floor board, but not before seeing Smitty's wiry frame bob up in sight. It was then she looked down at the brake. Two wrinkled brown hands clutched to it in a death grip that she was sure Hercules himself could not pry loose.

"Smitty, hang on. I'm coming," she promised joyfully.

The wooden brake began to crack. Her heart racing she dove for his hands, just as she saw the brake give a little more. Determined she reached out, circling his wrists with her hands.

"Let go of me you fool woman before we both get killed," he demanded in an outraged voice. She could just make out the top of his head through the cloud of dust of dead grass and rocks swirling around him. He coughed, then demanded even more firmly, "I said let go!"

She wasn't fooled in the least. He knew that as long as she held him, if the brake gave out he would be drug underneath the wagon to his death. It hardly mattered because she now saw the bushes running along the edge of the cliff.

"I'm not letting go, so you might as well make up your mind to hang on."

Smitty huffed in aggravation, "I always did say you didn't have a lick of sense." Then she heard him choke up a bit, "Well, girl I reckon we'd best be saying our prayers."

About that time, Elizabeth who had her head down on her arms, looked up through the dust and saw an angel. Adam. His face serious, he got a better hold of the saddle horn and leaned over. Looking her in the eyes, he winked and that vote of confidence gave her renewed strength.

"When I say now, I want you to let go, Beth, understand?"

She was so full of pride and love that all she could manage was a heartfelt nod.

"Okay. Now!"

Smitty and Elizabeth both let go at the same time. Too afraid to look and too afraid not to, she opened one eye and watched as Adam caught Smitty and pulled him away from danger before his arm gave out. Slowing down enough to drop the poor man to the ground, he spun his horse back around to come for her. Watching as Smitty rolled a little ways, but blessedly managed to regain his footing and limp over to a huge boulder, she sent a grateful 'thank you' heavenward. At least no one would die this day because of her.

The wagon jerked to the right and she fell to her knees. When she struggled up again, fear closed up her throat. The bushes were so near now; she could tell which ones were ripe for the picking. Adam would never make it in time.

"Stop fooling around, Beth, and jump."

His deep and demanding voice sounded like sweet music to her ears. Still, when she looked down at the racing ground beneath the wagon and Adam's arms so far away, she hesitated.

"I'm so very frightened Adam. I don't think –"

"I said jump!"

The horses reached the edge of the bushes. Leaning over, he grabbed hold of the bouncing wagon seat. "Either you jump or we both die."

She jumped.

Never missing a beat, his strong arms caught her and pulled her up in front of him, just as the wagon toppled out of sight. Elizabeth buried her head in his shoulder as she heard the silent echo of the wagon's wheels as they went over. Shivering, she moved in closer to Adam's warmth. He wrapped one arm protectively around her and kissed her forehead. "I love you, Green Eyes."

She reached up, caressing his strong jawline in wonder, "I know." Then with all the love in the world shining in her eyes, she kissed him.

A loud "Ahem" forced them to reluctantly pull apart.

Smitty, his ears a fiery red, shuffled uncomfortably from one foot to the other. He looked such a sight that Elizabeth would have laughed if she hadn't been so worried about him. The only parts not layered in mud or dust were two pale circles that once were eyes. His mouth busted and his short hair stuck up all over his head, with a huge goose egg poking out his forehead was not his best look. Stifling a laugh with his hand, Adam asked with a straight face, "Yes?"

"If you folks are through with all that kissing, I'd like to go home now." Puffing up like a rooster he added, "And the next time you have a secret meeting? I'd appreciate it if I wasn't invited."

Adam and Elizabeth couldn't stop themselves. They burst out in relieved laughter as a disgruntled Smitty frowned up at them absolutely certain they had lost their ever-loving minds.

Epilogue

Her wedding day.

Well, actually, her second wedding day. Adam still didn't seem to understand that it didn't matter what name was written on that piece of paper. She was married to him in the only place that mattered, her heart.

But her husband being bull headed and practical as usual, insisted on making sure it was legal. For a man who totally disregarded the law when it suited him, she found this bit of logic touching.

A timid knock sounded on the door, drawing Elizabeth back from her thoughts. "Yes?"

"It's me, Nicholas. Uncle Adam said to tell you he hasn't got all day, everyone's waiting on you."

Swinging the door open, she cocked a saucy hand to her hip, "He said that?"

Nicholas blushed. "Well, actually he said to see if you had escaped out the window."

Gently she tapped him on the nose and smiled. "Tell him, he's the only window I'll ever need from now on."

"That doesn't make a bit of sense." He screwed up his face. "You know I like you and all, but I believe Smitty is right. There is no understanding a woman."

She started to ask him what he meant by that, but quickly changed her mind. Maybe another time, because right now there was a wonderful man waiting below and she couldn't wait to spend the rest of her life loving him.

Reaching Christina at the top of the stairs, she clasped her friend's hand for reassurance. "Is my wreath on straight?"

Christina looked from the lovely peonies circling her mahogany head, to the light purple fabric lying in soft waves down her slender body before answering honestly, "You look beautiful."

Timidly Elizabeth began her descent down the half- finished church stairway. If someone had told her a year ago that she would be married at a church in the wilderness of Oregon and to a man twice her size, she would have called them a liar. Strange enough, none of that mattered anymore, just so long as Adam was the one standing on the other end.

Coming to meet her at the bottom of the stairs, Adam took her trembling hand in his. Giving it a squeeze, he gave a slow sexy wink and that cocky grin of his. Suddenly all her fears disappeared. She wasn't marrying some stranger this time. It was only Adam.

She winked back.

From now on everything would be just fine. Rawlings was headed for trial in Texas. Everyone, including Smitty had made it to the wedding and beamed at them now from the pews. Why, even Cornelia decided to start a newspaper. Now at least her nosiness would serve a purpose. Michael and Jana stood side by side at the back door; her glaring and him smiling. This probably had more to do with her being handcuffed to him than anything else. He was taking her to see the judge after the wedding.

Reaching the preacher, Nicholas handed Adam the ring and nodded his approval. Yes, even he accepted her now. Never mind she nearly died in the process. And Chelsea? How she adored the two year old who was methodically plucking the petals from her bouquet.

"Dearly beloved, we are gathered here to join..."

Life couldn't be any sweeter. She had real friends here who cared for her. A husband and family. But most important of all, she had found love. From this day forward she would lead a nice quiet, ordinary, everyday sort of life.

"Unhand her this minute, you scoundrel!!"

Everyone in the entire room turned. There, rudely pushing Michael aside stood a small elderly woman dressed in a nun's habit.

"Sister Agnes?"

Adam raised an eyebrow at his wife.

Still dripping from the downpour outside, the good sister was not in the mood for compromise. The tall angular sister with her followed close behind trying to ignore the embarrassed flush coming to her cheeks, not to mention, the shocked faces staring at them as the crowd parted to let them through.

Drenched from head to foot, with a wilted, winged hat bobbing limply beside her ears, the small sister strode forward and popped Adam over the arm with her umbrella. "I said; unhand that poor innocent child this instant."

He quickly jerked his hand away, rubbing at his throbbing arm. "I think you have the wrong idea." She raised her umbrella. He backed up a step and watched for another attack from the avenging nun he towered over.

Finally overcoming her initial shock, Elizabeth managed to ask, "Whatever are you doing here, Sister?"

It was then the good Sister noticed her surroundings. With a suspicious look, she surveyed the wide-eyed beauty in light purple. Elizabeth certainly didn't look like someone held against her will, or even mistreated for that matter. What she looked was radiant. Those facts alone made her frown deepen even more.

Shaking out the excess water from her skirt, she snapped, "What am I doing here, Elizabeth? I am responding to this letter."

She dug around in the pocket of her dress until, at last, managing to pull out the sodden letter in question. Recognizing her letter from the boat, Elizabeth groaned and began looking for an escape route. "I thought Rawlings took it from you."

"Now what makes you think I would trust that man with anything? Especially, the only proof I had against him."

"Oh, then you didn't go back to the convent?"

"Don't sidetrack me young woman." She put on her reading glasses and began to read. "I quote." She began dramatically, "Please sister, I implore you. I am being held prisoner in a small room over a saloon by a huge brute of a man and I fear for my very life."

Adam narrowed his eyes at the word brute. Interested to hear what else his wife had to say, he bent his head in closer with an encouraging, "Do continue, Sister."

Holding the soggy letter closer, she read, "You can't imagine the horrors I have suffered already at his hands."

Elizabeth was mortified. She placed her head in her hands, peeking out between fingers at Adam. He looked anything but pleased.

She had had enough. Snatching the letter away before anymore could be read, she explained, "I guess I might have exaggerated somewhat."

"Yes, it certainly appears that way, doesn't it Sweetheart? Would you care to explain?"

Unconsciously shredding the letter, she bit her lip in agitation, "Well, actually, no I wouldn't care to explain."

Adam brushed her aside and faced her clearly not-so-happy rescuer. "Sister, perhaps I can clear up this little misunderstanding for you."

So much for a normal wedding day.

"My wife does think I am a brute."

Elizabeth fingered her gown.

"And, I did hold her against her will. In fact, I even married her against her will."

Sister Agnes was feeling slightly better about traveling clear across the country. Elizabeth was feeling awful.

He looked the wise old woman straight in the eye, "But, the only horror she's suffered at my hands, she seems to beg repeating."

She would die right here. The man had no scruples whatsoever.

Sister Mary, who because of her height gave up trying to fade into the background, looked heavenward for help. Sister Agnes on the other hand, developed a slight twitch to her lips. She bowed her head as if in deep thought. "Then I suppose there is only one solution."

"There is?" asked an anxious Elizabeth.

Her mentor raised her head, dancing blue eyes looking into Elizabeth's wary face. "Yes. I insist on staying for the wedding."

Giving a relieved sigh, Elizabeth reached out and clasped the closest thing to a mother she had ever known. "Thank you, Sister."

Patting her cheek affectionately, and with tears clogging her throat, Sister Agnes asked, "Whatever for child?"

Now it was her turn to get all teary-eyed, "For putting up with me, and for coming all this way to save me. But most of all, for helping me recognize that if I wasn't meant to be a nun, that God would send me a window. I just never knew it would take the form of one huge Oregon Lumber Jack."

Adam kissed her on the cheek and Elizabeth turned an adoring face his direction.

"Elizabeth."

She turned respectfully, "Yes, ma'am?"

The small woman crooked a finger at her.

Perplexed, she cocked her head down to hear better. Instantly a smile broke out on a face so radiant that it rivaled the gloomy day with sunshine. After that, the wedding proceeded without any more interruptions. Sister Mary did lean over once to ask one question of her sister in the cloth. She wanted to know what she whispered in the young girl's ear to make her smile like that.

Her eyes twinkling with merriment, she answered simply, "I told her I was wrong."

"Oh', responded her still confused companion.

Sister Agnes looked up towards the heavens, her heart lightened by Elizabeth's new found happiness. "She would have made a fine nun, Lord. Nevertheless, only You understand how extremely grateful I am for that window."

About the Authors

Tammy Watson

Tammy lives on a state park in the deserts of Texas with the love of her life of over thirty years and two crazy weimaraners. Writing has always been her passion, but she also has a bit of a dramatic flair and studied theatre in college. Tammy has written numerous plays, novels, skits, and a bi-weekly humorous column in a local newspaper.

As a couple, they love traveling and adventure. They are always on the trail hiking, biking, rock-climbing, and camping. Her love for history and mystery has found its way into her novels as well, and she spends years researching for each of her books.

Melissa Phillips

Melissa lives in east Texas, is married and has three children. She enjoys reading, scuba diving and spending time with her family. This is Melissa's first book. She currently works as a psychiatric nurse at a mental hospital. Although it is a very challenging job, it is also very exciting, as one never knows quite what to expect from day to day. She appreciates the vast variety of people she encounters, and delights in observing their mannerisms and quirks. This inspires to create the many colorful characters in her book.